A MATTER OF ENERGY

Marco A. Miranda Sr.

PublishAmerica
Baltimore

First printing

ISBN: 1-4241-8990-X
PUBLISHED BY PUBLISHAMERICA, LLLP
www.publishamerica.com
Baltimore

Printed in the United States of America

This book is dedicated to my heaven-sent family members, for their love and support. Love is truly a matter of energy.

Contents

PROLOGUE
The Appearance

Washington, DC—The White House—05:00 hrs

Early morning activity at the White House starts with the automatic garden sprinkler systems that go off in symmetrical order around the grounds. The gardens close to the buildings receive special attention as they are inspected daily by both gardeners and security personnel. The gardening detail devotes special attention to the Rose Garden and its West End where French doors in the colonnade connect to the President's Oval Office. This is the preferred outdoor area where dignitaries are received and special events take place. It provides a unique setting for outdoor receptions and other functions.

The many trees around the grounds that are associated with former occupants of the White House are carefully inspected. Some of them date back to Thomas Jefferson, John Quincy Adams and Andrew Jackson. Within the White House, cleaning details move quickly from room to room completing the late evening tasks of the previous shift. The kitchens run practically non-stop from 4 a.m., and there is a great deal of hustle and bustle in all service areas.

In the private family quarters on the second floor, not much happens until around five am. If the President is not up, the valet wakes him and if there are no urgent matters to be dealt with at that time, helps the President get dressed in sports attire. The First Lady normally arises an hour later.

Ross Simonson, the President of the United States, woke up this morning at exactly five am. With no pressing early morning commitments, he welcomed the chance to do a few miles on his stationary bicycle. At 47 years of age, he was in great physical shape. His regular medical checkups disclosed none of the incipient ailments of men of that age. He was secretly proud of his physique and the fact that he had never carried an extra ounce of fat on his six-foot frame since the age of 18. He also took pride in the fact that he possessed the vitality of a 20-year-old athlete.

Ross Simonson's passion for race cars had been the only sportive obsession that had enriched his early years. After his service in the Air Force as a B-52 Navigator, he had owned an Offenhauser, 4-cylinder beauty which he ran on dirt tracks in the Southwest circuit, while still in college. That experience had left its mark on him. He often reflected that the thrills, the hard work and the satisfactions and disappointments, in equal measure, that racing a powerful machine could provide, somehow had prepared him for the rough course of political life.

He compared being at the helm of his race car to his present job. "Got to keep one eye on the road, the other on the instrument panel and the other on the rearview mirror. Three eyes are better than two!" A President needed more than three eyes, he thought. The problem is that the extra eyes he was forced to borrow sometimes did not match the vision of the first two. With these thoughts in mind he quickly dressed in shorts, sports shoes and a sweatshirt displaying Oklahoma State in large letters. He left the bedroom and quickly walked past the Lincoln Bedroom and Sitting Room, the Queen's Room and the Center Hall. He went up to the third floor Solarium and, immediately to his right, he entered the small room where he had installed the bicycle, a rack with weights and a combination TV/radio set. It was 5:31 a.m.

He turned on the TV set and switched channels until he found the 24-hour News Channel. Then, he mounted the bike and started to pedal, slowly at first and then vigorously. Somehow, the hard physical exercise stimulated his thinking at this early hour. He reviewed the major happenings of the previous day and also prepared for the activities of the coming journey while on the exercise bike. He found it easy to focus on specific items and to perceive matters with greater clarity.

He continuously forced himself to think that his job was like any other, knowing full well that it wasn't. He felt that by adopting the mental attitude of a 9 to 5 employee, he would be able to face problems and situations in an ordinary, down-to-earth fashion. While he was aware and proud of his personal accomplishments, first as Governor and now as President, he tried not to impart unnecessary transcendence to the job. That jazz about being the

Leader of the Free World, the President of the only Superpower on Earth, the Richest Nation, the Most Prosperous Country, the Omnipotent Leader and Negotiator, and all the hype that gushed out of the convoluted minds of an unpredictable media, would only introduce a false sense of security that could gradually evolve into arrogance.

He repeated to himself that his boss, the American people, expected from him an honest day's work and the proper use of the personal and professional qualities that had won him the election. He did not discard however the importance of his role, but was leery of the adoration of some and the constant scrutiny he lived under.

I must be turning into Constitution Avenue by now, he thought as he checked the speedometer and mileage dials of the bike. It was a game he played every time he rode the bike. He imagined the progress he would make from the White House. He would pedal down Constitution all the way to 23rd Street and then down toward the Lincoln Memorial. From there to the West Potomac Park, the Jefferson Memorial and back up to the White House on 14th Street.

He continued pedaling when all of a sudden he realized that the TV had blanked out. Only static hiss could be heard. He imagined it would be one of those temporary lapses caused by defective connections, electrical problems or even network transmission glitches. He was right. In few seconds the screen was back and the announcer, looking apologetic, delivered the familiar excuse about the temporary disruption of the broadcast.

An instant later, his imaginary voyage was interrupted by Manuel, his valet, who entered the room in an unaccustomed frenzy. His hands were trembling and he had acquired a pale color that overwrote his naturally dark complexion. His bulging eyes suggested a high state of shock. Manuel stopped in front of the President, and almost out of breath exclaimed, "Presidente algo raro está sucediendo!" In his state of excitement, he had resorted to his native language. Ross knew Spanish well and understood the phrase.

"What do you mean?"

"Please look outside, Mr. President. I don't know what to make of it!"

Without waiting for an answer, he rushed to the doors that faced the southwest garden and opening them, stepped somewhat out of balance into the small balcony. The President, puzzled and greatly surprised by Manuel's alarming fear, stepped quickly outside and looked up. A shadow of fear and amazement crossed his face. Used, as he was, to the awesome displays of nature's forces, what he saw above was nothing he could remotely understand. His mind was unable to identify some frame of reference that could shed some light on the phenomenon above.

His eyes opened wide as he examined the sky above him. A cold sweat came over him and there was a sudden blurring of his eyesight. He made an effort to calm himself down and with a trembling voice all he could say was, "I'll be damned!" The large object that seemed to cover the entire city transfixed both the President and Pablo, who had just realized that he was holding a cordless telephone. He handed the telephone to the President, who slowly raised it to his ear. Manuel meanwhile did not neglect his duty and was quick to hand the President a large towel. The early morning breeze could give anyone a chill. It could be someone perspiring like the President.

The Chief of Staff was on the line. Trying hard to control himself, Pan Rossi asked in a tremulous voice, "Mister President, something funny just happened. A few minutes ago, a strange shape or space vehicle has appeared and seems to be hovering over Washington."

The President, who had not taken his eyes off the strange object overhead, did not seem to find any words to answer to Pan. For a long moment he just held the phone to his ear while his mind was trying to absorb the impact of the strange apparition. Finally he said, "I know, Pan. Pablo just came in and we are looking at the object right now. The thing looks solid, like a giant aspirin tablet. We should be hearing from the Defense Department shortly. This thing must have triggered all kinds of alarms. I am going to get dressed and will be down in a few minutes. Try to get the Vice-president and the rest right away."

He clicked the end button and handed the phone to Manuel.

"What is it, Mister President?" was all Manuel could say.

"I told you, Manuel: I'll be damned if I know! It looks like a giant aspirin tablet and it does not seem to move. I better go in and find out what the heck this is all about."

The President rushed to the family quarters and woke the First Lady. She got out of bed quickly and opened the window, still groggy from sleep. Upon seeing the object, she was speechless for a moment and then in a voice that echoed the terror that was gripping her, cried, "Ross! What in the name of heavens is that thing?"

By then, the telephones were ringing. There are several lines connecting the President's quarters with the offices in the White House and they all seemed to be sending the same message of surprise, puzzlement and even fear. The messages all said the same. What is this thing? What do we do now?

"Tell everyone to hold on to their eyelids. I'll be down in a few minutes," he ordered Pablo and the Secret Service officer that had now attached himself to the small group in the President's quarters. He moved quickly to the bathroom and took a quick shower.

"Pablo!" he yelled, "forget about the massage and the shave. I'll shave myself."

He left the bathroom wrapped in a lush terrycloth towel and, in seconds was dressed in a dark gray flannel suit, the regulation white shirt with no cuff links, and a stripped blue and gold necktie. He adjusted the gold handkerchief on the breast pocket and with a quick look at the mirror, left his bedroom. The First Lady was herself dressed and waiting for him in the sitting room. Pablo busied himself in the inner chambers while the Secret Service Agent stood woodenly by the door, occasionally moving his head slightly and talking in barely audible tones into his lapel mike.

"I just don't know what to make of this thing," observed the President as he drank avidly a glass of fruit juice. "I hope it is not that invasion everyone has been talking about since H.G. Wells and Orson Wells put that show on radio years ago."

The First Lady, dressed in a one-piece Leslie silk dress and a beige cashmere cardigan, reached for the President's hand and squeezed it gently. Her light green eyes found his and conveyed tenderness and affection.

"I am afraid to be afraid. I can only think of two or three possibilities to explain the nature of this phenomenon. Like everything however, we must have more evidence before we can make a reasonable appraisal," said the First Lady, whose legal training was forever evident in her comments and even in casual conversation.

They were interrupted several times by telephone calls and the delivery of high priority e-mail messages and handwritten notes. Two more of his aides were already in the private sitting room, busy answering calls and taking notes.

The President and the First lady finished gulping their coffee and left the room in a hurry. As they walked past the Center Hall, the President said, "Please stick around, Earla. I'd appreciate it if you cancel whatever appointments you have and stay in the White House. Also, please call Mayfair at school. Just tell her to keep cool and that we will call her later or as soon as we know what the score is. I suppose this thing is going to be in all the papers in no time at all."

"Darling, I have already talked to Mayfair. She was sound asleep, you know. There is three hours' difference. She promised to call back later this morning once she finds out more about the objects and the reaction out there."

Mayfair Simonson, their 17-year-old freshman at UCLA, as an only child received a great deal of attention from her parents, but in such a manner that she never felt overwhelmed or fussed over. To her, being the daughter of the President of the United States did not mean unlimited privilege, except some occasional measure of convenience. She felt that there was more pressure from the surveillance of her Secret Service escorts than she had ever experienced from her parents.

At the elevator the President gave the First Lady an affectionate kiss on her cheek and pressing his body against her said, "Earla, I am as afraid as anyone. I want you to stay close by in case these things begin to blast us with their death ray machines or their giant microwave human scoopers."

"I'll be close," replied the First Lady as she put her arms around her husband. "There is surely a rational explanation. Besides, if these things were here to do harm to us, they would have done so the moment they parked overhead. Try to stay calm, Mister President."

As he rushed to the Oval Office, acknowledging salutes and good mornings delivered in somber tones, the President realized that the previous minutes had been unusually hectic. Practically every agency of the Government, the Media, the Church and every other institution, it seemed, had contacted the White House, collapsing the switchboard and also the mail voice system and even the back-up communication systems. The high speed fax machines had ran out of paper early in the morning and the e-mail messages streaming in at great speed, were about to overwhelm the bank of computers in the basement of the West Wing.

In the outer offices of the Oval Office there were already several members of the staff busy at the telephones, their laptops and the ever present cellular phones. Their faces reflected their puzzlement and fear. Mrs. La Vance and Pan were already at the Oval Office when the President entered. As in every crisis in his presidency, the very first appraisal was conducted by the President, Panaiotis "Pan," Rossi, his Chief of Staff, and Mrs. Martha La Vance, the President's secretary.

"OK, let us do something before these aspirins crash on top of us and give us a serious headache," began the President.

Mrs. La Vance looked up from the list on her note pad and read the names of persons and institution that needed to be contacted on a priority basis.

"Forget the incoming calls, Mrs. LaVance," advised the President, "let us do the ones you have. I only want a few minutes with each."

"That will take at least an hour," observed Pan Rossi. "You will have the Vice President, the National Security Adviser, the Secretary of State and the Secretary of Defense in here in a few minutes."

The President was silent for a moment. "Has anyone any idea what the heck this thing above us is?"

The Chief of Staff looked at the notes he had jotted down on an envelope and answered, "So far, Mister President, nothing at all. This object appeared over the city at exactly zero six am. Similar objects have also appeared over cities in the US, Canada, Mexico and we are getting reports of similar occurrences in the rest of the world. Now, as to their nature, they certainly don't look like space ships, but seem quite solid and impregnable."

"Whatever happened to our early warning systems, radar, shields and smoke signals? How can they get down and park without anyone noticing them?" asked the President.

"The Armed Forces Joint Command and the Strategic Services Office are now trying to determine what they are made of and attempting to establish contact," continued Pan. "Nobody has received any communication from these objects and no one has reported any lights, exhaust or even motion. They just appeared and parked above cities on the five continents. Their descent into the parking orbit must have been so fast that no one registered anything. It has been suggested that their speed is probably near that of the speed of light."

He stopped and looked at the President, then continued. "The various observatories are just getting underway to make a more detailed appraisal of these things, same as some of the specialized Air Defense and Reconnaissance Groups. There seems to be utter confusion all around. Fortunately, communications on earth have not been affected except for some isolated instances when satellite communications were disturbed by these objects. But the technology is such that communications can be maintained through back up connections. You see, we ourselves get a lot of satellite feeds that come in either through our own receiving antennas or through fiber optics or microwave. No problem there. Telephones lines and all other systems are working normally."

"Okay, how about the public?"

"So far, there is no panic. New York reports early morning crowds in Central Park and Times Square but they do nothing except look up at the objects. Here in Washington, the Mayor and the Chief of Police have raised an alert and will have all available personnel in the streets within the next hour. Most people have not yet realized what is happening above their heads. That is about all I have."

"How about the CIA?" asked the President. "Maybe for once they can tell us something we don't know."

They smiled nervously and after receiving rush assignments, left the Office. The President spent several minutes on the phone talking to world leaders, newsmen, party leaders and assorted religious, business and personal friends. He apologized for the little time he could spend with each and promised to keep them informed. Once finished, the President asked to be connected with Patrick Deschamps, the UN Secretary General at his home in New York. He was put through almost immediately.

"Patrick, excuse me for calling up so early..."

"I was up already, Mister President. I am now looking at the thing we have on top of New York and kept thinking about you."

"I have nothing to do with that, Mister Secretary General."

They both laughed and reverted to the familiar tone they used privately. Their friendship dated from years back when both had been active in "saving the world" as they often reminisced about their undergraduate days.

"My people are just getting started here," said the President. "No one seems to know anything about these things. To tell you the truth, I am a bit scared. Have never seen anything like it except in some of those movies when Bruce, Otto or Claude save the world from the giant Pepsodent spiders or some other loony creature."

"Ross, this is a hell of an invasion, if that is what it is. I am listening on short wave to reports from all over, and it is all the same. People are under shock and it will be some time before they react. Which is what I am afraid will happen. As an invasion, it is a funny one. They, whatever 'they' are, come to earth, park a few of these aspirin-like balloons, don't move an inch, don't say a word, don't make any noise they have no lights, no antennas, no landing gear, no exhaust pipes, no periscopes, *rien de rien*! Is it some kind of a joke?"

The President laughed. Patrick's Gaelic logic cut through extraneous considerations and arrived at the substance of the problem with no wasted words.

"Right you are. The problem is that we don't know if we have a problem. But we have those things above that could be the quickest way to promote panic and hysteria. I guess what I wanted to say is that as soon as you get to your office and get your staff organized, please give me a call. I am thinking of a public announcement and I believe a joint one on world television would help allay some of the fear and speculation. I want to hear what our iron generals have to say about these phenomena. Then, I plan to try to drop a couple of hints to our press corps to the effect that they should try to moderate their comments about the objects and attempt to maintain a sober outlook. What we don't need now is a non-stop parade of sensational speculations."

"Excellent idea. I am leaving for the UN just now and will probably call you in one hour's time. Give my love to Earla, and God help us!"

The President, with a somber expression on his face, replaced the telephone with a slow and deliberate motion. He felt that this historical incident had all the features of either a holocaust of the human race or the beginning of a new era in the planet. He could not believe that the objects were an isolated event affecting planet earth. He was quick to evaluate in realistic terms the disciplined manner in which the objects had appeared and their outward characteristics. He was convinced that something beyond a few aspirin-shaped flying objects was behind that incredible display overhead. His practical mind was already charting avenues of action that involved, above all, the safety and well being of the country and that of the entire planet.

This is the moment of "put up or shut up," he thought. *Here is where the Leader of the Free World earns his stripes!*

All other matters that had occupied his concentration in the last few weeks now appeared trite and banal. Even the peace negotiations in several areas of the world that had been foremost in his mind, had been relegated to a secondary level. He thought about pending legislation on domestic matters and could not help smiling when he thought of the sessions scheduled for that morning with committee Chairmen, leaders of the opposition party and the usual eager beaver senators from both parties. His smile however faded when he added the lobbyists to his thoughts. We are becoming more and more the executive arm of lobbyists and not a simple coordinating action. Whatever happens, these guys are not going to put off their meetings today.

"Here we have an event as momentous as the very creation of life on the planet and I have to face a squad of self centered senators prepared to haggle about minor bills, and the rights and concessions for some of the lobbies that propped them up!"

The irony of it all made him both sad and disgusted. He thought back to several events in recent history that had exposed fissures that mocked the term union. A term that had been proudly hailed for several generations. He shook his head and rang for Mrs. La Vance.

PART ONE
Surprise in the Sky

Washington DC—04:15 hrs

Richard Ferguson, the Nobel Prize Anthropologist, popular columnist and man about town, woke up in his Fairfax Station town house at four in the morning with only one thing on his mind. He wanted to complete the article whose deadline was a few hours away. He stumbled from his bedroom to his heavily curtained den in the back of the house. The cozy isolation of the den protected him from distracting noises and sights.

The article he was working on demanded his total concentration and made him forget about breakfast. He typed furiously for what seemed a brief moment but when he glanced at the clock on the wall, he saw that it was 7:25. He decided to stop and get ready to tackle the day's activities. Richard showered and dressed quickly in a practical combination of chinos, a button down yellow shirt and his comfortable black alpaca jacket. He took advantage of these moments to mentally program the day ahead: the routine meeting at the Academy in the morning, the lunch seminar and, with some anticipation, the late afternoon trip to New York and the chance to see Helen Lawrence again. He was also looking forward to the small dinner that evening, arranged by Patrick Deschamps, the Secretary General of the UN and an old classmate at Columbia University in New York and later a colleague at the State Department.

Patrick had not been "visible," as he put it, in the last few months due to a tremendously busy schedule. He had briefly explained to those close to him that he was trying to "make her honest," referring to the United Nations standing. Those dinners had been held with some regularity and provided those attending a welcome respite from their busy work routine. A work routine which, in the words of Richard, "all it did was to increase material wealth and professional satisfaction but it also made their clocks tick faster and fast clocks never help good digestion," but due to Patrick's frenetic schedule they had not met for several months.

As he started to make breakfast, he turned on the radio and was aware at once that the familiar voices now conveyed a nervousness that made him listen intently. The excited voices alarmed him as soon as he understood what they were talking about. The nervousness of the speakers denoted both amazement and fear. He was able to understand that they were referring to a phenomenon that had taken place barely an hour ago above the cities of the world. He rushed to the terrace of the town house and looked up. Parked above the city of Washington DC was a huge white object that resembled an aspirin, even though it had no discernible edges. He was at once puzzled and afraid. It caused his heartbeat to accelerate and his face to turn a deep shade of pink.

His first reaction was to force himself to accept what his senses had detected, but without making a conscious effort to interpret or decipher. It was an old technique that had proven valuable in his years as a field anthropologist. When dealing with tangible and intangible facts and objects it was necessary to observe some form of mental discipline to avoid hasty conclusions. "Let the neurons absorb the signals in their totality, before I put them to work," he used to remind himself. This was without doubt the occasion of all occasions to practice his mental precepts.

He went inside, poured some coffee and grabbed the US Army binoculars he kept in the closet in the hallway. He returned to the terrace and pulling a chair, focused the glasses on the object above. The adjustment was minor, as he calculated roughly the object's height at around one hundred thousand feet. The surface of the object was smooth and had no openings or external ports, exhausts, intakes, flaps, spoilers, or any of the familiar protuberances of airplanes, space ships or rockets. He also noticed the color of the structure which was neither white nor off white but something in between. It seemed to absorb daylight while at the same time providing an iridescent reflection that was barely noticeable. He estimated its diameter at about twenty miles, even though he felt that its shape was not totally circular but more like an oval.

The object did not move at all. He trained the glasses on the object for more than five minutes trying not to make any movement that would blur the image. Mentally he aligned one visible edge of the object with a landmark on the ground. No motion could be detected. By now, he was not only puzzled but also curious, and underneath these reactions he could feel a cold edge of simple, unadulterated fear. He got up slowly, stretched his six foot two frame, and thought about the matter: a very strange object appearing over most big cities on Earth, was not an ordinary occurrence. Scratch the whole thing as something conjured up by any one country on earth. He had convinced himself that it was no optical illusion. The thing was too solid to be the result of some clever mirror game. Besides it cast a very convincing shadow and reflected light in a very real manner. How about the crews of the things? Were they human? Were they good or bad? Were they vegetarians? How would they communicate? The incredible nature of the phenomenon elicited many more questions.

The telephone rang. He picked it up and with an effort to make his voice sound serene and calmly replied to the greeting on the other end of the line. To his surprise, it was Kathryn, the wife of Patrick Deschamps, the Secretary General of the UN, calling from New York.

"Richard," she said in a voice that revealed not only fear but a touch of desperation, "I guess you have seen the things above. I hear you got one over Washington, too."

"Yes, I have just spent ten minutes looking at it and trying to figure out what it is."

"Until we know, the consensus here is that we go on as normally as we can manage. That brings me to our long awaited dinner tonight. We have to cancel it, if you don't mind."

"No problem! This thing is bound to upset us all. I can well imagine that Patrick is going to have a busy day. The radio says that similar objects have appeared in cities all over the world, so we are not alone."

"Patrick is getting frantic messages from all over and no one has the faintest idea of what these things are. Anyway, if you are still planning to come to New York, Patrick suggests that we have breakfast instead on Saturday morning at the Essex House. I won't be able to make it Saturday but will see you later in the day." Richard interrupted, "Have you talked to Helen? I've been trying to reach her for the last half hour but her line is busy."

"Yes, I talked to her earlier. She and Mercedes decided to go to work anyway. They are both scared out of their wits. In any case they will be at the breakfast Saturday, that is, if there is no bad news from the pills on top of us!"

"You are right. I was planning to shuttle in to New York late this afternoon, but with this development I don't know if the airlines will be able to fly. If there are no flights I will drive in this afternoon. I just hope there won't be restrictions on driving. But you never know..."

They talked for a minute and then, recognizing the pressure she was under, Richard said goodbye. He was uneasy and a bit nervous. He realized that the thing above was beginning to intrude most dramatically into everybody's life. With a frown on his face he dialed Helen's number in New York.

New York—05:00 hrs

At quarter to five in the morning, Helen Lawrence lay deeply asleep. Ordinarily, at this time, she would be having an abbreviated breakfast followed by her morning jog. Her lavish blond mass of hair, splashed on the satin pillow, hid her delicate features and at the same time insulated her from the distant sounds of the awakening city. Deep sleep can only last a few moments but it can do wonders for the body and the mind. Deep sleep, defined scientifically as an almost total retreat from consciousness is a daily necessity for the human body. Absolute repose from normal physical activity allows for the replenishing of energy levels in the body (storing amino acids, sugars and carbohydrates). It also helps in creating a feeling of well being, which in turn affects ideas, thoughts and attitudes. This morning, her sleep met these requisites.

At 05:15 her telephone rang. By the fifth ring, the message entered her consciousness. She woke up and looked at the luminous clock on the elaborate telephone system by her bed. A glance at the time triggered her annoyance. She had set the alarm for 05:00, or had she?

"Helen." The voice was instantly recognizable. "Please don't open your eyes and listen. Did you know that at this time of the morning the soul of the city returns to the streets, parks, buildings and empty parking lots? Did you know that at this time of the day that soul of the city sets the tone and the rhythm for the rest of the day? Well, you lazy bones, I am sure you overslept and our jogging rendezvous will have to be postponed. I am also convinced that you spent half the night working on your latest project, instead of chaperoning me last night in my perfectly frightful dinner date."

Helen smiled and dreamily mumbled, "Mercedes, you nut, you are right. I even forgot to set the alarm. If you hadn't called I would have probably slept until noon. That jazz about the soul of the city is too much for this time of morning. I hope that soul returns in a good humor and does so after the sanitation department has completed its rounds. I know I would be in a foul mood the rest of the day if I had to listen to the early morning garbage trucks delicately loading and unloading, the screeching of the ambulances and the careful drop of newspaper bundles from the delivery vans in Manhattan. Forget about the jog and get your anatomy here. I can get a royal breakfast fixed in the next thirty minutes and we can have it on the terrace, if it isn't snowing."

"Nah, it is still dark but you know, you get that feeling that it will be a beautiful day. It will be daylight soon. And it is perfect for a terrace breakfast, as long as you give me real eggs and not those substitutes."

"Speaking of substitutes how was your date last night?"

"On a scale of one to one, I'd rate it a total minus. I find it hard to believe that an intelligent, educated person can fill an entire evening with the most egotistical concert I have ever heard. The guy only talked about his talents, his defects, his ideas about everything, his dog, his toothbrush. Not a single reference to a neutral subject. Is there any man on this city that is not totally immersed in himself?"

"There are a couple but they are in their eighties!"

Helen got out of bed and opened up the sliding doors that separated the bedroom from one of the coziest and most comfortable terraces in the Upper East Side of Manhattan. Mercedes was right. While the sun had not yet brightened up the skies, a soft light announced that a mild, cloudless day was in store.She quickly showered and, like she did every morning, studied herself in the full-length mirror in her dressing room. She was pleased. For a few weeks, she had been afraid that she had lost too much weight and that some parts of her well-constructed body may reveal signs of defeat and sagging. But such was not the case. Every contour seemed to be firmly established. There was just the right amount of bounce in the proper places to make sure that clothing would not hide but glorify those lines. She slipped into jeans and an Atlanta Braves sweat.Deftly, she made coffee from a large container of a decaffeinated blend of Venezuelan, Colombian and Peruvian coffee. She was putting the finishing touches on a courageous breakfast, when the doorbell rang. Mercedes had her jogging suit on and carried the day's newspaper editions and a fruit basket. But more than anything, it was the smile she had that made the day seem brighter.

Helen and Mercedes had been close for many years. Theirs was an easy relationship based on almost identical backgrounds. Both came from the same small New England town. Since childhood, they had formed a couple blessed with unique academic excellence and exquisite social graces. They had continued to excel throughout their college and post graduate days. Thus, they shared a wealth of common acquaintances, experiences and the special links that their growing up in the same small town had forged. At one time, Helen had helped Mercedes overcome a serious bout of depression as a result of the tragic loss of her older and much admired sister, Sarah, in a plane accident. Aware of the pain and the confusion experienced by Mercedes, she had remained at her side and helped her regain the sense of purpose in her life. She had been instrumental in getting Mercedes to make the change from Boston to New York and had helped her obtain a position in The New York Times. They became inseparable and, in time, Mercedes was able to regain her former enthusiasm and optimism. Her cheerful presence and welcome company alleviated Helen's frequent bouts of loneliness that most people in a city as full of people as New York often experience. In the meantime, they both enjoyed each other's company and, best of all, shared the joys and frustrations of living in the most exciting city in the world.Mercedes helped Helen carry the trays with the fresh juices, the coffeepot, the toaster and the chafing dishes with eggs, bacon, string potatoes and sausages. Helen handled the mushrooms that had just been through a delicate sauté session in a mixture of butter, small chopped onions and a touch of a light white wine.

The table in the terrace was strategically placed in a cozy recess that protected it from the occasional strong breezes coming from across the river and the sounds from the drive below. Helen was proud of her terrace and its unique personality. She often commented that she probably spent more time and money fixing the terrace than any other part of the apartment. It was well worth it. The terrace was an ample extension that surrounded the corner apartment and afforded a precious view of the East River, the UN building and the bridges downstream. Helen had resurfaced the floor with red all-weather tiles and had also installed motor operated awnings and self-standing umbrellas. The plants and flowers all answered to a carefully planned design that provided a restful and pleasant setting. The French wall light fixtures that blended with the awnings, the white French doors and the other two marbles topped tables gave the impression of an outdoor cafe in Lyon. She also felt grateful to the strange owner of the place, who had agreed to a very favorable lease and had also participated financially in the extensive remodeling she had insisted on.

The owner, whose occupation was not clear to Helen, was a charismatic man who vaguely informed her that he headed a Free and Easy Religious

Assembly, as he called it. She later learned that he was a street "Fire and Brimstone," preacher in the Park. But in spite of his strange manner, he inspired confidence and was sincere in his beliefs. These traits plus a forceful but gentle manner and a unique hypnotic look made him both attractive and intriguing. She understood that in New York City, a small dose of such traits could be parlayed into considerable assets.After setting their plates and pouring the mixture of orange, mango and papaya juices in their glasses and lacing them with a touch of California Spumante, and surveying the side table with the various appetizing dishes, Mercedes remarked, "I bet there are no more than a half dozen people in the entire city who are about to have, or are having, a ceremonial breakfast like this one. Of course, there is only one you and that puts all the other events in the so-so file."

At that moment, Helen's grandfather clock struck six o'clock. As the first familiar sound was heard, both Helen and Mercedes noticed a heavy shadow that cut down on the brightness of the white linen on the table and toned down the profusion of colors in the garden. They both looked up and saw this immense shape parked high above them. The object appeared to cover a large area and had partially reduced the still vague morning light. It seemed to extend over the entire length of Manhattan and it appeared wide enough from where they were to cover both the Hudson and the East Rivers. Its color was between light beige and off white, like an eggshell, or, in the uncertain light, like a huge aspirin tablet. For a moment they could not take their eyes off the object. Then, they looked at each other with unconcealed apprehension and amazement. Helen was suddenly pale and on the verge of tears. She tried to say something but could not manage. After a moment of involuntary hesitation she was able to blurt out, "Mercedes, I don't know what to say but all of a sudden I'm scared to death! What is it? It doesn't look like a cloud. Or anything..."

Mercedes had stood up and was again looking at the object as if by standing up she could have a better look. In a voice that did not have the usual forceful and confident tone, she said, "I don't know, Helen. It is definitely not a man-made object. It looks like a huge, eggshell colored aspirin tablet and it doesn't move at all. Let me call Information or the Police Central."

After a while, Mercedes picked up the small cellular telephone and standing by the parapet of the terrace made a number of calls, all in vain. All lines were busy. She tried JFK's Airport Information, the New York Terminal Radar Approach Control (TRACON), the Islip Long Island Air Traffic Center, the Police and even the Observatory in Staten Island. After a while she and Helen went back in and turned the television on. By then it was half past six.

The TV and radio stations at that time had just realized that the object above Manhattan was something out of the ordinary. Calls were coming into the studio at monsoon intensity causing an overflow of the automated answering system so that calls were stacked indefinitely. Stations with manned switchboards were swamped. The magnitude and the uneasiness caused by the event, added to the general confusion. Most radio and TV stations were forced to break into what remained of their early morning programming with special bulletins every few minutes. The anchors, disc jockeys and announcers had barely the time to scribble a few notes before receiving the "You are on the Air," signal from frantic directors and producers. Their messages however, were all the same, "An unknown, unidentified object has appeared high over New York City at exactly 6 a.m. today. This object—apparently a space ship—appears to be about 20 miles long and right now covers the entire island of Manhattan. Its width is estimated at about 10 to 15 miles and, from what we have been able to observe from the roof of our building, it covers both the Hudson and the East River and extends some distance beyond in both directions. It is stationary at an estimated altitude of well over 100,000 feet. Its shape is oblong and it does not seem to have any windows, ports or navigation lights of any kind. We expect a bulletin from the Civil Aviation Authority and the FAA any time now as well as information from the Defense Department. Meanwhile, we are trying to establish contact with the New York Terminal Radar Approach Control, the Long Island Radar Control Center and the National Transportation Board. There is no reason to be alarmed. We are sure that in a short while, the object will have been identified. Stay tuned."

Like the million New Yorkers who had been awake at six that morning, and had looked up to the sky, Mercedes and Helen, had drawn their own conclusions.

"It is not something we or anyone else has sent up. It is not a Christo stunt, even though it would be something he would like to author. It seems solid and smooth enough like an eggshell," said Helen.

Mercedes smiled.

"If it as an egg and it breaks, it will really be Breakfast in America!"

They both laughed if somewhat nervously and then the phone rang. Helen was quick to pick it up and listened intently without saying a word. Finally she smiled and nodded. She said, "Sure, no problem. I can speak for Mercedes. We'll be there. Bye."

She turned to Mercedes, still showing traces of a nervousness that would stay with her for some time.

"That was Patrick. I've never heard him so excited and agitated."

"Is our UN Secretary General already at his post? What does he have to say about these pills?"

"It seems this thing above us is not the only one. He says that most big cities in the world have acquired one of them just on top of their very center. He is still at home but getting ready to go to the UN and asked me if we could have breakfast Saturday morning instead of dinner tonight. It seems all the UN delegations have been on the phone to him in the last few minutes and will be lined up at his office throughout the day and probably the night."

She paused and with a fearful look in her eyes raised her head toward the object above. Then, she continued. "He does not have any information about the spaceships, or whatever they are."

"Is Patrick okay?" asked Mercedes.

"Yes, I think so. Nervous and trying to get his mind organized, he says. He has to try to fit in a million appointments in the next few hours. Everyone is alarmed and, he says, some are even hysterical. So, instead of dinner tonight he suggests breakfast at the Essex House day after tomorrow, that is Saturday morning at seven. OK?"

Mercedes, who had been looking at the object, lowered her head and nodded. As an Assistant Editor of the New York Times, Mercedes was already thinking about the avalanche of queries, comments and interviews that the phenomenon above was certain to bring about. She looked at Helen, whose puzzled expression and that slight edge of fear matched her own. She poured two cups of coffee, and handing one to Helen said, "Yup, I imagine poor old Patrick is going to have a hell of a day. This kind of thing can upset anyone! I wonder how the rest of the country and the rest of the world are taking this. I hate to think about it. Patrick has been going like a dentist's drill trying to straighten out the UN, against almost everyone's will except a few smart ones at the White House and the State Department, and now this!"

She shook her head and went on, "You know I've been trying to get him to think in terms of a series of articles about the remodeling of the UN. There is a great story in all the changes being made, and the effect they are having, but he is shying away from it at this time. I am sure he has tons of notes and juicy anecdotes about the shenanigans of his bureaucrats. They've been going on for more than fifty years and it is costing Patrick a lot to bring some order into that house."

She drank some coffee and continued. "We are all still recovering from the surprises Patrick has pulled on us the last few months. The way the UN is changing is simply incredible; we are getting reports from all over about projects underway that had been sitting in the shelves for years. He has entire industries coming to the aid of the UN which means the aid of the world. I wonder what kind of blackmail de has been using!"

"I think it has something that needed to be done. Patrick has probably found the formula. It is a good thing that against all precedent Patrick got the job. You know, citizens from the countries in the Security Council cannot be elected to the Secretary General post. It has been a great thing for the UN and for Patrick. Well, you know what Kathryn says, "If it hadn't been the UN for Patrick, he would have been bored out of his Guccis as an Ambassador somewhere or at some useless position with a pompous title in Washington, but as long as we stayed near each other, it would not really matter."

"Do I detect a bit of feminine envy? It would be natural, I guess. I also envy them and I am sure so does everyone that knows them."

After a pause that she used to take a sizable bite on a croissant and with her gaze fixed on Helen's eyes, Mercedes said, "And it will be great to see Richard again, as long as you two don't argue and flirt at the same time, like you always do. Perhaps our eminent professor can tell us more about these objects..."

Helen laughed, drank some coffee and moved toward the living room door. She muttered something about calling her mother in Connecticut and getting ready to go to her office, advising Mercedes to also call her mother before going to work.

"You'll probably be walking into the proverbial madhouse at *The Times*," offered Helen as she began to collect the breakfast items from the table.

"You can be sure of that. These days we even chase stories about shoplifting in candy stores, cute man bites dog stories and the love affairs of third rate performers," observed Mercedes and then, "I think I will give Flo Marsh at the Washington Radar Center a call later this morning. She should have all the details by then."

"Great! Say hello to Marshie for me. I hear she is doing well at the Radar Center; she was always nuts about science," said Helen and then she continued. "As for my office I can only guess that someone has already started writing the treatment for a documentary on the things above us. I expect Richard will be calling me at the office later today; he might have some information about these things from some of his contacts in DC."

Mercedes followed Helen into the living room and with a quick peck on Helen's cheek she left, promising to call her later that morning.

"Will there be time?" they both wondered as Mercedes rang for the elevator. At that moment, Helen's telephone rang.

National Radar Center—Washington, DC—05: 57 hrs

The complex where the Radar Center is located offers many advantages, one of which is its excellent parking facilities. You can choose the outdoor lots—ideal for spring and summer—or the multi-floor indoor parking. Today's forecast predicted a mild, sunny day so Florence Marsh, Radar Controller, Grade BG3, parked her Chrysler LeBaron outdoors near one of the waterfalls. She smiled to herself, anticipating her noontime snack soothed by the gentle murmur of the stream.

As she did every morning, Florence Marsh timed her arrival at her station at the Operations Lounge of the Radar Center a few minutes before the 06 00 a.m. start of her shift. After placing her light coat, lunch box and the morning paper in her locker, she went to the Bulletin Board and then quickly moved to her own station where the large Raytheon G5000 unit and the CTR had no messages for her. There was nothing of urgency or even of interest. At that time of the morning there was little traffic at either Dulles or National and practically no action from Andrews. The previous shift had completed the wrap up before leaving so all she had to do was to cut in the activator on her scope and make her hook up with the recording units.

As usual, she would warm up the screen for a few minutes so that she would be ready at exactly 06 00 hours to notify the various control points on the East Coast that she was ready to pick up incoming traffic and would be setting up the customary reserve and secondary routings. She said good morning to the Flight Data Controllers on her side of the room and accepted a paper cup of coffee from Sam, the junior NRC (Non-radar Controller).

As she often did, she smiled when she looked at the 36 inch scope or PPI, in the parlance of the R-people in the center. To her, the scope represented a triumph of sorts. Upon finishing high school she had been lucky to fall under the tutelage of Professor John Armbruster at Georgetown. The Professor was considered one of the leading authorities on Space Sciences and had been instrumental in the development of some of the deep space programs adopted by NASA. He and his wife Vi sort of adopted Florence and appointed her First Mate of their 45 foot Sail boat, that laid at anchor in St. Michael's in the Chesapeake Bay.

The Professor was quick to grasp the unique interest that Marsha had for

Astronomy, Astrology and Space Science in general. Since she was one of the best students he had, he was happy to arrange for summer jobs for Marsha at the Anacostia Naval Research Labs across the river from Washington.

She quickly earned a reputation as a serious and reliable worker whose interest in her small parcel of work and knowledge, was enriched by her own curiosity and scholarship. Soon, she was intimately familiar with the work of Nikola Tesla, who was the first to predict that radio waves could be used to detect objects and, later with the work performed by Marconi (who, in 1922 proved Nikolas' theories). Her fascination soon centered on radar systems and technology and, by the time she graduated from Georgetown, it was a simple decision to accept a position at the Washington DC Air Route Traffic Control Center. She rewarded herself with a month long holiday in Europe accompanied by two of her high school classmates Helen and Mercedes that now lived and worked in Manhattan. They had been close friends since their elementary school days in Connecticut. That month included all of those things that can make a vacation a glorious interval in one's life.

She enjoyed her work at the Center and only wished that she could have more time to pursue some of the theoretical work that she had pursued in college. She felt that a great deal of work was still to be done before radar systems throughout the country could be a guarantee of safe air transport. She daydreamed that some day multiple energy level pulses would be able to provide selective responses, independent of weather conditions, ground clutter and other factors that in this day and age, introduced some elements of doubt in radar detection.

By 05:59, Marsha's PPI or scope with its multicolor tracings and reference coordinates was ready to go. At the exact moment when her fingers were about to depress the sequence initiator—or at precisely 06 00—her screen seemed to go mad. Accustomed as she was to the occasional screen ghosts, ground clutter, and snow and flickering, she could not help letting out a loud exclamation as she saw the blink from a very large object that had appeared on the "Main Bang"—or center of her screen, from nowhere.

The sensation she experienced was unique. Later she could only compare it to those moments just before you lose consciousness. It was a dizzying spell, sudden and intense. She recovered quickly and mechanically noted the coordinates of the object. It was squarely placed in the center of the capital and it covered a fairly large area extending from highway 485 in the north to the 95 freeway in the south. Its width appeared to extend from Arlington to South Franklin all the way to Rockville. She could not figure out if the image was a ghost—a sometime reflective flaw in the screen or an unfiltered cloud shape. She also wondered if what she was seeing was not a major technical defect in her equipment. She knew that in spite of the extensive use of the airways in the United States, its radar systems were often antiquated and at times, unreliable.

Surprisingly few systems have been installed in the last twenty years, the rest belonging to the old and happy days when flying was not quite the preferred transportation for the masses. She quickly turned on her scanner while noticing that the object remained static. She fiddled with the controls quickly adjusting the receiver gain, the sensitivity button and the CPC or circular Polarization Control. Upon zooming in she read the coordinates that were so familiar to all the screen jocks in the Center. The White House! She also noted that the object's altitude was shown as 100,000 feet and that it had an oval shape.

Normally, all flying objects within the range of radar beams appear as dots on the PPI or scope and, as they move, leave a fading trail. This echo or target or just plain blip quickly identifies the position of the object, making the job of the controller a matter of establishing other flight data and proceeding to guide and control the path of the object. But this time, something was amiss. The signal that bounced back showed no power loss. There was no need to amplify the signal, as the object appeared to be stationary. No need to use the MTI (Moving Target Indicator) and it was useless to fiddle with Frequency settings or other adjustments.

At that point all hell broke loose in the room. The automatic scanners and identifiers had cut in milliseconds after the radar antennas picked up the shape. No one seemed to be able to report on anything that could serve to identify the object. No radio waves or any signals of any sort and no absorption or reception echoes could be detected. It was just a plain, strong signal. They were all amazed that the object, in spite of being bombarded by radar beacons, did not bother to acknowledge them. In technical terms, this was a case of an "Unassociated Track that provided data block." A rare occurrence.

It appeared as if the object were wrapped in its own electromagnetic field. Meanwhile, control centers from the entire East Coast of the United States were calling to find out about the strange shape that had suddenly appeared on their scopes, even if not directly above them. Messages were coming in via their own FDP facilities, radio, Internet, fax, telex and telephone and no one in the room—where more than a dozen operators were working—could provide a logical explanation for the appearance of the objects.

Identical objects had suddenly appeared over all the major cities in the

United States. It seemed that every city of some importance had its own object overhead. The descriptions were always the same. It was about 20 miles long and about 15 miles wide. Its thickness was estimated at about 2 miles and was sitting on a stationary position at approximately 100,000 feet. No one had reported any form of signal or even motion from the objects. Because of its oblong shape and color, operators throughout the world were calling it several names; the most popular of which seemed to be the "pill," as it did resemble an aspirin tablet.

Late that morning all operators and other personnel at the Center were asked to remain at their posts. It was suggested that they arrange to eat their noon meal at their positions. Florence had managed to overcome the moments of anxiety she suffered during the first hours of her shift, but she could not shake the gnawing suspicion that she was witnessing the beginnings of a space odyssey.

The Oval Office

That evening, the President and members of his inner circle sat in the Oval Office having the last coffee of the day. For the entire day they had discussed the phenomenon overhead and filed innumerable notes about cabinet meetings, calls from US embassies overseas and all sorts of private communications from Heads of State and political leaders from all over the world. They also had to contend with a press that was anxious to extract from the White House any information that might be available, or, failing that, simple opinions about the objects.

"I don't see how we can prepare any defenses for any form of aggression perpetrated by these ships. For one thing, they seem to be impregnable and also, they have not shown any form of animosity toward us. Impossible to tell what they are up to."

Ross Simonson, the President of the United States refused to be drawn into the state of extreme alarm that had been created by some of the more apprehensive members of his Cabinet. He maintained that sooner or later some form of communication would be forthcoming. He did not believe that all of a sudden, giant purple spiders or three-eyed scaly customers would descend on planet earth and begin feeding on its population. Once the initial shock created by the abrupt arrival of the pills had worn off, people did not fail to notice that the presence of the pills over so many cities created a special feeling where fear, suspense and curiosity blended together. Some did not fail to notice that there was some beauty attached to their presence in the skies. As sunlight acquired different intensities in the various time zones of the planet, the pills managed to provide a golden edge to the skies while appearing to float harmlessly.

The tension and puzzlement of the situation was almost palpable in the room. They quietly poured coffee or tea from the beverage containers in the side table and then sat down in the sofas in the middle of the room. Michael Pashley, the National Security Adviser glanced at the President, who at the moment was deep in thought and then, clearing his throat said, "Mr. President, I am convinced that there is a plan here. These objects haven't just parked on this planet for the hell of it. I think that whoever or whatever, they are studying us and probably deciding how to make contact. Any aggressive action on their part would have taken place the moment they arrived. You know; the element of surprise and all that. I would not be surprised if they decide to establish contact through the UN or some other international organization."

"Other than the UN the only ones I can think of are the NATO Organization, the Vatican, the Red Cross and maybe some Interdenominational Church Group," remarked Alan Clayton, the Secretary of State.

They all nodded. If there was a purpose behind the appearance of the objects, it would have to be exposed sooner or later. If it was a contact of a peaceful nature, it would have to be communicated to the peoples of earth.

Michael Pashley reached for his briefcase and pulled out a sheaf of printed pages that had the familiar red Top Secret strip at the top. He turned to the President and said, "Mister President, these are the reports received throughout the day from the various space agencies. You already received a summary. If you let me I would like to pass some of this data on to our colleagues here."

The President nodded and Pashley continued. "The first object recognition alarm was automatically triggered by our Reconnaissance Satellites. There are several birds that detect anything that moves. Even field mice. They are part of a series that picks up all types of communications and are run by the NRO or National Reconnaissance Office and translated by the National Imagery and Mapping Agency and the National Security Agency."

Vice President Ursula Walters asked, "But aren't these birds looking down only?"

"Actually they have sensors that can be activated to check in all directions. The size of the objects did not escape them, except that their arrival was so swift that it approached the speed of light and no meaningful images were obtained as they took up their position above the cities of the world."

He paused for a moment and then continued. "Keep in mind that few things can move undetected by the eyes and ears we keep above, especially if they approach the planet. We have in addition to the NRO, a string of Communication satellites, early warning launch satellites, infrared detectors and locators and then there are the Special Communication Satellites, the Milstars System, the Defense Meteorological Sats, the Navstar GPS and a string of UHF birds doing all kinds of privileged communications work. You see, we have a good umbrella. But it must be kept in mind that it is part of an information network. It is not reactive and it does not alert strange objects or contact them."

The President spoke. "Yes, we can see the objects but we have not heard them. But I am convinced that they will soon let us know that they know we know they are there. And, I agree that they'll probably contact us through some supranational agency. It would have to be something like that. I don't think that they'll buy a page in the New York Times and explain to us what they are doing here. Nor do I think they will they hire a Media Communications Consultant to arrange for a Television special."

Ursula Walters drank some of her coffee and made a face.

"All due respect, Mr. President, but coffee at this hour begins to taste like Arabian crude."

They all smiled. She continued. "In my mind it is clear that there is a purpose behind this unexpected visit. The question for the people of the planet is what to do. And the more we review the situation, the more I am convinced that there is nothing we can do. We see no signs of life behind that hermetic electromagnetic shield and the damn things don't move an inch!"

The discussion continued for a while but without any enlightening conclusions. The consensus was that the best option was to wait for some form of message from the objects.

"I am sure that before long, they'll give us a holler," joked Alan Clayton.

On that note, the President got up and with a weary and tired look thanked them all for attending that impromptu meeting. Then he added, "Go home and on the way there, don't look up! Good night!"

As the President turned toward his desk, the telephone rang. It was Patrick Deschamps, the UN Secretary General calling from New York City.

"Mister President," began Patrick in his usual friendly tone, "just a short one. There is nothing to report from our side. I guess you are getting the same from your Embassies and offices abroad."

"Nothing at all. I guess you have seen the reports I sent you from our military and scientific people. They are just as dumbfounded as we all are. Again, the question about what we do or should be doing boils down to the identity of these things. Without having an inkling of their nature there is nothing we can do."

"My feelings exactly," answered the Secretary General. "The European Union and NATO have nothing to report; their findings are still the same as earlier today. I guess it is a question of time. Sooner or later those pills will have to say something."

"I hope so too," retorted the President, then added, "As long as no one gets hurt. By the way Patrick, we think it a good idea if we released a joint statement in the next few days not saying much but expressing some optimism about communications form the objects. It might help defuse some of the wild speculations the public has to swallow. What do you think?"

"You are on! Let us say next week, OK?

"OK."

The Secretary General of the UN

The presence of the objects was a situation that had no precedent in human history. It was easy to interpret it as a menace to the inhabitants of the planet even though it remained a very tangible and to date harmless unknown. To Patrick Deschamps, the UN's Secretary General, this crisis appeared to be a test of mankind's capacity to adopt a common attitude before an unknown phenomenon. It would also test people's capacity to look after each other. At least he hoped that it would be so, even if recent conflicts suggested the opposite.

While he refused to dwell in formless speculation about the nature and purpose of the objects, he could not ignore the responsibility that their very presence implied. He was aware that a purpose of some sort was behind the sudden appearance of the objects, but he did not wish to go any further in ascribing motives and reasons to the phenomenon. He felt that idle speculation would be more appropriate for the horse races or the British Soccer pools.

After a long and tiring day made even more anxious by the demands of a press thirsty for knowledge about the objects, Patrick Deschamps arrived in his apartment in upper Madison Avenue. Kathryn, his wife was having dinner out with a friend, so he planned on spending a quiet evening alone.

After a long and relaxed bath, he dressed in comfortable clothes and fixed himself a scotch and water. As he frequently did after a specially busy and tiresome day at "the shop," as he termed the UN building, he sat down at the shiny, black Yamaha Baby Grand in the living room. With no servants about, he felt both tired and pleasantly relaxed. The perfect mood for some piano playing. He sat down and began to play a few chords and to experiment with some of his favorite jazz sequences. Then he moved to the more relaxing sequences of one of Mozart's concerts for piano and violin. He loved to imagine the violin part in the concert. He felt that it helped him apply the right tempo and emphasis to the piano part.

After a while he switched to more popular melodies and then to his favorite piano game of playing a popular melody as it would be interpreted by the great masters. This time it was Georgia on my Mind, an all-time favorite. He applied the Schubert technique first, with its soft and sweet cadences and then moved to a violent Rachmaninoff, then to a romantic Haydn and finished with a vibrant Gershwin mode. As he switched to a variety of compositions, he could not help thinking about his life and shuddered to think that it might end up in the sudden flash of a nuclear explosion if the objects above had some belligerent ideas about planet earth.

As a boy growing up in Virginia, Patrick Deschamps had shown a unique talent for music in all its forms. At the age of 4 he could play Schubert's Serenade on the piano with sufficient technique and feeling, even if he could not reach the pedals to provide the added emphasis and accent to the composition. He was equally adept at the guitar and the violin. This talent, however, was not exploited by his parents who felt, wisely, that Patrick should grow up without the rigors and impositions demanded of child prodigies. His parents' attitude was not improvised and was the result of extensive testing by educators, child psychologists and even expert physicians in the US and in Europe.

Patrick's childhood and early youth were spent within the comfortable confines of a well to do, harmonious family life in Richmond. By the time he reached adolescence in the mid fifties, the memories of the Second World War were beginning to fade from public consciousness and new attitudes and perspectives dominated the world scene. His schooling at St Andrews in Delaware had prepared him for the more formal needs of a college education.

After a while he moved to his bedroom and once comfortably installed in his bed he reviewed today's events and made mental notes about pending matters. One was the joint announcement with the President of the US, another was the press conference in the morning and later that week a breakfast meeting with Richard Ferguson, his prep school classmate, Helen Lawrence the charming TV producer and Mercedes, the lovely Times journalist. It was the sort of reunion that he always found stimulating. As an Anthropologist, writer and man about town Richard brought the urgency of current events along with his wise and often amusing comments. Helen was a lovely presence enhanced by a first class intellect and a unique sense of humor, same as Mercedes whose journalistic excellence had made her a popular figure in New York's intellectual circles.

Breakfast in New York

Patrick, Mercedes, Richard and Helen looked forward to having breakfast in New York that Saturday morning; days after the appearance of the objects. It had been a busy interval for all since the day the skies were darkened by the mysterious shapes. Fortunately, there had been no signs of aggression or animosity toward the people of earth. The objects remained stationary and did no more damage than create a shadow as well as provide a new tourist attraction.

Breakfast in New York has a special significance. It is the meal of the day when visitors and residents alike greet the day with some measure of anticipation, optimism and high spirits. New York City boasts some of the best breakfast stops in the nation. The top line includes a few private clubs, exclusive tea rooms and the rapidly disappearing Breakfast Rooms in some of the better hotels.

The entire breakfast sequence in most of them becomes an exalted ceremony. Sober and unique importance is attached to common tasks such as the squeezing of fruit juices, the offering of fresh fruits, already peeled, cut and placed in decorative motifs on fine china plates, and the serving of the varied fare that makes breakfast a gourmet experience.

Unlike the lesser category hotels and even the better appointed cafeterias, the major hotels have gone to extreme pains to provide an atmosphere of elegance and decorum. The noise levels combine the discreet conversations with the muted sounds of cutlery and crystal, and the careful jostling of the morning papers. The dominant feature however is the exquisite service and attention by the expert personnel. Such thoughts crossed Richard Ferguson's mind as he sat in the lobby of the Essex House Hotel, waiting for Patrick, Helen and Mercedes.

He had spent a short and restless night in the habitual corner suite he occupied on his frequent trips to New York. The presence of the strange objects overhead had caused the airlines to cancel all flights, so he had had to drive from Washington to New York in a rented car. Other than the chaos that the suspension of airline service all over the world had caused, there was that unmistakable feeling of doom and fear evident everywhere.

With some bitterness, he remembered the terrorist attacks on New York's World Trade Center some time back. They had shocked the nation and dispelled once and for all the notion that terrorism was a distant and occasional nuisance. The American people reacted with dignity and compassion and quickly organized an international anti-terrorist coalition that soon established an acceptable approach to a problem that up to that point had been ignored by most, except by those nations that had experienced it in their own soils.

He reflected that such event had created an unprecedented sense of unity among the industrialized nations. It also underlined in blood the wide texture of the differences that existed among nations. It showed that fanaticism can be taught in schools and that the diabolical appeal of terrorism was based on selfish aims like nationalism, and misguided religious beliefs. Its allies were the misery, hopelessness and the despair that affected a large part of the peoples of the world. He recalled a favorite thesis of his that could also be summarized in a simple sentence, "Barriga llena, corazón contento" (Stomach full, happy heart). On a long term basis, terrorism could be diminished if not defeated if all emerging nations could attain a reasonable level of prosperity that would result in acceptable employment levels and living standards. Social and political maturity would ensue. But it could only be accomplished with the help of the wealthy nations of the planet.

The sight of the objects parked motionless and silent above the entire human race, while not sinister, was unsettling. There had been no attack and there were no victims, yet these apparitions created a sense of powerlessness and bewilderment before an unknown phenomenon whose nature could not be understood.

Richard could not help recalling his initial reaction to the sight of the objects over Washington. He also remembered vividly the frantic television accounts of the phenomenon. By noon of that fateful morning, Washington had been almost deserted. The early crowds, after waiting around the White House and the Mall, and not receiving any meaningful reassurance from the stream of news report and bulletins, had wisely decided to return home. Most people felt that the nearness of the loved ones would at least provide a measure of comfort and serenity if the objects above of all of a sudden decided to take some form of action. The early traffic gridlock had dissipated by mid afternoon so that he was able to drive out of the city without major problems. It had been an eerie drive, as most service stations and shops were closed and there was little traffic on the freeways.

He was anxious to see Helen again; the very idea did revive his optimism and filled him with that familiar blend of excitement and anxiety that her image inspired.

He had arrived late in the evening in New York. He was amazed at the deserted look of the city and after checking in at the familiar Essex House hotel, went straight to bed. He telephoned Helen and talked to her for about an hour.

The next morning, a few minutes before seven o'clock, Patrick Deschamps arrived at the lobby of the hotel, accompanied by his chauffeur and security personnel. There was genuine pleasure in their greeting, which was expressed in an affectionate embrace.

In a few minutes Helen and Mercedes appeared. They all greeted each other effusively while Helen and Richard shared a fleeting tender moment.

At the table, each one expressed his personal feelings about the objects above. All through the previous days and nights, radio and television stations had provided continuous information about the appearance of the pills above 300 of the major cities on earth. As usual, the eternal news channels offered the widest world coverage, even though their reporters had little to say except to regale the audience with an irritating display of their ability to say the same thing for hours in many formats, tones and expressions. The networks did not miss the opportunity to call up countless experts who were asked to express their opinions about the objects. A parade of retired this and retired that ensued with the corresponding increase in the level of inanity and repetition.

"So far, all we know is that they are there and no more," observed Patrick.

Helen, half seriously, offered her view that such large objects would probably contain some lethal gases and that at a given moment they would be discharged above the cities and wipe out the human race. Sort of fumigate the place before landing.

"But," interjected Mercedes, "what if instead of gases or lethal weapons or belligerent beings, the things are full of friendly extraterrestrials who wish to pass their superior knowledge on to us and help us become a decent planet?"

"I just try to picture what Columbus felt when he first landed on the American continent. Did he question his right to be there? Was he prepared to observe the natives before making any decisions? Was he concerned about their reaction? Would he in any way bring about changes that the natives would not accept? Did he realize that his arrival would change their lives forever? Are there any beings inside those pills thinking like Columbus?" asked Richard. He paused, then continued. "I hate to be pessimistic but all I have is history to back my perception of this episode. In the history of the human race, every discovery and every conquest has exacted a price. History shows that a continuous and implacable chain of abuse takes place whenever a new world is discovered, a new territory is conquered or even a major invention, social concept or precept is adopted. We might be in for some rough times."

"History is a wise companion, I agree," added Patrick, "but you are assuming that our visitors behave like humans, so…I feel that our best course in any case is to wait until there is some communication. We can speculate until the next century. That is, if these pills allow us to see the next century."

"What plans do you have, if any, about these things?" asked Richard.

"Really very little. I have asked some people to help me keep an eye on this phenomenon. I want to have near me a sort of an informal committee made up of people that have deep knowledge of Space Science, Medicine and Biology, and World History; an advisory group that can help me interpret matters when and if they happen. Nothing formal; I should know more about it in a few days, I expect."

Mercedes interrupted to say, "The only one missing in your Committee is an Anthropologist."

With a side glance at Richard and a broad smile, she continued. "I hear they are very good at divulging secrets and going out for coffee and doughnuts!"

They all laughed. Patrick looked at Richard and said, "How about it, Professor?"

Richard nodded in agreement.

"Truly, there is not much anyone can do until some form of communication is established. My feeling is that they, whoever or whatever they are, will make some form of announcement not very long from now. So, happy to be on your Committee, Mister Secretary General!"

"Are you still going to Paris?" asked Patrick.

"It all depends on whether there will be any flights. This morning I heard on the radio that all the airlines have been in constant conference with the NTSB, Air Control Agencies, Government Departments, and others, trying to decide whether they ought to start rescheduling flights or wait. I hear that the FAA in Washington is in favor of having most flights restored. It doesn't seem that much is about to happen, and if it does, it's better to have people back in their homes."

"We sound terribly somber about this whole thing. I think I might spend a few minutes at St. Patrick's later today," concluded Helen.

What About the UN?

Smiling, Richard said, "Patrick, you have produced the largest collective shock in history. To take over the job of Secretary General of the UN and in less than a year turn it from a paper tiger into the most dominant and formidable force on earth is better than any script Hollywood could dream up. In stead of eating give us a short take on what and how this has been accomplished!"

Everyone laughed but at the same time stopped eating. "This I want to hear," was on everyone's mind. The substantial changes made and being made at the UN answered to Patrick's undeniable vision, ability and cunning. From a moribund international institution that at one time had held the promise of promoting, protecting and aiding peace and well being on the planet, the UN had become an irrelevant effort and now it had miraculously been transformed into a hard hitting and powerful arm of world justice, peace and progress. Patrick smiled and aware of the interest everyone had in his words said:

"There goes the lobster bisque, the canard a l'orange and those cheerful asparagus! So I'll make it as short as possible!" He drank some water and with a smile continued, "I simply created another superpower. I have put the UN on a par with the European Union, the United States, China, Japan, Russia, India and Brazil or those who cut the bacon on the planet. I enlisted the help of people who have the heart, the soul and use clean credit cards. What do you think you can do with a hundred Bill Gates? Buffets? Prince Alwaleed Bin Talal Alsaud? Carlos Slim Helu? Paul Allen? Li Ka-shing? Lakshmi Mittal?" He paused and then continued:

"It did not take a great deal of convincing. I had my objectives and general plan in one single sheet of paper. In less than a week we had installed within the UN the World Health Center, the Human Research Center, the Educational World Plan and the World Energy Plan. In another month we had acquired more than 1,500 institutions throughout the world, including entire universities, pharmaceutical companies, and research companies and enlisted the most qualified people to be part of this new UN."

Richard interrupted to say, "Yes, it was a frenetic pace you set. But, what happens to the thousand committees, study groups and commissions that the

UN usually employs to supervise any change that needs to be made beginning with the purchase of toothpicks, toilet paper and instant coffee?"

Patrick laughed and said, "Remember how the media broiled me about the supreme authority I demanded as a condition of my employment? They called me everything, you will recall. But I got it and then I was able to wheel and deal as needed. I did and voilá! The new UN!"

Everyone at the table recalled that period when almost every country opposed the sketchy proposals made by Patrick to turn the UN into a truly world organization with enough teeth to deserve the respect of every one. Patrick continued. "In a way it was easy. Money talks they say. And they are so right. In no time at all we were able to control the manufacture of all major medicines, medical aids, medical research programs, medical schools and above all attract the needed talent and expertise. I will not go into the details but just remind you that more than 95 percent of all drugs used in the world today are made in UN facilities spread throughout the world and those facilities belong to all nations. Add to that the research effort, also in our facilities, and you are providing the people of the world a real service. We were also lucky that the cure against cancer, the new stem cell developments and their revolutionary applications, and the medicines and procedures to eradicate just about every infectious disease on the planet came from our laboratories. If that does not make the UN a major player, I am Count Dracula!"

Helen laughed and asked, "How about all those other centers that seem to keep the world going in the right direction?"

"Same thing. One page plan, lots of rupees and a new song is sung. You see, most nations in the world were waiting for something like this. A supranational body with no special interests or addictions operating strictly in the service of nations. For instance, we just bought outright Singapore's Biopolis a multinational research center that has come up with new stem cell developments At the same time we acquired a number of multinational pharmaceutical laboratories, that are now busy developing the drugs and medicines coming in from the research centers. Talk about Universal care! We are on the way!"

"How about energy? Food, communications? How did you manage to gather all under the UN roof?"

"Simple enough. We had to use the big stick at times. You sell or else. Also, the prospects we brought before their eyes were such that they could not afford to refuse. Another major achievement for instance was nuclear energy; we had in our hands the process to recover spent fuel and recycled it so that a gram of uranium would be turned around indefinitely. The disposal, which was one of the major drawbacks, had been solved and we had the key. That plus lots of coins and the whole enchilada was ours. Solar energy was another. We stumbled into a unique process to convert the sun's radiant energy into electricity without going through dielectric receptors like solar panels, photo cells, accumulators, converters and the such. Soon you'll have a simple varnish that will take care of your power needs. And so on with every industry. Did you hear about the new electromagnetic engines? We own its technology. Once on the roads, the new cars and trucks will reduce oil consumption to one tenth of what is now. The new organic fertilizers based on a combination of just air and a bit of that and the other? Light weight, transparent steel? The recovery techniques for most metals? The new vaccines? Veryical farms?"

"How about the effort to administer and manage all those activities new to the UN? I am referring to their management, supervision and planning?"

"Again, we just annexed every major institution dealing with management sciences. Harvard Business School was the first. We just bought Harvard and threw it in with the French Academie, the Ecole Superior, London School of Economics, the Zurich Technology Institute, the Russian Academies, etc. etc. You can imagine the joy of their faculties when they discovered that they had to forget about their old disciplines dealing with assets analysis, unredeemable liabilities, net present values and swift stock exchange maneuvers. It was a new ball game; management for a world center was serious business. And the emphasis was not solely on profits and the bottom line. In short, we accumulated muscle. And it belongs to all nations, no more shady deals, exorbitant salaries and inequality of rewards as had been the practice in the private sector. The new Harvards are now looking at a different set of parameters. And they love it!"

Jokingly, Helen added, "Patrick, you sound like Goldfinger or Doctor No. You are about to own every walking soul on the planet and all its resources!"

"And what is wrong with that if it means improving conditions on the planet? We have turned the UN into the only superpower in existence and it belongs to every nation on earth. It has no army, navy, air force nor uniforms, national anthem, religion, or softball team.

Everyone was silent for a moment until Richard observed, "In the process you must have made a few enemies. People just do not give up their gold mines without a fight."

"Surprisingly enough we ran into very few of them. Most were self made men empire builders who did not want to play. There are a few left."

Richard observed, “A federal judge said, not long ago, that what societies crave is ten per cent of thought and ninety per cent of action. If that is the case we should all be happy, for that is what Patrick is accomplishing. Organized societies have always needed a steering mechanism that would allow its people to exploit resources, seek new horizons and look after whatever rights and privileges exist in their society. A few years back no one would have thought that this could be accomplished in this scale.”

They ate in silence for a few moments and then Mercedes asked Patrick, “By the way, Secretary General, how are the inmates reacting to all the changes you have made at the UN in the last few months? There must be great stories about resignations, suicides and disappearances, from what I hear.”

“I know what you are leading to. You print hounds are all the same. I even had The Enquirer tempt me with much bullion to give them an exclusive on what I am doing. We have uncovered so many petty and not so petty transgressions that we could keep the Enquirer doing nothing but the UN for a few years. So you’ll have to triple what they offer if you want the real stuff.” Everyone around the table laughed, enjoying that moment of levity. Patrick continued. “Seriously, most countries are taking the UN’s actions in a positive way. True, we are giving them proposals that they cannot afford to refuse. We have mapped out what our experts call a ‘black hole program.’ You see, we have uncovered so many funny arrangements, sanctioned by the governments of many countries, that the only alternative is to go straight to the responsible ones and ‘black hole’ them. In some cases we go straight to top ministers, presidents and even bishops that are known crooks.”

He paused and, pointing to Richard, said, “Our anthro-physicist friend here can explain the ‘black hole’ results better than I can. Well, we have reduced personnel from more than 50,000 to around 15,000 and expect to cut that down by half in another six months. The budget is now estimated at around 2 billion bucks and is about to become even smaller.”

“But, won’t this affect the effectiveness of the organization?”

“What effectiveness? Other than very few successes and actions that have had a positive impact, the UN has been a colossal failure. A former undersecretary defined the UN as ‘a rather ridiculous bunch of foreigners enjoying free parking in New York, eating at the best restaurants and living high on the hog tanks to funds provided by gullible nations.’”

He paused for a moment and then, with a smile continued. “Well, if it is any consolation the US did not pay its dues for years! Someone else must have financed those great dinners.”

"I was really glad when they announced your appointment," observed Richard. "I knew you were not going to sit on the suite on the top floor and start worrying about your image. I did not think for a moment that you would be getting someone to write articles for you and begin a non-stop round of conferences, meetings and big state dinners all over. I still remember our days at the London School of Economics and later at all those committees at the State Department. You were a ferocious administrator, and a sharp one. I still wonder about the complexity of the UN problems and the solutions you dreamed up, or how to change that costly administrative merry go round into a useful tool for humanity?"

"Well, it cost me some overtime, many lost week-ends and hours listening to endless committee reports. I realized the need to mobilize Washington's influence and to zero in on constructive recommendations. I was lucky to obtain the support of the US president, which also made things easier when it came to enlisting other nations. I then created a gold plated ask force that put on the table key proposals to restrain the proliferation of nuclear and other weapons, plus peacekeeping and peace-building schemes along with the creation of the world centers I have mentioned before. There was also a major practical charity and health care program aimed at poor nations. We wrapped all this in very realistic human rights protection, economic development and new lines of authority: this last aimed at strengthening the U.N.'s badly discredited management systems."

He paused for a moment and then continued. "As expected, the major countries screamed to high heaven. Some questioned my authority to undertake these major changes without previous consultation with them. As you will recall, the Security Council was one of the first mass firings I engineered."

"But, Patrick, we knew that great battles were being fought at the UN, that companies universities and research centers all over the world, were participating on a major project with the UN. The complaints were quite noisy and you were targeted as public enemy number one. How did you manage to steal all that know how and set up that incredible powerhouse? How did you avoid the endless consultations, study groups, think tank evaluations and what not before you could even buy a hot dog stand?"

"It was easy. By the time that the reactions set in it was too late. At a crucial meeting I just announced that most agreements creating the World Centers had been signed and that we were proceeding with their implementation. The pharmaceutical companies could not believe that from that moment on the manufacture and distribution of every suppository, AIDS cure or special treatments were out of their control. It was no longer a business that appeared to be exclusively devoted to the generation of profits. And the same happened when other sectors were quickly incorporated into our structure. All those plans that seemed unattainable in education, scientific research, social endeavors, food, transportation, communications and all the other chapters were now a reality. We just redefined their objectives and they all bought it!"

"What kind of help did you have?"

"First and foremost was the president of the US. The fact that we have known each other for a long time and have worked together at the State Department, helped a great deal. He saw the advantages of the new UN structure and endorsed it heartily. Most other countries followed but with absolute discretion. No sense creating a conflict between the new UN and private industry all over the world. The lubricant we applied to get things rolling, for your information, looks green and is printed on nice pieces of paper and has lots of numbers!"

He paused for a moment to taste the bisque, drink some of that delicious Sanserre and butter a piece of bread. He applied the napkin to his lips and continued. "An important chapter included the creation of an independent audit and oversight board along with a new assessment of military peacekeeping operations. We also improved access and new rules for inspections by the International Atomic Energy Agency and other international bodies that monitor the proliferation of unconventional weapons. All this underlines stronger cooperation between the United Nations, the World Bank and other international agencies. This time around we found most countries quite cooperative."

Richard observed, "It sounds like a very ambitious agenda: something that was sorely needed. I can also imagine that formulating new policies is not a simple matter. Their enforcement is the painful part along with securing the needed support."

Patrick nodded and said, "I am trying, but getting modest support. Keep in mind that the role of the UN has changed from the original purpose. Initially, the UN was envisioned as a forum where conflicts and problems among nations could be explored and discussed and, with the help of world opinion, arrive at satisfactory settlements. It was a practical approach at a time when the world was deeply divided; the UN somehow managed to bring some common sense and open up the floor to discussion. It was not contemplated that the UN would act as a policeman everywhere, that it would train platoons of people to look into food supplies, medicine, agriculture, drug prevention, bad movies, education, sports, technology, basket weaving and who knows what else. But, you see, for lack of another entity whose door would be open, the UN has had to do more than what it was designed for."

Helen interrupted to say, "Yes, but its presence has been felt in one way or another."

"Right. But it must be recognized that without the UN the history of the past few decades would have been much different and probably more conflictive. Now, corruption, mismanagement, an unwieldy bureaucracy, and all kinds of side deals gave the place an image that is proving hard to change."

"Why do you thinks this has happened?" asked Helen.

"Do not lose sight of the fact that the UN exhibited all the attractions of a religious organization, an international corporation, a silent military system, an educational system, a debating society, a travel bureau and even a Gourmet testing facility and therefore it has been the ideal subject for a variety of ills; bureaucracy is the first one. Bureaucracy satisfies two key desires; one is the perception of power. The more people recognize your position in the pecking order, the more your sense of importance and personal power are stimulated. The second condition is a fairly usual one and is called nepotism. Why keep your wife, or Cousin George idle if they can come to the office to shuffle a few papers, get a substantial salary and eventually begin to develop the feel for the reverence expressed by subordinates and nurture their own taste of power. Combine the two and you have chaos on 34East. But other than its obvious deficiencies and incompetence, we must not forget that the UN remains an international forum accessible to every country and group on earth."

He paused for a moment and then, "As I see it, the UN is not a simple forum where endless debates take place, or an enforcer, or a charitable institution and certainly not a political force. In abstract term it should be the instrument that is accessible to all and that is in a position to detect threats to peace and security, stimulate the development of the poorer regions of the world through the active collaboration of the wealthier nations and, above all, analyze and propose changes as they occur in the world. The UN cannot afford to become a venerable institution whose guidelines remain forever written on stone. It must become a dynamic, changing entity."

"What major changes did you contemplated when you took over?"

"First, I had to keep it alive. It does serve a purpose. Winston Churchill once said about the UN that 'it is better to jaw-jaw than war-war.' Second, the UN demands a drastic change in the mentality of its officials. I want to do away with the practice of using it as a catchall for spent politicians, people who are appointed to UN posts because they are considered potential threats to government leaders. You know, the best way to neutralize or annul a political adversary is to make him invisible, and an appointment at the far away UN is the best solution."

"How about your famous overhead? It eats a large part of your budget, from what we hear," observed Richard.

Patrick added, "I also wish to get rid of professional bureaucrats, second hand celebrities and retired friends and relatives. You are right Richard, we have too many termites in the building. I want to upgrade the quality of the people involved in UN work. The creation of the centers and the availability of highly trained personnel will certainly help. Besides, the centers will be self sufficient, requiring only a small layer of control and supervision. In a few years I want a class of people characterized for their integrity and competence as UN people. I want a Delta Force touch in the troops. Honesty, dedication and competence is what I am after, so that the most menial job will be handled by an employee that is fiercely proud of being a 'Unie.' It is clear that all these changes will have to come under the umbrella of a new conception for this circus."

He drank some water and in a serious tone continued. "The UN, in my view, should not be responsible for a number of operating units that rightfully belong in the private sector. They can benefit from the hard ass dictums of private enterprise. What the hell are we doing with 29 entities devoted to the supervision of food and agriculture programs worldwide, for instance? A single well oiled unit would do. I don't think we need a fancy printing establishment when we can have all our work done by private companies and that way we won't have to pay a couple of dollars for each visiting card that is printed. In my view, dear Professor, all we need now that the centers have been installed is a lean and sharp Economic Council capable of detecting the theft of paper clips anywhere. We need a Social Council to deal with Human Rights, Health, Child Education, etc and reassert and recreate the Security Council to serve as the major international mediating body. I am getting rid of the overabundant agencies, commissions, councils, Trusteeships, Foundations, branches, field offices and all kinds of totally superfluous activities, and personnel."

"This is ambitious," added Richard who had been, like the others, listening to Patrick with great interest.

"It is," replied Patrick. "The UN is to grow into a highly respected supranational body with enough muscle to dictate its own terms. It will be ready to listen, discuss, suggest and arrange for implementation. Keep in mind that the world is no longer divided into two major camps and that at last, the political climate is characterized by a desire to deal, or should be."

He paused for a moment and then continued. "Yes, we have a new world and without doubt a new test for democratic principles, don't you think so, Professor?"

Richard smiled and replied, "Absolutely, but we must not lose sight of the effort it took to arrive at democracy as a philosophy and a way of life. Let us not forget that modern society has reached its democratic texture after many centuries and it is to be hoped that beyond installing democracy in the rest of the world—only half the countries on earth live under democratic principles—a better distribution of resources and wealth will result. We have to remember that arriving at democracy by way of the universal suffrage was never an easy process. It was not very long ago that most countries operated under an electoral system based on a public census. The ones entitled to vote were those who paid a certain amount in taxes. Later, it was agreed that all those who paid taxes, no matter the amount, could vote. Finally, the right to vote was extended to those who could read and write. And all this happened during the 19th century!"

"You are right," agreed Patrick. "It was not long ago that democracy was adopted by European countries in various forms. Universal suffrage changed the styles of government: for the first time, voters had a say in public expenditures, taxes and social services."

Looking at Helen and Mercedes, he smiled and continued. "At that time, only men were allowed to vote, which says much for the influence of existing taboos and traditions about the role of women in society!"

Patrick shook his head and continued. "Universal elections in those countries resulted in immediate improvements in the distribution of wealth and resources and the serious evaluation of labor and social laws. So, my friends, a lesson that must not be forgotten is that elections are the fuel of democracy and it is only through the vote that a true democracy can recognize individual values and initiatives."

"How come in the last centuries only the democracies became rich and powerful?" Helen asked.

"Democracy is based on freedom and strong doses of juridical guidelines; these elements help protect the rights of all citizens and provide the climate for confidence and security. Under those conditions, all kinds of scientific and social development can prosper and can lead to the creation of wealth, which in turn leads to investment, employment, tax revenues for the state to subsidize public services, etc."

"How does the system affect the UN?" asked Mercedes who had been taking notes all along.

"Ah! Good question, Mercedes," replied Patrick. "Listen, the UN is made up of a number of international entities where most countries are represented. It is therefore a representative parliament, so to speak, but it is not democratic at all. You see, the thing is ruled by veto and the veto or decisive vote is in the hands of the winners of the last major wars: China, France, Britain, Russia and the US. We could call it a multi-language monarchy, if we wish to be facetious. The rest of the countries have a vote each, whether the country is a large one or a tiny one."

"How about the economic organizations?"

"The system is just as bad. The vote depends on quotas paid by the member countries. The amount depends on their Gross National Product, which makes the whole process similar to the electoral census, or a clearly discriminatory system. It is not surprising that under those voting conditions, privilege and abuse exists, because the stronger and richer countries will tend to look after their own interests."

"So, Patrick, are you intimating that a world government is the solution?"

"It will have to be. In time."

In a reflexive mood, he continued. "If a responsible democracy is installed in most countries, a responsible world government is the next step. Its foundations are already here, you know. Organizations like the UN, the economic institutions like the World Bank, the WLO, the FMI and the WTO, along with the European Union and all the other groups that operate within democratic principles. I plan to buy their mortgages and induce them to join us."

"But do you think that it will be easy to install democratic governments in most countries?" asked Mercedes.

"It will be an uphill battle all the way. We have to deal with many totalitarian regimes, some of which date back thousands of years and others that are the result of convenient arrangements in recent times. To most of them, their ideologies hide their conviction that the end justifies the means which, in a democracy the means represent no lesser value than the ends. But above all, installing democracy will imply that individuals will willingly accept the rights and responsibilities of the democratic system and also learn to respect the rights of other communities."

"You are not asking for much but I certainly hope so," added Mercedes. "Here is where a respected institution like the UN can stimulate the tide of democracy in most of the world. I can also see where the UN can play a moderating role among those countries or alliances that become too powerful and rich. Even heroes need someone to make sure they remain heroes."

Mercedes raised her hand and said, "Tell me, Patrick, how about Germany and Japan?"

"It is now in the works. It is part of a new realism I am trying to implant. It no longer makes sense to keep Germany and Japan without a voice in the UN. My intention is to unite not to divide and I don't want to allow past practices to maintain alive the seeds of resentment..."

"How about peacekeeping and security, etc.?"

"I am elevating the involvement of the UN in these matters to another level. Fortunately I can now count on total support from the US, the European Union, China, Japan, Russia and India. Political maturity seems to be here at last!"

Richard observed, "Patrick, the recent agreements about those nations have been mainly the result of your own personal diplomacy. How did you manage to overcome sticky problems like China and Taiwan, North and South Korea, Iran, Pakistan and India, the Palestine problem, Islamism and religious extremism, the control of energy resources, agreements on universal institutions and the climate of suspicion that has hindered international relations for years?"

"Pure luck. I just happened to find that the governments of the major nations was in the hands of a new breed of realists and that the leaders shared legitimate concerns about world security. Somehow they were looking for a formula that would reduce if not eliminate their costly commitment to weapons and some form of bond with the other countries that would go beyond signing treaties and attending peace conferences. All I did was to parade before them the history of the last few decades and point to them their indifference in some cases, their intransigence in others and the fact that a minimum effort on their part would have saved millions of lives and bring hope to billions. Once they were properly chastised I sprung the deal, whose features I copied from Alexander Dumas and his 3 Musketeers!"

"You mean one for all and all for one?" asked Helen.

"Right. Except that I added a few items that I presented in my best Don Corleone's fashion: I made some offers that they could not afford to refuse! The UN will continue to propose and enact policies and assist in resolving conflicts but, when it comes to knocking heads, there are now in the world new perceptions and new attitudes."

Richard interrupted Patrick to ask, "If it is not a secret, give us a glimpse of the techniques employed."

"When you happen to own the playground, all the toys in it, the refreshments plus having your children as the biggest and strongest boys, the others will willingly play the game you want."

"That is blackmail, not enlightened politics for a world entity, Patrick," said Mercedes.

"One way to call it, but ask yourself what is politics? How has the social order developed? Remember that to eat an omelet you have to crack a few eggs!"

They all laughed and marveled at the same time at the extent of Patrick's guile. He nodded and continued. "Remember that the centralization, and globalization if you wish, of essential goods and services gives the UN unprecedented priority in practically all matters. That is why we can count on the military might of the more powerful nations to provide the proverbial stick. It benefits everyone to prevent all those nations suspect of nurturing international terrorism and illegal production of deadly weapons from becoming a real threat. It is also to their advantage if any action is coordinated. We have seen that unilateral measures tend to widen the differences that exist among countries."

"True," interrupted Helen, "even the US has run into serious problems in the last few years. Its unilateral policies, born out of specific interests, did create for a while a climate of antagonism among peoples that had been allies for years, if not centuries."

Richard nodded and added, "This would not happen today when a strong UN has the means to prevent any of its members from adopting policies that go against the established aims. The world can no longer be viewed as anyone's private domain."

Helen said, "Well said, Professor. History teaches us that the dominant powers become the targets of collective animosity from the less privileged nations the moment they stray from the accepted patterns; in addition, inequalities between rich and poor and the inevitable comparisons on standards of living, create a permanent current of envy, which as we all know can easily turn into resentment and even hatred. In my view, the more powerful you are, the more responsible you have to be."

Patrick smiled and drank some water from the glass in front of him. He cleared his throat and said, "Fortunately, we must not forget that, traditionally, the United States has always been a good neighbor and a helpful friend. There are no indications that its preponderant position in the world today might lead to abuse and indifference. Besides, the age of globalization is here to stay and the US, whether it wants or not, has to join the game."

"I guess you refer to the recent war in Iraq," said Richard, "which in some way spelled the end of the United Nations, or rather the Old United Nations, same as the old Europe and the Old War Plan as someone used those terms to reject further discussion and let the dogs of war loose."

"Exactly. The Iraq episode has been a confusing one not only for the US but also for most of the rest of the world. It is a pity that all the available diplomatic tools were not used and in the end the war turned into a more or less single initiative, creating some worrisome precedents. But this episode also points to the fact that an international body like the UN must develop uniform criteria arising from the very basic premises on which it was founded. Good versus evil to put it simply so that it can act with decision and with a minimum of blah blah."

"For a while there, it looked as if the UN would prove to be as irrelevant as some people claimed it was or would become," observed Richard.

Patrick looked at Richard and smiled, "In a way, it had it coming. Fortunately the drastic changes that have been made since that phrase was composed have brought the UN back to the front lines. But the creation of the UN super team together with recent successes and accomplishments have overcome what looked like a hopeless impasse. Also keep in mind that it took a tremendous coordinated effort to defuse the insularity and radicalism of some religions and to instill respect for Human Rights everywhere."

"How about those isolationist tendencies that, like mushrooms, appear seasonally in the US?"

"Well, not only in the United States. We all know that the moment a country enjoys a comfortable standard of living and profits from prosperous economic perspectives, it starts peering at its belly button. I think that growing social enlightenment will trigger collective responses to world crises and these responses will aid the UN and others in their quest for appropriate solutions. The UN will benefit also from future military-economic alliances throughout the world. It will no longer be necessary for the UN to develop and maintain occupation or observation forces. I just can't see myself as the Chief of Staff of a gang of MPs chasing bandits in the hills or directing traffic in some remote nation."

He smiled and continued. "One of my priorities is to continue the fight against terrorism. Since the time that New York was made the target of one of the most inhuman attempts by terrorists, the entire complexion of our society has been altered..."

"No question about it," added Richard, "but the problem I see is that most people have no understanding of the nature of terrorism. It is nothing like fighting against another nation for whatever reason. Terrorism has no nation and it exists as a bloody reaction to a losing cause and also as a form of expression against real or imagined grievances. The worst part is that it can take root in any nation and operate from there; then, that nation can be conveniently blamed for whatever terrorist actions have been committed within and outside it."

Patrick raised his head and with a serious look said, "Right. Terrorist attacks have exposed the vulnerability of even the better organized societies and ushered the era when small groups of people operating outside any known country or even nationality are in a position to shatter existing social structures. The uncomfortable status quo with which we lived for years is no longer there; deterrence, which is a one-on-one stand off, is no longer a valid solution. How can you deter a terrorist group? Also, the availability of nuclear weapons, and its illegal production, gives the terrorists a powerful argument to threaten, negotiate and intimidate. Only a combined effort by all nations can help eradicate this scourge. We must identify the organized bands, dissension groups, cults, and underground organizations that employ violence to express their grievances. We have also to seek the countries and financial groups that in one way or another support and encourage terrorists…"

How would you plan to accomplish all this?" asked Mercedes.

"Actually there are two ways in which to face the problem. They are perhaps a bit idealistic, and even unreal, but are valid options nevertheless. You see, terrorism is the result of social, political or religions circumstances. Any one of these is used as the excuse for resentment, envy and hatred. From there to organized violence is a mere step. Its environment is not necessarily restricted to poor countries. The only way to inject some form of rationality is through education and through the improvement of those environments where these tendencies develop. I am talking about a universal Task Force armed with strong economic tools that pave the way for change. Sort of a book in every child's hands and a chicken in every pot."

Helen interrupted. "Right, but this is easy to say. For thousand of years we have had tribes, social groups and even entire civilizations suffering from isolation, misery and the contempt of others. The best efforts to bring some detached view through education have been total failures. The fact that slavery continues to exist is latent proof of it. Not much could be done against the fanatic monks during the Inquisition days and the witch hunters in our country in the 18th Century. No arguments could convince the societies that prospered as a result of slavery, of the injustice and abuse this represented. Education could do even less when political ideologies were the driving force. Millions of Russians, Chinese, Persian, French, British and others that supported their colonial or autocratic policies, managed to justify their beliefs in spite of universal pressure to introduce improvements. And let us not ignore religious sects and beliefs. In our own time, we ourselves think that we are always right and parade our self-righteousness and piety as the only God-given mandates that are acceptable. You would have to educate the hell out of the uneducated as Yogi Berra would say!"

Patrick laughed and said, "I am surprised that you quote Yogi Berra. I thought that his quotations belonged to the more senior citizens in the village!"

They all laughed. Patrick continued. "If we are successful in maintaining an international and efficient anti-terrorist front we can blend it into regional organizations that will be created in all regions of the world. I think we are at the moment when the creation of an international force, sort of a World Foreign Legion, begins to make sense. In addition to providing a military presence, it would create a common experience for men of all cultures and origins. Fortunately defense organizations are no longer necessary; the idea of creating armies for a few countries is a thing of the past."

"I guess you are thinking back to the Roman Legions and more recently to the French and Spanish Foreign Legions, the Gurkhas and other multinational armies."

"Yes of course. By having an international military force a great deal can be accomplished. That way, the moment a terrorist group is detected in the jungles of Brazil, or a fjord in Norway, the regional group will plan and execute the necessary action. The hard part of all this is to get all countries to take the matter seriously. Terrorism has gone unchecked for too long. Also, it hides behind long time beliefs and dogmas. The best protection against terrorism is keeping the ear to the ground. If you don't have operatives near the sources, all these unhealthy movements will grow and develop. The prosperous countries have been a bit indifferent, thinking that a kidnapping here, a truck blowing up elsewhere were things that happened to others, or to those who have on-going conflicts. They don't seem to realize that their very prosperity and well being are resented by less fortunate countries. And resentment is at the root of all violence..."

"Isn't there a danger that the UN will assume the role of the conscience of mankind?"

"I doubt it. I don't see our coordinating and supervising job as becoming the conscience of mankind, as you call it. This is a problem that affects all nations. If the UN can provide leadership and coordination and is able to define common purpose, establish the objectives and develop practical guidelines, we are all doing our job. If you wish to call that the conscience of mankind, fine with me."

He paused and, noticing that everyone around the table was following his every word, he continued. "We are working on a mechanism that will make enforcement a fair and effective process in the hands of existing or new military alliances in various parts of the world. We now have the tools to make us credible and, most important respected. And those tools belong to everyone. Remember that the effects of the so called globalization must be harnessed into effective measures. It makes no sense to expect that the United States and a few other industrialized nations, as the more powerful, must resolve every conflict, everywhere. That is why I think it is important to develop common policies on a world level. If not, we all become irrelevant."

He turned to Richard and asked, "Wouldn't you think so, Professor?"

"Clever students I have! But yes, in one form or another, most countries nowadays, are closely linked to one another. The criteria for developing common approaches that might involve military action are already there. All that needs to be done is to identify the problem and assist in the overall execution of whatever plans are developed. I think that after the campaigns in the Middle East, the world will have developed a few instruction manuals on the assessment, detection, protection against and eradication of terrorism based on the tactics that have been practiced by the warring factions. Still missing is the manual on preventing it!"

Richard paused for a few seconds and then continued. "To me it sounds like a good strategy. The idea of having regional alliances within an international army to handle conflicts in their regions is of course a logical expectation, however, do you think that individual countries are prepared to air their internal problems and, worse yet, allow foreign alliances to settle their disputes, prevent violence and arrange for peaceful solutions? How about the cost of enforcement and, when it happens, operations?"

Patrick replied, "Let me be clear on one thing. My idea is to prevent Kosovos, Timors, Chenyas, Basques, Amish, Corsicans, Irish, Guerrillas, Revolutionary Armies, Militias, Religious sects, KKKs, Tutus, Zulus, from resorting to violence. It is a policy of total prevention, which I consider as important as any of the efforts being made to protect our environment, or the vaccination for infants."

"Why don't separatist movements prosper in the US, or in many other countries?" asked Mercedes, whose small notebook was running out of pages by now.

"Cohesive forces in the US and many other countries are supported by their economic and political structures. Developed nations, where living conditions are satisfactory and social justice is observed, are rarely receptive to drastic changes or the revival of ancient feuds and hatreds."

Richard observed, "Even in the United States we occasionally witness the appearance of extreme creeds. Our leading political parties often act as enemies and seem to pride themselves in rationalizing their beliefs into articles of faith. Both the liberal and the conservative factions can create powerful doctrines who, at times seem to forget that their existence is solely due to the allegiance they owe to the people. But let us not forget that unless the more developed countries cease to worship their own wealth and all those traits deriving from it, they are fomenting resentment and eventually social unrest."

"What traits?" asked Mercedes.

"The richer you are, the easier it is to misjudge the measure of your own accomplishments. At one point, arrogance, selfishness, a sense of infallibility and a superior attitude take over and from being the subject of, let us call it, healthy envy from others you become an easy target for resentment. In a way resentment points to the lack of human charity, and if you want me to get biblical, let me remind you of one phrase that has been so blatantly ignored: love thy neighbor!"

Richard, who had listened quietly to the various exchanges, spoke. "The great risk I see in all this has to do with human nature. There have always been tyrants, dictators and evil leaders and they will continue to appear. This will be a major challenge you will face. It suggests some form of future pre-emptive system to avoid the appearance of these evil souls. It also brings into the picture the moral and material aspects of any pre-emptive system; there are still too many banana republics quite susceptible to the creation of cliques and the emergence of tyrants. Especially if it is all tied into the age-old practice of dividing up the pie among a few."

"They don't have to be banana republics," muttered Mercedes. "We have seen modern and prosperous democratic countries adopt the questionable practices of lesser countries. Greed is always around."

"See?" asked Patrick. "We are looking at some of the problems we will have. I am convinced however that drastic reforms will help reduce if not eliminate the danger of autocratic regimes and widespread corruption. It will take years if not generations to have people accept a few rules that can benefit not only them but also others."

"What reforms?" insisted Helen.

"Well, we have to take a good look at those areas that must be returned to their original purposes I see as major failings at this time the attempts that are committed daily against freedom, against its desired result which is democracy and against its necessary control mechanisms, meaning governments. They are not what their creators had in mind; on top of that add the tremendous inequalities in practically all aspects of human endeavors from the color of the eyebrows to the performance of 5 million dollars yachts, and you find a very sick planet. We all talk freely about democracy which is supposed to reflect the expressions of a majority, yet in most elections throughout the world, which is where democracy is proven, less than half the people vote, therefore making it easy for opportunistic groups to act. Governments are no longer social instruments devised to provide public services; they have been corrupted beyond hope and are viewed as the means to legalize and protect enterprises, dynasties, people and institutions whose idea of public service is to own the means to disseminate their ideas and products. The driving force is simple greed!"

Helen spoke. "I guess you are right. It is gong to take a great deal of effort on your part. I can only wish you *Bon chance*, Patrick. But how about the things above? Are there any plans? What are we supposed to do? To tell you the truth, I am secretly hoping that you confess that it is all a Disney promotion announcing a new movie…"

Patrick looked at Helen and, with a sad expression, said, "It is something beyond our comprehension. We'll have to wait…"

World Reaction

The sudden appearance of the objects over the skies of 300 cities in the world created a collective shock that manifested itself in popular demonstrations and gave way to a current of fear and suspicion. The first few hours were hard to describe. Activity stopped in most cities and people abandoned whatever they were doing to rush to the streets and seek dubious reassurance by mingling with the silently amazed and fearful crowds. Fortunately, most public services continued to work, averting certain chaos and confusion.

While Governments, press, churches and public institutions could not provide an explanation for the phenomenon, people resorted to all sorts of speculation, most of it based on an end-of-the-world theme. In some places, the usual troublemakers took advantage of the confusion and passivity that dominated society and went on rampages of destruction and pillage. Order was fortunately soon re-established but not without the usual broken ribs, gas-poisoning injuries and a few cracked skulls. Since the objects were located above large cities only, the more serious disturbances took place in those cities. People in rural areas, other cities, small towns and villages received only a second hand impression of the phenomenon through non-stop television and radio, and copious press coverage.

After the initial shock had worn out, the governments of most countries realized that, some sort of position, whether social, political or even religious, had to be assumed. People needed some form of reassurance. But the big question in all cases had to do with the unknown nature of the objects and their absolute silence. What sort of pronouncements could be made? What manner of advice, leave alone guidelines and regulations could be provided? What should the people and the authorities do?

In the end most governments relied on well-reasoned premises aimed at removing fear and instilling some measure of confidence. Authorities pointed out that since their arrival, the objects had not caused any damage and had not been responsible for any sort of direct or indirect disasters. Obviously, their intentions could be considered peaceful since they seemed capable of behaving otherwise.

In a short time, other consequences of the object's appearance became evident. Each country developed its own interpretation of the incident and took measures that were as disparate as they were futile. For a while most countries shared the universal feeling of bewilderment and even panic but, after a few days, those feelings began to fade and were replaced by suspicion and a deep fear of this unexplained phenomenon. Somehow, the dialogue and normal exchanges that characterized the relations among neighboring countries suddenly ceased. Suspicion arose in many cases as the objects afforded an excellent opportunity to open old arguments and revive forgotten offenses.

Canada felt for a while that it was the United States that had decided to test new surveillance technology by placing these huge objects over every one of Canada's major cities. Mexico quickly backed up such claim, afraid that the US had finally decided to plug the holes in its borders and to do away with the profitable drug trade that used Mexico's extensive border with the United States as a convenient and hard to police entry point.

Russia, India and Pakistan were quick to blame the Chinese for the appearance of the unsettling fixtures above their key cities. The reaction from

Europe was swift. Media coverage of the phenomenon reflected, as usual, the unique perspectives of each country. Official communiqués adopted the official tone that barely concealed a panicky attitude and a "save yourself, if you can" attitude. In the clamor, the latest prescriptions offered by the European Union, the bland statements from NATO and the individual interpretations of the phenomenon advanced by the scientific institutions in the old continent were ignored. The only voices of reason that found eager audiences were those of the Vatican and the Church of England who advised the Christian World to remain calm and to wait for further developments.

Japan accepted the appearance of the objects with stoicism. There was a large dose of fatalism in the pronouncements of the various Government entities. The Emperor advised calm and prudence and reminded the public that it was about time that one or more deities come down to earth and prepare the empire of the Rising Sun for the entire millennium.

In South America, where regional animosities and conflicts among neighboring states, was a cherished tradition, a rash of declarations and accusations were quickly made. Chile and Argentina went quickly at it, each one afraid that a new border intrusion was being perpetrated by the other. Their bone of contention was a forgotten tract of barren real estate in Tierra del Fuego and its few hardy inhabitants who were totally indifferent to the unusual event. Chile mobilized its Armed Forces, fearing that either Perú or Bolivia had something to do with the strange objects. Perú and Ecuador with their irreconcilable differences about some jungle extensions in their borders went at once on the alert. And so on.

While near panic had shown its unsettling signs the world over, no attempt had been made by the occupants of the "pills," or "pancakes," to communicate with anyone on earth. Day and night, radio, radar and electronic surveillance was kept by a score of countries, not to mention the around the clock alerts that called for special flights by the Air Forces of most major powers. The fact that 300 of the major cities on the planet had suddenly acquired an aspirin-looking object overhead created a feeling of insecurity and fomented all kinds of speculation. The silence maintained by the strange objects added to the surprise and the fear. The sight of the objects which—depending on the lighting conditions—resembled an aspirin tablet or a light colored wheat pancake at 100,000 feet of altitude evoked all kinds of reactions.

All efforts to communicate with the objects had failed. Even radio-commanded helium balloons with high-power radio, radar and laser transmitters were maneuvered to within a few thousand feet from the objects but their signals, beams and echoes were not able to penetrate the electromagnetic shield that seemed to enshroud the pills.

Satellites did not fare any better. Other than high resolution photographs that showed the smooth surface of the objects from above, the satellites did not provide any meaningful data. Their thermal profiles based on infrared technology drew a blank. It just wasn't possible to penetrate the shield covering the objects.

Landsat and its digital-imaging capabilities proved useless as its high definition black and white photographs could only provide a closer look at the smooth texture of the pills and no more. European and Japanese satellites tried their own digital photography in radar, visible and infrared light, which ordinarily would allow computers to see beneath most surfaces, but with similar negative results.

The US Air Force was quick to place on alert a wing of its high performance U-2 Reconnaissance planes and, as in the old Curtis LeMay days, kept around the clock surveillance on some of the objects. The 34 million dollar Lockheed Aircraft all-weather plane is specially suited for high altitude work and operates day and night. But its sophisticated electronics and unique flying characteristics were useless since the photographs they took did not disclose any clue as to the nature of the objects. It appeared that the objects had been placed at an altitude slightly beyond the reach of the most advanced high-flying plane. The U-2 itself could barely reach 100,000 feet and all it could do was to point its cameras and instruments at the underside of the objects.

Attempts were also made with the highly secret unmanned aerial vehicles that the US Air Force keeps in reserve. The Global Hawk and the newly developed Dark Star vehicles possess a fascinating collection of state of the art detection devices that do not require a pilot at the controls. The work done by Raytheon, Hughes, GE and General Dynamics to equip these heavenly eyes, ears and noses is without precedent in remote control technology; but no luck. The pills did not disclose anything. There were no vapor trails, no exhausts of any kind, no motor vibrations to register in the ultra sensitive bipolar sensors and no sounds that the equally sensitive acoustic membranes could detect.

As in the case of the U-2s and the unmanned vehicles, other countries had launched all kinds of remote-controlled Helium balloons to photograph and try to approach the ships. Upon getting to within 5 thousand feet however, their crafts would begin to show the effects of the electromagnetic shield that would not allow them to get any closer. While no accidents were reported as a result, and no harm was done, control of the balloons became a hairy adventure; their instruments would cease to function when reaching a certain altitude, somewhere near 100,000 feet, and there would be sudden power failures, forcing the crafts to become erratic and to begin uncontrolled descent.

Adding to the confusion, civilian flyers all over the world saw this as a wonderful opportunity to log a few hours doing something that was totally useless as their prop aircraft had limited altitude ceilings and the best they could do was to get up to around 16,000 feet. It gave the pilots at the numerous Aero Clubs throughout the world the chance to strut around announcing in self-important tones, "We will never find out about these beings if we do not show them we are interested. I am taking the old Navaho up to 16,000 today for a few minutes. Maybe they'll decide to throw me a radio beam or something."

Secretly, every one of them hoped that the first contact the world was expecting would happen during one of their flights up. They imagined being the first to have a glimpse at the visitors from the strange space ships. And in keeping with the celebrity culture of the times, most of them fantasized about the attention and adulation they would receive. They thought of the TV interviews, the magazine articles, the endorsements and merchandising of a variety of products. It was easy to daydream in this way when coaxing the old crate upward.

Once commercial flights were resumed, the pancakes became a convenient beacon for navigators and controllers alike. They even entered the lexicon. "American Alpha Zulu 331: maintain altitude at 25,000 and stay on present course until you come under the pill..."

Almost three months had gone by since that day when almost every major city on the planet had acquired its own static "pill," overhead. Even the committee created by the UN to monitor world reaction had lost some of its vigor. Gone were the almost hourly communiqués from distant cities reporting non-events; the objects could only go so far in stimulating fresh news. Radio and Television interviews with astronomers, anthropologists, gurus and priests and ministers took up most of the airtime. Speculation laced with apprehension was the keynote.

Expectantly, the lunatic fringes of every society saw the objects that by now people called aspirins, or pancakes, as God-sent opportunities to proclaim their dubious beliefs. The silent presence above and the multitude of theories that sprouted from all corners, paved the way for the development of new religious sects that ascribed spiritual qualities to the objects while at the same time extorting funds from a gullible and fearful public.

Such was the impact of the unknown objects that academics were quick to advance a complex set of hypotheses relating to world history, religion and astronomy. It was not strange to discover in a University in California that the objects overhead were being used as basis for a graduate course on "Appreciation of Space Ships, Their Purpose and their Meaning."

But the objects brought with them not only the awareness that our planet is not an isolated corner of the Universe, but also the belief that whoever caused them to appear and remain over planet Earth, were here for a purpose. By then there was no doubt in anyone's mind that the objects were clearly steered and controlled by a crew that was apparently observing us, and learning our language and codes of behavior, prior to making contact.

The only instance that had been detected—and recorded—of one of the objects deliberately moving to another location, had occurred in Santiago de Chile. Hours after the object appeared over Santiago and had taken up its position overhead, it began to move westward in a slow and majestic manner, away from the range of mountains on whose lap the city rests. The reason became evident first to the controllers at Pudahuel, as the Arturo Merino Benítez Airport was popularly called, who had noticed that the ship was causing excessive interference with their radar, making them almost useless.

Arturo Merino Benitez Airport, sits on a narrow strip between the high range of the Andes and the Pacific Ocean. Both the original and new position of this ship had been recorded. But in the excitement caused by the appearance of these objects, this small incident had gone unnoticed. It was more than a week later that the scientists at Princeton, working with various supranational weather agencies, flight control centers and military units in all the countries hosting a ship, completed a detailed report on the arrival and exact location of every ship.

It was at that time that Santiago de Chile reported two positions on the same date. All other reports showed one single set of coordinates that had not changed the proverbial inch. Since the event in Santiago had been carefully recorded and filmed by both Government agencies and private citizens, there was a wealth of images showing the slow repositioning of the object.

The Religious Issue—The Church

The overwhelming presence of the objects, now familiarly referred to as "pills," brought about a myriad manifestations of human response. Churches that up to the moment had been on the brink of going out of business—so to speak—recovered their appeal to a public that had become suddenly fearful and doubtful.

People quickly turned to the faith that had nurtured them and found that some comfort was deftly dispensed by glib ministers, who managed in most cases to allay their fears and apprehensions. Special services were held every day in most churches in order to accommodate a growing number of people who felt that the end of the world was near. As expected, charlatans sprung like condominiums in Collins Avenue. The number of insurance scams, protection schemes and even soul salvation policies—sold through a 900 number (at the convenient rate of $8.75 a minute)—became the rage. As usual, the United States led the way in developing the most preposterous systems and the most sophisticated scams; it used its space age communications technology and the ever present Internet to reach the pockets of a public that was softened by the impact of a really awesome phenomenon.

Most of the leading notables of the Church in the country staged impromptu prayer meetings everywhere. The presence of the pills caused a sudden wave of religiosity all over the world. Faced with a phenomenon that—in spite of the presumably advanced technology available on the planet—had no simple explanation, a current of doubt mixed with fear seemed to impregnate human society.

In this sudden upsurge of religious fervor, no one could match the extent and quality of comforting messages like those offered by the Reverend John S. Toe.

To the Reverend John S. Toe, the arrival of the ships and their silent presence were a godsend. He knew that a secret Senate Investigation Committee had been formed, instigated by a number of prominent politicians in Washington, to look into all of his activities. This included his complex and not too clear web of financial arrangements and, worst of all, the extent of his private life with special emphasis on his sex life. He felt that the objects above would somehow distract the attention of that group in Washington and force them to postpone or abandon an inquiry into his activities.

For too many years his respected and admired public image had shielded his deft maneuvering in the management of the many enterprises in which he was active. At the same time, the aura of respectability, high morality and ethical conduct he had managed to project had concealed an incredibly complex and intense sexual life. A scandal at this time, when his personal fortune was increasing effortlessly with geometrical pulchritude, would be catastrophic. The chance to become the spiritual voice of America would be forever lost.

For more than thirty years, through the Church, the Foundation, the

University, the Sanctuaries and numberless institutions, joint ventures and cooperatives, he had amassed a fortune that at this time exceeded several billion dollars. His frantic business activity behind the scenes had been complemented with sexual commitments beyond the wildest fantasies of most men.

He quickly rationalized the appearance of the strange ships with his own situation. As he had done throughout his life, he mentally set himself up to create the basis of his own deception. The technique had never failed him. You had to make yourself believe in order to be convincing. He also felt that here was a unique opportunity to do the ultimate in the soul-saving industry. The space ships represented some divine form of salvation to the Reverend.

"If you are able to interpret any type of signal in your favor, you are actually establishing yourself as its messenger and can make use of it for your own purposes."

This advice had enabled him to take advantage of the subtle way in which a personal conviction can affect others; at the same time it aided in transmitting a sense of honesty of purpose.

He remembered his first experiences with the technique. While in college, a serious incident took place involving several faculty members and some uninhibited coeds. As the scandal became publicized, the pressure on the Administration became the target of a vociferous media and a concerned Board of Regents.

John was able to detect the urgent fear that dominated the members of the Board of Regents. They were more concerned with the possible loss of valuable contributors and sponsors to the various academic endowments, than with preserving due processes. They were quick to accept John's proposal to rally the student body and the faculty around a religious issue arising from the incident.

He simply offered his own interpretation of the events and linked them to the temporary lapse of religious fervor that affected the youth of the country. He enlisted the school newspaper, the local radio and TV stations and through the Campus Religious Student organizations he led a campaign that practically put the blame for the incident on the lack of religious beliefs on the campuses of America. Soon, the case was a matter of omission of faith in the academic world rather than the sordid affair it was. He directed the attention to himself by proclaiming that, as a student, he felt entitled to share the guilt but equally entitled to develop avenues of atonement.

This well orchestrated plan managed to stop further lynching by the press and allowed the entire situation to defuse itself in a short time. In the process, John assumed all the exposure and notoriety that he could muster and came under the interested attention of the Chairman of the Board of Trustees, Elmo Saks, a well known billionaire, senator and humanitarian.

His success as a preacher of dubious causes, later on, carried him to the forefront of America's moral crusaders. His mentors, under the vigilant eye of Elmo Saks, were careful to pave the way for his success. He was gradually introduced to the power circles in the State. Soon, he was being called to organize fund raising campaigns for all sorts of religious coalitions that were, in fact, fronts for political organizations. That small group of members of the Board of Regents of his Alma Mater viewed with possessive pride the steady and sure manner in which their protégée was becoming a national icon.

Thus the Church of Unlimited Faith was founded in Nashville, Tennessee. Before any attention could be devoted to the development of its religious activities, a recruiting campaign was undertaken to select and hire some of the more notorious and successful Wall Street business managers, Harvard Business School Grads and a few of the up and coming Ivy Leaguers staffing key Government departments in Washington. Before long, a campus for a University was added to the church, followed by a radio station, a 40,000 seat stadium, a 200 room Residence Hotel, a Medical facility and an Agricultural and Animal Husbandry Extension that controlled 266,000 acres of pastures and 12 experimental stations in the state.

As Head of the Church and President of its University, John was quickly honored with a number of Honorary Degrees and Academic distinctions. These achievements enabled him to get the attention of the national press and that of the powerful political groups in the State. Soon, John was the conscience of the State and a frequent guest at White House parties, meetings and other occasions where his brilliant expression and his sense of humor gained him a growing retinue of adherents and admirers. John, however, was not a religious man in the sense that he acknowledged a divine presence in his daily life or lived scrupulously by a set of ethical and moral rules. Since early childhood, he had learned the value of setting and achieving goals without great concern for ethical guidelines, personal loyalties or the recognition of others' efforts. He considered himself an accomplished actor, whose natural talent had added a new dimension to the practice of religious faith in the country. And all this time, he had maintained constant, if not daily contact with Elmo Saks, who continued to use his personal wealth and his influence to bolster the University's varied causes.

But he was in trouble. For several years he had maintained three mistresses in three different states. While his marriage had been uneventful and childless, it had provided him with the necessary image of the devoted and considerate husband. Liza had met him when he was still in college. She had been seduced on their second date. She never expected that the most popular campus leader would pay her any attention. While her physical attributes were modest and not lacking certain attractiveness, Liza possessed a sharp intellect and a refined manner, product of a careful upbringing, a happy family life and the training and conditioning that the best Eastern schools offered. Her parents had made sure that she would benefit from additional exposure to refinement and culture through carefully chosen European Summer school programs.

Theirs was a wedding of special resonance in the social circles of the Eastern United States. But soon after they had settled into the more familiar and usually rewarding marriage relationship, John began to long for the excitement he experienced from seducing women and initiating them in the uninhibited application of unique sexual techniques that ranged from ultra sensitive caresses to peculiar variations worthy of some Polynesian tribes or sumptuous Mediterranean brothels.

He recognized the power of his instinctual drive but was simply unable to exercise any form of control over it. He compared himself to Dr. Jekyll and Mr. Hyde in the sense that he embodied 2 personalities whose differences were the result of an abnormal sexual appetite. He possessed that rare quality of being physically attractive and at the same time able to instill confidence and trust, and respect for his intellect. These qualities were enhanced by his dialectic ability as a Minister of the Lord. Further, he seemed to project, albeit reluctantly, a subtle insinuation of wickedness and perversion that many women found curiously enticing.

Over the years he had used this unique appeal to further the aims of the Church and, in the process, to seek and obtain release to this passionate and uncontrolled facet of his personality. All along he had taken infinite pains to maintain the utmost discretion in his affairs and escapades, and thus had managed to protect his reputation as a national religious leader and saver of souls. In time, he began to develop special feelings toward three of his many lovers to the extent that he arranged for Meetings, Sermons and Special convocations to take place in the three cities where his mistresses lived. His busy schedule camouflaged to perfection his regular bouts of adultery in the three cities.

When he thought about his poligamy, he felt curiously happy and totally free of remorse. In his mind he had rationalized his situation in such terms that, he could always come to the conclusion that he was contributing to the happiness of four human beings and that they in turn were giving him the measure of physical satisfaction and solace he craved.

Maintaining a consistent love affair with three women simultaneously, outside marriage, is indeed a daring and complex adventure. Besides, being a public figure, easily recognizable, added to the need to play the game with exquisite discretion and secrecy. He had become a master at deception and a formidable strategist.

His monthly trips to the West Coast lasted, as a rule, 4 days and included Sunday when he delivered a sermon and held a luncheon meeting with the Church Council at their Newport Beach Headquarters. He preferred to fly into the crowded Los Angeles Airport where he would be less noticeable. He refused chauffeured limos, and discouraged people from meeting him at the airport. He also made it clear that he would not accept any appointments nor attend any functions the day of his arrival. He would rent a car and drive to the Marriott in Irvine where he usually stayed. He preferred the Marriott in place of the more luxurious Ritz Carlton near Dana Point as the lively rhythm of the Marriott's business clientele offered some measure of anonymity. Shortly after checking in, he would leave the hotel and drive a few miles south on the coast highway. The road to Meg's townhouse winded up the hills for a few miles. He would drive into the three car garage and once inside, would activate the automatic garage door closing mechanism. Until early the next morning, he and Meg would rediscover each other, talk about his and her activities and make love in several episodes charged with suppressed desire and stimulated by passions that inspired all kinds of refinements.

Their suppers were memorable, for after an afternoon of lovemaking, a restful sleep and a refreshing shower, their appetites were greatly enlarged. Meg would prepare novelties such as Chicken and Green Rice, marinated seafood, mango and ice cream desserts and would have a selection of wines and champagnes. Once in a while, he would attach a small mustache to his upper lip, wear a pair of glasses and they would go to the restaurants in Dana Point.

All this was possible thanks to the generous arrangements that the Reverend had made to enable Meg to collect a substantial fee as Deputy Director of the Church's Foundation. This arrangement, quite common with most influential men that maintain a parallel personal relationship, worked to the satisfaction of the Reverend. He did not feel that he was breaking any ethical guidelines as Meg was being paid to do useful work—even if all she had to do was to attend one session a week at the Foundation and arrange for a monthly mailing to a list of 25 college administrators in the area.

Meg was the only mistress of his that had questioned his conjugal relations and the nature of their affair.

"Reverend, what I do not understand is how you can preach about sin and all the time you are a champion offender of the sixth commandment. Does it bother you?"

"Not at all. Look at it this way. Our physical love is the result of the pure love we have for each other. If you deny love, my girl, you are denying life itself. Our lovemaking is an expression of our love and it certainly does not go against any moral or ethical consideration."

"It is a very convenient rationalization. How can you not call our affair unethical, or immoral? You are a married man and on top of that you are supposed to be an example of good behavior to your flock."

"Well, yes. I agree that our relationship attempts against some principles, but they are social principles. When love enters the picture, a different set of values apply. Imagine that I have real affection for some people in my congregation. It is different from our kind of love only in that no physical intimacy is present but is still love. And no one objects to it!"

"Reverend, you are so glib with words that you could twist an Oklahoma tornado quicker than you can say fornication!"

To him Meg was not only a willing and eager lover but a reliable information channel into the doings of the local organization.

Just as intense was the affair that he maintained with Stella, the petite real estate agent and popular hostess in DC that to him represented the icing on the cake of his multi-layered infidelities. Stella possessed a rare combination of natural beauty and a formidable intellect. But the quality that made her uniquely attractive was the fiery breath of sensuality that she exuded. It was almost palpable. Men could not look at her for long before becoming aware that they were in front of a highly charged, erotic woman. As ordinary a gesture as picking up an object from a table became a sensual sequence with Stella. Her movements, perfectly natural, somehow projected nothing but sexuality. To top it all, her face and body were in themselves blueprints of anticipated joys and an expression of a quality difficult to define that hinted at wildness and total abandonment.

She paid minute attention to every detail of her appearance. She knew that such care would cause men, and, why not, also women, to keep their eyes riveted on her. For instance, aware that the first look from men follow almost identical patterns, she made sure that her frontal exposure was much in evidence. Her cleavage was carefully measured, and arranged to emphasize the soft merging of the two breasts; this vision was perfectly complemented by the subtle insinuation of round and appetizing nipples which she took pains to make sure would emphasize their presence regardless of the fabric of the dress, sweater, or plain blouse. Similar attention was paid to that part of her anatomy that suggests inviting motions and gentle thrusts; she made sure that her pelvis area, her barely noticeably lower abdomen bulge and her round hips were always in such position that a message seemed to be coming from them. She knew that the view from the back was just as important. She used specially made undergarments that provided an almost invisible profile as seams were practically non-existent. She wanted freedom of her hips and buttocks and had developed a walking style that emphasized the enticing quivering motion of her well shaped cheeks that drove some men to pine for a caress, a feel or a pinch.

From the beginning, her relationship with Reverend John Toe acquired the features of a sexual carnival of unlimited joys. Stella had carried on affairs with some of the powerful men in Washington. Her curriculum was strewn with the broken hearts of Senators, Cabinet Secretaries, almighty legal eagles, celebrities, etc. But she adhered religiously to her practice of treating her affairs as just that: affairs. She always made it clear that after the cruise, the trip to Athens, the vacation in a hidden ranch somewhere out West, or the relaxed week end in some secluded Bed and Breakfast in the Bay, was the beginning and the end of the episode. But these severe restrictions that she had imposed on herself, and her suitors, vanished when she met the Reverend John Toe.

She often thought about the circumstances of their first encounter. She would never imagine that the funeral services for a common friend would not only bring them together but also discharge a current of attraction that was as immediate as it was ardent. From the moment Reverend Toe reached the pulpit at St. Francis, Stella noticed, or rather, detected, that concealed wildness that John possessed. Her infallible instinct conveyed an urgent message to Stella. Here was a man worth knowing. She tried hard to delete these thoughts from her mind, but the moment she heard his voice, her resistance evaporated.

On his part, the Reverend had not missed the attentive glances from the beautiful woman in the front pew. He instantly felt the strange but enticing aura of physical sensuality she projected. Several times during his sermon, he made a sub-conscious appraisal of the specimen in front of him. She was elegantly dressed, which reassured his predilection for women of good taste. It also meant that the good taste could be a by-product of a good education, some cultural depth and possibly some personal accomplishment. These were all ingredients that enhanced his admiration and commitment to women.

After the service, she approached him and said, "Reverend, yours has been a great eulogy. Most of the time, on these occasions, all we hear are clichés upon clichés and a string of platitudes. You must let me know next time you are doing another service of this kind!"

The Reverend was not surprised by the approach. He more or less expected to meet and talk to the beautiful woman in the front pew.

"Very kind of you. And you are right. Often we let ourselves get carried away by the easy, pre-fabricated phrases."

He got closer to her and, looking at her and her frontal charms, said, "Just to have the pleasure of seeing you again, I am ready to officiate at a service at the nearest gas station!"

She laughed while her eyes acknowledged the message.

Their coming together was thus inevitable. They began an intense affair that benefited from total abandon on both parts and a simple desire to introduce exciting variations into their love-making. In weeks, Stella had given up on her policy to limit her affairs to only one night, or one week-end stands. To her own surprise she turned down all proposals from the many Washington men about town who courted her and concentrated on the visits that the Reverend John Toe made to the area.

Their relationship matured into a highly satisfactory arrangement where there were no demands from either party. Their obsessive purpose was to extract the most pleasurable sensations from their bodies.

In time, their affair became known to others. Washington, like New York, is not the ideal place to conceal an illicit love affair. Those who have succeeded can probably be counted with the fingers of one hand. An eager media and an avid public have turned both legitimate and illicit love affairs into a thriving industry.

The Senate elite, besides, maintains an efficient intelligence service that keeps tabs on affairs and situations that could easily become national scandals. Often, the secrecy of some affairs remained well protected by colleagues and peers. They go to great lengths to make sure that some remain unknown and forgotten, while others are kept under wraps to serve as elegant blackmail in later occasions.

Most confidential reports of this nature are first brought to the attention of

Senator Forsyth, as the Senior and most respected member of that small elite that in one way or another has a lot to say about anything that goes on inside and outside the Government. While he was never pleased with the honor of learning of the improprieties of Government officials and national public figures, Senator Forsyth felt a responsibility for the handling of some of the items that entered his confidential files. His colleagues trusted his judgment and generally accepted his well thought out appraisals and decisions.

When he received a fresh report on the Reverend John Toe and his torrid affair with Stella, the well known Washington hostess, he was flabbergasted. It was hard for him to believe that the respected Minister, self acclaimed as the conscience of the country, whose power extended beyond the boundaries of faith and religion, had maintained a mundane love affair right under the noses of the most influential people in the nation. He requested verification and additional details. Almost at once, he received a sheaf of investigative reports, video tapes, telephotos, transcripts of telephone conversation, copies of letters and E-mail messages. There were also innumerable copies of hotel bills, restaurants and shops in Europe, the Virgin Islands and the eastern part of the country. The Reverend disguised as Mr. John Taylor had left a wide trail, easy to detect and even easier to follow.

In spite of the many reports on the bedroom shenanigans of elected members of the government, the fresh report on the Reverend John Toe and his torrid affair with Stella, the well known Washington hostess, did manage to raise his eyebrows.

Once he was sure of the veracity of the information, he invited Elmo Saks to his home where he felt they could talk openly about the matter. Senator Forsyth was well aware of the close relationship between Elmo and the Reverend. He had on many occasions, aided both of them in matters of national interest.

"Elmo, this is a very serious matter. You must stop John from keeping up this affair. Right now, only a few people know about it, but sooner or later it will become known to others. I am holding on to the information that has been collected and will make sure that none of it leaves my office safe."

After discussing the details and the recent history of the affair, Elmo agreed with Senator Forsyth. He summed up his thinking with, "Senator, this is a tremendous shock to me. I had not expected anything like this from John. I have known for sometime about his weakness for a pretty woman and even some brief escapades, but never thought he would carry his sexual adventures to such a risky level. I shall have to have a talk with him."

The senator looked at Elmo and, nodding his head, said, "Elmo, it is a messy affair. Just remember that a scandal at this point will cause irreparable damage to too many people. I, of course prefer to be totally removed from all this. You know what to do."

In the next few hours, Elmo traced the Reverend and located him at one of his sanctuaries in New Hampshire. He asked him to meet him in Washington as soon as possible. Reverend Toe had planned to fly directly to Nashville but instead changed his plans to include a one day stop in the capital.

Two days later, the Reverend was met at National Airport and taken to Elmo's estate in St. Michael's. Remy, the driver was unusually silent during the trip, unlike other times when he would chat about unimportant matters. It made the Reverend uneasy. Elmo had not given him any hint as to the purpose and urgency of the meeting. Upon arriving at the estate, he was quickly ushered into Elmo's private office on the second floor.

Elmo, did not waste any time in disclosing the extent of the offense and, what he considered just as censurable, the careless manner in which the affair had become known. Elmo abstained from offering moral judgments or approaching anything close to a sermon. He just enumerated the possible consequences of a major scandal and the damage it would do to the number of respected institutions in the country that they had worked so hard to create.

The Reverend was silent and seemed to be under shock. After drinking a glass of water, he acknowledged the relationship in few words and agreed to end the affair at once.

"We have heard rumors in the past about some indiscretions of yours, John, but have always felt that you were capable of managing any situation that could lead to a scandal. You realize that this could be, considering the media, one of the juiciest scandals of the decade. Stella's bedroom curriculum covers a wide spectrum of personalities in practically all walks of life. Besides, we understand that she maintains detailed dossiers on every encounter she has had. She is nothing short of a weapon of mass destruction!"

Elmo then proceeded to question the Reverend about Stella's home in Washington and the bungalow she kept in Martha's Vineyard. He extracted detailed descriptions of both places and also about Stella's work habits, schedules and itineraries.

It was late in the evening when the Reverend John Toe, preoccupied and exhausted, boarded a flight to Nashville.

Early the next morning, Elmo called Remy into his private office on the second floor. Two hours later, Remy left the office with his usual expressionless face while Elmo, stared emptily into the chimney.

The Saturday morning editions of the metropolitan papers and also the national press headlined the mysterious fire that had caused the death by asphyxiation of a famous Washington hostess. Preliminary investigations indicated that a gas leak might have been the cause of the fire. The house was totally destroyed and burned to the ground.

Twenty four hours later, and as a strange coincidence, Stella's bungalow in Martha's Vineyard also burned to the ground during a violent storm. It was believed that lightning had struck the house and caused the fire.

Assessing the Potential

Only a few days had passed since the appearance of the space ships above the major cities on earth when a meeting took place in the luxurious library of an impressive estate in the Chesapeake Bay. Elmo Saks, the billionaire ex-Senator was holding an informal meeting in his estate in St Michael's. Present were the Reverend John S. Toe and Dr. Sam Zellner, the Chairman of the National Science Foundation.

"Elmo, what does your hyperactive brain tells us about these objects above us?" asked Dr. Zellner as he poured more scotch in his cut crystal glass.

Elmo, who had spent many hours analyzing all kinds of hypothesis concerning the origin and purpose of the objects, answered the question in his usual brief but forceful manner, "One, they come from outside our known universe. Two, they are here for some purpose. Three, they possess technology way beyond our present levels. Four, they cannot hover above forever; sooner or later they will make their presence known. Five, who they are and what they look like is anybody's guess. As far as I can see, they do have access to mental processes of some sort; the fact that they have placed objects above very specific locations indicates the use of deductive processes. You know, size of the cities, location, even their altitude has been carefully established for the purpose of making sure that we on earth know that they are there and also to allow regular airline traffic to proceed."

"Yes, that is more or less our same conclusions at the Foundation. We have been in contact with both military and civilian institutions in this country and abroad and no one can provide any insights into this thing. We can only speculate about the kind of technology they have developed. Care to comment on it?"

Elmo stood up and walked to the large picture window that offered a magnificent view of the bay. He thought for a moment and then said, "One, the pills appear to be vessels of some sort that must have been made somewhere. That means a manufacturing process, which in turn means technology. Their electromagnetic shield is no small accomplishment. Two, there must be an exquisite control system that keeps all these things in the right place. Three, if such is the case, there is some unique communications systems linking the damn things."

He paused to sip his scotch and continued. "Whatever the nature of the phenomena, there is advanced technology that we would do well to keep in mind. Four, if you ask me, there is also deep reasoning and thinking; a brain of some sort, either organic or otherwise, must be directing this episode."

"I suspect that a soul must also be involved," interjected the Reverend Toe. "All the planning to get those things in place above us and what you just said, somehow brings us to that thinking process and by consequence to some form of guidelines, which could be moral or not. That is where I feel that a purpose and a meaning are involved in the rational way this surprise has been sprung on us."

Elmo nodded and added in a jovial vein, "Leave it to the Reverend to bring in the abstract into this! Next you can tell us about which commandments they are here to check up on!"

They all laughed and followed the uniformed waiter to the dining room where a splendid supper was waiting.

The London Meeting

Ross Simonson, the president of the United States had opposed from the beginning the proposal to hold a meeting of the industrialized nations to discuss the objects above and what sort of common policies ought to be considered in dealing with the objects. He felt it was premature and that it was better to wait until whoever was manipulating the objects above announce their presence. He also indicated that the UN must be included in any possible plan to establish contact with the objects. He felt that their intentions did not appear hostile as they would have acted well before then. He let Simon Ross, the British Prime Minister know his feelings and tried to convince him to consider the alternatives he favored.

While not totally satisfied with the US President's reaction, the Prime Minister hoped that once in London his attitude would change. He felt strongly that the UN, in spite of its current level of efficiency and spotless reputation, would not be in a position to deal with the objects and whoever was behind, or more likely, inside them. He was also aware of the pressure exerted by the other nations to celebrate a meeting devoted exclusively to the objects.

The Foreign Office in London put into effect their emergency plans to cope with a meeting that had the eyes of the entire world upon it. Advance groups from the various governments began to arrive hours after the Prime Minister in a simultaneous press conference with the other world leaders had announced the meeting to be held 48 hours thereafter.

The placid routine of the various departments at Whitehall was severely disrupted. For one thing, this emergency was taking place at the beginning of the summer season when London hotels are beginning to receive the package tours and tourist throngs that wish to avoid the July and August crunches. Even so, the Coordinating office had to employ all its muscle to make sure that there would be room for everyone. The executive staffs numbered more than 1000 persons, not counting support personnel such as Security, secretaries, liaison and Press officers attached to the offices of Prime Ministers and Presidents. Within hours London was invaded by reporters, anchormen and women, observers, TV crews and the rest of the media fauna. Also, within hours, most of the bars from Green Park to Trafalgar Square were doing three deep business and most restaurants were refusing any more reservations.

"This is like the day before the Olympics"—observed Muir Sutherland at the London Times offices in Pennington Street. Like most newspapermen, Muir had a theory about the object parked above London. In spite of the cynical outlook that 20 years in journalism had engraved on his personality, there remained a trace of deep religious beliefs in him that had been imbedded in the course of a happy and secure childhood in Yorkshire. The appearance of the pancakes, or pills or aspirins, as the objects were being called, had triggered in Muir an unexpected craving for quiet meditation. He went through a confusing moment when he could not rationalize the physical characteristics of the phenomena with an act of faith. For those religious beliefs that existed deeply within him made him lean toward a purely spiritual manifestation, as most churches were suggesting. The appearance of the ships was being considered a miracle. A miracle that wore the colors of whatever church group, minister or sect proclaimed it. Every religion on earth had astonishingly adopted the phenomena and somehow managed to use its presence as corroboration of whatever creed they had been dispensing.

Muir's theory was diametrically opposed to his convictions as a journalist. He believed—and felt—that God had finally decided to make its presence known on earth at a moment when conflict and human misery were rampant on the planet. He was convinced that whatever the occupants of the ships were, they had been assigned a divine mission. Of course he was careful not to let his opinions transcend the severe impartiality of the newspaper' s philosophy. His articles—while full of details and valid quotes and opinions—remained an example of reporting at its most objective level.

The announcement of the meeting of the Big 8 filled him with with joy and anticipation. It meant that in addition to the exciting stream of news coming his way, he would again have the opportunity to see Mercedes, the assistant editor of the World Events desk at the New York Times. She would probably be arriving that same evening and—chances were—that a message was already recorded in his answering machine at home. Theirs was a unique relationship. It was not often that common professional interests and the personal traits that colored their relationship—plus an ocean and a culture apart—could survive the frenetic pace of modern day journalism. He checked British Airways timetable out of New York as he wanted very much to meet Mercedes at Heathrow. By then, incoming air traffic into London's International Airport had been rationalized as every flight would have to approach the airfield under the space object. No major difficulties had been encountered as all flights never reached altitudes in excess of 35 to 40,000 feet, except the Concorde which flew at higher altitudes but never within the confines of the British mainland. The only variation had been the shadow that the object created, but it was only in evidence during sunny days, which in London are not really missed.

Sure enough, there was a cheerful message from Mercedes when he accessed his answering machine through his cellular phone. "Hey! My favorite bald man of the British Isles: how about picking me up in the morning. Arriving on BA 906 to attend the space barbecue organized by the eight dwarfs, or whatever. Un beso. Say! hope these plane phones work. Couldn't call you before because I did not know I was coming until a few hours ago. Ciao!"

Getting out of London at 8 in the morning is no problem. The real congestion is caused by the number of cars and lorries, as trucks are called in England, that occupy every inch of every roadway coming in to the city. Even the clever ones who choose exotic shortcuts, eventually find themselves immobilized and staring at the license plates of the car, or lorry in front of them. This chaos lasts until about 9 a.m. Muir had no problem negotiating the old familiar route from his three story townhouse off Banbury Park. A quick dash across Oxford Street and smooth sailing from Bayswater, Kensington, past the Museum and on into A4 to Heathrow where the incoming traffic moved at the traditional snail's pace.

He quickly made his way to Heathrow's inner belt to the terminal 2 parking lot. He parked the Chrysler Voyager van and walked across the walkway to the Terminal. Most overseas flights arrive at that time of the morning. And all of a sudden, the quiet halls with their polished stainless steel, Rochdale marble floors and quiet background music take on the appearance of a railway station in Istanbul during the evening rush hour. Muir stopped briefly in front of the arrivals board to check that the flight was on time and to verify the gate number. He had done this so many times that he knew by heart the arrival times from New York of Delta, American, British Airways, Air India, ElAl, Paki Air, JAL, etc. Mercedes was responsible for this unwanted piece of knowledge. She delighted in trying different airlines, claiming that if she was going to arrive in London groggy and with an upset stomach she preferred not to indulge in targeting her hate on a single airline.

"No airline deserves to have an exclusive on my hate," she joked.

She arrived at the gate fresh and lovely as ever. She was wearing a comfortable combination of a tight fitting navy blue alpaca skirt, a light blue silk blouse with fine white lines and a white linen three quarter loose jacket. Two tone Italian pumps completed the loveliness of her image. She carried a fine leather Molteni bag, of the kind that can be used as handbag, business case, and even overnighter.

"I am not going to ask how was your flight," Muir said, as they started the long walk to the Baggage Collection area. "It seems to me that it is the most wasted expression of the airplane age. If it was the Challenger Space Shuttle, I can approve, but not when you spend a few hours sitting on a comfortable flying sofa sipping French Champagne and making eyes at the Austrian Baron sitting across the aisle!"

Mercedes laughed in that peculiar two tone melody of hers.

"No matter. I am going to tell you anyhow! First, there was no Austrian Baron. Most of my first class team were the typical tired businessmen from New York. They looked as if they had not slept for a week when they downloaded themselves on their first class seats. They slurp a few, pick at the food and pass out. Ah! the joys of being middle aged and successful!"

"Nothing wrong with being middle age, flower of my garden," replied Muir. "Remember how you used to admire the first gray hairs I sprouted? Later, they gave me a distinguished look as they suggested added maturity. You swore that I became more interesting. Mature men are more understanding and affectionate. They make better lovers. They have good golf handicaps and good credit ratings. They know wines, fine leather shoes, poplin shirts and those selected phrases that make women change the expression in their eyes and their appreciation of soft-voiced insinuations. And, my love, a lot of etceteras which I shall not discuss at this time of the morning..."

"It is all true, with some exceptions, of course," teased Mercedes. "But I must tell you. I sat next to one under Secretary coming to London to attend the Pancake meeting. By the way, you should see the sight the space ship provides as you approach Heathrow. I am surprised the Airlines have not added a surcharge to their fares. It is a fabulous sight. There she—or it—sits on top of London as if it was an artificial cloud. As the sun rays hit it, the reflection brings to mind the magnificence of the Taj Mahal in the early morning. As you approach London, you can see the thing in all its beauty; from the distance it looks much lower than its real altitude and, of course, smaller. But as you get near, you realize you are flying well below its height. I never saw so many cameras come out of hand bags in my life. All the windows were crowded for a full half hour."

They collected the luggage, loaded it on a cart and made the short trek to the parking lot.

Once in the van, Mercedes said, "I telephoned Ginny from the plane and told her I was on my way. She wants us to have dinner tomorrow night at her place."

"Great! It is always good to see Ginny and enjoy her fabulous cooking. I also hope Andy can make it one of these evenings. We'll probably see him at the meeting but I am sure he will be babysitting with the PM most of the time. By the by, I ran into them at the airport in Geneva a few days ago. They'd been to the slopes in Megeve and both looked tanned and happy."

Mercedes smiled and said, "I am glad to hear it. They are one of my favorite couples. I only hope that their relationship is not taken out of context by the nosey press here and make life uncomfortable for both of them. Even a Cabinet Secretary has a right to a private life and our Sir Andrew Blott and Ginny deserve any happiness they can enjoy."

"Quite so. It could be a dangerous game for both of them. But a full blown scandal is doubtful. Remember that Andy has been a widower for over four years and in all this time, he has never strayed form the straight and narrow. Besides, the English public is mature enough to accept a relationship that hurts no one."

Mercedes looked at Muir and observed, "If they keep a low profile, not much can happen. You know how the sensational press tries to find dirty linen where there is none. He is after all a prominent member of the government and by all concepts, free game!"

"You are probably right. Even so, there is no chance in this country that the Judicial authorities, or an opposition party can set up some maniac prosecutor with a budget large enough to support a dozen Third World countries for a full semester. You know, love, illicit affairs in Britain, as fodder for scandal, only count if there is high treason committed, if homosexual activities are detected or if the Royal Family is somehow involved."

Mansion House

Mansion House, the residence of the Lord Mayor of London had been selected as the site for the meeting of the leaders of the industrialized nations, a group also known as the Big 8 or the Group of the 8. It included the U.S., England, Germany, Russia, France, Japan, Italy and Canada, even though most people wondered why this last country was included in such group. Canada is neither an economic giant nor a major player in the world scene.

Someone had observed that England and the U.S. wanted to accumulate a bit of Anglo-Saxon voting power and, having failed at promoting Australia and New Zealand as world powers, had obtained a small victory with Canada. Fortunately, Canada is a sound and stable country with strong ties to the UK, France and the United States and can be counted upon to support those policies that reflect agreement among those countries.

Mansion House is an old stone barn built in 1735 by George Dance the Elder, who was at the time the Surveyor of the City of London. Up to that time, the mayors of the city lived in their own homes and were never comfortable as they had to conduct meetings, receive citizens and hold banquets and ceremonies there. Design and construction of Mansion House was an involved affair. Since the London fire in 1666, reconstruction of the city had progressed in uneven bursts with the result that no recognizable architectural features had developed. Originally, Palladio, the 16th century master architect was invited to develop a design for the Mayor's Mansion in what was then known as the Palladian Style. But Palladio did not get the approval of the city's notables because, as an Italian, he was accused of being a Papist. Nothing to do with architecture but just another instance of irrational prejudice.

Later, the Mayor of London, who was also the Keeper of the Royal Seal and Secretary to the King's Council insisted that the City's Surveyor prepare the plans for the Mansion and not spare any effort in obtaining the services of the best craftsmen and in selecting the best construction materials.

Eventually the job was given to George Dancer, who was probably a good surveyor but a lousy architect, judging by the slightly grotesque aspect of the finished product. Mansion House is a stone structure that sits on the corner of Poultry and Queen Victoria Streets, next to Wallbrook Street and to one of the churches built by Wren, St. Stephen Wallbrook Church.

Completed in 1752, Mansion House received an indifferent reception from visitors and locals alike. Dancer exaggerated a bit on the use of classical columns and stuck 6 Corinthian columns on an imposing but unattractive colonnade. Further, he included a portico that was too large and cumbersome.

Somehow, the structure reminds one of the architectural excesses of the nouveau riche, whose mansions easily confirm the suddenly affluent status of the occupant by supporting everything that needs it with Corinthian, Ionic and Doric columns, and crowning them with marble pediments.

In 1934, Mansion House underwent its fifth renovation and was equipped with a new electrical installation, a security system and air conditioning. It houses more than 150 tapestries of Flemish, Dutch and Spanish manufacture that require a precise humidity control to offset the humid breath of the Thames River and London's ever present morning showers. At that time also, the roofs were rebuilt and the attics remodeled so that they could accommodate offices, a modern communications lounge and several large storage and file rooms.

During the Second World War, damage was inflicted on its West Wing but mainly on the roofs and some of the meeting rooms. An incendiary bomb caused some damage in 1944 but the Mansion was spared the V-bombs. In 1986, a complete renewal was undertaken. Its weather and pollution-scarred facades were sand blasted, old windows were reinforced or replaced and new carpeting was laid on some of the exhibition and display rooms. A new air conditioning system was installed and its basements were totally remodeled. The old coach houses were transformed into well appointed offices and meeting rooms, including several plush private apartments.

This day, Mansion House was resplendent with all its flags flying at high mast. The ceremonial drapes hanging from the ornate balconies and the imposing columns, added a touch of medieval color to the windows facing the small park in the front.

The conference had been scheduled to take place in the comfortable Banqueting Hall or Egyptian Hall, where its 400-year-old solid oak round table—claimed to have been one of the tables Richard III installed in several

London palaces and residences—would again witness important deliberations. It is claimed that Winston Churchill once was caught carving his initials on one of the legs of the table. When confronted he is said to have exclaimed, "It is just a small but lasting scar in a beautiful leg and I am partial to beautiful legs!"

At 09:00 hours, the motorcades began to fill up the courtyard of Mansion House. Steel-armored Cadillacs, Mercedes and Nissans entered the stone paved area and discharged their occupants in front of the entrance colonnade and portico. As each leader arrived, he or she was taken to the Central Lounge where they were greeted by the Primer Minister and his Lordship the Mayor of London. Once they were all assembled, they were asked to pose for press photographers, paparazzi and television cameras that then proceeded to offend everyone's retina with their flashes and Klieg lights. Reporters were not allowed to ask questions, thus limiting the session to a photographic exercise.

In a few minutes the session was finished and the leaders of the 8 industrialized nations were taken to the Cornwall Lounge. True to tradition, the British Prime Minister occupied the chair facing South and the other dignitaries sat around the table with their aids and assistants sitting some distance in back of them. The round table served its purpose admirably. Its shape did not allow for any feeling of ascendancy or supremacy. Everyone sat around it and felt that the tone of the meeting was one of equality, even if each one of them felt different about the matter they were about to discuss.

Sitting right behind the British Prime Minister, Sir Andrew "Andy," Blotts, fiddled nervously with the tooled leather note book on his lap. As Whitehall's Cabinet Secretary, he had every reason to be nervous. If the blasted things above made or caused any damage and were responsible for panic among the population, it was his department's responsibility to make sure that all emergency services operated under a coordinated plan. The Cabinet Secretary has the tremendous responsibility of maintaining equilibrium between the country's public services and its politicians. As Head of the Home Civil Service he commands a large and powerful sector of the Government.

The present meeting was also a cause for concern. To him, anything that smacked of improvisation would invariably result in harried decisions and, eventually, in embarrassing reversals and the unavoidable situations where blame for the errors that were made would be placed on the unsuspecting. Besides, the Prime Minister had been vague about the purpose of the Summit at the cabinet meeting the previous day. Even though the agenda mentioned prominently the need to develop a coordinated world policy in respect to the objects that had appeared so suddenly, it did not go into detail about why the Group of 8 should take it upon itself to set a course when the UN, Russia, China, Brazil and many other countries, not to mention the entire human race, were as involved as the blessed 8. Or was there something that he did not know?

For the next 10 hours, interrupted only by short breaks devoted to visits to the lavish buffet and the equally lavish toilet facilities, the Presidents, Chancellors and Prime Ministers of the most influential group on earth debated the need to assume the leadership in what they all feared would be a crucial episode in the history of mankind. The debate was intense and at times heated. The main thesis, proposed by a disturbing majority, was simply to have the Group of 8 to act on behalf of the rest of the world, when and if, some contact was established with the unknown objects and its crews.

As anticipated, the question of why the UN had not been invited to the London Summit, was rised. While they all agreed that the UN had been transformed into an effective world forum, they still felt uncomfortable with the recent past history of the organization. It was felt that unjustified importance in the past had been bestowed upon nations which cultural and economic development left much to be desired. Some also felt that the spotted history of the UN represented no guarantee to the rest of the world. It was felt that only the 8 more industrialized nations on earth were in a position to negotiate with the visitors with some degree of authority and also, with the backing of their substantial resources. This thesis was introduced subtly at first and then with certain vehemence. It became clear that, with the exception of Italy and the United States, the other countries had arrived at some form of tacit understanding regarding the matter. Italy and the United States did not agree with such course of action.

"This is the equivalent of a coup d'etat," argued the Italian Primer Minister.

"That is ridiculous!" replied the French Prime Minister. "The UN is not the Government of Earth and if it wasn't for us, it would not exist!"

The arguments were presented, discussed and again reintroduced in another tone. But the idea was the same: to prevent the UN from assuming a position of leadership in any situation that might possibly develop.

A similar argument and a similar rebuttal were presented when it was mentioned that the European Union should also be included in the deliberations regarding the objects overhead. The Group of 8 insisted that the EU was already represented by having some of its members at the meeting. It was obvious that they opposed having all 21 EC nations represented at meetings and at later deliberations about the space visitors. Some felt that some of the smaller countries like Portugal, Greece, Spain and the Low Countries would be at a disadvantage if at a later date, it they had to pledge substantial resources.

"I explained to each of you personally, that I felt that this meeting was somewhat premature," Ross Simonson, the President of the United States, finally spoke, after having listened patiently to the lengthy presentations, the vociferous arguments and the occasional rebuttals.

"For one thing, we are still in the dark about the identity of these things. If contact is made, they, or whatever, might just choose anyone. And as far as the UN is concerned, I think that the Secretary General has done such a superb job that for the first time we are seeing positive results in every one of the missions it has undertaken. Besides, Patrick has assembled one of the finest management teams anyone could expect and has also underpinned the top echelons with the most effective support groups ever seen. Each of you has had ample opportunity to experience in vivo, the new UN in action. If there is a truly world representative that has the welfare of the peoples of this planet foremost in his mind, that is the Secretary General. He could deal successfully with anyone, be they green little men or giant truffles with aviator sunglasses!"

There was silence around the table. Most of the leaders were aware of Patrick Deschamps' outstanding record and recognized the fact that the UN had become a tremendously lean, concise and humanitarian instrument that applied its precepts with fairness and impartiality. Some, who had been caught with their skirts soiled, as the saying went, resented Patrick's and the UN's perfect record and for that reason alone, opposed the idea of having the UN speak for the rest of the world. It was the usual mixture of vanity, jealousy, envy and suspicion that has forever impregnated the guidelines of International Relations.

The President sighed and continued. "I don't need to go over all this, gentlemen. You are all too familiar with Deschamps' successes in the last couple of years. But it isn't the record that he has achieved but the fact that almost all nations on earth have for the first time in the history of civilization, recognized the presence and the authority of an international force that they can turn to with confidence and trust."

Sir Andrew Blott, the Cabinet Secretary, listened attentively to the President of the United States and to the other arguments. To him, the entire sequence appeared too elaborate. *There must be a proposal somewhere but no one wants to be the one to table it*, he thought, remembering the Prime Minister's unusual reserve about this reunion.

Ordinarily, the Prime Minister would prepare for a meeting in a most meticulous and detailed manner and would drive everyone to focus on the million details, options, escape clauses, projections and historical precedents attending whatever topic was being discussed.

Finally, and well past dinner time, Simon Ross, the British Prime Minister approached the subject, "Gentlemen, let me be clear. Our civilization might be threatened and possibly in danger of being obliterated by the objects above our cities. There is no doubt in my mind that soon we will be asked to come face to face with the visitors and will have to defer to whatever demands they might have in store for us. I have been thinking about the possible reasons that have urged these beings to park above our planet. I am inclined to discount all those reasons all too familiar to us that have been the cause of continuous conflicts among the peoples of Earth. You know, extending land holdings, conquering new worlds, looking for natural resources, controlling means of production, conflicts over trade and new markets, the desire to acquire wealth and power and, in many cases, the desire to use and exploit technological properties."

He glanced at his handwritten notes and continued. "It is obvious that these beings possess superior scientific knowledge and are not likely to be seeking nuclear fuels, high octane gasoline or plain old matchboxes. Air, water, minerals, vegetables, etc. are not—in my mind—reasons to justify an invasion or, as it is, a presence here. Even if they are methyl ethyl ketone-breathing beings or need to live in a perchloroethylene atmosphere, they should be in a position to synthesize or somehow produce such gases. Any group that can place these incredibly large flying objects at the drop of a hat all over a fairly large planet like earth, and use an electromagnetic shield to keep the natives away, must have developed sophisticated technologies. I have also thought about those remote possibilities so popular with science fiction writers: flesh eaters, blood suckers, escargot munchers, etc. I still cannot see it."

"How about just plain conquest of a new planet?" the Italian Prime Minister asked.

"That is a plausible hypothesis. However, I should think that if such was the case, more direct action would have been the appropriate procedure. You know, the softening barrage, the neutralizing of defensive forces and the massive landings. Of course we are all assuming that these beings are similar to us. For all we know, they may be just plain old robots or ships manned by some form of living organism. But I cannot help thinking about the impeccable way in which they appeared and the way they have positioned themselves above the principal cities on the planet. Somehow, in my view, it takes planning, resources and training...The whole episode has to follow some rational explanation."

The German Prime Minister, revealing a touch of impatience, raised his hand and spoke. "Well, we could continue speculating for the rest of the night. I suggest, Mr. Prime Minister, that you formulate the plan that has been discussed privately among some of us."

Upon hearing those words, Ross Simonson straightened up in his chair and in a severe tone asked, "I was not aware that there was any pre arranged plan or that even discussions had been held. I thought that this meeting was more in keeping with the idea that we would collectively decide on a course of action, meaning that we would face this situation as a group, or if I can be more clear, as the entire planet. What is the plan?"

The tone of his voice clearly revealed his annoyance. *Here we go again*, Ross thought. *We are in front of the most important event in our history and those responsible for assuming some form of united criteria, engage in the old devious ways.*

"Well." The German Prime Minister, a bit sheepishly, looked around the table and said, "Mister President, we are convinced that the intentions of these visitors are peaceful. We are also convinced that it must be us, the 8 industrialized nations who must deal with them on an exclusive basis. It is not only a guarantee for the rest of the world but also protection for our own well being. Besides, we are better prepared to take advantage of exciting new forms of scientific knowledge."

He looked around the table and, pleased with the nods given by some of those around the table, he was about to continue when the President of the United States stood up and said in a clear voice, "I am sorry but I cannot become a part of this plan. For the same reasons that I refuse to subscribe to any attempt that would exclude the UN or anyone else for that matter. Besides, like I said before, we haven't heard from these beings so I repeat this is as premature as it is a futile occasion. It is like eating the turkey before it has been caught."

The Canadian Prime Minister also stood up, and under the somewhat sheepish glance of the others, said, "I share wholeheartedly the feelings of the President of the United States. We can't eat the pasta before it is cooked. I suspect that this entire episode has been triggered by the pressure some of us are under. The pressure applied by our private sectors eager to latch on to the new technology that these beings are certain to bring in."

The Japanese Prime Minister raised his hand and, without waiting for acknowledgment, said, "Of course we are all interested in exploiting new technologies. While no one has said it, it is clear that additional sources of technology must be developed on this planet and not limited to our pressing energy problems. Fresh inputs are needed in the fields of telecommunications and space and computer sciences where US monopolies have expanded beyond reasonable limits. There is no bank transaction, electronic communication or transmission of data or images that is not in some way controlled by a few multinational corporations. We owe it to ourselves to seek and employ alternate sources. Competition, after all, has been the driving force of our societies."

The French representative was next to speak, "Gentlemen, we don't gain anything by quibbling among us. Let us be pragmatic. France is very much in favor of establishing direct contact with these pills, that is, the industrialized nations of which France is one. Nothing would be gained if some poor or backward nation is allowed to set guidelines for future policies with these objects. We are also opposed to the United Nations assuming the role of spokesman for the rest of the world. Its function has been and is strictly a forum for the nations of this planet and not the appointed and anointed representative of the human race. Besides, we feel that any technological benefit should be first offered to the industrialized nations, or rather, those countries in Europe that are in a position to provide the necessary guarantees to the objects of our good intentions. Any technological advantages will eventually benefit other nations. After all, it is the industrialized nations of Europe that bear the load of huge receivables from Eastern Europe, Russia, Asia, Africa and Latin America."

After another two hours of discussion, at well past 9 p.m., the meting came to an end. While no unanimous agreement had been reached on the plan to have the Big 8 act as sole world representatives before the objects, it was agreed to draft a press release signed by all those present indicating their willingness to collaborate with each other once the objects made contact.

The Prime minister, Sir Simon Ross, thanked them for attending the meeting and apologized for the long day and the missed opportunity to enjoy British hospitality. He regretted that a formal dinner had not been scheduled for that evening as no one had any idea of how long the meeting would last.

An hour later however, five of the seven met again, this time in Lambeth Palace, located twenty minutes from the center of the City of London The meeting was restricted to the Heads of Governments and their closest advisers. Notoriously absent were the Presidents of the United States and the Canadian Prime Minister.

Sir Andrew Blotts was not terribly surprised when told that another meeting was to take place at Lambeth Palace and that he had been requested to attend. He arrived in a few minutes and after meeting privately with Sir Simon Ross he joined the group in one of the ornate meeting rooms that had just been sanitized by a team of Special Forces.

The Prime Minister had not appeared too happy about this meeting and said so to Sir Andrew. "Andrew, things are getting complicated. First, it was a matter of taking an initiative before the objects. It meant having the industrialized countries deal with whatever is coming instead of having the UN assume that responsibility. But the US and Canada insist on waiting until these things communicate with us and let us know what their intentions are. They also insist on keeping the UN and other countries involved. We want to deal directly with the beings manipulating those pills."

Sir Andrew thought for a moment and then said, "Simon, let me be candid about this. I think it is premature to try to forge alliances before we know what we are dealing with. In that respect, the US and Canada have adopted a reasonable position. Now, I fear that some of the members want to enlist the rest of the world, so that when and if our upstairs visitors make themselves known, there would be an overwhelming majority that would keep the UN out of the game. I also think that there is a current in favor of keeping the US out of this situation. I don't think that it is the type of involvement we should either pursue or sanction."

"Thanks for putting it so clear. You know what? I agree. Up to now it was a matter of making sure that the industrialized countries could have access to the technology these objects might bring. But we must not lose sight of the bonds now existing between the UN and the United States. You know, those two, Patrick and Ross, have been close friends for years and it would be very easy for them to keep a hold on the whole situation. My concern has been all along that whatever technology appears, must not be retained in the hands of a single power, or the UN for that matter."

"So what is going to happen now? Who organized this meeting?"

"Everyone except us the US and Canada. The idea is to bring the Asian countries, Russia, the Middle East countries into this, along with Africa, Latin America, Australia, etc. and create a block solid enough to force the UN to defer to it. Let us see how this thing develops. I also suspect that each country has been pressured by their own industrial giants who do not wish to be left out of any new developments."

"Sir Simon, this smells to me as another trade war. I think the European powers and Japan are only following a tradition that at this time is reinforced by their own importance in world affairs. It is clear to me that they are afraid that the US, by virtue of its power and importance will end up dealing unilaterally with the objects."

"Yes, it is more or less what is behind these maneuvers. There is a tremendous thirst for novel technology, including us. And there is the fear of becoming even more dependent on US science and technology. While I would not go as far as calling this a trade war, it does make sense if Japan and the European members of the 8 are made to participate in any new developments."

Sir Andrew had listened to the carefully thought arguments presented by the Prime Minister, but he felt that some subtle element was missing. He decided to be candid about it and bring his own perceptions in the open. "Well, it is clear that most of the industrialized countries would love to get their hands on whatever new technologies these object will bring. But it does not escape me that the arguments that we have heard all day long seem to have a common fiber. While no specific mention has been made of either industrial companies or financial groups, some of these arguments maintain a common thread. To me it smells as a major prompting effort by a large supranational group that knows how to pressure all these governments and probably how to flash the carrots in front of their eyes. It seems like a masterful plan that profits from the legitimate aspirations of the governments involved and that unfailing appeal to collective greed."

"You are not too far off, Andrew," replied the Prime minister, who had a similar impression. "A well established global concern, with strong bases in the European Union, Asia, the US, Canada and other countries would know that by having the Big 8 and, in particular the European nations, deal with the visitors, they can have easy access to whatever new technologies are obtained. My question is which large group is involved, if any?"

"If we are both thinking about the same man and the same group, Sir Simon, how has he managed to line up all these heads of state?"

"You said it before. The carrots, Andrew, the carrots!"

"How about the sticks?"

"Do not worry, Elmo has plenty of them. Don't forget his influence with the US Senate, his reach everywhere through his banking network and the control he exercises over the global telecommunications sector. And that is not all, my friend. Don't forget the strength and power he commands in practically every major city of this world through his association with the world religious movement led by the famous Reverend Toe."

Sir Andrew smiled. He had of course been thinking about Elmo Saks and was pleased that the Prime Minister had the same thoughts. After all, there were very few moguls in the world that would step beyond their commercial interests and reach for a position in the unknown and the unpredictable.

"Andrew, in addition to these things on top of us we are going to have to worry about Elmo Saks and his bottomless bag of tricks."

With these words, Sir Simon picked up his briefcase and, followed by Sir Andrew, went up the red carpeted stairs to the meeting room on the second floor.

The meeting went as planned. It was agreed that China would be contacted at once, same as the major oil producing countries in the Middle East. Other contacts included Brazil, a number of African countries, India and the various nations in Southeast Asia. Sir Simon expressed some reservations but in the end agreed to remain within the group.

Oddly enough, Italy had assumed the role of major supporter of the world coalition proposed by France, Germany and Japan. It was agreed that after obtaining the support of the other countries, a special committee would be formed and that this committee would negotiate with the UN for the right to establish contact with the visitors, when and if they made themselves visible. After two more hours of discussion and, having promised to maintain their negotiations confidential, the participants left Lambeth Palace.

As the Prime minister was about to enter his car, he turned to Sir Andrew and said in a low voice: "Andy, I know it is a hell of a thing to ask, especially at this time of the morning, but cold you somehow get our meeting notes typed by noon tomorrow? You know we don't want detailed minutes at this point, but I want for everyone who was here just now to get a copy of our notes."

"No problem. Computers and printers nowadays are like kidneys, everyone is got at least one. I can get it done in plenty of time. In the morning you can revise it and have the final draft printed in your office."

The Prime Minister thanked Sir Andrew and, with a friendly punch in Sir Andrew's kidney entered the vehicle.

Sir Andrew went back to the meeting room and spent another two hours with officials attached to the Prime Ministers, Presidents and Chancellors that were by now busy revising and comparing their own notes.

Sir Andrew's Romantic Life

Sir Andrew Blotts gave a sigh of relief when the last car had left the grounds. He sat down in one of the chairs of the terrace and with a wary gesture lit a cigarette. He smoked quietly for a few minutes, allowing the aromatic poison to assist his nervous system to regain a quieter mood. With little concern for the hour, he then made a number of calls in his cellular phone to his associates and colleagues at Whitehall, giving instructions about the next morning. He planned to be at his office at about eleven in the morning.

He finished the cigarette and dialed another number.

"Ginny, it's me!" he whispered. He knew that Virginia Louise, the attractive executive of one of the British Television systems, would not begrudge him his calling at this hour of the morning. For more than two years, Virginia Louise had provided Sir Andrew with the companionship and understanding that a man prematurely widowed was certain to need. On his part, he had sought at all times to become a cheerful and reliable presence in Virginia Louise's life. Theirs was thus a mature and well balanced relationship reinforced by a surprisingly passionate edge.

He knew that she would not be annoyed at being awaken at dawn. Their affair was graced with a great deal of understanding and a serious tone of personal commitment. At At 40 years of age, Sir Andrew felt at the top of his physical form, and while the relationship with Virginia had initially started as a sexual carnival, it had given both the necessary outlet to their passionate natures and the emotional balance they both craved. His high pressure job required cool detachment and emotional stability and these could only occur if a sound mental and physical state were maintained.

On her part, Virginia Louise had simply fallen in love with Sir Andrew. Her successful career had provided her with numerous satisfactions. Her busy schedule provided a convenient outlet for her energy and professional zeal. For sometime prior to meeting Sir Andrew she had wondered whether there would be another man in her life. She made a conscious effort to erase from her mind those years of a failed marriage that almost took away her self esteem, and more important her prodigious energy and optimism. "Mejor sola que mal acompañada," was a Spanish proverb she often flashed in her mind. "Better alone than in bad company," brought to her the image of her Castillian grandmother who used it as a warning, a command and a suggestion.

"Andrew! What the...!" She sounded sleepy but her voice to him conveyed that indescribable sense of welcome he had become accustomed to in the last few years.

"Don't tell me those pills or space ships have finally landed."

"No such luck, dear. And forgive me for calling this late, or this early. We just finished our sessions. Would you mind very much if I come round in a few minutes. I am at Lambeth Palace so it is but a few minutes to Richmond."

"Of course I don't mind. Besides, I haven't seen you for 4 days and, let me tell you, Sir Andy, I do miss you!"

"I know. I also miss you. You have no idea what these few days have been. International conferences that are short, interesting and fruitful are one in every 376, according to some Australian pollster."

"How about this one?"

"Way off. Everyone trying to get hold of what at this time is plain old air. Great speeches but not much substance. Will tell you about it."

"Well, I have received a good report from Mercedes and Muir who said they had seen you but could not talk to you at Mansion House. They complain that all your press officers are very stingy with information or sidelights. Something must be cooking."

"Yes, but it too shall pass. Glad to hear Mercedes is in town. I had promised Muir some weeks ago that we all would have dinner when Mercedes arrived for the EPG Congress, but I guess that these objects have upset all plans."

"Well, everything is on hold, for almost everyone until we know more about the objects. But, in any case Mercedes and Muir will come for dinner tonight. There are also some friends in town that I have asked to come over. Wish you could make it. They would all be thrilled."

He smiled and said, "I am sorry to miss another of your enchanting dinners. The PM has arranged a small dinner tonight for some of the chiefs that remain in London until tomorrow. In any case you must give them all my love, except those who might take it literally. While I am in the mood to pester the most lovable woman in Richmond and vicinity, I wonder if I could use your computer. I have some notes that I have to prepare before noon tomorrow."

"Of course you can. What is more, I will type them for you. I have seen your two finger efforts and timed your speed. If I recall, it takes you about 5 minutes to type your name."

Sir Andrew laughed delightedly and felt grateful to Ginny that she volunteered to do the typing. He wanted to spend as much of the vanishing night with her. Not exactly typing.

Her cheerful tone removed the fatigue he was beginning to feel. Instead, that delightful feeling of anticipation took over his consciousness. He always felt that such feeling blended the essences of his love for Ginny. It included, without clouding, the gentle desire to see and admire her physical beauty. To hear not only her words but her meanings. To enjoy her softness and the depth of her intellect. It triggered the desire to embrace her and feel her lips on his. And it also flashed the catalog of tender gestures and intimate caresses that made his blood pressure move up a few mm of Hg.

The few hours until morning passed quickly for Ginny and Sir Andrew. Promptly at seven, they enjoyed a great breakfast and, immediately after, Ginny and Sir Andrew worked on the report. By 11, they had completed the draft and had made two copies in diskettes and another two on paper. Sir Andrew then left in something of a hurry and promised to have dinner with Virginia Louise later in the week. He forgot that a copy of the report had remained in the hard disc of the computer.

Only a few guests attended Ginny's dinner that evening. In addition to Mercedes and Muir, there was Trisha Friswell, another TV executive, accompanied by David Nogueira, also an executive from Spain. There was also, Carmen Ilera a stunning multilingual model from Madrid and her escort, a patently homosexual American painter who spoke with a strange accent that reminded some of Andy Kaufmanns impersonations.

At dinner, Mercedes asked Ginny to let her use her computer to send a couple of E-mails on last minute happenings. After dinner while they were all drinking coffee in the living room, Mercedes went to the small den and found that the computer was still on and that a Word processor program was on the screen. As she opened a file, she noticed that a "London Meeting" file was listed.

Mercedes debated with herself for a fraction of a second. To open or not to open that file. Her ethical fiber protested against looking into that file, while her professional commitment ordered that she learn about those facts that the file was certain to contain. She quickly opened the file and the screen revealed the substance of what was discussed at Lambeth House. She reached for the box of clean diskettes and inserted one in the computer and made a copy. She took the diskette and placed it in a pocket of her coat, before returning to the living room were the others were engaged in animated conversation.

Later that evening, Muir and Mercedes returned to Banbury Park relaxed but anxious to continue the exciting process of exploring, discovering and conquering the heights of the pleasure they knew how to dispense to each other. In the car, Mercedes commented, "I feel like a twenty-year-old bride, dear man. It has been a great evening and I feel that the proper ending could be written, directed and acted by you and I. Or is it you and me?"

Muir laughed and answered, "Please, darling, I am driving and your words will start a chain reaction with my hormones, blood pressure, muscular control and will introduce clouds of passion in my feverish mind. Change the subject before I start driving on the wrong side of the road like you Americans do!"

But their anxiously expected session could not be. As soon as they reached

Muir's townhouse, the answering machine spewed out several urgent messages. Muir was to meet at once with the editorial board at the newspaper's office. Something had come up that had to be discussed before the next edition of the paper. Muir looked at the answering machine and said in a tone that did not leave room for any doubts about his disappointment, "Gee, potatoes! I take great pains to let everyone know that I am unavailable tonight, disconnect the cellular phone, hide the damned pager and still, they chase me. Just when my passion index was beginning to assume the proper operating mode!"

"That's all right, darling. I have some work to do anyway. I'll use your PC and get some more E-mails off. Just let me know if there is anything I should know about. We'll postpone the ending to today's chapter. Vaya con Dios!"

Minutes after Muir had left, Mercedes established an Internet connection with Richard Ferguson's computer in the US. Thanks to the Internet technology, her message could be privately read by Richard from any point on the planet. She knew that the information she was sending would cause a lot of ripples in the fermented pond of Washington speculation.

Back at the White House

While the meeting at Lambeth House was taking place, the President of the United States decided to cut short his visit to London and return immediately to Washington. There were the usual last minute preparations and shortly after midnight, Air Force One was heading west. After a buffet dinner prepared by the plane's kitchen staff, the President, Alan Clayton and Mike Pashley, sat in the private lounge that is also the President's office and reviewed the events of their short visit to London.

"Well," announced the President, "we must prepare ourselves for another round of shifting winds. This has been a waste of time. I wonder what is behind our partner's proposal."

Alan Clayton looked at the ceiling of the luxurious cabin and said, "I feel that it is more the fear to be left out by some of the countries in the club than anything else. It is clear to me that they wish to prevent us and the UN from taking any initiative once more is known about these objects. Certainly, that fear is also caused by some strong economic currents one of which is the pressure from some of the large European multinationals and banks that, feeling like independent countries, wish to be in on anything that develops with the objects."

"You are right," said Pashley, "I can see where any kind of new technology can be tremendously attractive to governments and corporations alike. Without wishing to appear cynical, they have fed on each other since day one," As an afterthought, he added, "On both sides of the pond."

The President thought for a moment and then observed, "It looks that way. If they want to by-pass the UN and be the only ones to deal with the objects and its crews, troops or whatever, they are of course free to do so. Except that it would not be playing by the rules that we have worked so hard to establish. As far as the US is concerned, I think we are right in reserving any judgment until we know more. When that happens, we'll play our hand."

"Meaning?"

"We will make sure that the UN and other all other countries on the face of the earth are not left out, no matter what contrived excuses are made by anyone." The President said these words in a tone that betrayed the annoyance he had felt when he learned the real purpose of the London meeting.

After a moment, Clayton said, "I think it is the right attitude to adopt. But I don't discount some attempts to isolate both the UN and us. We are already seeing a lot of that strategy in the business world. Most business conglomerates outside the US are now seeking to obtain the kind of power our own corporations possess and the maneuvering capacity it entails. And, just like in our bailiwick, corporations, banks and large commercial entities, be that insurance, health or even religion, have a lot to say in Government affairs."

Pashley added, "I am sure that pressure from those groups is forcing our partners to follow this course of action. I don't say that those groups are dictating policy to their governments but the carrots and sticks they use cannot be ignored!"

The President smiled. "It might be a mixture of many factors. I see from my own experience here that if I shut my eyes and ears to the factions in my government that in their own perverse manner uphold the interests of the groups that sponsor them, I am liable to find myself on the microscopic sights of a Remington. Or what is worse, being put on trial for stealing the two ashtrays I lifted from the Oval Office to give my sister-in-law!"

They all laughed, aware that Ross Simonson was deeply concerned with the subject they were discussing. The man had that extraordinary quality, reminiscent of FDR, HST and even Ike, that enabled him to conclude a statement or observation with an unexpected touch of sarcasm or levity, that nevertheless provided a hidden corollary to a real situation. He continued. "I just question if this free global economy, free market and global wheeling and dealing cannot get out of hand. Corporations are turning the governments of earth into nothing more than bureaucratic janitors or housekeepers. All the original ideas about creating a just world with reasonable distribution of wealth and a more humane profile, seem to have evaporated. Any one of the International Fortune 500 compadres has within its power the ability to shut down the planet. Based on historical facts, all that is needed now is the appearance of the right tyrant to turn the planet into an Orwellian nightmare."

There was a moment of silence and then Mike Pashley said, "You know, our various advisers are seriously concerned about the direction and scope that all these mergers and associations between giants will take. Local governments will find it increasingly difficult to control and regulate these mammoths as they are spread all over. Their power will not only affect thousands of people that depend directly on them, but entire nations. Someone jokingly said that in 50 years, corporations will have a department called Government Services, which will replace Governments as we know them now. The job descriptions for its members would include simple coordinating functions among branch offices and subsidiaries. Government as we know it would entirely disappear."

He stopped to pour himself some coffee and continued. "It is evident that with the space ships parked above, the large corporations, financial groups or what have you, are asking themselves how to get at the technology these beings most certainly have. In all this, I am sure they all want their fingers in the pie and wish to leave the Governments out of it. Also the UN."

The Secretary of State that had sat with a frown on his face, nodded and observed, "During the discussions and in the many side conversation I had, I could not help notice that most Heads of State employed similar arguments. They all pursued the same objectives; while the objectives satisfied their national aspirations, they seemed to have been designed by the same hand. I could not help thinking about our ever present Elmo when it comes to grabbing new global opportunities."

Pashley got up and pointing his finger at the Secretary of State said, "You have let out what was in our minds all along!"

The President sat up and poured himself another shot of Scotch. He shook his head as if trying to remove the concerns he had and said, "Well, all we have to do is wait and see. There is nothing Elmo can do except wait until our friends above show up. Meanwhile, a little Scotch will help me get a couple of hours' sleep. I suggest you do the same. Sleep, I mean; leave the bottle of Scotch here! Good night!"

Air Force One landed at Andrews AFB at 02:30 hours, Washington D.C.time. The helicopter that was to ferry the President and the others to the White House was sitting on the tarmac waiting for its passengers. In a few minutes, he had deposited them on the White House lawn. In minutes they were all in their homes, tired and somewhat disappointed.

Early the next morning, after receiving Mercedes' e-mail, Richard contacted Mike Pashley, the National Security Adviser and requested an urgent meeting with the President. In spite of his crowded agenda, the President agreed to see Richard during the morning. The meeting was attended by the National Security Adviser, Ursula Walters the Vice President and the Secretary of State, Alan Clayton. Richard did not waste any time. He briefly explained that the source of the information he was about to disclose came from as legitimate a source as Sir Andrew Blotts himself. He carefully avoided mentioning Mercedes' accidental discovery of the cassette in Ginny's house. He read the report slowly and in a firm voice. The President and the others listened with serious, if not worried looks.

"Well, there you have it. Just what we talked about this morning on our flight in. Another extra-official deal."

For the next forty minutes they discussed the contents of the report and took notes about possible strategies to consider. As they were leaving, at the door, the President turned to Ursula Wolters and said, "Now how the hell has Elmo Saks managed to insert and exert himself into all this?"

"The Foundation, Mr. President. He's all over."

"But how is the darn foundation involved with the European Governments? I always thought it was more of a religious effort financed by Saks but run by that weasel Reverend Toe."

"It goes well beyond our borders, Mr. President," added Alan Clayton. "Elmo is very much involved in entire industrial sectors in Europe and elsewhere. Telecommunications, Television and Radio, Publishing, Banks, Insurance, Airlines, Shipping, hell, you name it and he's there!"

Alan Clayton looked at the President and said, "We are keeping an eye on Elmo. He has become much too powerful. He has made sure that his support of political parties in Europe extends into practical politics. In other words, he helps someone get elected and then begins to inject ideas, propositions and positions that both make him richer and more powerful. That is why I would not be surprised if some of the basic outlines of the European project can be traced to him."

The President shook his head and opened the door.

PART TWO
The Message

Exactly 90 days after making their appearance, the objects announced their presence in a unique fashion. At 16:00 hours Greenwich Mean (GMT) Time, or Coordinated Universal Time (UTC), corresponding to 11 a.m. in Washington, D.C., all television sets and computer screens the world over were activated. Even those that were not plugged in suddenly came to life. It was an eerie experience. Not only TV and computer screens were lit up: digital watches, computer game toys, microwave clocks, radar scopes, large liquid crystal displays, airplane flight indicators and every digital or electronic screen on the planet suddenly became bright and empty.

The bright screens were blank for exactly 60 minutes while a puzzled world excitedly attempted to turn them off, change channels or make adjustments, to no avail. The image was uniform throughout the planet; it had the same egg shell color of the ships and did not seem to be the result of the usual electron sweep in the cathode ray tubes or the newer liquid crystal systems or plasma systems in their digital formats. It was plain but steady and did no flickering at all. There was a hypnotic fascination to it as it did not cause any eye strain. In a mysterious way, it attracted the attention of the viewer and induced a sense of well being.

The moment the screens lit up, a current of expectation and also fear gripped the entire planet. After 90 days, the brightly lit screens brought a sharp reminder to the world that the objects overhead, by now almost ignored represented a presence whose nature and intentions were still not known.

The blank screens in themselves embodied a message. Besides causing all TV, computer and other electronic screens to loose their image, they removed any doubts about the presence of someone manipulating whatever controls the objects possessed. Unlike the day when the objects made their appearance, public reaction was hardly felt. It was more of a subjective reaction rather than the exteriorization of personal fears or apprehensions. People seemed to be glad that the objects had finally decided to make their presence known and adopted a wait and see attitude.

In the White House, the bright screens caused an immediate alert. Teams were quickly assigned to key dependencies, even though no one could explain why. Just having Secret Service and Staff people in front of blank Television sets and computers, seemed to provide a small amount of reassurance. Not so fortunate were the Air Control Centers throughout the world, the airborne commercial and military aircraft and all other vehicles that relied on navigational aids that depended on computer screens. Wild and intensive shuffling took place at most airports, radar control centers and airplanes aloft.

Most flights were asked to maintain altitudes on their established routes, and then circle safely and switch to visual modes at their destination. Radio communications was not affected so that some measure of control was still possible. Radar operators had to resort to hand tracing of positions and vectors and managed to maintain airplanes safely in the air. A large number of flights were ordered to land at the closest airports and were laboriously guided in by their controllers.

Sixty minutes after the screens all over the world had come to life, the message appeared. It was written in the language of the country where the screen was located. At 12 noon in Washington, the President of the United States, Ross Simonson, who had been sitting in front of the large TV set in the Oval Room with Vice President Ursula Walters, Mike Pashley the National Security Advisor and Alan Clayton the Secretary of State, suddenly stopped talking and pointed at the large screen, where the message had suddenly appeared:

There is nothing to fear. We are here to help. It is our intention to meet with your representative soon. Our contact with the peoples of this planet will be exclusively through the United Nations, which we understand is the only organization where all nations participate. We will contact you again at 22 hours GMT tomorrow. Have a nice day!

In seconds, practically all telephone lines, fax transmission systems, satellite and e-mail links were running at full capacity. Everyone was online to ask, comment or simply to obtain reassurance from others.

The message remained on the screens of an anxious world for exactly sixty minutes and then it disappeared. Then, frenetic, non-stop radio and TV coverage began. Conjecture assailed the entire human race and created again an atmosphere of doubt and suspicion. Many, who had accepted the objects as some strange manifestation from the heavens, now were able to indulge in limitless speculation. "They know who we are," "They say not to fear," "They express themselves in human tongues," "They are definitely friendly," "Are they the envoys of heaven, or the other place?" "Why don't they move those buckets so that we can get some sunshine?"

The President turned to Mike Pashley, his National Security Adviser and said, "Mike, you were right. Whoever or whatever they are want to contact us through one single entity. I guess they realize the futility of trying to contact hundreds of leaders in as many languages and frames of mind. This bears out what I said in London. If I was in their shoes, I would also attempt to establish contact through a single person or agency…"

He paused and the continued. "This announcement also tales care of the hopes of those in the Big 8 to become a welcoming committee, partner and associates to the visitors and, more important, eliminates Elmo's possibilities to engage in galactic intrigues."

Mike smiled and nodded. He had felt all along that these ships were more than just a strange mechanical contraption that through unknown guidance systems had parked above three hundred cities on earth. He had correctly assumed that some intelligent form of life was responsible for the appearance of the pills and that the time they had allowed to elapse since their arrival was probably employed in learning about planet Earth.

The President continued. "Of course, we still do not know who we are dealing with. Are they human? What is their biological make up? Their attitudes, habits, thinking patterns? From the message it is clear that their thinking processes are orderly and clear. They don't leave room for second guessing or misinterpretation."

He stopped for a moment and pointing at the message on the screen said, "Another thing that bothers me is that Patrick Deschamps, the UN Secretary General has his hands full with the thousand conflicts the UN is monitoring and will definitely need the support of all nations. I just don't buy the idea of our European compadres to nudge the UN aside and take over direct contact with our visitors. I also don't agree with the old tune that this matter is too important to leave in the hands of the UN."

He was silent for a moment, absorbed in his thoughts, and then as if talking to himself continued. "I just don't see how our friends from the Group can go through with their plans to override the UN. All that talk about amending the Charter, signing a covenant and all that other garbage they proposed—I am afraid—is not going to be good for much now. You see, it is obvious that the objects possess technology more advanced than anything we have on this planet."

He paused and then continued in a thoughtful tone. "The Group has also envisioned the commercial implications of the bloody objects. Here we have 300 objects that are totally impenetrable, and are placed at a fixed altitude without motion. And now we learn that they are capable of turning on several billion TV sets, digital watches and all types of screens on the planet: they represent a formidable expression of scientific achievement. The fact that they act as a super communications network and could conceivably provide who knows what other services makes them a most attractive ally. I can just imagine the Ma Bells, AT&T, MCI, Time Warner, Worldcom, Telecom, Murdoch, Disney and a few others thinking about this deal as the one that could help them keep Gates from plastering his Microsoft on every gadget on earth. You get to control such system and Bingo! you become Goldfinger! You control de world!"

Alan Clayton smiled and observed, "It'd play hell with the satellite, cable, DBS, Internet and all the other gold mines that have been devised. Not only that but we have seen what they can do to rockets and missiles, meaning that they can easily neutralize all offensive and defensive weapons from their little aspirins above. It is really mind blowing! And somewhere there is Elmo Saks ready to pounce!"

Ursula Walters, the Vice President, had remained still in her chair, with her eyes fixed on the screen. Her expression did not reveal any emotion, as she appeared hypnotized. Her very silence caused the others to look in her direction. The President looked at her with a knowing smile. He knew that she would not fail to provide an incisive and pondered judgment. Her capacity to analyze in a fraction of a second the most complex of situations and cases, and the solidity of her arguments had been some of the reasons why he had chosen her as his running mate.

She suddenly turned and clearing her throat said, "Mister President, this message is full of meaning. In a few lines they have managed to convey an entire program to the people of this planet. First, the fact that they only wish to deal through a single entity denotes an extensive knowledge of how things work down here on earth. It implies also a no-nonsense dictate as to how they expect us to react. Most important, they are letting us know that they possess technological resources well beyond our present capabilities, something we learned when the objects appeared, and now they are demonstrating a unique power to control all communications on the planet. And last, gentlemen, it is clear that there is a specific purpose to this visit. What that purpose is, remains to be seen. My feeling is that we better avoid internal squabbles and be prepared to listen to them."

Clayton, sitting next to her, nodded and observed, "You are thinking what we all have been thinking. But, what sort of visitors are we to expect? Will they show up as peaceful and kind adventurers, or beings of the other kind?"

She looked at him and shrugged. "Impossible to tell. They could be kind an patient, show us how to get rid of disease and other ills or they could unleash who knows! Death rays from above, nuclear explosions, toxic gases, a storm of fleas, termites, rodents and or human flesh-eating butterflies!"

Turning to the President she added, "And I agree with you that Patrick has his hands full trying to enforce the reforms that he has made at the UN and will need all the help we can muster for him. More than ever I feel that your personal relationship with Patrick is going to be a valuable asset in the days to come. In other words, Mister President, the ball is on your court!"

The President, who seemed hypnotized by the message on the screen, observed in a low voice, "Ursula, Alan, you said it. Thank God that Patrick is the way he is. He has more common sense than all the Ivy League faculties put together and a few hundred Nobel prize winners to boot. And as far as the UN is concerned, I like its new look. Patrick has turned the old mammoth into a sleek and dynamic world organization. I for one will give Patrick all the help he needs. I am sure that we can work together. The question is work on what? Those pills must also be aware of how things work down here, as our VP suggested. I suspect that is the case."

He stopped and turned to Pashley. "Mike, I am puzzled. Who are these beings? Why don't they identify themselves? Gee, any well-educated little green man from Mars would be considerate enough to let us know who he is. And what he is doing here. Then again, I question if this is not a man-made con job."

"Mr. President, since these pills parked overhead last June, we have had all the Agencies and all the key Scientific Institutes working on viable hypotheses about these things. You have seen the reports. They all draw blanks, both in this country and abroad. There is no response or feedback of any kind to indicate that the objects are mechanical structures or that there are humans or some other form of life in them. High power laser, radar, radio, optical scanners, ultrasound, infrared and every knock-knock possibility has been employed. Tight as the proverbial drum. Even when those maniacs in Beijing sent the rocket, we were following every millisecond of the flight. I was just as surprised when the thing seemed to run into a brick wall and turned into a pretty display of fireworks over Beijing. The films are great! I just don't know what to make of them."

There was a knock on the door and after receiving permission to enter, the Marine guard ushered the Secretary of Defense, General Sam Colbert. He was tall enough to change light bulbs without a ladder and vain enough to have his uniforms designed and made especially for him by a well-known New York designer. As a military man heading what, for a long time had been a civilian post, he was conscious of the barely noticeable reserve that the other members of the cabinet exhibited in his presence. He greeted the President and the others, if somewhat stiffly, and sat down on a sofa opposite the President. He spoke. "Mr. President, I don't know if you wish to make any changes in the agenda in view of this," and he pointed to the TV screen.

The President asked, "Any reaction so far, or any other incidents anywhere?"

In his usual mechanical tone, General Colbert rattled off a report in the familiar terms of "militarese," English that sounded to those present like the accurate reply of a third grader to a beaming teacher. He continued. "Nothing so far, sir. It is still early to receive inputs from our field offices, other than Embassies and other agencies. Just in case, cryptographers are standing by, same as members of the Army's Psychology Warfare Unit. We continue to maintain an alert in the Continental United States and all overseas military installations. Now that the message has been received, we can relax a bit. It is clear that these beings want to talk first."

He launched into a detailed report on recent activity by several Armed Forces groups in locations around the world. He described the various reports from the joint US-Canadian DEW (Distant Early Warning) System for air defense cooperation and those received from NADGE, the NATO Air defense Ground Environment system in Europe. None of them indicated any changes or activity from the objects overhead."

The President nodded and thanked General Colbert, then, "Well, they clearly state that they wish to work through the UN. That is going to ruffle a lot of feathers and make many stomachs nervous. Again, we will have to wait until the next message."

The Vice President added, "This message is going to trigger a great deal of nervousness and speculation. The end of the world theme is finding more and more fans. I think that we will be called upon to do something, Mr. President but I don't know what."

The President nodded and replied, "For the time being all we can do is keep our eyes and ears open. The fact that they state their wish to deal through the UN, at least initially, is a relief. I'd hate to see everyone scrambling to establish direct contact with these objects and start cutting deals. Going through the UN will give us time to prepare for an eventual extensive dialogue with them. We just have to wait until we hear further from them about who they are and what the heck they are doing in this neck of the Universe. Assuming also that they are visitors and not invaders and that they are here for peaceful purposes."

Pashley spoke. "Mister President, you are right. The whole episode hinges on the identity of the visitors and the purpose of their visit. I hate to think that they could be strange forms, or some unimagined mechanical entities. Until they let us know who they are and let us catch a glimpse of their appearance, there is absolutely nothing we can do, except to try to instill some calm and patience in the general public. I think we are witnessing the most important event in the history of mankind."

The Secretary of State, Alan Clayton had followed with interest the various exchanges and now he said, "In a nutshell, we sit and wait. However, we must advise our allies and partners that this situation suggests the necessity of maintaining continuous contact in the event that we might be required to act. If you agree Mister President, I shall release a note to the key governments of our position. I think that we should defuse the big 8 plot and confirm our support of the UN. Besides, I don't see how our friends could expect to neutralize the UN's participation in this situation. It would be going against the expressed wishes of the visitors."

"You are absolutely," replied the President." The message is clear and it would be a daring thing to challenge it! You go right ahead. Meanwhile I will prepare a short note for the Press Conference after the Cabinet Meeting. Really, there is nothing I can say to anyone about these darn objects. Maybe our members of the Cabinet have some ideas, but I doubt it. This thing on TV must have caught them on their way here for the cabinet Meeting."

As an afterthought, he added, "Mike, please remind me to call Patrick at the UN."

As he did often, he glanced at Charles Wilson Peale's portrait of George Washington and wondered what he would have said about all this. The President rose and nodding towards the door announced, "Let us go cabineting!"

Later that day, the President spent an hour on the phone with the Secretary General of the UN.

Uncertain Times

When the second message appeared and the screens all over the world suddenly lit up, it was exactly 22 Hours GMT or 5 p.m. in New York. At that moment, the UN Secretary General was presiding a meeting of the Security Council. The dark 52," screen in one end of the room, suddenly came to life. It became—as the day before—bright and silent and stayed that way for a full hour. The Council members sitting around the table could not take their eyes off the screen and Patrick had to discontinue the meeting, "Gentlemen, I don't think that we can accomplish much now that we know that a message is coming. I suggest that we remain here until the message appears. It will save us having to be recalled later, as we will have to discuss whatever it is that our visitors tell us."

The agreement was unanimous. Various degrees of expectation, nervousness and anticipation were in evidence. The fruit drinks and beverages on the large table were quickly consumed. Oddly enough, in a deliberating body that was quick to express opinions and to incur in stimulating exchanges, few comments were forthcoming. Everyone seemed to retreat into himself to assess the impending event in terms of his or her own personal perspective. There was just a minor note of apprehension, which under the circumstances, was amply justified

Time seemed to drag in the room. At times, there was total silence except for the familiar rhythmic echo of the large grandfather clock in one corner of the room. The nervousness around the table was palpable. And no less evident, was the concern reflected in the faces of all those present. An unexplained event of this magnitude would naturally introduce a note of fear to the degree of uncertainty that was felt by all.

"I suppose that the new message will appear 60 minutes after they lit up the screen, just like they did yesterday," observed Patrick. "Maybe this time, they will be more explicit and disclose details about their identity and purposes."

Baron Carini, the oldest member of the Security Council and its Chief of

Protocol turned to Patrick and said, "Since they made it clear that they only wish to deal through the UN, their message today will probably tell us when and how. It might no be an easy task, you know. The darn objects are so large that they can probably land only on the ocean or on the Nevada desert."

Patrick nodded and said in a thoughtful tone, "In any case, we must be prepared to listen and analyze whatever they propose. The President has been most cooperative and has made sure that the US Armed Forces will provide whatever facilities are needed. He doesn't think that there will be a landing. Their reference to the UN is clear and that means that they will be arranging something right here in New York. He thinks that they might be sending an envoy or envoys down to Manhattan. But it is only speculation."

The Baron nodded and said, "It stands to reason. If they want to deal with us, New York is the place."

In a few minutes, the second message appeared on the blank screen. This time it said:

The Secretary General of the United Nations is cordially invited to attend a meeting at the ship above New York City. A transport vehicle will collect him at the UN heliport at exactly noon tomorrow. That is 12:00 hours EST. He is to come alone. We expect we will abuse his kindness and keep him with us until mid-afternoon. He will be returned in the same conveyance to the UN Building. Have a good evening!

All those present in the Council room turned to the Secretary General without saying a word. While not overly surprised, Patrick Deschamps felt a special concern that went beyond his own role in the situation. All of a sudden, the weight of the responsibility thrust upon him, made itself felt. His mind made an instantaneous review of the task assigned to him by the visitors and analyzed the options before him. How can I prepare to negotiate if I don't know what it is I am negotiating? Who I am negotiating, or even establishing contact with? What am I expected to agree to? I don't even know if they look like human beings or motorized sardine cans.

In a few minutes, and after everyone had commented on the message on the screen, Patrick gently tapped his pen on the table and spoke. "Gentlemen, in a way I am greatly relieved that there is now tangible contact between the objects and us, the people of Earth. I think that our organization is well prepared to meet whatever challenge is brought to us by these objects. Let us just make sure that all regional UN groups are coordinated and, above all, that they continue to set the example. The world needs a strong sense of security and large doses of calm and patience."

All those around the table nodded their agreement and then proceeded to offer some suggestions about the impending meeting. After a while, when most comments were beginning to extend into pure speculation, Patrick spoke again. "Gentlemen, I really don't think that we can do or say much until the meeting takes place. I think, if you all agree, that we should concentrate now on tranquilizing the media and to provide them with comments and reports that reflect the unified position of all members of this Council. It is also a great opportunity for the United Nations to assume, for once, a primary role in the affairs of this planet. This appears as a test for us as an organization and also as humans. I move that we close this meeting and go on to tighten up our respective ships. As agreed, we will meet again at 9 p.m. this evening for the press conference, which, incidentally, will only take 15 minutes, since there is not much to say and speculation can only bring distortions, misinterpretations and errors. Until then good evening!"

As in the previous occasion, the message remained on the screen for a full hour.

Public reaction was instantaneous. The Press, the embassies, everyone wanted to speak with the UN. Again, switchboards were flooded with calls and messengers crossed the city with tremendous urgency in their mopeds, bicycles and motorcycles.

Back in his office, Patrick took a few moments to sit alone and reflect on the last message and all it implied. He felt no fear as such but a strange feeling of anticipation blended with a peculiar anxiety. After a while, he placed a call to the White House. In a moment he had the President of the United States on the other end of the line.

"Ross, I guess you have seen the message. I also hope that our friends in Europe and other latitudes have seen it. I guess Ursula and Mike hit it on the nose." He was referring to the Vice President and the NSC Adviser, who had predicted that the visitors would insist on establishing contact through the UN.

"Yes, we have seen it, and I am glad it confirms what we hoped for. I am also glad that it is you who will be opening the doors to what I pray will be a mutually beneficial dialogue with these beings, or whatever they are..."

"Thanks, Ross. All I have been able to do here is to make sure that our people are prepared for whatever happens tomorrow. We know that this is a peaceful approach and all I have to do is find out who they are and what they want. I really have not bothered with details about their appearance, as much as the content of the message. They sound polite enough, don't you think?"

"Well, Patrick, I am with you. In a way, the pressure is off. You will be able to gauge the extent of what comes next."

For the next few minutes both men talked about the visit and briefly outlined joint action concerning press communiqués and media reports. They agreed that their press officers would be in constant contact to allay any wild speculation from the traditional rumor mongers.

First Visit

From 23rd Street to 45th Street, the crowds had taken over sidewalks, rooftops, side streets and many had climbed on the few hardy trees that were still standing. Those New York trees, so typical of the city, miraculously survive both the elements and the incessant attacks of those obnoxious ground level fumes. Also at ground level, they withstand the abuse from dogs and the occasional bladder output of furtive passersby.

Fortunately, it was a sunny day with the temperature in the balmy sixties, which helped swell the crowds in mid town. There did not seem to be enough space to fit a closed umbrella. The area around the United Nations Plaza and the surrounding buildings was a homogeneous mass of humanity, eager and anxious to find out about the space ship. The East River also seemed to be totally paved with boats, rafts, yachts and every form of vessel that could float and sustain the maximum weight its shape and volume could stand. The general mood, however, was not that of a crowd on a holiday. Or even a religious event. A combination of fear, reverence and curiosity permeated the air.

The expectation could be felt. And as noontime neared, the subdued roar became a soft rumble and just before 12:00 o'clock, total silence descended on the entire area and all eyes were focused directly towards the UN Building. Through portable radios, some could follow the incessant reporting of the newscasters that had been lucky to obtain the accreditation that allowed access to the heliport and the chance to report on the first visit to the space ship by the Secretary General. They were broadcasting directly from the helipad on the area in the North Gardens, where the space vehicle would pick up the Secretary General. Presumably, the big object would send some form of smaller ship to pick up the Secretary General.

"What will they send? Some form of helicopter? A flying saucer? A rope ladder?"

People's curiosity was manifested in many ways as they kept up an incessant dialogue about the objects that also revealed their badly concealed nervousness. To many, the transcendence of the event had not made any impression. They were more concerned with the imagined technical characteristics of the transport vehicle.

In his office, the Secretary General felt the clammy sweat of his hands and the slight tremor in his voice as he answered last minute questions from the members of the Security Council. He asked himself repeatedly if he could really believe what was about to happen. For too long—it seemed—he had lived under the enormous responsibility of having to steer the entire world on a path of moderation and prudence while at the same time undertaking a painful and thorough reorganization of the UN.

But in the last hours he had been overwhelmed by the frantic calls from several Heads of State and the subtle threats that they conveyed. He had refused in no uncertain terms to attend a meeting with some of them and had also turned down the idea, advanced by them as a last resort it seemed, to be accompanied by a group of their leaders in his visit to the ship above New York. He also rejected the idea of asking the visitors for a postponement of the visit while the big Powers reviewed the matter and planned an adequate strategy. He emphasized the fact that the message was clear and did not leave room for misinterpretations nor schedule changes. The invitation was pointedly personal.

He had had to calm both Government and private agencies from those countries that were clamoring for the privilege of attending the "meeting," in the ship. He had also had had to convince several foreign envoys that it was unnecessary to prepare a set of terms and conditions to be given to the unknown visitors. And—most important—he had had to allay the fears and almost panic of his family. His wife Kathryn had practically assumed that the visit to the ship meant sure oblivion, while other members of his family felt that he would be subject to unspeakable indignities from those beings who had remained aloft for over 90 days without giving signs of their existence and who had paralyzed world activity while creating fear, apprehension and despair.

His aide, Mrs. Nelson, appeared suddenly at his left and in a soft but firm voice said the words he had been dreading for the last 18 hours: "Mr. Secretary, it is time to go. Remember that the message said that they would have a conveyance at exactly noon today."

The entire group, made up of the Secretary and Mrs. Nelson, members of the Security Council, his Chief Deputy, Chief of Protocol and representatives of four countries, entered the private elevator and were quickly taken to the ground floor. From there they walked to the North Gardens where the heliport area had been cordoned off. The area had been surrounded by policemen, security officers and UN officials. Off to the right—next to the huge cooling towers and air conditioning exhausts and filters, a section had been roped off for the TV cameras and the press.

A few minutes before noon, the entire group arrived at the landing spot in the helipad and in ominous silence; each one raised his head toward the shape more than twenty miles above their heads.

At exactly 12:00 o'clock, a blurred shape appeared on top of the landing area seemingly from nowhere. It appeared to slow down from some extreme velocity and, in the last few feet; it reduced speed to the point where it became clearly visible. It hovered gently over the big X mark on the pad floor and softly landed on it. The people in the immediate vicinity were unable to form a clear image of the small ship as its arrival happened so fast. It was like a slow motion sequence but only during those seconds it took the ship to make contact with the floor. The human eye obviously could not cope with the speed of the arrival, it being a blur that suddenly slowed down and acquired its container shape as it covered the last few feet.

The conveyance was far from the shapes and forms of science fiction space vessels. It appeared to be a rectangular box about 8 foot high, 8 foot wide and about 6 feet deep. It had no windows and its edges were all soft and rounded. Its color was definitely a strange combination of soft hues with no dominant tone and gave the impression of an egg shell molded into the container shape and, not at all unpleasant to the eye. It reminded one of those eggs on top of the walls of Salvador Dali's Museum in Figueras. Its sudden appearance—even if it was eagerly expected by the crowd—caught everyone by surprise.

Its appearance was so swift that it took a moment for most everyone to associate its high speed with the fact that it only became visible when it was about to land. The crowds in the streets, on top of nearby buildings and even those some distance away were not aware of the arrival of the ship as it left no trail and only became visible in the last few seconds of its descent

The container shaped ship was in effect the shuttle that would take the Secretary General to the space ship parked above.

As people gaped at the strange vehicle, an opening materialized on a side of it. There was no perception of a door sliding or a hinged action on a moving door. The space just appeared. The secretary General—who was standing behind the safety rope some 40 feet from where the shuttle had landed, could clearly see the opening but could not discern any thing inside the vehicle. The knot in his throat signaled the tenseness of the moment.

He tried hard to remove form his thoughts the unbelievable circumstances that had placed him a few steps away from what he considered the greatest moment in the history of man. Instead he made a conscious effort to think of the forthcoming encounter as a routine meeting with a Head of State of some country. It should help him retain a certain detachment.

He turned towards Baron Carini, his Chief of Protocol, smiled warmly and without a word extended his hand. The handshake—firm and strong conveyed a sense of confidence. The gesture was such that it elicited a round of spontaneous applause from the crowd.

He smiled again to the crowd and with well measured steps reached the opening of the ship and without turning entered it.

There was a hush in the helipad. Only the occasional bursts of wind, the rattling of some of the supports of the cooling towers and the whirring of movie cameras were the only sounds. There was not a single pair of eyes that was not riveted on the Secretary General. A few tears were also in evidence.

As soon as the Secretary General had entered the ship, the opening, whose symmetry and structure were curiously studied by those near it—seemed to dissolve and the outer wall became whole again. It was not possible to gauge the thickness of the walls of the ship. Those near it had peered intently into the opening but could not make out any sort of structure around the opening. The wall seemed to be as thick as the ship itself giving the impression of a tunnel.

In no more than 2 or three seconds, the ship had lifted from the pad and at a vertical speed impossible to measure and hard to believe, it disappeared from view. Again, there was no trail and no way to visualize the object as it traveled up towards the space ship. Only the radars in Long Island were able to record the milliseconds it took the shuttle to take off from the heliport at the UN building and presumably reach the space ship.

As he entered the shuttle, the Secretary General felt again the apprehension that had accompanied him the last few weeks. But he was alert enough to make an attempt at recording everything he saw and felt. The floor of the ship seemed to be made of a material whose properties would resemble something between a multi knot Oriental rug and soft pine wood. He realized the door or opening had closed behind him just as he was inside the ship. Strangely enough the walls were transparent and allowed him to look out to the crowd in the ground but only for a fleeting instant. The next impression he had was that the crowd had vanished and only the familiar contours of Manhattan were visible. But only for a fraction of a second.

Inside the Ship

The shuttle's interior did not resemble anything he had seen nor imagined; either in fact, fiction or in some of the more daring space adventure series on Television. There were no instruments of any kind nor structures and no crew. The interior was of a color similar to the outer shell and had no chairs nor lights or even handholds. He did not feel the motion upon ascending nor did he have any sensation at all about moving upward at what he imagined was very high velocity. Somehow he felt as if he was being held comfortably even if he was standing up. There was absolutely no tension from any direction and his weight appeared to be well controlled by the invisible forces that kept him upright but as relaxed as if he was lying down.

Next, he noticed that the opening had again appeared. He assumed that the small ship had reached the space ship. Before leaving the small ship, he looked carefully at the landing area. The shuttle seemed to be inside the larger vessel but again, no structures of any type were visible. The walls—if that is what they were—seemed to extend indefinitely. They seemed to blend with the ceiling and the only different texture was that of the floor. It appeared like a strange combination of a cotton rug and some harder fiber that was easy on the feet and not slippery at all. The light inside the small vessel and in the larger ship had the same pleasant hue and intensity.

He sighed and stepped outside, while his heart beat at an accelerated rate. At that moment it came to his mind the numberless conceptions of extraterrestrial beings by artists, scientists and a number of UFO enthusiasts. He imagined little green men whistling the la-si-sol-re-sol, or maybe a lobster type being with horn rimmed glasses and a briar pipe. A quick image went through his mind of ET but 10 feet tall.

No one was there to meet him. He stopped in what appeared to be a long corridor and at that moment, an opening appeared to his left. He entered it. This area could be called a room. It appeared square in shape and you could see walls and ceilings somewhat differentiated. In one end of the room there was a dark area where he could barely make out the outlines of what appeared to be a glass enclosed area. As he neared it, he could see in front of the enclosed area a good old sofa, complete with carved legs and comfortable side arms upholstered in light colored velveteen. A polished oak coffee table in front of the sofa completed the furnishings. His eyes quickly took on the objects on the table. He was a little surprised to see that day's edition of the New York Times and the Washington Post. There was also, amazingly, a crystal ashtray and a cigarette box. The silver vase with what seemed fresh violets completed the decoration.

The Secretary General advanced slowly towards the center of the room where the sofa was. As he moved toward it, he looked intently at the enclosure trying to define some distinguishing features in the shapes that appeared to be sitting motionless in the podiums. The light was so poor in that part of the room that it seemed artificially contrived. The enclosed area brought to his mind the podiums where jurors sit. As he stopped in front of the sofa, a little more light seemed to bathe the podium and he could distinguish several shapes—human shapes—sitting down. He counted 2 on the front pew and 4 in the back, but the area had been deliberately made dark so that he could not make out any clear features. They just appeared human, even if he could detect no eyes, mouth or other features. Only vague outlines in shadows. He felt reassured. If these beings had human shapes, it could well be that they had other human attributes and that it might be possible to establish some form of normal communication with them.

As he reached the sofa, a voice coming from the direction of the enclosure said, "Please have a seat, Mister Secretary General."

The voice he heard was as close to the sound of a human voice as a synthesized version could get. The Secretary General's trained ear was able to gauge with almost total accuracy the subtle variety and combination of tones and sounds making up the words he heard. It was—without question—a superb job of synthesizing the human voice.

To the Secretary General, the inflexion, tone and all other characteristics of the voice appeared of supreme importance. He felt that the sound—like the first look at one of the visitors—would be of crucial importance. To him, the way the words were pronounced and the "intention," tone, or call it what you wish, would disclose to him something about the visitor's attitude. While he realized how difficult it would be to read these elements in a synthesized voice, he also felt that anyone able to elaborate such message would do so instantly so that the "translation," from the phrase in its original conception, would carry the subtle nuances of tone and intention. Mentally he was reassured as the message had been delivered in even tones but with clearly a touch of cordiality.

The Secretary General sat down. A few, interminable seconds passed before he again heard the voice, "Thank you very much for coming, Mr.

Secretary General. We have been most anxious to establish contact with the people of this planet. I also wish to reiterate that you should not fear our presence. We have no designs on your planet and its inhabitants other than some energy adjustments we are to undertake."

In anticipation of this moment, the Secretary General had several phrases ready for delivery, but the excitement of the moment had somehow deleted them from his mind and all he could say was, "We are all relieved that your presence poses no threat to the safety of the people in this planet. I am also curious to learn why you did not contact us as soon as your ships appeared."

The Secretary General was conscious that this was not perhaps the most diplomatic sentence he could emit but such had been the tension created by the appearance of the ships that he felt it was important enough to be said.

He looked at the podium and could only detect a slight motion from one of the beings that appeared sitting in the front row. Oddly enough there seemed to be a crystal carafe and glasses in front of him. He felt that this one would be the speaker so he peered with more intensity in his direction feeling that he would be the one answering him. He was right, the shape moved slightly as the voice was again heard. "Yes, I believe we should explain. The days that we have been in your planet correspond—in our time frame—to a few seconds. It took us these seconds to adapt to your dimensions and absorb the major elements of your culture. We did not wish to create any problems to your people by appearing all of a sudden and, worse of all, by being ignorant of your customs, history and idiosyncrasies…"

The Secretary General felt that at least the beginning of the dialogue with his extraterrestrial visitors, if that is what they were, was cordial and not devoid of the usual parsimony that characterized diplomatic talk on earth. The myriad questions in his mind began to sort themselves. He started to feel the elation and the excitement of the moment. He felt he was operating at his full level of perception and wanted anxiously to begin a long exchange with the visitors.

As if reading his mind, the one who had revealed some motion and obviously the one acting as spokesman for the others, said, "I am aware that you and your people must have many questions to ask. We will be happy to satisfy your curiosity and allow you to learn about us as we have learned about you. For the purpose of establishing normal communications among us, we have adopted human forms and have even acquired those traits that make the human race the unique phenomenon that it is. I must warn you however that our true nature and the levels of energy in which we exist will be more than confusing to you and they will be absolutely impossible for you to conceive and understand."

Again, he paused as if to collect his thoughts and then continued. "We certainly do not wish to create confusion in your planet. Especially, we do not wish to create conditions that might give way to mass hysteria and panic. As we proceed with our dialogue, you will find that there are many matters that we wish to review with you. In doing so, we both must make the effort to use a commodity that seems scarce in this planet: understanding."

These sentences were delivered in an emphatic way not devoid of friendly undertones, but without being patronizing. As he absorbed the meaning of each sentence, the secretary General felt that his own apprehension and suspicions of the last 90 days were not totally allayed. Those days since the arrival of the ships, had created an avalanche of speculation and conjecture in the world. So much had been imagined and assumed that now that he was face to face—in a manner of speaking—with the space visitors, he felt the weight of the responsibility thrust upon him. It seemed that the reference to "many matters to review" pointed to some form of plan.

The visit was clearly not an accidental occurrence. His mind raced through the endless conclusions that the learned wise men of Universities, churches and Institutes had reached. Because, after the initial shock of having the key cities in the planet covered by the strange "pills," all kinds of theories were at once set forth. The key question—in his mind all along—had remained a simple one. What was the purpose of the appearance of the ships and their crews? He never allowed the myriad assumptions, hypotheses and—supreme conceit—conclusions to cloud his thinking. Further, he had expected all along that a meeting inevitably would take place between the visitors and representatives from Planet Earth and that he would be part of it.

"Indeed we have many questions as you so well assume. On my part, I believe that you already know my identity and—evidently—a great deal about our planet. We would also like to know about your own identity. You must know that your presence here has created a great deal of turmoil and even fear. You must also know that in the history of this planet—or at least since the human race became its dominant species—no contact has ever been made with inhabitants or beings from other planets."

This time the voice acquired a neutral tone. Also this time, the cadence was deliberate as if an effort was being made to make sure that its message was understood.

"To be honest with you let me state that the nature of our identity is really beyond your comprehension. I do not wish to appear arrogant or give any impression of superiority. But to be absolutely clear, I must use a comparison that will certainly seem offensive to you. It is not intended as such. It is a poor effort on my part to make things clear for you and the inhabitants of this planet. Just imagine that you attempt to establish contact with amoebae, your simplest form of life. Such protozoan represents just about the simplest being in the animal scale and—I would venture—has limited capacity, mental and otherwise to be able to maintain a dialogue with humans."

He stopped and with a familiar gesture rubbed his eyes with his left hand. Then, "What I am saying is that our relative scales—and I refer exclusively to mental development—conform to that comparison. We have had to make an effort to adjust our own perceptions to your mental levels and also to the dimensions of your environment. We are not made of flesh and bone, as the inhabitants of this planet. In time, you and your collaborators will get a better notion of our make up. A clear understanding of our nature and the environment, from which we proceed, is beyond your present state of mental development. As far as our purposes is concerned, I must inform you that our visit answers to what you would term a process of rectifying some equilibriums and balances in this planet. Later on it will become evident to you that conditions in this planet do have an effect—as infinitesimal as it might seem—on other forces and equilibriums beyond your dimensions."

He paused, ostensibly to give Patrick a chance to absorb and reflect on what he had just said. After a moment, he continued. "As we set out to do our tasks, we would like to limit the amount of official contact with humans. Even though all of us have already become familiar with the planet, the human race and its history, and have actually visited many places at different time periods, we feel that the proper thing is to conduct our dialogues with no more than a few people of earth. Preferably, as we have already indicated, through a supranational entity like the UN and its representatives. We are convinced that the UN can present our case to the people of earth and can also assist us in accomplishing the objectives we have."

He paused as if expecting a comment. Patrick thought for a second and said, "Our organization has already assembled a team. It was one of the first things we did when your ships appeared. I shall provide you with detailed profiles of each one of its members. I also understand your desire to deal with only one entity on earth. Our planet is made up of many countries and just as many interests, attitudes and points of view and it would be difficult to elicit from them some common responses."

The visitor continued. "Thank you, Mister Secretary General, or may I call you Patrick?" Without waiting for an answer, he continued. "Also, we would like to ask that you arrange for one person—to be universally selected or elected, as you wish—to be our permanent liaison. Please keep in mind that we are not at all reticent about disclosing our identities. But, like I said before, your degree of intellectual development will not permit you to understand fully who or what we are. We have adopted human forms—your old flesh and bones—only to make our relations with humans more acceptable. We have no physical shapes or mass such as you have on this planet...For the purpose of identity and communications you might call me—if you have no objection—Adam."

"Thank you, Adam," replied Patrick in a tone that hid a great deal of relief. In addition to a very polite reception, he was extremely relieved to detect Adam's evident friendly manner. He decided to ask one of the many questions that crowded his mind at the moment.

"Evidently you have become familiar with our makeup since you have adopted our physical shapes. Have you had opportunity to observe the people of our planet at close quarters?"

"Yes. All of us have spent a lot of time 'amongst them,' as you say. It has been a unique experience for us. Since we were able to assume the roles of humans in their entirety, and I mean—besides the physical attributes—all the characteristics possessed by humans like its active mind, the ever present conscience, the array of virtues, complexes, defects, fears and reactions, we have traveled and met all kinds of people without being detected. Some of us can now spit off baseball league statistics another can talk for hours about literature, painting and all the plastic arts. We also have acquired expertise in Cuisine Provencale, three-wire landing jets on a carrier deck, speak in 20 languages, eating with chopsticks and making passionate love to lovely females on the planet!"

Patrick could not believe his ears! His feelings were a mixture of amazement, relief and a thin edge of concern. The light manner in which Adam had answered the question and the way he described their activity on Earth, helped reduce Patrick's apprehension, but the fact remained that they were obviously employing infinitely superior means to "land" on earth.

"I hope it has been a pleasant experience," was all he could blurt out.

Adam nodded and leaned back. Somehow, the lighting in the area had improved. Patrick peered at the elusive shadow and this time he was able to distinguish Adam's features. A high forehead was crowned by well groomed hair parted on one side. It looked light brown in color. The features were regular and—by any standards—handsome. The face had a force in itself that underlined the quasi perfection of the features. Patrick wanted desperately to be able to gaze into Adam's eyes, but the prevailing shadows did not let him. The old adage about the eyes being the windows of the soul was clearly on his mind. He wondered about the content and meaning of a look that presumably came from a synthetic being. "If they are able to assume our very essence, they should be able to include as important a feature as the power, subtlety and meaning of a look," he mused.

Adam raised his arm and in a sweeping gesture pointed at the other visitors seated on the enclosed podium. He said, "Patrick, these are the troops. There are six of us and each has acquired his own human appearance that corresponds to some of the ethnic groups on this planet. We have selected varying ages and personal preferences. My colleague to my right is Emosh and the four sitting in back of us are Evan. Eldon, Earle and Ely... This is the team on this planet. Plus these marshmallow shapes that we have placed above the major cities. Incidentally, their function has been that of antennas and let me assure you that they do not represent any danger to the cities they service. Sorry, but there is no little men, no death rays and no insect-like invaders."

A sudden chill paralyzed Patrick Deschamps. It dawned on him that these beings were here for a purpose. It also shocked him to hear that there were only six of them. Which meant that the other ships were on automatic pilot if such thing was possible? But the sentence that was etched on his mind was what they termed "equilibrium and balances," that appeared to be a little out of kilter on planet Earth. His mind tried hard to assimilate the meaning and import of the phrases he had just heard.

"We have adopted human forms," "We have no physical shapes or mass." If so, what were they? How could they move about the Universe if not through some form of physical means? What were the ships made of? How were they controlled? How did they communicate among themselves?

The questions were quickly becoming a crescendo that caused him to close his eyes. It remained in the forefront of his thoughts the statement made by his visitor that the human mind was not capable of understanding the nature and make up of these beings. Worse yet, he is comparing the human race to amoebas! The lowest forms of life! And what about their human shapes? He had glimpsed some facial features in Adam as he talked. He seemed to move his head in various directions and also his mouth moved as he enunciated the words. Patrick felt that once his eyes became accustomed to the gentle darkness that shrouded his hosts, he might be able to identify more features such as nose, ears, hair, etc.

Patrick made an effort to regain his composure and concentrate on his next words: “I am sure that there are great differences between us but that is no impediment for us both to use that commodity to which you referred a moment ago: understanding.You can also be sure that I will do everything in my power to assist you in carrying out the task you mentioned, once it is explained to us in more detail. What you have said, Adam opens a world of curiosity, not only to me but to our entire species.”

The initial exchange had put Patrick at ease, even if an avalanche of thoughts and questions seemed to come to the front of his mind. Where do you start? He made an effort not to become intimidated by the sheer transcendence of the occasion and tried hard to control the awe he felt about his hosts.

As if guessing Patrick’s confusion, Adam spoke. “Patrick, we wish you to feel as if you were talking to another human. We have assumed all the traits of your species. It is the only way in which we can talk to you and explain in your own words and with the appropriate feeling what we are and what we wish to accomplish here. To become as you humans are has been quite an experience, believe me. Some of us cannot believe that you are able to exist at all. As we see you from our real identity, we wonder about the parameters of evolution on this planet.”

Patrick could not hold back his curiosity and asked, “And how do you see us humans?”

“Well, I shall do my best to translate our perception into your way of thinking and the way you see things. But you must keep in mind that our first impressions are usually from the standpoint of our real identity and not at all from our acquired human perception. You humans appear to us as random organic masses covered with living organisms that—fortunately for you—you cannot see nor detect. It causes some amazement to us to focus on any part of your anatomy and find you full of the most incredible collection of bacteria, dead cells, dust, oily compounds and myriad cultures of microorganisms that seem to thrive on your epidermis. If you were to look at Cindy, Jennifer, Catherine Zeta or Claudia with our perception, your entertainment and modeling industries would go the way of horse drawn tramways…Not to speak of what would happen to your peculiar reproductive exercises and simple cohabitation…But, as I said, you are not aware of these things. As they say in Brooklyn, what you don’t see, don’t hurt you! It is better that way.”

Again, the tone was cordial. Again, Patrick felt a strange affinity for this being. He asked, “I am wondering if your knowledge of our language and customs are the result of observation and study or do you have other techniques that you use. I am of course amazed at your command of the language and your ability to detect both our feelings and our thoughts."

"Patrick, I said before that it would be useless to try to explain to you about our nature. Our best intentions to enlighten you are limited by your mental capacity and neuronal development. We can only use your levels of knowledge and—most important—the physical references and environment in which planet Earth has evolved. As far as your languages and customs are concerned, we simply employed a technique that I can only describe as mental and cultural absorption."

"That means that you had to learn almost everything about the human race," interrupted Patrick, still amazed at the facts revealed by Adam.

"Yes, in other words, we were able to assimilate all expressions of mental and neurological activity from the moment the most rudimentary form of life appeared on the planet, along with many forms of vocal expression, particularly in humans. We have had to learn—if I can call the transfer process we use, learning—the ancestral forms used by your Stone Age people and go on from there to the Indo European languages and finally to the Germanic groups and the present form of the English language. We also followed a similar process with all the other languages."

Adam smiled at Patrick's surprise and amazement. He continued. "In a sense, it is amazing to us that it took ages for Homo sapiens to be able to translate thought into sounds. It is more amazing than the fact that it took your species a longer time to connect up some simple neurological activity into thoughts. The evolution and quality of those thoughts in the last few thousand years—you will admit—has been a sad experience, only brightened by occasional flashes of reason."

"You mean to tell me that you have recorded brain activity and speech from the very beginning?—It would mean that you have been around since life appeared on earth."

"See, here you assume—properly—what your mental capacity allows. We have not been here more than the 90 days of your time. For us to absorb planet earth in the manner we just discussed, we used our own dimensions and parameters. It is interesting to us that you exist within four simple dimensions and that one of them is irreversible."

Patrick was simultaneously amazed and relieved. Adam had mentioned other dimensions and indicated that they were able to compress time and—if his understanding was correct—go back in it. The irreversible dimension. He could not help thinking of Albert Einstein and his e = mc2 and his admiration for him took a quantum leap. He smiled to himself at the pun. Einstein had vaguely made a stab at the essence of time, maybe unwittingly in the formulation of his energy equation because speed, is a rate that includes time.

"I guess you are right, Adam. We on earth tend to think that the universe revolves around us. I am beginning to understand our limitations, though I feel proud to have evolved from amoebae to a thinking being."

"Touchè!" Adam exclaimed and laughed as heartily as any human.

"Sure you must be proud of being a thinking human being. I must admit that since becoming a human I have found innumerable traits that are most endearing. To let you in on a secret, amoebas do have their own level. I just hope that my reference to them in a comparative manner does not offend you, or them. All this ties in to our presence here."

"There is a little contradiction concerning our having adopted human manners—so to speak"—Adam continued

"As we turn human, we assimilate your way of thinking and feeling, which in a way makes us more conscious of the real differences between us. We have made a transition from our existence levels to yours. In the process we have acquired a variety of desirable and undesirable traits that are unknown to the real us. For instance, your flesh and blood structure seems to divert energy to your peculiar emotional make-up, creating a variety of reactions and feelings that lurk in both your conscious and subconscious minds. There is a whole catalog of those. Like envy, love, indifference, hatred, etc. And then there are infinite currents that mold those feelings and reactions in all directions, in many cases in contradiction to themselves, repetitions and distortions. It is really a complicated brain system you got beneath that hair!"

He stopped for a minute while he drank water from a glass in front of him. He used his handkerchief to dry his lips and then continued. "For instance, we notice that somehow, as we turn human and occupy your flesh and blood suits—to call them something—we become aware, automatically, of a feeling of superiority towards the human species. It is not a feeling known to us in our real identity. Somehow, the fact that once our human form detects that we belong to other spheres of existence that enjoy more advanced qualities, it triggers that sense of superiority. If not consciously controlled—another of your mechanisms—it leads to a patronizing or contemptuous attitude toward humans or other beings in your planet. In other words we experience being a human being. I also have noticed that within your species you delight in accentuating superficial differences and—in more cases than is necessary—you allow your nature to develop those feelings of superiority I mentioned before. But we cannot be too critical. Your evolution has obviously been faulty and has not yet reached its proper level."

He paused and lit a cigarette. The gesture was so unexpected that Patrick almost fell off the sofa, while gripping the armrests. Adam inhaled deeply and put away a Zippo lighter with the White House emblem on it. He smiled at Patrick and said, "This is one of the most curious habits that we have seen on earth. Naturally it makes sense in your species since you have the olfactory capabilities, the lung mechanism for ion exchange and a peculiar brain action regarding the act of smoking. I tell you that I do not find smoking unpleasant, but I am very much aware of the damage it is doing right now to my human shape. It is a typical trait of your species, I guess. You deliberately—when you smoke—introduce poisonous agents into your system and for milliseconds deprive parts of your brain of its essential oxygen."

He laughed and coughed at the same time, causing Patrick to laugh with him.

"Now, if you put together all those milliseconds and measure the damage, you'll find that smoking and the normal loss of brain cells in every human are as bad as being hit by one of your Express Amtrak trains; they seem to hit a lot of things anyway."

Adam then put the cigarette out by pressing its lighted end on a metal ashtray that seemed to have been in front of him.

"Adam," said Patrick, "smoking is one of many things we do that harm either us or our environment. Our race—as you have noticed—is a continuous contradiction."

"We are aware of your unique mental processes and for that reason we wish to proceed with all the necessary caution and patience. Our task—while not earth-shaking, as your media would say—is very important and also delicate. We need the cooperation of your entire species."

At that moment Patrick realized that the room was now brightly lit. He could distinguish clearly the features of the other visitors sitting behind the glass enclosure. The lighting that seemed to come from nowhere afforded a comfortable level of luminosity.

He was gently interrupted by Emosh, who spoke for the first time in a pleasant synthetic voice a little different from Adam's. "Patrick, we are aware of the impression and tenseness that this meeting is having on you and on the entire planet. I think that as a first contact we have set down the basis for further meetings. We want for you to address your General Assembly and inform them of our meeting. Also, explain the reasons for our being silent these months and—above all—assure them that we are not here to look for gold, uranium or some other element. We are not flesh eaters and we all dislike curry dishes."

Patrick and the others could not help laughing at this last reference. Then Emosh continued. "You may also wish to mention that our presence here is due to the need to rectify some conditions created by your species. This will be done once we have jointly established some guidelines and formulated some plans. We view your personal role in all this as a senior liaison with the governments of Earth, which role fits in with your position as Secretary General of the United Nations and the excellent rapport you maintain with most governments, religious groups and other institutions in the planet. We know your life in detail. Better than that, we admire your integrity and honesty in all things. Also, we value the forcefulness of your personality and the ample intellectual capacity that you have always used for humane purposes. We trust you. We realize that the United Nations has had a peculiar history and that more often than not it has been a body that has presided over funerals rather preventing them. We are also aware that."

Patrick felt compelled to interrupt Emosh. Long years of practice had enabled Patrick to develop a personal technique for interrupting others without appearing rude. It also helped him to be able to inject his comments into a given trend of thought, without the risk of having to wait until further thoughts and expressions had diluted the main subject and—worse yet—he had forgotten what he had to say.

"I know what you are going to say. You are right of course. The United Nations is one of many attempts in the history of mankind to seek a collective way of addressing the problems of the many and varied societies in the Planet. Unfortunately, the unhealthy influence of power and special interests has not always been as positive as we would have liked. It has forever been a challenge to induce societies and their leaders to observe the basic guidelines developed by our species and, more recently to adhere to the ideas and hopes expressed in the Charter of the United Nations."

This time Emosh leaned forward allowing Patrick to see his face clearly. Emosh had a youngish look with a trace of Latin facial characteristics. An aquiline nose and high cheeks under a well combed mass of light brown hair. He appeared well tanned and healthy. Patrick was able to see the eyes, and that pleased him enormously. Emosh eyes were light green-gray and had a peculiar shine. The look—which is what Patrick wanted desperately to evaluate—was deep and conveyed an inner serenity. And Emosh was wearing a Nike T-shirt!!

Emosh nodded and said, "Yes, it has been that way since day one. And that is precisely one of the reasons why we are here. It will be all explained to you in due time. Meanwhile, we would like for you to transmit the message that we wish to deal only through the United Nations, with you as the responsible officer. Also, we would like for the team that you have assembled to arrange for the creation of a special committee, Council or huddle or whatever, to have all countries on earth delegate the required powers on such group. We do not wish to have to deal with the many countries on an individual basis. You are therefore our political link. Adam has already mentioned that we also wish to accomplish our task with the aid of a special person, that will have to assume day to day tasks and also be in a position to guide and advise us. This person must have the depth of knowledge and intellect to be able to help us make our plans and also to apply some of the measures we plan to suggest."

Patrick interrupted to ask, "About this coordinator, since you seem to possess unique powers, could you not locate this person for us?"

"Yes, we could but we prefer that the selection be done by the people of earth. Worldwide elections would be ideal. It would force people to participate in this project. Besides, elections seem to be an ingrained collective reflex of the human species and some people find them joyful occasions. If only more people participated in them you would not have some of the problems you seem to have." He smiled and continued. "Before I forget, you must be able to tell your people who we are. This is a difficult part. Maybe at this point I can best tell you what we are not. We are not from another galaxy or some such nonsense. The ships are energy configurations even if they look like things out of the Rose Bowl, a pharmaceutical company or one of the fantasies of Jules Verne, Arthur C. Clark or our admired friend Steve S. In our habitats, or what would be our worlds to you, we have no physical shapes. No green little men, no ETs and no monsters with fangs attacking semi-demented ladies in earth ships flying the asteroid belt."

He laughed and Patrick also smiled at the quaint manner in which such knowing references were made. Emosh continued. "Suffice to say that cosmic energy plays a major role in our make up. Brains? Back to energy. The Universe as you know it—or imagine it—is really much different. Here again energy has much to do with things. There are continuous mirror effects that create varied conceptions of things. It is the case with your entire system and your ideas about your universe. Let me put it this way: You are riding a van in one direction and looking through a windshield that has only an opening the size of a quarter. This gives you a view of a minute portion of what is beyond the windshield. To rationalize what you see you naturally apply the time-space dimensions which are your only references. As a result your conclusions are bound to ignore what there is around the windshield, the road you are traveling on and where you are going. No wonder your conclusions, and beliefs, are peculiar...But do not bother with these things at the moment. Just let your people know that we are good little aliens."

Patrick could not help but smile at the humor and the simplicity with which Emosh explained unexplainable topics and the assurances he implied.

"You will be taken back to the UN building. And, if at any time you wish to speak to us or even come up to this ship, all you have to do is call us at this 800 number."

Patrick was taken aback as he took a small piece of notebook paper that contained in very ordinary style of handwriting the 800 number. He recovered quickly and thanked Emosh.

At that point, Adam smiled and said, "There is another way you can also get in touch with us. You just concentrate in our names and repeat them to yourself, so that momentarily they are firmly on your consciousness. It is just like ringing us. Then, mentally, just send us the message that you wish to be brought up to the ship or even that you wish to talk to us on your telephones. You know, it isn't that we don't trust your AT&Ts, Bells, MCIs, your ubiquitous cell phones or other carriers. We want to avoid that infamous tabloid publicity you have down there! We are just being cautious my friend, so the idea of wearing belt and suspenders is not so outlandish!"

Patrick could not help laughing out loud, while at the same time marveling at the relaxed familiarity with which both Adam and Emosh used colloquial expressions and Earth customs and habits.

"I think we should meet again once a coordinator has been elected and the Committee is in place. Also, we would like very much to meet Kathryn, your wife. We believe your wife to be an outstanding representative of your species and we would like to make sure that women are as involved in this matter as men. Ask Kathryn to feel free to invite another lady to join her in her visit to us. Often, the women of your planet obtain more reassurance from a person of their own sex than from the claimed superior strength and fortitude of their male counterparts."

Patrick could not help smiling as Emosh was patently doing a tongue in cheek routine in an effort to obtain some reaction from his guest. Patrick said, "I happen to agree wholeheartedly with you on this last point. As important as women have been in the development of civilizations in this planet, they have often been relegated to secondary roles."

Emosh looked at Patrick and added, "Yes, we have had the opportunity to observe that subtle and almost undetectable animosity that exists between your two genders. While their complementation is well understood and sought after, there is that sliver of something complicated that feeds on a negative this and a bit of that. Unfortunately human society remains a very primitive exercise, where guile, the imposition of personalities and the obsession to dominate convert life in an everyday battle."

"It is a complex relationship, Emosh. As you say, there are subtleties that if not viewed under the proper perspective, lead to deeper feelings, not always good. Don't forget that since the beginning, man, because of his superior physical strength, assumed the role of provider and protector. The females remained in the cave taking care of the offspring while he was out chasing game, fighting intruders and animals. In this scenario, women tended to adopt a passive role."

Emosh nodded and pulling out a silk handkerchief from the back pocket of his chino pants wiped his brow gently, as if caressing his tanned forehead. He said, "Well, dear Patrick, things have not changed much except that the cave is now a 10 room duplex in Manhattan, or a Villa in Cap D'Antibes, or a 2 bedroom single family home in a subdivision in Akron, Ohio. The hunting, the stalking, the unmerciful thrust and the collecting of the prize, is now done on carpeted floors, or in machine shop floors, or other corporate havens that include everything and everybody from the Government, the Church, the Academic institutions and even the Insane Asylums."

Emosh stopped for a second and then continued. "For too long males on this planet have considered women as a sub-species, not realizing that by recognizing women's unique perceptions they could have benefited from contributions that could have helped to reduce the inequalities that exist. Besides, we wish to meet Kathryn in person; your profile includes your wife as an integral and very important part of your life."

Patrick was not at all surprised to hear this last request. He was aware of the outstanding qualities possessed by Kathryn and was also objective enough to evaluate and treasure Kathryn's undeniable role in his success as a man and as a public figure. Kathryn was the essence of modern woman. Equipped with quick wit and an above than average intelligence, she had never allowed the circumstances to make her a simple complement in their marriage. From the beginning, in subtle and delicate ways, she had assumed the role of active partner and, later on, as his public responsibilities increased, she struck on her own in a sustained effort to support her husband's work in the exhausting job of cleaning up what should be the most important institution on earth.

"Good day, Patrick." It was Adam's voice that interrupted the pleasant contemplation of the woman he truly loved. It made Patrick feel good to be able to distinguish their voices. As he heard Adam's words, he noticed that the lighting in the room had lost intensity and it was hard to make out Adam's shape.

If I could only see the color of his eyes, he thought.

He rose and moved a few steps to an open door leading to a passage. He looked around once more but could not find anything other than the curving walls blending into a luminous ceiling. Not a nail, or valve or rubber mats. It felt like being inside a solid cream puff. The shuttle door was open a few feet away.

He entered the small ship and just as in his ascent, he found himself at his destination in a fraction of a second. He looked at his wristwatch and was surprised to note that more than two hours had elapsed since he set foot on the helipad at the UN.

As in the departure, the arrival of the shuttle at the helipad was as swift and silent. Before he had a chance to focus on the island shape beneath him, he was already on the helipad and could see the anxious looks on everyone's faces.

Return to New York

As the opening appeared, photographers approached the shuttle and thrust their cameras and recorders in Patrick's face.

"Mister Secretary, have you seen our visitors?" "What do they look like?" "What is it that they want?" "Did you have lunch?" "Do they look like Mister Spock?" "What were their first words and—by the way—what language did they use?"

He managed to step aside and taking advantage of the quick action by the Security officers who formed a protecting ring around him, he shouted, "It has been a great experience. They look just like you and me! There is nothing to fear. I thank you for coming and I trust you understand that I have to report first to the Assembly. I hope you will be at the press conference right after it. I will then give all the details of this first meeting with our space visitors. Thank you!" As an afterthought, he added, "No lunch!"

"Cheapskates!" someone muttered.

He was whisked to the door leading to the stairway and in a moment he was again inside the private elevator that would take him to the upper floors. As the elevator began its controlled ascent, he could not help thinking about the incredible comfort and speed of the shuttle. *Here I go again!* he thought. *It is so easy to become accustomed to space age comforts!* He smiled to himself at this play on words. Kathryn would certainly chide him for it and—he just remembered—Kathryn had been invited to come up to the ship with him accompanied by a woman of her choice. She will be thrilled. And he was sure she would make him proud. Kathryn's qualities, personality and physical beauty, would impress the space visitors, whether they had their flesh and blood uniforms on or not!

The hallway and corridor leading to his office were crowded and noisy, but turned silent the moment he appeared. Officials from many departments, Ambassadors, delegates and others were anxious to greet Patrick and to hear from him some details of his meeting with the visitors. He thanked effusively all those who shook his hand and patted him on the back, and all the others who had managed to sneak through Security into his Office suite. He had no recourse than to plead with them to wait until the General Assembly to learn more about the visit.

Mrs. Nelson quickly steered him into the large reception room next to his office and allowed only the closest collaborators of the Secretary General to remain. She gently asked the others to let the Secretary General rest and collect his thoughts. She reminded them that the General Assembly meeting would take place in a few hours.

The expectation that had arisen from the first encounter was beyond description. Practically all TV and cable systems worldwide, computer web channels, web sites, networks, satellite feeds, links, transponders, Ku bands, optic fibers, radio waves and all forms of transmission had been deployed in and around the UN Building. The crowd was as heterogeneous as you could produce in New York City. In addition to the idle and curios there was also the large number of camera toting professional and amateur photographers. The video nuts were everywhere pointing their camcorders in all directions. And if you were perceptive enough you could identify just plain nuts, religious freaks, mumbling cases and just normal people. They had waited patiently from early in the morning until they were finally told that the shuttle had appeared and taken off. The whole sequence was so swift that nobody saw the shuttle arrive, except that quick flash when it landed on the helipad.

And it was the same when it returned. No one saw the shuttle arrive, not even those who had set up powerful binoculars, telescopes and other optical devices. The efforts made by networks and photographers were useless as the only sequences of the shuttle were those obtained in the few moments when it landed and again when it took off. They were all unable to obtain images of the contraption in flight.

Patrick reached the reception room adjacent to his private office and was glad to be again in familiar surroundings. Even though the visit to the space object had been pleasant and informative, he now felt the tension of the last twenty four hours. He dropped on a sofa and reached for the water carafe. Mrs. Nelson, the Deputy Director and his Chiefs of Staff and Protocol were silently standing in front of him with an anxious expression on their faces. He realized that they were hoping he would offer some comments about his journey to the ship.

"Listen, this whole episode is really beyond anyone's imagination. That shuttle is an incredible vehicle; it just took off and landed in what seemed to me the same instant. More sleigh of hand than aerial transport. The interior of the ship above is just as strange. It has no tubes, pipes, controls, lights, nothing!"

"How about the visitors? What are they? And where do they come from?" asked Baron Carini.

"As far as I can understand, they are energy. Energy configurations that exist somewhere in some energy pocket who knows where. They have adopted human forms. They look and act like human beings, but are not. And they talk and act like well educated Americans, if there are any left. And believe it or not, there are only six of them."

"Only six?" asked Baron Carini. His tone reflected the amazement of those present.

"Yes, six of them. Somehow they have installed all those three hundred objects all over the planet to obtain, as they claim, a full understanding of the nature of our world."

"But, what do they look like? You mention that they look like humans, now, could they be really humans playing the alien game? Maybe we are being sold a bill of goods by some of our clever competitors."

"Not a chance! While they look very human, their voices betray them. Do not forget that I have a very sensitive ear. I could detect a synthesizer modulation and tone that a human could not possible imitate. I am convinced they are the real McCoy, as we say in Kentucky."

They all smiled, used to Patrick's spicy comments. Patrick added, "My conclusion is that there is nothing to worry about. Not at this time. They have clearly indicated that they are here to do a job and that they'll describe it to me in time. Other than that I must confess that I am deadly tired. I must beg you to let me rest a while and also prepare some notes for the General Meeting later this afternoon."

Patrick excused himself and asked Mrs. Nelson not to let anyone in his private office. He was anxious to sit down and dictate the incredible experience he had just lived. He went in and locked his office door. Kathryn had been there all along. She had cried tears of relief when she saw him on the TV monitors as he emerged from the space shuttle. Her embrace had been tender and also anxious; like everyone else on earth she could not wait to find out about the space visitors. Patrick sat heavily on a sofa and sighed. More than a sigh it seemed a signal for his mind and his body to release the tension that had gripped him since the moment he stepped on the shuttle. His youthful demeanor had left him. He looked exhausted.

In a voice she could hardly recognize he said, "Kat, I don't know if we are dreaming or what. This could be the greatest thing that has ever happened to mankind. Or..." He stopped in mid sentence and the look in his eyes filled with sadness.

"What is it?" inquired Kathryn, concerned that her husband's poise and self control had deserted him.

"We have visitors that look exactly like us. They have assumed our physical shapes so that we do not become alarmed. From what I understand, they are not made of flesh and blood like we are but some form of energy capsules, pills or who the heck knows. Their intentions are not in any way threatening, or so they say. But they are here to do a job. Something to do with balances and equilibrium on this planet that will be explained later, they said. There were 6 of them. Two did the talking."

"What do you mean that they look like us humans?" asked Kathryn.

"Well, just what I said. They have assumed the appearance of several of the races of this planet. But they are not humans. And, according to them there is no such thing as a universe as we conceive it. No voids beyond. I still don't understand the kind of void we live in. These beings have learned all about humans since the first cell appeared in the primordial ooze—if there was primordial ooze, in the 90 days they have been parked above this planet! They have gone back to that first moment of creation and picked up the essence of all living things on the planet. If those first cells talked to each other, these beings have managed to hear what they said."

"But what do they want from us?"

"It is not clear to me yet," replied Patrick "They have mentioned something about some equilibrium on earth being out of order and that they plan to make some adjustments, whatever that means."

Remembering one of the visitor's requests, he continued. "And they want to meet you. They seem to know all about our life together and, what is also important, they seem to have evaluated woman's role in our society and seem to be critical of the way women have been treated by men."

Kathryn put her hand on Patrick's shoulder and, applying a gentle pressure, said, "See, I told you so. You should have been nicer to me all these years! They probably know all about the time you lost my wedding ring at the beach in St. Augustine, the time you checked out of the hotel in La Napoule leaving behind my slippers and nightgown and the times you faked the proverbial headache!"

Patrick smiled and immediately felt a wave of relief invade him. He savored the moment and reflected on Kathryn's unique talent to calm him down and give him instant solace.

"You know, these fellows behave so naturally human that they could fool anyone. If it wasn't for the barely noticeable synthesizer accent they have when they speak, they could be from Cincinnati, Buenos Aires or Port Cerbere...They also suggested that you bring a lady friend with you. They think you would feel more comfortable and, I suspect, they want to evaluate first hand women's behavior in a decidedly stressful situation."

"Of course I shall be delighted to come up to their ship. And let me think about who I can invite to make the trip with me. It places a burden on me, you know. Everyone not chosen will feel slighted. But let us not worry about that just now."

"Yes, we'll talk about it later. I want it to be a personal choice of yours and not a public decision."

Kathryn had listened with great interest, but noticing the tiredness and contained emotion in Patrick, she said, "Patrick, you must be awfully tired. I am dying to hear about your visit but I prefer to wait. In a little while you will have to address the General Assembly. It will be your report to the world so you must put yourself together and put your thoughts in order. Now, you better lie down on the couch for a few minutes and just look at the ceiling. I suspect this episode has been too much for one person."

Obediently, Patrick lied down on the couch and holding Kathryn's hand, looked at the ceiling and said, "What, no mirrors?"

She laughed and leaned down to kiss him on the forehead. She then moved to the small alcove off one side of the office where a small kitchenette was installed, and busied her with the tea kettle.

The General Assembly

At exactly 5 p.m., the tension in the Main Auditorium where the Assembly would convene was at its highest. The nervousness that saturated the atmosphere in the crowded room was evident in the way some sought the relief of a cigarette in the smoking areas next to the auditorium; others looked at their

Rolexes every few seconds and a few chewed their fingernails all the way to the elbow. In addition to the bona fide members of the UN Assembly, the entire diplomatic corps was present. Ambassadors, envoys and Plenipotentiary delegates were all packed in the upper left gallery, along with their assistants and interpreters. The press section could not hold one more number two pencil and the special scaffolds built to accommodate additional Television cameras looked dangerously loaded with technicians, equipment bags and cases.

The Secretary General appeared flanked by the current Chairman of the Security Council, the Secretary General of UNESCO and the Chief of Protocol. There was an immediate silence as everyone in the chamber fixed their eyes on the main podium.

Without any preliminary openings or introductions by anyone—as he had insisted—the Secretary General stopped in front of the bank of microphones and for 55 minutes held his audience spellbound.

His report was detailed, accurate in every respect and not devoid of the humor and pathos that this first ever contact had contained. His delivery was spontaneous and he did not use a prepared speech, only some notes scribbled on his personal agenda.

Toward the end, he exhorted all governments on earth to collaborate with the UN in carrying out the proposals made by the space visitors. He quickly outlined a plan to conduct the election of the Earth Coordinator and to take the first steps in making a preliminary selection of potential candidates. The announcement of his decision to create a Committee to monitor all matters related to the visit of the objects was received with enthusiasm by most countries. He concluded with a plea to everyone to do their utmost to delay, resolve or postpone any pending conflict domestic or otherwise. He emphasized that he intended to follow the requests made by Adam and Emosh and would immediately start work on the mechanisms needed to make sure that subsequent contacts with the space visitors and the carrying out of whatever requests were made by them, would be met with immediate compliance. He also vowed that no information would be withheld and that all decisions would continue to conform to established UN parliamentary procedures.

His last words were met with applause from the majority of those present. As the applause and the murmur of comments subsided, the Secretary General broke a long tradition of the General Assembly by throwing open the floor for discussion. This in itself created another ripple of low voiced comments and an occasional cheer.

Almost everyone wanted the floor. Patrick had no option but to ask for silence again and said, "Gentlemen, this is no ordinary session of this August body. This is no ordinary occurrence. I feel that everyone who has a question should ask it and I will do my best to answer it. It does not matter if we have to remain here for the next 24 hours. This event affects us all and I must again remind you that our visitors expect the UN to be the entity that will have the responsibility of getting the cooperation of all the nations in this planet."

Again, his words were received with enthusiastic applause.

The questions—as so often happens—reflected the entire catalog of man's insecurities, arrogance and pride. Long speeches were made to end up asking a simple question about the type of clothes the visitors wore. It struck Patrick that not until this moment had he realized how imperfect human nature appeared. Faced with an occasion of such momentous import, the general understanding and appreciation of the event was insignificant. Most of the questions were preceded by long harangues that inevitably enhanced and promoted the questioner.

Were the Roman and Greek forums like this? thought Patrick. *I must ask Adam.*

Fortunately, there were some questions that exposed some intelligent thought behind them. Great concern was expressed by the feeling that the UN was supposed to carry out "requests" made by the visitors. Are they requests or orders? What is the exact purpose of the visit? Why should they deal exclusively with the UN? Did they not recognize the existence of individual nations? Why was Patrick the only one chosen at the moment? Why could not a delegation meet with them? Wasn't Patrick assuming powers that made him in effect the spokesman for the entire human race? How do we know that these beings are not really human beings that have managed to build such contraptions and probably want to institute some form of control over the nations of earth? Do they believe in God? What is all this about energy? Don't they know that the world and the heavens were made in seven days and that all those theories of evolution are only subscribed by liberals and eggheads?

The essence of the questions revealed the convictions and beliefs of the innumerable sects, political parties, creeds and organizations of this earth. It saddened Patrick to observe the banality and naiveté of most delegates. It concerned him that faced with such diversity of attitudes and interests, his role of link with the space visitors would be fraught with the petty arguments, jealousies and intellectual vulgarity displayed habitually by the representatives of most countries.

He made an effort to dispel these notions as he listened to more questions and answered them automatically. In the back of his mind—and as a stabilizing influence—he felt the presence of Emosh and Adam and the backing and endorsement that this last seemed to have extended to Patrick.

By 11:30 that evening, and after exhausting all avenues of discussion, he ended the session. He insisted once more that little was known about the visitors and that subsequent visits should disclose their plans and desires. He asked the members of the Security Council to meet with him in another hour and with a cordial good evening to those present, he left the room.

There was the usual rush of reporters and others out of the auditorium.

Patrick's exhaustion was patent. He had spent the last 48 hours under tremendous tension. The transcendence of the first meeting ever with extraterrestrial beings had almost been lost in the whirlwind of public appearances, UN sessions, meetings, telephone conferences and—worst of all—the persistent demands of a hungry media. He had barely had time to dictate into his pocket recorder the events of the last days. This habit of his—which he considered more a responsibility than a simple practice—had provided him with fresh and accurate versions of conversations, events and impressions in his dealings with the multiplicity of matters at his UN post. He looked at the old recorder and smiled. He remembered that sunny morning when General DeGaulle had presented him with it. Observing the worn state of the recorder he muttered, "Just hang on while we live through this episode."

Finally Home

The session with the Security Council and the phone calls afterward, had kept him at the UN building until 4 o'clock in the morning. After about three hours sleep, Patrick woke up with the guilty notion that he had overslept. While the curtains in the bedroom of his spacious apartment in midtown Park Avenue were drawn, he could perceive the brightness of a clear day beyond.

He quickly got out of bed and dashed into the shower, still half asleep. As he fine tuned the temperature of the almost violent stream of water, his mind went back to the hours spent in the space ship. He could not help wondering if his alien hosts were also taking a shower at that same time. If they have acquired all the traits of modern human beings and wear a flesh and blood uniform, they must have learned the way to keep the uniform clean and neat. He smiled as he wondered about the kind of deodorant they would use, if any. He could not remember any specific scent or odor in the ship. He recalled that the air in the shuttle and in the "pill" was always fresh.

He looked at the clock on his night table and saw that it was almost eight o'clock in the morning.

As he was finishing dressing, Kathryn walked in cradling a bunch of newspapers. Behind her, Dolores, their maid, pushed the little food cart to the sitting room next to the bedroom.

"Bon jour, Monsieur Secretaire General!" Kathryn's happy greeting and lovely presence quickly removed from Patrick's mind all thoughts of the recent events. He embraced her and felt the freshness of her skin and the familiar feel of her soft body. She kissed him on the cheek and, smiling, said, "Patrick dear, I did not want to wake you up, but I am glad you woke yourself up. Remember that you have a telephone conference with the White House at nine o'clock. I have blocked just about everything else and told Mrs. Nelson to keep everyone at bay, at least until ten or ten thirty."

Patrick held on to their embrace and the fatigue of the last 48 hours retreated at once. They both felt the stirrings caused by the close embrace and with some unrestrained passion they kissed. It was a compromising kiss, but not very opportune. Patrick smiled and whispered to Kathryn, "Can we make the President of the United States wait a little?"

Kathryn laughed and, aware that Dolores the maid was enjoying the encounter, replied, "I am sure that the President of the United States would not make us wait if he found himself in similar circumstances."

"Well, Kathryn! Just what do you mean similar circumstances?"

Still embracing they both laughed.

Later that morning, Patrick placed a call in his secure line to the President of the United States. By then he had received several calls from leaders around the world who wanted to comment on his report the night before. He had asked Mrs. Nelson however to advised them that he would return their calls later. He wanted to speak to Ross Simonson first.

"Mister President."

"Mister Secretary General! Punctual as ever. Before anything, let me tell you that your report before the General Assembly, and the world in general, was a magnificent piece of realism. You were able to paint in sharp colors the entire episode inside the pill above New York. Congratulations!"

"Thank you, Mister President. I just hope I was able to allay some of the fears that grip all of us. You see, I still don't know what it is that they want. I am afraid that there is little that can be done to prepare the world for any action they might wish to take. You see, their powers, are something never imagined on this planet…Dear Ross, I don't know what the hell to make out of these energy envoys!"

"Listen, I have read the transcript of your report a couple of times. It is surely a very puzzling situation. We are both however obligated to provide some guidance in this entire affair and, somehow, must find a common thread. This whole thing may call for truly United Nations."

They talked for a few more minutes in the informal and honest manner they had employed since they first met several years back.

"Just one more thing," said the President, "will it be possible to have other people attend these sessions? I have been getting requests from everyone and his purple turtle, to have me sell you the idea. Other than the usual publicity-seeking weenies—and you know we have shitloads of them in Washington—there have been some serious requests. What do you think?"

"I personally feel that these fellows above—or whatever—are full of wisdom, information and data about planet earth that I would love for them to explain it all in world television. My feeling is that the more people know about our visitors the more they will be able to understand them and the less they will fall for wild speculation. However, whether other persons accompany me or not depends on them. I shall mention it to them during my next visit. So far they have only invited Kathryn and a friend of hers, on the basis that women feel more comfortable in new surroundings if they have a close friend along. So, Kathryn and a friend of hers—don't know who, as yet—will come up with me."

The President said, "Yes, you are right. They are calling the shots. I shall pass it along. You know, I have had requests from Senators I hadn't seen in years, Ministers of some remote churches, insurance executives, bankers, golf commentators and even some Television cooks. By the way, have you heard from Elmo Saks?"

"Oh, yes, a stack of messages, notes and handwritten faxes. This time he is not going through one of his powerful lackeys. He wants a personal meeting. I shall talk to him on the phone in the next day or so. I guess we both know what he wants. The Ambassadors from Japan and 4 European countries have been very insistent. You know the connection with Elmo."

"Just keep him on a string. He's also called me but I'll have Mike McClellan deal with him tomorrow. He is beginning to place his chips on the table."

After a few more minutes, Patrick hung up and returned to the crowded agenda for the day.

Patrick's report on his first visit to the ship above New York had caused not only surprise but also apprehension and fear. The effect it had on world opinion was beyond measure. Patrick's vivid description of the appearance and nature of the occupants of the ship above New York had been received with silent amazement and, in some places, with some skepticism. The fact that there were six beings that resembled human beings in the object above New York City caught everyone by surprise. It was hard to understand that these beings controlled the entire fleet of the pill-like ships sitting atop 300 cities of earth.

Patrick had been questioned about the "energy presence," as the New York Times had named the visitors. Not only the media had shown the greater insistence but also the Academic Institutions and, most vociferous of all, a large number of religious sects and church denominations.

"Is Deschamps telling the truth?" "How do we know that they are what they claim to be?" "Maybe they are just a few yuppie puppets maneuvered by a mogul somewhere," "Is this another Yankee happening?" "Why don't they come down and meet the people of this planet face to face?" Most headlines reflected the failure of most reporters and editors to accept in their totality Patrick's detailed descriptions and reports.

Voices of Dissent

In the middle of this uproar, a strong voice was heard. The Reverend Toe arranged for a one hour televised message sponsored by one of the major networks and a number of multinational corporations and religious groups. On the day of the broadcast, the Reverend met with Elmo Saks in one of the latter's offices in New York.

"John, we have gone over the message you will deliver tonight. I think it will strike the right chord. For one thing it will make people realize that whatever these energy things want affects all of mankind and not only the UN. It is not too late to make people understand that there is another option."

Elmo was frantic. He had opposed having the UN as the sole contact between the visitors and the people of the planet. He had hoped that the informal consortium he had managed to organize among some of the industrialized nations would be the one that would assume the responsibility to represent the planet before the "energy things," as he called them. He and the Reverend had worked hard to make sure that the Television Message would enjoy the widest coverage possible. Elmo's considerable resources all over the world and the Reverend's own organization that included more than 500 sanctuaries in all five continents, counted on the interest and support of millions of people.

The highly touted television Message however did not bring about immediate expressions of agreement to the proposal it contained. In spite of the elaborate show business presentation and the carefully rehearsed interviews of famous people, impassioned speeches, marvelous choral and solo performances, the Reverend's message fell into deaf ears.

"The people are still under shock!" sentenced Elmo after the broadcast. "They are incapable of reacting the way we wanted." All the new committees, fronts, commissions and delegations that had been meticulously organized in almost every country of earth, had been primed to create a popular movement that in the end did not receive popular support. People enjoyed the show but nothing else. Only a few seemed willing to follow the Reverend's urging to force their governments to support the creation of the New Force. Most people needed reassurance and, in stead, the Reverend asked them to rebel against the established order.

Strange Requests

Approximately two weeks had elapsed since Patrick's first visit to the ship above New York. In that period, the Committee had been organized and quartered in one of the wings of the UN building on 34th Street. New lines of communication had been established by the Committee with most Governments. An efficient UN regional network of representatives and delegates was in place.

Also during this period, Patrick had been in almost daily contact with Adam and Emosh, and had received more concrete ideas about the "preliminary steps" required to straighten out the energy balance problem. He had long discussions about these with the President and with Richard, and arrived at the conclusion that the visitor's presence simply involved the removal of negative and evil elements on the planet. The question remained as to how this would be done and what was expected of the UN and the Governments of the countries of Earth.

At one of these sessions, Richard had explained in simple terms, the many and varied effects of energy manipulation, or "conduct," as he called it, both from the purely physical standpoint and from the consideration of its intangible, non material essence.

"These boys have detected an inordinate amount of conflict in this planet and, worse, a strong current of evil or negative elements. Somehow, this has caused some problem elsewhere, where, I can assume, the levels of existence do not contain such elements. The big question is how do you deal with billions of tainted souls, sick minds, violent attitudes, arrogant behaviors? I shudder to think what I am thinking!"

"Whatever the path they will follow, we must be prepared. I suspect that these preliminaries will involve identifying the problem areas, cataloguing them and studying the appropriate techniques for rectification, whatever they might be. This means having our house in order and being in a position to do as they say," said the President.

Patrick was silent for a moment and then turning to Richard observed, "Ross is right. They have told me that they need to look into the world's criminal records in recent history. They are also asking for some definitions on current morality, ethics and human relations. You should be able to clarify a number of areas that, to them, appear gray and confusing. In a couple of days, we'll go up to the ship with Kathryn and Helen Lawrence. You will be able to see for yourself how deep their knowledge is of our history and their perception of us as thinking human beings. We will probably hear at that time about their "energy balancing act."

Richard was silent for a moment. While Patrick's report of his visit had been finely detailed and well analyzed, there were still many points he did not understand. He felt that some of his doubts would be dissipated once he faced these strange visitors. In his mind, any form of corrective measures applied to a given situation, or restoration of conditions of a certain environment, would inevitably imply strong or drastic actions. The energy unbalances on Earth had been caused by its inhabitants, themselves the product of energy configurations. If you act upon people, you are also acting upon energy. Would this be the key to what the visitors planned on doing? He said, "I am really at a loss about what these beings wish to do. Correcting balances might mean almost anything. It can apply to people, as well as to other living creatures or maybe even physical and inanimate entities on the planet. Just suppose that they consider that oceans cause a great deal of damage to people and to property all over. This would be a negative expression of energy. A tornado or a typhoon is definitely bad energy. Or are they solely concentrating on the quality of energy levels that are inherent in humans?"

Their conversation continued for some time with none of them able to point to a plausible understanding of the intentions expressed by the visitors.

Meanwhile, Kathryn had decided to have Helen accompany her on the visit to the ship. She felt that the idea of having another woman along on this important visit was a good one. While Kathryn was an independent-minded woman, she realized that there would be so many new experiences unveiled during the trip, that another witness was a good idea. There was also the reassurance factor. Someone she trusted implicitly would be the perfect complement. She thought about all these reasons, but only after she had decided on Helen. *Typical woman,* she thought to herself. *Decide by intuition and then analyze and justify!*

She asked Helen to lunch the following day. They met in the lobby of the Pierre and walked the few blocks to Ellis Island, the cozy restaurant where they often met. Kathryn did not beat around the bush. "Helen, I want to ask a big favor of you. I want you to come with me when Patrick, Richard and I go up to the ship or pill or whatever, next week

Helen's surprise was painted all over her face. It took a moment before she was able to say

"Why, yes of course. But I thought that your visit was an official one and also, I understand that the visitors have made it clear that they do not want anyone else other than Patrick and Richard."

"In the last visit, they asked Patrick to bring me along, and that is the official version. However, they also suggested that I invite someone close to me to accompany me on the journey. They know that we girls can perceive and see things that most men would miss. They also realize that two women can energize and comfort each other when it comes to facing unknown situations. So that's it, my girl!"

They talked excitedly about the trip and speculated about what was expected of them. Their conversation was not without an edge of apprehension, barely overcome by the curiosity they both felt. In typical woman's fashion, Helen asked, "What about clothes, Kathryn? Has Patrick said anything, or suggested anything? What are we to expect?"

Kathryn smiled and answered, "Good question. I asked the same question. Patrick just said that I should dress comfortably. He mumbled something about doing some traveling but without leaving the ship. So, I plan to stay with skirt, blouse, cardigan and low heeled shoes. I should think you'd like to do likewise, except do not wear a plaid skirt with white cashmere turtleneck and beige cardigan. We'd look like the Kessler twins, remember?"

On the given day, a brunch was arranged at the UN by Patrick and Kathryn, to which the President of the US and Cardinal Ludlam had been invited. Richard would also be present. They all met in the executive dining room on the 3rd floor of the UN building. The shuttle was not expected until noon and so they were able to enjoy a leisure breakfast and extend the session into a "sobremesa," about which Cardinal Ludlam commented, "You know, back in the old days, my predecessors made it almost an obligation to have a 'sobremesa,' or post meal conversation. They assumed correctly, that as digestion proceeded, the relaxed mood of a friendly conversation did a lot to improve digestion. It also helped to summarize matters discussed, seal agreements and maybe even tell a few anecdotes. It is a custom that seems to have been lost. My lunches or other meals in the company of others are always timed to the second, with little chance to enjoy a BS session afterwards."

Helen smiled and added, "The rhythm of our lives is such that we are losing some of the things that at one time made life bearable, if not enjoyable."

Richard, knowing what was coming, asked, "Such as?"

Helen was quick to reply, "La siesta, for example. In some countries, the siesta automatically provides an extension to the workday. If you work from, let us say 8 in the morning, by one or two you are ready for food. So you have a leisure lunch, do a bit of 'sobremesa' and then spend one hour or so sleeping. By the time you get up, around five or so shower and look at yourself, you are ready for another 6 hours of work. So, you see, la siesta is not all bad. You can even consider it a pleasant way to enhance productivity."

They all laughed. Then Patrick said, "I want to thank the President and Cardinal Ludlam for joining us at breakfast today. I feel that having both of them here, we are getting some divine support on one end, and also some material reassurance on the other. I don't know what is coming and I not afraid to confess that I am still scared about this whole chapter. Also, to have Kathryn and Helen with us, gives me also a great deal of confidence. I also count on Richard's wisdom and boundless energy to aid in unraveling this mystery."

They were all silent for a moment and then the President spoke. "First of all, let me say that I endorse the 'sobremesa' and most wholeheartedly support la siesta! I just don't know how to modify the Constitution to make both obligatory!"

Again, they all laughed, enjoying the moment while at the same time aware that time was running out and soon they would be embarking on the most important adventure in the history of mankind. The President continued. "All four of you will carry not only the concern of the human race but also the hopes of those in this world that have observed and continued to observe the Golden Rule. If these visitors come to diminish or eliminate evil from this planet, welcome! For too long, we have lived under false standards and have managed to create generations of people with little or no principles. The question of God is certain to come up. This morning, Cardinal Ludlam and I had a long discussion on the subject. We both agree that the hand of God Almighty is evident in this situation and that in time the visitors will confirm it. I can only say to the four of you that I envy you, in spite of whatever dangers or risks are involved. I think that as delegates of the human race we could not do better! Bon voyage!"

The Ladies Visit the Ship

At exactly 12 noon, the shuttle materialized on the heliport. As in the previous trip, the area surrounding the UN building was crowded and, this time, noisy. Since it had been established that the visitors were here on a peaceful mission, or so it seemed, much of the apprehension and fear had vanished from the public and the media. This time, there were street vendors peddling T-shirts with pictures of the objects, Beanie babies with the imagined appearance of the visitors, the Reverend Toe's videos and pamphlets in several languages, the ubiquitous hot dog and fast food carts and the usual contingent of beggars, pickpockets and con men.

The shuttle door opened and Patrick and the others quickly entered. Without any sound or motion, the vehicle lifted off and remained visible for a second or two, then it disappeared.

All four were silent inside the shuttle. Once the door shut down, they felt as if they were being supported by an unknown force, so there was no sense of acceleration or motion. They looked carefully all around the strange object but could not detect any mechanical device, controls or joints of any sort. The amazing part was that the walls of the shuttle were totally transparent and, for a fraction of a second they were able to see the outlines of Manhattan, the Bronx and Staten Island too.

All of a sudden they reached the ship above and realized that they were inside of it. Helen stepped out of the small vehicle and could not help exclaiming, "And I thought our building on Fifth Avenue had the fastest elevators in creation!"

They all took a few steps and to their left an opening sort of materialized, or maybe it had been there all along. They entered it and found themselves in the large room where Patrick had his first encounter with the visitors. Patrick was quick to notice that a number of bookcases had been placed around the walls of the enclosure. They were all full of books of all kinds. He could see expensive leather bound volumes, paperbacks, school textbooks, thin publications that looked like manuals and one large bookcase full of the larger coffee table books.

They moved slowly toward the center of the room, where the large sofa and the coffee table were. As in the first visit, the lighting was soft and its source unaccountable. At one extreme, they saw the podium where all six visitors were seated behind the glass partition.

Emosh got up and came forward to where the guests had stopped and shook hands effusively with Patrick and motioned the group to move into the room. It was Richard's first opportunity to observe one of the visitors up close and in motion. Emosh was about six feet tall and weighed approximately 180 pounds. He was dressed casually with chino pants, loafers with white sports sox, and a light blue golf shirt with the letters United Nations in white letters above the left side pocket.

Adam was at his usual post in the podium and seemed to be reading from a single sheet of paper. As the group moved into the room, Adam got up quickly and came to greet the delegation from Planet Earth. He smiled at Patrick and patted him on the back as they shook hands. He looked appraisingly at Kathryn, Helen and Richard, and said, "Welcome to the Big Apple's Aspirin! My name is Adam." Then, looking at Kathryn, "You must be Kathryn, so nice of you to come." He turned to Helen and said, "And you are Helen Lawrence and next to you our prized Coordinator Professor Richard Ferguson." He bowed to the ladies and shook hands with Richard.

Kathryn and Helen made a striking pair. While Kathryn was a few years older than Helen, she possessed a subdued beauty enhanced by her refined manners and sunny disposition. At 39 years of age, she was in the prime of her life. Her beauty and lovely figure elicited not only admiration by men and women alike but also that special appraisal by most discriminating men.

Helen, on her part had the freshness and attractiveness of well bred American women. Her physical beauty had none of the cheerleader gloss but the more appealing features of a beauty that appeared casual and sensual. The slight reticence, barely noticeable in Kathryn's manner complemented Helen's more forthright demeanor, with the result that as a pair they projected a charming blend of self assurance tempered by obvious intellectual prowess.

"Let me introduce the rest of our crew." The other four visitors descended from the podium and came to the area where they shook hands with the new arrivals as each introduced himself. They pulled up some of the chairs around the room and sat down around the large coffee table, except one who remained standing behind Adam. They all looked casual and relaxed.

Adam spoke. "Welcome back, Patrick, and welcome, Mrs. Deschamps, Miss Lawrence and Professor Ferguson. We are really delighted that our mission here is becoming a very pleasant experience. The cooperation and help we have received from Patrick has been valueless. We are also delighted to meet Mrs. Deschamps and Miss Lawrence and to welcome Professor Ferguson, about whom we have heard great things."

Richard knew that a short speech was expected of him. The other visitors seemed to be following the exchange with a great deal of interest. He said, "Thank you, Emosh and Adam. You must know what a thrill this is, not only for me but for our entire planet. It is the first contact ever with beings from beyond our solar system and it makes us feel that we are not alone in the void of space."

Emosh smiled and in a gesture that they all took for that unconscious awkwardness that often underlines first encounters, busily rearranged the books and ashtrays on the table. Adam cleared his throat and said, "We are pleased that we will be working with a group of people from Earth such as you. I must reveal that we know a lot about each of you and feel honored and impressed to make your acquaintance." He paused, and with a smile continued. "And, ladies, may we call you Kathryn and Helen?" Both women nodded and smiled back. He then said, "In the weeks ahead we will be working together to implement an energy program that we described to Patrick during his first visit. I want to ask you to please let me know of any needs you might have, either up here or down on Earth."

Patrick remarked, "We are all glad to have this opportunity to meet you, to learn so many things about our planet and also to be able to help solve the problems you have identified. You all can count on our total cooperation."

At that, Emosh faced Richard and said, "You are both Doctor Ferguson and Professor Ferguson. May I call you just Richard? We will be spending a lot of time together and we can afford to dispense with the formalities."

Richard was glad to hear both the light tone and the question itself. He thought to himself: *Here I am going through what is certainly the greatest experience of my life, talking to an alien of unknown shape but looking like a weekend yuppie! And he calls me by my first name!* He smiled pleasantly and replied, "Of course, formalities have their place and time. Just feel free to make any request of me. Patrick has already explained that we have been empowered by the Governments of the planet to comply with any request that you have."

Emosh turned to Ely, who had remained standing a few feet from Adam, and said to him, "Ely, Richard here is the author of those books on Cultural and Physical Anthropology that you found so absorbing. He is also the one who has been raising all that hell about cooking shows on TV. Pull up a chair and join us. You look better down here than on that pedestal of yours!"

Adam and Richard could not help laughing. Without saying a word, Ely approached the group seated around the coffee table and said in a voice that was deeper than either Adam's or Emosh's, "It is a great pleasure to meet such lovely ladies and you fellows. I am an admirer of all of you. My name is Ely. I have read almost all the articles written by Richard, Helen's scripts and treatments, Kathryn's column in some of the Hachette publications and of course Patrick's articles and public memorandums. They treat me as sort of a walking reference library around here." They all laughed as the tension of the moment began to disappear. He continued. "As I said, my admiration is divided equally between your personal traits and your public or professional accomplishments. You see, I have observed that an inordinate amount of people in this planet are unable to establish a rational correspondence between those facets of their existence. In a sense they sort of live a contradiction. You know, great artist, lousy person, respected jurist and at the same time immoral person. Then popular minister but miserable human being, etc. Talk about ghosts and closets!"

He laughed gently and continued. "Please forgive me for running away with generalities."

Both Patrick and Richard were delighted with Ely's candid comments. Patrick said, "What you say is true. Inconsistencies of the species, I guess."

Adam laughed out loud and said, "I guess you gather from Ely's comments that we are very fond of the anthropological sciences in this planet. Seen from our perspective, your planet is a fascinating laboratory of cultural, social and biological differences. The fascinating part is that the process of evolution has occurred more as an accident than an orderly development. For us, it has been a great opportunity to be able to see the entire episode from zero hour to this date."

Richard had listened with special interest. Here was a being that claimed to have seen the evolution of the species since that first cup of nothing was suddenly turned into a cell with a code within. He was awed by the idea that these visitors had traveled through time and seen the primitive societies on earth, and observed the great events in history, same as the great catastrophes.

As if reading his thoughts, Ely declared, "Yes, we have seen the development of the species since second one. We have also seen how your history was made and have listened in person to some of the great individuals your species has produced. Since the days of old Australopithecus through the jumping Neanderthals to the more sedate and judicious Homus Erectus."

While he spoke, both Richard and Patrick observed Ely. He was a handsome man by any standard. He was about 30 years old, with a lock of dark brown hair decorating a wide forehead. His features suggested a bloodline with a touch of Native American.

He appeared well tanned, which made his light green eyes more noticeable. He was dressed in chino pants, an Oxford light blue button down shirt open at the neck, a sleeveless pullover and expensive loafers with matching color socks. He could pass for a college professor or a corporate vice-president in weekend wear. The body message was relaxation pure and simple.

Richard looked at Patrick as if asking for permission to speak and seeing Patrick's ready nod, said to Ely, "As an anthropologist I can only say that I envy your ability to see our species in its various stages of development. I must clarify however that the label of anthropologist in my case does not quite conform to the general conception of such animal. Anthropology is a recent discipline and until few years ago was a narrow field of study."

"Yes, I know," interrupted Ely and, smiling, said, "I am aware that not too long ago you people were considered crackpots looking around for tribes to discover and digging for lost cities mostly in the Middle East, Mexico and Perú."

They all laughed at Ely's sharp comment. When the laughter had died down, Richard said, "Well, yes. For many years Anthropology centered on the study of old or vanishing peoples in remote areas of the world; for some time it consisted—as you so aptly put it—in collecting artifacts that would be used to reconstruct the details of everyday life in old cultures. But in the last decades, it has been recognized that Anthropology, the study of human social life and culture could not be detached from the social sciences and from the humanities. Both Cultural and Physical Anthropology have broken their more traditional boundaries between disciplines and—in my opinion—have become more practical. They have also become more useful. Cultural Anthropology, for instance, now deals equally with conditions like poverty, ecological crisis, population explosion, urban disintegration, etc. same as it does with symbolism, religions, arts, rituals, etc. It now provides the basis for the development of philosophical thought and a better understanding of social and economic sciences."

They talked for a while about current trends in education, crime prevention and health care, subjects that seemed to interest Ely.

The conversation continued in the usual amiable tone adopted by the visitors, who, in spite of the resources they had that enabled them to learn and know matters in their utmost details, preferred to exchange ideas, facts and opinions with Patrick and Richard.

"It allows us to feel the cloth, so to speak. Somehow, a mass of facts acquire more meaning and depth when it is discussed with you all," replied Adam when queried about their unique capacity to know.

They dwelled into the not-so-orderly development of societies on Earth, a matter that interested Adam a great deal. In particular, he wondered about the extraordinary development of American society and culture that in a relatively short time had evolved as one of the great civilizations in the history of mankind. He seemed fascinated by the turmoil associated with the Revolutionary War and the way an enviable system based on law and order managed to survive and flourish. He wondered about the cohesive forces that were able to blend the widely different cultural backgrounds of the peoples of America.

Patrick observed, "Yes, it has been an interesting aspect of the development of the country. First, various backgrounds began to blend after the first generation. The natural leaders that emerged were deeply religious and smart enough to understand that as a force in society they were accomplishing things no one thought possible. So it was a combination of strong religion and quality education, that created a ruling elite imbued with sound religious principles. One example is Harvard University. It started as a religious institution and grew into a great University. In colonial days, it also provided a link that unified aims and criteria. You know, the beginning of the Establishment in this country."

Adam nodded and replied, "You see, you are fortunate that what is generally known as 'The Establishment' in the United States, has been and is a silent and almost invisible fountain of control and restraint in a society that is increasingly more varied and complex. Even today, it serves a function similar to that of pre-Revolutionary days. It is still the game of having the right person in the right spot at the right time, especially if it is someone you know."

Patrick nodded and cleared his throat. He said, "I think that Richard, as a respected American academician and pundit, can probably discuss this subject better than I can. See, in countries like France, the so-called 'Etablissment' has a history infinitely more complicated than that of America. It has its own peculiarities, resulting from a more complex history, old traditions, and the unique character of the French people."

Adam listened with interest and, pointing at Richard, said, "From checking up on the past of the human race, we have found that some sort of invisible order, promoted and inspired by some members of a given community, group or society, has always been present. In most cases it has safeguarded the observance of basic principles, such as respect for the neighbor's property, respect for the elder, care for the infirm, and the children, protection against outsiders, etc. We see the Establishment in America as an invisible brotherhood whose self-imposed role is that of guaranteeing among the various forces and tendencies existing in American society, a certain degree of equilibrium. You can probably tell us more about it."

Richard had often thought and had in numerous occasions written about that vague and nebulous term that, at least in America, had its origins in one of the great Universities of the East Coast of the United States. He mentally reviewed the exciting fabric of the term and the myriad facts associated with it. After his own Harvard days, he had attempted to understand that intangible web of subtle influences and innuendo that attached itself to the typical Harvard education. He was aware that the term in itself had raised questions among practically all segments of society and that society, when faced with vaguely unknown situations, developed some form of prejudice against it. He was also aware that in the last decades, the so called establishment in America had abandoned some of its elitist restrictions and was now open to those whose merits and accomplishments were noteworthy. It had created an important and essential set of standards.

Adam, in a light tone, interrupted Richard's thoughts. "What is the matter, Professor? Are you afraid to talk about your Alma Mater and its web of influence in American life?"

Before Richard could reply, Helen said, "I was just thinking that some form of 'establishment' exists in all forms of life. Some are ruled by instinct and others follow some form of tacit discipline where influence by some of its member is exercised, be it a herd, a flight, a community or just a bunch of hungry hyenas in the savanna."

After a while of enlightened discussion, Emosh signaled to all and said, "We are forgetting our manners! It is about lunch time and no one has said anything about food. How about it?"

They had been so engrossed in the discussion of many topics that they had forgotten about food, except Patrick who had looked at his wristwatch a couple of times.

"I thought you'd never ask!" exclaimed Kathryn.

Adam got up and led the group to the end of the room, past the podium. He stopped and, again, an opening materialized and they all entered a large room brightly lit and decorated in soft white and green tones. It had large windows that were in reality frames superimposed on bright landscapes. There were several tables with bright white linen and shiny cutlery and glassware. Comfortable chairs in green velveteen along with Crystal chandeliers and foot lamps completed the decor.

Adam suggested that they all sit at one of the large circular tables and at the same time pointed to a buffet on one side of the room.

The visitors from earth could not believe their eyes. The effect of that dining room was unique. It combined the elegance of some of the best dining lounges in the French Riviera, Switzerland and the US. The image was warm and distantly suggested a summer resort.

They were in for more surprises. The buffet was a masterpiece. Not only was the arrangement of the many dishes an exercise in beauty and good taste, but also a statement about the quality and variety of the items it contained. I took the guests some moments to admire and review the large buffet area. They carefully chose from the various hot and cold foods and returned to the table. For a while there was a constant stream of people going to and from the buffet and the table.

"Adam! This is really a treat!" exclaimed Patrick once they were all seated. "You must have one of the best cooks in space!"

Adam laughed and replied, "This is all courtesy of Planet Earth, really. We borrowed a few dishes from here and there. Listen, since coming to Earth and becoming humans, all of us have gained weight!"

They all laughed heartily. Wine was poured and the meal proceeded amidst comments, anecdotes and laughter.

After lunch, they returned to the living room where a cart with coffee, tea, juices, cognac bottles and a large crystal bowl of Marron Glazé and After Dinner Mints had been placed nearby.

After coffee, Emosh and Adam suggested that Patrick and Richard begin a review of some statistical profiles they needed. The four got up and left, led by Emosh. Evan and Earle excused themselves and left the room, leaving Kathryn and Helen alone with Ely and Eldon.

Ely said, "A good host would ordinarily invite his distinguished guests to visit the manor. Unfortunately our manor is really a come-as-you go facility. In other words, we conjure up the rooms as we need them. The dining room where we just ate, is no more, for instance. But if we need it again, it'll be there."

"And how do you do that? Who clears the table and do the dishes? I'd like to do the same thing in my apartment!" joked Helen.

"Ah! It is an energy game too complicated to explain," replied Eldon. Then he said, "Let us talk about history and other things that interest you."

He got up and led them to another part of the ship, to an area tastefully decorated as a lounge. The floor was covered by several colorful and rich Persian rugs. Several damask-covered wall sections contained fine mahogany bookcases, paintings by some of the world's great artists, prints and an imposing Marlborough portrait of the Duke of Wellington above an elaborate Florentine marble chimney. The flowers in the Belgian vase looked fresh and were artfully arranged. After they all sat down, Ely smiled and observed, "One of the things we have learned to appreciate and admire on this planet—besides its lovely ladies—is that peculiar and admirable tendency most everyone has to seek and enjoy comfort. Every time I sit on this sofa and breathe in the beauty of the room, I experience a sensation of well being. The kind of feeling you can also get in the lobbies of first class hotels in London, Paris and New York, same as in the first class seats on a plane, a stretch limo, and even the waiting room of some physicians' offices in Beverly Hills."

Helen and Kathryn listened with rapture to this impromptu confession from Ely. Both women were still trying to recover from their initial contact with the visitors and the incredible lunch they had just enjoyed. They found strange that the visitors exhibited all the traits of humans and the only faint indication that they were actually "non-human," was the barely noticeable echo their voices emitted. It took a trained ear and a great deal of concentration to be able to perceive such flaw. The synthetic sound was almost too perfect to Kathryn's and Helen's ears. The small flaw occurred when they interrupted a phrase with a new thought or idea. What is usually a millisecond of hesitation and, at times, an imperceptible change of tone and cadence in most humans, such change in the visitors was infinitesimal so that the delivery was almost atonal.

As if guessing what Kathryn and Helen were thinking, Ely said, "We were able to turn ourselves into humans in practically all respects. In spite of the complexity of the human anatomy, I think we succeeded in creating several human types. Sounds however were a bit hard to reproduce, especially when it came to what we termed sound in motion."

"Well," said Kathryn, "it is almost impossible to detect. The amazing part is how well you have managed to acquire different accents. We love all of them and for me, it is kind of homey. The United Nations ambiance, you know..."

Ely nodded and continued. "For instance, Earle has been given a soft English accent and English looks. Emosh exhibits slight Latin looks. I am supposed to be a sort of neutral American type with a little bit of Native

American blood, a pinch of Scottish, some Jew and some Dutch. Eldon is our Oriental oracle while our leader Adam, has been made to adopt a run-of-the-mill Anglo Saxon cut while Evan with his dark skin and his romantic eyes reflects some African heritage."

Helen looked at Ely with interest and asked, "You just said that Adam, and the rest of you, were 'made to adopt' different human characteristics. Who or what made you do it?"

"Clever young lady, you are!" retorted Ely. He raised his hands and sort of spread them so as to signify some form of immensity. He said, "We are just an energy pool, split into six entities. Think of a baker. He makes doughnuts that come from the same dough. But he can add chocolate to one, glaze others, etc. But they are all doughnuts!"

Kathryn and Helen laughed at the curious explanation. Helen looked at Ely with a mischievous look and said, "Well, your energy pool did a good job in making up some human doughnuts. You all look very good, by the way!"

Ely bowed his head and was quick to reply, "You are making me blush! You see, we are human for all purposes. We adopted all your features. Please do not think that we are animated dummies. The bottom line is that we and you all are all from the same dough. We call it energy. And, by the way, has anyone told you that you and Kathryn could easily enter and win a Miss Universe contest?"

Again they laughed and then Ely added, "Speaking of doughnuts, how about some more coffee?"

As he finished asking, a wooden serving cart with silver trimming appeared. It had a plate full of doughnuts of several types, a fine porcelain coffee service of undoubted English origin and a bottle of Carlos Primero, the excellent Spanish cognac.

"Voilá," he said as he pulled the cart in front of the sofa where Kathryn and Helen were sitting.

"You mentioned that since adopting human forms you have experienced every one of the infinite sensations of human consciousness. Is that it?"

"Yup, everything, dear lady. Including losing at Wimbledon, missing a 6 inch putt at the Augusta Masters, surviving a quintuple by-pass and dancing with Jennifer López!"

Helen laughed with that special and endearing crescendo and, with a mischievous look in her eyes; asked the question she had been preparing for a while. She felt sure that Kathryn had the same question in mind: "Ely, have you made love to a human?"

The question remained in the air as if it had crystallized. There was no motion from either Kathryn, nor from Ely. This last had been looking at Helen and his posture and gaze remained still. For a few seconds, not necessarily awkward to them, there was silence.

Then Ely, in a light tone, replied, "Yes."

"Is that the answer?" asked Kathryn with a slight tone of disappointment.

"Gentlemen don't tell, you know," retorted Ely with a bigger smile on his face.

"We grant you that, but we are asking because we are curious about your reaction and whatever conclusions you draw from it," insisted Helen.

"OK, OK. I shall be more constructive. Yes I have made love to a number of women on this planet. Gee! It is something we did not expect at all. We knew about your peculiar coupling, like the rest of the fauna on the planet, but were totally unaware that beyond base instinct, other forces come into play. We are still amazed. But let me clue you about my curriculum in this subject."

Kathryn and Helen were by now hanging on Ely's every word.

"First of all, I began to feel a certain attraction for a young saleswoman in Via Veneto in Rome. I tried to figure out what made me, a piece of galactic energy disguised as an earthling, develop this unusual desire to see, be near and talk to this creature. My initial analysis showed a lot of things. Visual perception, impacting a brain circuit that has to do with pleasure centers and also with a couple of survival links, then a touch of male vanity, self assertion, hormonal activity, intellectual curiosity, tendency to apply olfactory capabilities, a subtle form of hunger for her lips, currents of tenderness and also a dash of fury. Not to mention that strange urge to touch any part of her. But above all to keep her image in my retina."

He paused, and a longing look painted his features. "You know, I knew that you kept an arsenal of feelings and intentions within you, but never imagined that the sight of another human could trigger such avalanche of desires and sensations. You people are really complicated!"

"We know," said Helen, terribly curious now to learn more about Ely's experiences. "Please continue."

Ely seemed to blush and then he said, "After my analysis, I decided to let human nature and inclinations take over. I went to the shop several times with one or another pretext. Once I was sure that she acknowledged me and that I detected a slight bit of interest, I went beyond the simple conversations we had been having about silk neckties and alligator belts, and asked her to have dinner with me. Here, another sensation enters the picture. Before asking her

I felt an annoying cold inside me. Not fear but expectation laced with anxiety. When she agreed, the feeling disappeared and another took its place. I felt light-headed and happy; I could even detect sharp stabs of optimism and self-confidence. Really the funniest damn thing I have ever experienced. But wait, that ain't all."

By then Ely was fully into the subject, which he seemed to be enjoying immensely.

"We went to dinner that evening. She told me her name, about her family, school, food preferences and type of books she read. With every revelation of her life, I felt a greater degree of pleasure at being with her."

"How about all the other sensations you mentioned before?"

"Oh! They were still there. Some manifested themselves sharper than others but they all were there. But remember that I tried not to remain in an analytical mood, otherwise some of my own enjoyment would not surface."

"Did she ask about you, and what did you tell her?"

"Yes, she did ask about me and was full of curiosity. She tried to identify my accent and to guess my national origin. She though that I had a trace of Milanese accent and that I looked Latin but with many Anglo-Saxon and American mannerisms. I told her that I was visiting from New York and that my looks reflected my mixed racial background. You see, I didn't lie and, fortunately, she did not insist on additional details."

"Then what happened?"

"Well, it was a great meal. Italian food remains a great experience. Specially those carcioffi all'olio, the gnocchi a la Romana with Pesto and fresh truffles, la Sogliola al Cartoccio, the bottles of Gattinara and Verdicchio. Then, il gelato and that fabulous café espresso. Mamma mía! I could stay with that menu for years!"

"Hey! Don't get carried away," interrupted Helen in a good humored voice. "We want to hear the rest of the story. Also if you keep talking about Italian food we will be asking for pizzas in a minute."

"Patience, lady, patience," offered Ely as he poured himself some Carlos Primero.

"I found that you people get as much pleasure from telling stories as you do from living them. And anything that has to do with romantic, sensual or erotic happenings adds to their enjoyment. It is an interesting trait, that strangely relates to the very early civilizations on this planet. Storytelling was in a way some form of group therapy and at the same time a convenient way to transmit information to new generations. But the seed is still within that jelly computer in your pretty heads. An amazing interlocking of impulses representing almost any possible sensation or reaction interact when things happen."

He drank some more of the amber liquid, and continued, After dinner we walked around Via Veneto and after listening to a jazz singer in the Cafe de Paris, she suggested we walk up to Galleria Borghese on the northern corner of the park. We walked around the great palazzo and sat down on a bench in the park in back where a dozen statues of emperors, princes and thinkers kept looking in the distance with those eyes devoid of pupils. We talked with great zest. I was wondering about my comments and stories, while she very naturally described recent events at the shop and a trip she had recently made to the Costa Brava in Spain. At one point, she held my hand to emphasize a point and I took advantage of that to kiss her hand. That changed everything. She looked at me in the eyes and said some words to the effect that I was a very nice man and that I exhibited a touch of mystery. She said these words as she moved her head closer to mine so that when she finished the sentence, her face was only inches away. Then we kissed. Well, she kissed me."

"We guess you had never been kissed up to that point," commented Kathryn half seriously.

"Nope, first time. And it was great. It seemed to turn on all the switches and activate all the circuits. It was such a sweet gesture. In no time at all I had learned to kiss a woman on the lips. Kisses that ranged from the gentle brushing of corners to the more compromising approaches with open lips that reveal surrender, or something."

"Now you are being cooperative!" exclaimed Helen. "What happened then?"

"Nothing unusual, I walked her home and we kissed again as we entered the 'portone,' of her apartment building. We agreed to have dinner the following night and planned to spend the week end visiting the Roman sights."

"So?"

"We met again the following night. This time she took me to a restaurant on the Coline overlooking the city. It was another marvelous experience. The food was excellent. The company fascinating and the view from that terrace could only compare to a gift from the heavens. I think."

The ladies laughed and by their looks suggested that he continue. "We went back to Via Veneto and had another coffee at Mario's, all the while talking about many things and laughing at her observations. She had a great sense of humor and was quick to make witty remarks. I told her that I had never met a woman as attractive and witty as she and that I enjoyed being near her. I kissed her gently on the ear and held her hand in mine. She looked at me and asked me if I wanted to accompany her to her home and maybe have a drink there. I was immediately overcome with a form of excitement that I could not control. We left the colorful café and walked to Piazza Barberini in the direction of her place."

"This is getting to be like a Danielle Steel novel," said Kathryn to Helen.

"I hope it ends well, like all her novels," added Helen. Ely laughed and continued. "Hers was a small apartment on the first floor. It consisted of a large dining-living room with a small kitchen at one end and a bedroom, a utility room and a bathroom on the other."

"How old was this woman?" asked Kathryn.

"She told me she was 28 and I think she was telling the truth. I did not check. Besides, it did not matter a great deal. Well, we had a drink and then she gently led me into the bedroom. She kissed me again but this time standing up so that both our bodies pressed against the other. Her hands were very agile and knowing. I can tell you that in trying to keep track of my sensations and paying attention to what was going on with her hands and her body, I was an excited piece of energy! The funny thing is that it was all pure pleasure. Even the ordinary action of removing my shirt or her blouse, represented a rainbow of sensory experiences. It was just great! Then..."

"I guess we have seen—or heard—enough," said Kathryn. "We can imagine the rest, Ely."

"I suppose you could. I was just trying to give you as detailed a description as I know. She was a most lovable and lively partner. I must tell you however that the end result was incredible. I understood at that moment a great deal about the human race. Here is a powerful drive within each one of you, quite difficult to define as it creates changes within you and at the same time it is changed by circumstances. I see it as a threat, a need, a reward, a solution and often a curse. But I don't want to get philosophical. Whatever it is, dear ladies, it is a great exercise!"

"How about your other affairs?"

Ely smiled and slowly shook his head.

"Like I said, gentlemen don't tell. There have been some and all of them most pleasant. You know how it works!"

Learning About the Past

Soon, the conversation turned to the ability of the visitors to travel in time and the possibility to be able to witness events of the past. They seemed to be able to conjure them at will.

"It is a necessary tool for the task at hand," explained Eldon. "You see, proper measures can only be adopted if we are in possession of as many facts as possible. This is a unanimous opinion among us, so we try to be as exhaustive as we possibly can. One of the best ways to get at the truth is simply to be there if it is a matter of precedent or to examine all judgments at once if it is a matter of criteria."

"We understand that you have gone back to the very beginning not only of life on earth but to the origin of the solar system," said Kathryn, with a touch of awe in her voice.

Helen looked at Eldon with curiosity and asked, "Is there anything or anyone in your time travels among our kind that you would consider as unique or outstanding?"

Eldon thought for a moment and then with a sad smile answered, "Not one but many. Perhaps the greatest impression upon me has been that of a man that by himself and from a tender age, was able to instill in a good part of the people living in those days a special conception of the uniqueness of the human race. Just as admirable was the way he gathered around himself a group of disciples that understood and interpreted his thoughts and feelings. They also were unique in that they possessed the ability and perseverance to spread this conception and the messages it contained, all over the world. I am of course talking about Jesus of Nazareth…"

Both Kathryn and Helen did not seem surprised. They more or less expected such reply because in their hearts they had always felt a special love for the tragic figure of a man who against all odds, had remained true to his beliefs and whose word was nothing but a plea for love and reason.

"Did you by any chance see him, or talk to him?"

"Yes," replied Eldon. "It was a real experience. I ought to write a book about it," he concluded as he smiled, reflecting upon the unique and pleasant memories of his encounters with Jesus.

"Tell us about it," urged Helen, whose curiosity had been aroused beyond anything she had ever felt.

"You probably know more about Jesus than I do. Keep in mind that I have only witnessed a few fleeting moments in his lifetime. Since then I have thought about Jesus a great deal. I think that anyone who met him could not erase his memory easily…"

"Were you able to see and experience the environment of the time?" asked Kathryn, to which Helen added immediately in a pleading voice, "Please, describe these encounters to us and don't miss a single detail. We want to know about the air you breathed, the people's attitude, did they appear happy? How about the children? The food?"

Eldon smiled and nodded. He said, "I don't want to sound like a college professor, not that there is anything wrong with that, but I don't wish to get lost in the myriad things that come to mind. To begin with, I was impressed by Jerusalem and the historic aroma it possessed at the time and still possesses today. It is almost an overpowering sensation. Almost every wall, brick or roadway suggests a long past, then, as it does now. Then the people. Almost everyone you meet in the Old City is a study in itself. Somehow you think at once of some of the more used clichés your writers use. You know, things like 'eyes that reflected a complex or tortured soul, a smile that embodied the sadness of centuries' and the ever popular 'his wrinkled face exposed unusual serenity' and 'something was etched in the million wrinkles of his race.'"

They all laughed. Helen commented, "I know what you mean. The first time I visited Jerusalem, I ran out of film in the first couple of days and batteries for my digital cameras. I never tired of taking pictures of people. They were such unique studies of expression, mystery and beauty. After posing for me, I asked a venerable man with a long, white beard and the aristocratic demeanor of a noble man, what he did for a living. I almost dropped the camera when he replied that he was a computer programmer."

Eldon continued. "You are right; it has always been a city of contrasts. Then as now I observed a never ending stream of visitors of varied nationalities and creeds that emphasized the universal nature of the city. Jews, Christians, Muslims intermingle peacefully. The weight of its history is evident. Remember that Jerusalem was at one time conquered by Egyptians, Assyrians, Pharaohs, Babylonians, Romans, Persians, Greeks, Mamluks, Ayyubids, Crusaders and Ottomans. Not to mention the original hundreds of tribes that fought each other for centuries…"

"You seem to have absorbed the city's history," observed Kathryn. "Jerusalem is probably one of the many places in antiquity that have seen more tears and bloodshed than one thousand years of bullfighting!"

He paused while he seemed to concentrate. He continued. "Since Heterodotus first termed the area that extends between the Mediterranean and the Syrian desert, from Mount Hermon to the Dead Sea, or from 'Dan to Beersheba' as Palestine, there have been incessant fights among the peoples that have inhabited it. Check this: since the beginning of the Bronze Age or around 3,000 years before Christ, the various nations of Semitic speech, known as Semites, occupied the place, but not peacefully. They battled each other constantly. There wasn't a single 3 year period without a war of some sort. But other than fighting each other, they had invaders, greedy traders, corpulent farmers and sly merchants all fighting for the area."

He was interrupted by Helen who asked, "I vaguely remember that the main reason for all the fighting was to control commercial routes in the area along the Jordan, and not necessarily religious differences."

"True. The quick look I took showed me that at the beginning, all these people fought for a right of way, more than anything else. Later, there were so many others besides the Amorites, the Hebrews, the Arameans and the Arabs that I have trouble remembering who they were. You have no idea. Every few years or so a new tribe or group would suddenly appear over the undulating dunes, as they say, and start another war. Guerrilla warfare was the order of the day. There were Horites, then Hurrians, Hittites, the Philistines and once in a while some Sudanese or Upper Nile gang would join in. After a while, religious beliefs appeared and added to the tenseness of relations among people."

He paused again as if to reorder his thoughts and spreading his palms said, "But what happened to Palestine is not an isolated example. When I looked at the Roman Empire I almost lost my cookies. For several centuries, the history of the Roman Empire discloses some disturbing facts. I am not an Anthropologist or a Social Scientist and even less a moral authority, so my conclusions are strictly based on superficial observations of that civilization. One is that political power in any human society exercises one of the strongest attractions to the individual or to the group."

He stopped as if to make sure that his observation had been understood. Helen took advantage of the pause to say, "That old saying about how power corrupts and absolute power etc., etc. is so true! We begin to see it in kindergarten and it never ceases to influence people."

Eldon smiled, and continued. "The Roman dynasties and ruling classes engaged for centuries in an orgy of assassinations, poisonings and murder in a scale seldom found in the history of other civilizations. And it was all done in the quest for power. Second, it seems that material progress, establishment of social customs and civil rule, plus development of arts and sciences takes place at a quicker pace under these conditions. Thirdly, I would venture to say that all this takes place as long as there are subservient masses of people who provide the labor and the sacrifice."

Helen observed, "Yes, we know that the Roman Empire, and before it the Republic, was run on constant intrigue, murder and deceit. But what we learn in school, unless you specialize in Ancient History, does not really go into any kind of detail about it..."

Eldon nodded and replied, "It is an incredible history. True enough, there was enough intrigue to keep one thousand scriptwriters turning out scripts for as many years."

"Please, tell us about it."

"OK. Let me go over an interesting period of the Roman Empire. It is really a fascinating piece of history. It combines just about everything individual human beings and human societies are capable of achieving and, at the same time, demonstrate their unique capacity to destroy not only themselves but others as well. Somehow, the balance between what was good and what was evil has never been fully understood in the history of the civilizations that have given this planet its present substance. To me it is still incomprehensible how a superb social complex such as the Roman Empire was able to achieve greatness in practically all of its endeavors and yet allow its ruling classes to engage constantly in intrigue, murder and all kinds of evil acts. Who knows! is evil a desirable ingredient in the minds of those responsible for the welfare of many?"

Kathryn leaned forward and said with some vehemence, "Even today, morality and ethics as guiding components of what is good, often fail to recognize, or simply ignore, evil doings. Could it be that evil made its appearance before good was recognized?"

Eldon looked at Kathryn and raised his hands in an inquiring gesture. "Ahh! what came first? The chicken or the egg? Do you have to break the eggs to make the omelet? Must you cut the leg to save the patient?"

He looked at Kathryn and Helen and smiled. Then, "I hope I am not boring you."

They both replied at once, "Not at all, bore ahead!"

"Right! For almost a thousand years, Rome was the dominating force in what we know as Europe and the Middle East. Its influence reached everywhere and affected almost everything. Style was set in Rome, educational guidelines were prepared in Rome, and health care systems were developed in Rome, same as standards for building, transports, roads, food and beverages. But it took oceans of blood and numberless wars to create the Empire. And also great doses of intrigue, treachery, deceit and plain old cussedness, as Mark Twain would say."

Smiling, Helen interrupted. "Fine, let's get down to cases."

"Look, in the space of 70 short years, there were so many tragedies and plots, it is hard to keep them straight. You remember what happened to Julius Caesar. He teamed up with Crassus for the purpose of doing away with Pompey. At the time, Julius Caesar and Crassus were trying to get the Senate to approve either one for the top job. So Julius Caesar is installed and things go well for a while, in a manner of speaking. In this period, Julius Caesar eliminated all opposition through exile, poison cocktails, stabbing in the night and accidental drowning. Enter Marcus Junius Brutus and Gaius Cassius Longinus and a few stabs later on the marble steps of the imposing Senate building, Caesar is done and so is the Republic. But, in comes Mark Anthony and Octavian. They chase Brutus and Cassius until both are forced to commit suicide. Octavian takes over as Imperator Caesar Augustus and for 41 years does a great job."

Kathryn and Helen had listened attentively. It was indeed a period like no other in history. After a few moments, "How about Cleopatra? Where does she fit in?" asked Kathryn.

"Ahhh! Sex enters the equation. Without doubt an extremely clever and calculating woman. What you call a survivor. Since the age of ten, she developed a unique technique to get men's attention. The Egyptian court in those days was a very staid and imposing affair. While there was the usual amount of illicit affairs, adultery and secret trysts, the court frowned upon promiscuity and licentiousness. But our girl was quick to capitalize on the anxious and often lascivious looks she invariably received from the older members of the Court. She conquered them first. She was a beautiful girl with hypnotic eyes, a smile that could open heavens of joy and a body that hinted at untold pleasures. She knew how to parlay her sexuality into uncontrollable desire on the part of men…"

Helen interrupted to ask, "Did you have the chance to see her?"

Before he could answer, Kathryn asked, "What impression did she make on you?"

Eldon flashed a smile full of healthy teeth that did not quite conceal a touch of guilt and replied, "Yes, I was very curious about that period in your history that I felt I had to take a look. Well, the banks of the Nile in those days were something to behold. Practically the whole river was packed with cargo vessels coming and going. The cities were like beehives with traders, merchants, craftsmen, tourists, slave traders, builders, you name it. And of course Cleopatra's name was on everyone's lips. So I showed up in court as a wealthy Tunisian builder. I was invited to meet with her almost at once. It seems she had instructed her vast network of spies, collaborators and servants, to let her know the moment someone rich or important arrived in Egypt."

"Where was the meeting?"

"In one of the palaces she had in Luxor. We met at noon the following day.

I was taken to a chamber totally covered with damask, silk hangings, gold chandeliers, perfumed oil burners and lovely sofas of lacquered black wood. As I examined the silk hangings and the furniture in the room, I had the impression that I was being observed. After a while, she made her entrance, accompanied by two maids and a tall Nubian soldier."

"What was she wearing?"

"I remember every detail. She had a transparent white silk robe with very subtle gold trimming and, it seemed to me, nothing underneath. She was short but her self assurance and radiant beauty made her appear tall. Also, her sandals helped; they had an inch of two of platform soles."

He stopped and blushed slightly but not so that Kathryn and Helen would not notice. He swallowed and continued. "We talked for a while about Tunisia, the problems with the caravan routes and the new sails being tried in the Nile. She was well informed and very charming. To tell you the truth, it was very difficult to concentrate on caravan routes and sail surfaces. The robe, and the way she wore it, was designed to showcase her lovely figure. It had a hypnotic effect, as she made sure that her body motions were somehow amplified and hidden at the same time. It was terribly disturbing!"

"What happened then?" Both women were mesmerized by Eldon's reminiscence.

"She offered me some mint tea and pieces of brayan with honey, while all the while she looked at me the way you appraise a slave you are contemplating buying. You know, the teeth, the shape of the head, the hands and arms, the waist, the loins, feet, etc."

"Eldon, we wouldn't know. We have never bought any slaves!" Helen laughed as she made the observation. Kathryn and Eldon joined her. Then Helen asked, "Don't keep us in suspense! Go on!"

"After we ate, she called one of her maids and whispered something in her ear. I could have learned what she said but decided against it. I wanted to enjoy the moment 'au naturel,' if you know what I mean. She then said to me that she did not have any appointments until sunset and, it being early in the afternoon, she felt that we could refresh ourselves in a bath. Well, I was a little surprised. There I was, a supposedly wealthy builder, but in reality nothing more than an energy conglomerate about to take a bath with Cleopatra, no less!"

"And then?"

"She led me to another chamber in the middle of which there was a beautiful and ornate marble tub flush with the floor. It was full of water and the surface was covered with floating rose petals and water narcissus. An attendant helped me disrobe, while Cleopatra stood in front of me watching every detail of the sequence. I cannot bring myself to say what I saw in her eyes and the way she appraised me. You can imagine it, I am sure."

"Don't be too sure," interjected Helen. "It seems modern women's appraisal of men start with the job description, net income, legitimate assets, IRA, retirement plans, insurance, make of car, location of his home in the city, schools attended, brand of shoes, type of wristwatch, etc. Then a quick look at the physical attributes. Probably the last thing women look at is at the person per se."

"Well, they are missing a lot! But to make a long and lovely story short, let me say that the bath was an incredible experience. I never imagined that two bodies in a tub of water could extract so much pleasure and excitement!"

Kathryn, with a little color on her cheeks, said, "I suppose the next part of the episode deals with the sexual encounter. Unless, there was something unusual, we probably just as well imagine it rather than get you to relive a personal experience. We are curious but not to that extent!"

Eldon laughed out loud. "You are right! But there are a couple of features of the episode that deserve mention. Please forgive me for allowing my description of a very private act to attempt against your sensibility..."

He paused for a moment, in which Helen said, "Listen, Eldon, no one in his or her right mind would miss a first hand account of one of Cleopatra's sexual encounters, as detailed as the account might be. We are talking history! Go ahead and enlighten us!"

Eldon laughed again and proceeded to relate in a tasteful manner the details of Cleopatra's superb technique in the art of love. They all fell silent after he finished, slightly embarrassed but wiser. Eldon smiled and, shaking his finger at the ladies, said, "See, you make me do an ungentlemanly thing! Now, where were we?"

He reached for a Sprite, deftly uncapped it and drank it all in one thirsty gulp. He continued. "By the time the Roman Generals appeared in Egypt, Cleopatra had developed such a mystique about herself that a few minutes were all she needed to have the most indifferent Roman at her feet. I would show you a holo picture of Cleopatra in action but I fear it would be too risqué."

"No need to do that," said Helen with a smile. We saw what Elizabeth did to Richard. Please go on."

"She ruled for a while with her brother Ptolemy XIII and then they quarreled and fought a war. Then a Roman General shows up. Pompey the

Great was his name. He was assassinated by Ptolomey. At that moment, the Big Boss, Julius Caesar invaded Egypt and fell for Cleopatra, head over heels plus helmet, tunic and sandals. Meanwhile, back at the back of the Nile, her brother Ptolomey drowned somewhat mysteriously. As Caesar's mistress she wielded much power and began to think seriously in terms of ruling the entire Roman Empire, but they stabbed the old man and she returned to Egypt."

"Talk about murder and intrigue! The only thing missing is Inspector Clouzot!"

They all laughed at Kathryn's comment. Then Eldon continued. "After a while, Mark Anthony shows up in Egypt and was promptly seduced by Cleopatra. They began to plan for a merger of empires, provinces and protectorates, when Octavian appeared and defeated Mark Anthony at Actium in 31 BC. Old Marc killed himself, while Cleopatra made a try for Octavian, who, wisely stayed away from her. Despondent and aware of her failure, she let an asp (cobra) bit her and put an end to one of the more fascinating chapters of life and love on this planet!"

He paused and then said, "But let us go back to good old Octavian or Augustus. The moment he died more intrigues appeared. After Tiberius, his son, came Caligula, a certified nut. So Claudius I took over. He didn't watch his back, or rather his diet, and his wife Agrippina gave him an arsenic cocktail in order to have her son Nero from a previous marriage, become the Emperor. But Nero turned mean, burned Rome and arsenified his mother Agrippina, his half brother Britannicus and his mentor Sextus Afranius Burrus. To round out the cycle, he kicked his second wife Poppaea Sabina to death."

"Wasn't Nero the Emperor who started the persecution of the Christians?"

"Yup. After he burned Rome in 64 he blamed the Christians. You will recall that Saint Peter and Saint Paul were his victims. After all this carnage, he committed suicide in 68 AD."

"Is it true that he fiddled while Rome burned?"

"Naw. That is a tale invented by the violin lobbies. Old Nero was stoned and drunk when Rome began to burn. Remember that about one million people lived in Rome in appalling circumstances. No running water, no heating, irregular food supplies, high unemployment, and so on. The houses were 2 or 3 stories high and many had rotten beams, straw roofs and poor structures. Fire just happened a day when the wind was blowing and most of the city went up in flames."

"How about the great things the Romans did?"

"They were so many that it'd take a while to catalogue the more important.

Their civilization is the foundation of today's Western Civilization. They were military geniuses, well disciplined, brave and possessed great initiative in the battlefield. They developed the logistics of military support in battle and after. They produced military leaders of the caliber of Napoleon, Wellington, Eisenhower, Colin Powell and many others. They were not only outstanding strategists and warriors but were well versed in policy-making of entire nations."

"But what was their motivation?" asked Helen.

"Let us say that at the bottom, they were all driven by a desire for stability in which to practice their crafts, trades and the art of politics. Logically, they had to conquer as many territories as possible in order to be able to reach that stability in the surrounding areas and above all, avoid more wars. They recognized that losing a battle meant having to fight another a later day. But winning a battle meant doing a lot for the conquered peoples. They raised the standard of living of all conquered territories by introducing agricultural techniques, arts, education, transportation, manufacturing, etc. In this they depended on a well organized bureaucracy and the support of an enterprising middle class. It was not long after a war that colonies were established and the conquered nation began to benefit from the technical superiority of the Romans."

"How about their guidelines?" Insisted Helen.

"They were crafty, diplomatic and decisive. And they were also driven by a desire to do good for the conquered people and for their Emperor. It was the Romans who set down the basis for Jurisprudence and Civil Law. Their law, seen from my Harvard Law School prism, was an exercise in accuracy of thought, weighed argumentation and strong logical premises. More important, they created a political system that attempted to reflect the voice of the people. In all this they were influenced by Greek culture and traditions. While the Greeks devoted much effort to developing philosophical theories about the human being, the society he lived in and the means and forms in which society can best be governed and administered, the Romans had a more pragmatic approach to the realities of their time. They emphasized the strength of legal proceedings and were able to profit from the power that emanated from their conquests, their organization, their commercial ability and their superior intellect."

Helen interrupted. "I guess it is an accepted fact that emerging civilizations are tempered by excesses and that in some instances these excesses contain positive elements. In the case of the Roman Empire, for instance, if they had not expanded their empire and in the process created higher levels of social justice, intellectual expression and culture, the entire Mediterranean culture and Western Civilization would have had to wait a few centuries to exist."

Eldon nodded. He smiled and said, "What I am getting at, is that there has not been one, repeat O-N-E social group on this planet that has developed in a peaceful climate. We have been trying to get at the essence of mankind and we find that, cynically, the human species that has evolved on this planet serves only the purpose of doing away with the other members of its own species."

Kathryn and Helen were silent. In a mellower tone, Eldon continued. "Please try to look at your history and your present day society from an objective point of view. As if you had just landed here just like we have. What is the first thing that you notice? I don't care where you land. The people that you find send a very clear message about themselves, first. It is fine with me. But then, underneath that message, you begin to uncover feelings and attitudes that involve others. And in nine out of ten cases, those are negative feelings."

"Give us an example."

"All right, you asked for it. Let us look at Grand Central Station at 8 a.m. There are people rushing to work. We just do a random selection. Let me read you some scripts that come straight from their minds. This is what they are thinking at exactly that time. No editing."

At that moment a large screen appeared on the wall behind Eldon. It showed people in constant motion inside Grand Central. Then, Eldon proceeded to enumerate at a rapid pace, a long list of thoughts from some of the commuters, as he pointed at them. "Hell, I hope that s.o.b., Donaldson, breaks a leg today and doesn't show up! I need the afternoon free to meet up with Daisy."

"Gee, it's good to get to the office. One more minute listening to that old bag in Greenwich and I would have choked her!"

"I gotta switch some more accounts from Mrs. Lindmast's portfolio. I need to do some transfers and replenish my own account. The old bag does not need so much money anyway!"

"I have to raise their prices today. Those buyers, goddamn fags from San Francisco, are nothing but monkeys dressed in Armani suits. Fuck them!"

"Got to move fast today and unload all those Bruckert shares, after what we learned yesterday. Not exactly kosher, but better grab it when it flits by!"

"How am I going to explain to Bee that my wife is pregnant again. I'll have to change the story about sleeping in separate rooms and not having screwed in years!"

"What am I gonna do with a six month pregnant secretary? And she is the daughter of our minister in Rye. Elsie will not only kill me but I will lose my partnership in her old man's law firm! Hell! I am going to need a bunch of lawyers!"

Eldon looked at the girls and with a sad smile said, "Got enough?"

They did. In one short moment, Eldon had demonstrated the shallowness and evil of modern day man, or woman. Eldon continued. "If it is not a racial difference, it is a matter of superficial values. If it is an economically advanced country, you perceive waves of selfishness that are almost visible. The man in the expensive car and clothes is wrapped in himself, his immediate aims, his personal gratification and his only exterior gesture toward others is to flaunt his well being in search for admiration, adoration and envy so that he can easily trigger his mechanism to despise others." He paused for a moment as if to collect his thoughts and continued. "As you move from one social enclave to another you perceive defensiveness, animosity, greed, envy, in practically the majority of the people. Where are the virtues that a generous God instilled in the beings in his pet project? How about love, compassion, good will, respect, sharing, attention and all the other elements of what I would term being a good egg?"

Helen could not contain herself. She raised her head and, laughing, said, "Eldon, don't forget you landed in New York! It is not the best showcase!"

"Don't worry. I've tried other cities, rural villages, and even a couple of monasteries in unreachable places. Somehow, the vibes are more or less the same. That's why it seems a waste to have had someone like Abraham, Moses, Jesus of Nazareth, the Prophet Muhammad and a few others who tried to instill some measure of love and respect among humans. Because, my dear ladies, the situation since planet earth went on its own, has not changed a bit!"

Amazing Invitation

Kathryn and Helen remained silent as they absorbed Eldon's words. It was a harsh dictate and indeed colored by Eldon's cynicism, but nevertheless true, as they each acknowledged on their own. Who could deny that the modern world did not suffer from the same ills of ancient cultures? Things had taken a different form and content but the principles remained the same. Finally, Helen said, "You are right, of course, but you neglect to include in your evaluation all the elements of good will, compassion and civility that accompany the development of all modern societies. Somehow, this topic reminds me of a book written some time ago about Jesus' return to earth and his reactions to what he found. It was written in Spanish and was called 'Y

Jesus Regresó.' It would make interesting reading. In it, Jesus finds tremendous disappointments but also some measure of hope for the human race."

"You know," interjected Kathryn with a serious look that also denoted a bit of anxiety, "we have so many theories and legends about Jesus Christ that, sometimes, it is hard to distinguish fact from fiction. Maybe you can help us get a real perception of the man and his times?"

Eldon smiled and nodded agreeably. It was obvious that he was genuinely interested in the subject and that he would enjoy a serious discussion about Jesus.

"Of course, Jesus Christ is probably the most important figure in the history of this planet. And, yes, there have been many versions about him. You see, his coming was announced in the Old Testament and, of course, Matthew, Luke, John and Mark talk about him in the New Testament. I can assure you that he did exist. Maybe he was not born on December 25 of that first year but exactly 5 years before."

Helen raised her hand as if asking for permission to say something and, seeing Emosh nod of agreement, said, "That is specially intriguing, since there are almost no records that can shed some light on the subject. I guess you know that a key reference is the Star of Bethlehem."

"Well, let me pass on to you what I know about this. The astronomer and theologian Dionisyius Exiguus originated the Christian calendar in 525., but you see, old Dionysius did not take into account year 0, a bit like your computers and YK2. As a matter of fact, year 0 was not recognized until the ninth century. He also goofed when he missed the four years when Roman Emperor Augustus reigned under the name of Octavius. All this plus the fact that Jesus was at least two years old when Herod ordered the murder of children under that age, and that Herod died immediately after a lunar eclipse in 4BC. So, we can pinpoint Jesus birth date during the fifth year BC. I checked on the eclipse, and it fits."

Kathryn and Helen listened with a mixture of amazement and curiosity. The revelations made by Eldon were indeed astounding. In a sense, they both felt that they had uncovered a fountain of truths about civilization but realized that facing the truth is not always a pleasant experience. Particularly in a society that used the truth in many strange ways, not always commendable. Their curiosity however overrode their reticence. Curiosity is not only a sign of intelligence but also a clear form of self gratification. Kathryn spoke. "There are some astronomical facts that are still nebulous, never better said, about the bright star of Bethlehem, that is supposed to have appeared on Jesus birth date, and had guided the three Magi from Persia."

"Well, yes. Between the year 7 BC and 5 BC there were three major astronomical phenomena. First, there was a Nova in the Capricorn constellation that became quite visible for a time on earth in 5BC. Before then, Jupiter and Saturn in the constellation of Piscis, went through a triple conjunction and as such became so bright that, from earth, they appeared as a single star. This phenomenon is really unusual since it happens about once in four thousand years. The next year another bright star. This time it was Mars, Jupiter and Saturn around Piscis, in another conjunction that happens every eight hundred years. So you see it did happen. If you add to all this the fact that Hebrew mythology associated these stars with Moses and enabled them to interpret their appearance as messages, you have your answer. The Magi considered the Nova the definitive signal. They didn't miss."

"How about Jesus' early life?" Helen, with typical writer-producer mentality, was anxious to order the information that Eldon was dispensing.

"From almost his Day One, Jesus was under the influence of an intellectual elite in Nazareth, where he was born. Even his baptism was an event. John The Baptist officiated and gave the new born the name of Jeshua ben Joseph. In a few short years, those around him realized what an extraordinary human being he was."

"Was he extremely gifted? A precocious child? A genius?" asked Helen

"A bit of everything. Above all, he was very natural. There was no affectation of any sort or any visible desire to impress or show off."

"Then how did he acquire his knowledge at such early age?"

"He possessed boundless curiosity, a prodigious memory and a capacity to interpret and judge concepts and events. He was also a great listener. And he was surrounded by the intellectual elite of the most important social and cultural center of the world."

He paused and closed his eyes in what appeared to be an attempt to visualize Jesus in his early years. He continued. "But Jesus was not an encyclopedia, nor a glib master of platitudes. He was a communicator of selected concepts, expressed in such direct manner, without being offensive, that he immediately captured the attention of his audience." Then, "He was able to talk on an equal basis with the teachers, prophets and priests about science, politics and especially religion. The clarity of his ideas and his command of Aramaic and other dialects caused a distinct impression on all those who met him. Soon, his learned discussions overshadowed the attempts of others to discourse and he gradually found himself in the position of lecturing others at their own request."

Eldon was obviously enjoying his subject. "Keep in mind that he lived in Nazareth, which at the time was a Roman garrison and there was great tension between the locals and the conquerors. However, the period was exciting in that there was also a great deal of intellectual unrest, which created a receptive atmosphere to new events, ideas and the appearance of new leaders."

"How did the name Jesus Christ come about? There are several theories, not always from highly reliable sources," interrupted Helen.

"The name Christ was added in his teenage days. By then, his followers were convinced that he was the Messiah of Israel or the chosen by God to save his people. Christ is Greek for the Hebrew Messiah, which also means 'anointed one.' The Roman historians of the time, like Tacitus, Suetonius, Pliny the Younger and others, made reference to a rebellious teacher with revolutionary ideas and a great deal of compassion that was capable of assembling a large following at a moment's notice."

The two women had listened with great fascination. Their curiosity was boundless. As Catholics, they were modern day followers and admirers of Jesus. Kathryn wondered aloud about the nature and source of Jesus' youthful drive that turned him into a revered master. Eldon smiled and was about to say something when he stopped, raised his head and sneezed with some force.

"I beg your pardon, ladies. This barn gets drafty at times and I may be catching a cold. Heck of a way to lose some of my precious energy!"

They laughed heartily. Kathryn and Helen enjoyed Eldon's special humor and the elegant manner in which he acquiesced to their smallest wish. He continued. "See, Jesus was not a salesman, nor a genius. In other words he was no Bill Gates, nor a pitchman like Ed, Dick, Lee, Al, Fidel or Bob. He spoke from the heart and what he said made sense. He added a philosophical insight and a unique content to his teachings. You heard him and you felt that whatever your situation, things would get better all around. He planted the seed of Faith and Hope in all. Believe me, you felt what he said. I can tell you that we haven't found anyone remotely like him in all the centuries this planet has been going around the furnace."

Kathryn asked, "I know it would be difficult to highlight a specific trait, but could you give us your own impression of Jesus and what you consider his charisma?"

Eldon smiled and replied, "Jesus, to me, was a presence full of content. He could be a block away from you and totally removed from your field of vision but somehow you felt his presence. And it made you feel good. Like you feel when you have had a good night sleep and for a while enjoy a sensation of well being, enthusiasm about yourself and optimism about everything. That was the first impression. But when you heard his voice, things around you lost their focus and you sort of became part of him and you were drawn, irresistibly, to share his feelings and pledged yourself to his ideas and his words. The message was pure wisdom, reality and compassion. It was not a matter of a pleasant voice, a studied delivery or a hypnotic tone. His voice was like the music of a symphony orchestra. It included myriad notes and nuances and, somehow, went straight to the hearts and souls of those around him.

An Invitation to the Last Supper

Eldon stopped and thought for a moment. He then smiled broadly and said, "How would you like to be present at the Last Supper?"

Both Kathryn and Helen remained motionless for a moment. They could not believe their ears. They both knew about the capacity of the visitors to materialize any period, or person or object from any time in the past. They had heard from Patrick the glowing and detailed descriptions of previous "trips" made by the visitors, and while those voyages remained an object of awe and admiration, the offer to be present at the Last Supper was well beyond their capacity to be amazed.

They were silent for a moment and could only nod their heads in agreement.

All of a sudden, a large hall materialized in one side of the area where Eldon, Ely, Kathryn and Helen were. It was as if one side of the walls of the room had suddenly expanded but in such smooth and subtle manner that its appearance did not cause any surprise. It was sudden but at the same time it sort of fell into place as if in slow motion.

The room, obviously a large dining room, measured around forty feet by thirty feet and had two large windows and two opposite doors. One side opened into a terrace and the garden beyond. The smell of lemon, orange and jasmine quickly assaulted their senses. They knew they were there!

"Let us take a look," said Eldon. "It will be at least two hours before anyone shows up."

"What time is it supposed to be and whose house is this?" asked Kathryn in a voice that revealed some nervousness.

"The house belongs to Joseph of Arimathea and it is half past one in the afternoon. You know, supper in those days was between five and seven.

Joseph of Arimathea was a close follower and friend of Jesus. He was the one who convinced the Roman authorities to let him recover Jesus body from the Calvary in order to bury him."

"I seem to recall that he was a wealthy merchant and some manner of sponsor of Jesus," added Helen.

They stood in the middle of the room absorbing all the details. Kathryn and Helen were impressed by the orderly arrangement of furniture and chairs, and the cleanliness of the room. Almost immediately, they had sensed the unique flavor of the room, which in their minds blended the aromas of Jerusalem and the powerful projection of its historical value.

Kathryn interrupted to ask, "You know, there has been a long controversy about the exact date of the Last Supper. Even the Bible is not clear on this as the accounts from some of the Apostles differ from each other."

Eldon replied, "It is a rather involved story and I am not surprised that there may be different versions. Let us not forget that the days after the last Supper were terribly painful for Jesus' family and his followers. You see, Jesus came to Jerusalem for the Passover. However, he had the premonition that on Passover he would die, so he decided to offer a banquet to his disciples the day before. He arranged with Joseph of Arimathea to hold the banquet at his house on the afternoon of the 14th. The date is further confirmed by an old Jewish custom that took place the day before Passover."

"What custom is that?" asked Helen.

"An old tradition; you see, Passover could only be celebrated if the place where the meeting took place was completely deleavened. In other words, the occupants of the house had to seek and remove all traces of the substances they used as yeast, which could be something like baking soda or some fermented dough. They did this the day before the Passover day which was Nisan 15th. I think that this had already been done in this house. So you see, we are on the 14th and it is Jesus' last day."

At that moment a tall man with a neatly trimmed dark beard and wearing the flowing off-white robes of the successful merchants of Jerusalem, appeared at the door and with a questioning look asked in Aramaic, "Are you looking for someone? You are obviously strangers. Kindly identify yourselves."

Eldon answered in Aramaic, "We are visitors from a northern province. We understand that Rabbi Jesus is coming to supper this evening and we would like to see him. We know he will be busy with his disciples and we do not plan to interfere in any way. And please do not worry about us. We are not Roman spies or members of any of the groups that oppose the man from Nazareth."

In a low voice he translated for the benefit of Kathryn and Helen. The man had listened attentively and now said, "Thank you for telling me. I am Joseph of Arimathea and this is my house. You are invited to spend as much time as you want in this property. I am also anxious about tonight's supper. There is a bit of tension not only at the temple but also at the Prefect's Palace, so I hope Jesus of Nazareth can bring some relief."

As he said these words, he kept looking at the attire of the three visitors. With a puzzled look, he inquired, "Please tell me why you are dressed so strangely. You know, women are not supposed to show their bare legs and their hair must always be covered. Also you wear sandals that are not only funny but also look uncomfortable. And you," as he turned to Ely, "you are wearing Turkish pantaloons and no robes."

Ely answered the best he could, insisting that theirs were traveling clothes and that they were looking for appropriate robes. To which, Joseph of Arimathea suggested that they come into the house and select some robes.

"I am a merchant, you know. There are always plenty of robes and sandals in my house." He turned to the women and said with a mocking smile on his lips, "And you, my ladies, if you want to really enjoy our city and its people you must learn our language!"

Ely translated and, at once Helen shot out a reply, "Tell him that the moment we get the robes we'll be ready to start learning the language!"

Ely again translated to Joseph, who laughed out loud and motioned them to follow him.

They went into the house while all the time Joseph kept up a non stop commentary in a pleasant voice and cheerful tone. He led them to a large storage room where a variety of items were orderly placed in shelves. There were rugs, vases, copper and bronze instruments, robes, sandals, saddles, crystal sets, bolts of cloth and innumerable small bottles containing essences and perfumes. In the back, robes of many kinds were neatly hanged. He pointed at them and said, "Be my guest," which needed no translation. After each had selected a robe that they put on top of their casual clothes and tried it on, Joseph was quick to compliment the women while apprising both of them with a look they all knew. They thanked him profusely and Helen, on an impulse, kissed him on the cheek.

For a moment, Joseph was at a loss for words. He flushed a deep pink and with a sheepish smile thanked Helen. Claiming that he had matters to attend and again expressing his wish that they enjoy their stay, he left.

Kathryn had chosen a silken robe with embroidered edges that once wrapped tightly around her body, revealed her attractive figure. Helen on the other hand had selected a light cashmere robe that she had artfully placed around her shoulders and allowed it to flow down around her pretty figure. They selected a couple of lovely shawls to cover their heads and carved ivory pins. They both looked stunning, causing Eldon to observe, "Ladies! You look great. Just make sure that a Roman General does not see you or you'll have a platoon of his flautists, lyrists and drum musicians serenading you for days!"

They went back to the main house and feeling less noticeable by the servants and other people of the household, went to the main lounge. They stepped into the room and observed with more than casual interest every feature of it. Strong brick columns supported a simple ceiling structure of wooden beams. The floor was covered with Egyptian red tile that was quite popular in that period. The walls were rough stucco and the roof was a combination of wooden planks, large shingles and gesso tiles, all of it cleverly enmeshed and supported by the large wooden beams. The windows faced each other. One faced north and the other south. On one side there was a wide staircase of brick and tile that led to what seemed from the floor below a large room. The view from the windows was colorful and relaxed. They both showed the different angles of a lovely garden where olive trees and a few orange and lemon plants in ceramic pots were carefully located in a simple design that bordered a narrow walk. Some twenty meters from the house, a narrow creek provided the soothing sound of a gentle stream.

"You know," observed Helen, "somehow the vision most of us have of the Last Supper is that depicted by Leonardo's great fresco in Santa Maria delle Grazie in Milan. The long table with the white table cloth, the large windows in back, the ornate ceiling."

"Well, Leonardo's conception was not too far off, as you can see. Of course he painted The Last Supper using references of his time like the Savonarola-type chairs, the tableware, the Florentine ceiling and a few other items. It is a shame that that magnificent fresco cannot be restored nor kept from deteriorating any further. You see, Leonardo experimented with a new fresco technique that wasn't very fresco, and it failed."

"How was that?" asked Kathryn.

"Normally you apply water based paints to wet plaster so that the colors blend with the base material when they dry. Since the Last Supper covered a large area, he could not keep large areas wet. By the time he got to some parts of the painting, the plaster was dry. What happens is that he had to resort to painting on dry plaster. In time the paint began to come off the dry surface, with only small parts blending with the plaster. That is what gives the painting that faded, incomplete look."

He walked toward the center of the room and stopped to look at the texture of the plaster that covered the walls. He carefully scratched the surface and rubbed the powdery material between his fingers. He turned toward Kathryn and Helen and said, "You see, Leonardo was commissioned to paint a fresco in the dining room of Santa Maria delle Grazie in Milan around 1478. His intention was to paint a scene that would blend with the dining room, sort of make it look as if Jesus Christ was having that last supper right there. So he painted glasses, dishes, embroidered tablecloth and other items of that time, not of the time when the last supper took place. A small matter of misdating objects. A glitch that reminds me of a movie I saw once."

"What movie was that?" asked Kathryn.

"Oh, some period thing about the Roman Empire. In one scene, where Caesar is reviewing his troops, one of the Roman legionnaires holding an infantry lance, is seen wearing a wristwatch! I think the actor's name was John Douglas."

Eldon then suggested that they look at the room upstairs. He explained, "The last supper took place in the room above. Where we are now is sort of a lounge with the kitchens in back. It is also used as a dining area, even though the room upstairs is supposed to be the formal dining room. It is also the place where Joseph of Arimathea conducts some of his business luncheons; sort of the executive dining room."

They ascended the stairs and found themselves in a large room with several windows. The room did not give the impression of luxury of any kind. On the contrary, it looked as if it was an everyday dining area, as there were several wooden tables, a large hearth where the subdued crackling of the logs in the fire provided the only sounds. There were few chairs and benches around the stout wooden tables whose surfaces revealed their function through the well known rings stamped on them from wet cups and jugs. The only decoration in the room were the palm trees in large clay pots, an irregular camel skin rug on the floor around a large table, and several earthenware jars full of water and wine.

On one side of the room there was one table full of dishes containing a variety of delicacies. There were several earthenware plates of simple design containing sauces of different colors, probably oil and vinegar with species, mashed capers, cheese and onions, etc. There were also chestnut paste dishes, dry figs, honey cakes, dried pieces of duck meat, a large platter with the tasty Bethlehem crumbly cheese, several types of goat cheese, some plain some with spices and olives. There was also abundant fig bread, dried fish, and several plates full of oranges, apples, pears, grapes and fresh plums.

They also noticed a number of small reclining sofas or triclinia for the dinner guests. These were comfortable couches with pillows that would allow the guests to eat while reclining. Helen observed, "I thought the custom of reclining while eating was practiced only in Rome."

Ely moved toward one the couches and sat down acquiring the reclining position. He said, "Well, at this time Roman fashions are widely imitated. Don't forget that Judea is under Roman rule. Also, it is a sign of good taste to dine reclining on these sofas, but you can see that also benches and individual chairs are used," and he pointed at the other tables. He put his feet on the end of the sofa and said, "I don't know. Maybe if you had a lot of wine this posture might be more comfortable. I rather eat sitting down."

He smiled and then added, "But not on a plastic chair!"

Kathryn and Helen approached the large table and studied with great attention the objects and the food on it.

"Look at those olives!" exclaimed Helen, pointing to one of the plates that contained large, lush and juicy green olives. The plate was decorated with salvia leaves, slices of red pepper and peppercorns.

Eldon reached for an olive and quickly popped it into his mouth. He pointed at the plate and motioned for them to taste the olives. Kathryn and Helen took each one olive and tried it. Their expressions said everything.

"What on earth do they do to these olives?" Kathryn could not help exclaiming once she had tasted the olive.

Eldon looked at her and popped another olive in his mouth. He said, "It is bad manners to speak with your mouth full, so please forgive me. I shall explain things as I savor these delights! These olives have had their pits removed and then are marinated in vinegar, wine, herbs, spices, including garlic, cilantro and hot peppers. Before they are served they are filled with pepper, anchovies, almonds or pineapple. The end product, as you can appreciate, is worthy of the best New York watering hole, as you say!"

"Listen, what happens when we eat these olives? We are disturbing the past!"

Helen's question did not stop her or Kathryn from eating more olives and tasting some of the pieces of cheese on the table.

Ely smiled and gestured to his guests to sit down at one of the tables next to the large narrow table in one side of the room. Since the room was warm, they removed the outer robes and folded them next to them. They kept the shawls covering their heads. Ely then reached for the clay jars and poured some water into each cup.

"Actually nothing happens. The olives you are eating are of course the real article. The entire process however is under a travel deal too involved to explain…Drink up, dear ladies. This is water from a nearby spring. It is supposed to cure lumbago, gastroenteritis, acne and rheumatism!"

At that moment two women dressed in linen tunics, sandals and a colored shawl entered the room and, noticing the small group at the table, approached them. One of them smiled and said in Aramaic, "You people are early. The Master is still at the temple but should be here before long. Are you the ones from Dimashq?!"

Ely laughed and stood up. He bowed and replied in Aramaic, "We are just taking a break. I was showing Joseph's home to my friends here. We are from another province and love to see as much of Jerusalem as we can. We don't have many chances to visit this part of Judea."

The women looked intently at Kathryn and Helen and seemed fascinated by the clothes they wore under the robes. They paid special attention to the jewelry Kathryn and Helen wore, and particularly to their wrist watches. One of them approached Helen and said, "Can I feel the material of your dress?" referring to Helen's all-wool skirt and her Cashmere Cardigan. Helen looked at Eldon expecting a translation but before she could say anything, she understood what the woman was asking for. She nodded and in a friendly manner extended her arm. The woman felt the material and asked the other to do likewise. They admired Helen's entire outfit and then moved over to inspect Kathryn's clothes. They seemed to be enjoying the experience. One of them said, "You must have gotten these clothes from some of the eastern traders. They bring around material as fine as these. You are not Romans, are you?"

Eldon shook his head and said, "No, we are not Romans. We are from far away places." He changed the subject quickly by asking the women if they were in any way connected with the Passover Eve festivities there.

"Yes, we have to help the servants get everything in order. The Master will be coming soon. You know, the poor man has been terribly busy these days."

"What is happening?" asked Eldon, while also providing a translation to Kathryn and Helen.

"Well, since arriving the Master has been arguing a bit with the priests at the temple. You know, the Sadducee priests are a bit haughty. They think that they are better than the other priests because they are the official link with the Roman Prefect. They are also distrustful of Jesus who has been critical of the way the Sadducee use the temple for their own purposes. Jesus has insisted that the temple is a vehicle to encourage people to worship, and not an end in itself."

She paused and looked at the other woman, as if asking that her comments remain among them.

"You see, there is also trouble with the Romans. They are convinced that Jesus of Nazareth is a revolutionary and is plotting against them." The other woman added, "The Romans are very suspicious but in this case they are wrong. Jesus of Nazareth plots against no one and all he does is help people and teaches us the way to be good persons and to worship God."

Kathryn and Helen listened with fascination to Eldon's translation into English. They realized that they were living a moment in Christianity that has been etched in traditions, dogmas and entire rivers of belief and faith. Their faces were flushed and they could hear their hearts racing. And more was to come!

The women took their leave with the traditional words, happy to have seen visitors from far away provinces. Eldon sat down and, smiling, said, "It is time for a little wine. My Aramaic is a little dusty, you know, and these ladies have forced me to exert myself."

He laughed aloud and reached for one of the clay jars on the table and poured a glass for each of them. They tasted the wine much as modern day gourmets savor it in 5 fork restaurants, and nodded approvingly. The anchovies, olives and figs had left in them the subtle urge to wash them down. Then they got up, put on the robes and went to the garden.

They walked around admiring the view of Jerusalem. It was a beautiful afternoon and they felt terribly excited.

As they were returning to the house, Helen said, "Even if I know what is about to happen, I feel like an opera star, or a singer, or the actors on opening night. My blood pressure must have been way out of range in the last few hours. The suspense is killing me!"

"You took the words right out of my mouth!" added Kathryn. She turned toward Eldon and asked, "How about you, our energetic friend?"

Eldon laughed and, pointing at the house, said, "I feel the same way you do. What is about to happen here will be one of the more enlightening episodes in the history of mankind. It is hard to imagine the effect that one evening of wisdom will have on generations to come. I have a knot in my throat just thinking about seeing Him again."

They sat silently for a while near the stream and listened to the gentle sound of the water as it found its way around the pebbles and the weeds. Each one thought and felt, within their own perspectives, the impact and meaning of the event they were about to witness. They also felt a bit out of place. Their clothes and the unfamiliar robes caused them to feel self conscious and awkward. They returned to the house and went up to the cenaculum on the second floor. They found a table in a corner where they would not be in evidence. The long narrow table in the center of the room remained empty. Some of the tables in the room were already occupied by men in different styles of clothes. Eldon explained that the clothes indicated the area where they came from and in some cases their occupation. They all maintained lively conversations which, unlike public places in Jerusalem, were controlled and quiet.

Kathryn and Helen could not believe their eyes. In moments, shortly after five in the afternoon, the dining room began to fill with guests. Both women had pictured in their minds the appearance and physical aspect of those around Jesus. They had been depicted in million paintings and invariably followed the conception of artists in the Middle Ages.

"Helen, I don't know if we can identify the Apostles. All those here don't look at all like the ones in the paintings!"

"Yes, I have noticed."

After a while, some servants came in bringing plates and wine jugs. They went straight to the large table and arranged dishes and cups carefully. Eldon suddenly stood up and motioned the others to do likewise. They approached the window and looked out. A number of people were seen by the stream, some of them washing their hands and their faces. One of them stood out.

Kathryn and Helen were speechless. They immediately understood what Eldon meant when he described his feelings about Jesus. Even at that distance, the presence before them was overpowering. Jesus of Nazareth stood by the stream talking to one of his disciples. Kathryn and Helen could not believe their eyes. For a moment, their senses seemed to fade and the view before them appeared fuzzy and irregular, as if seen through a gauze.

The man they saw possessed a unique aura that combined the smooth strength of his personality and an impression of self assurance without the slightest hint of arrogance. His manner was relaxed and attentive. He was about six feet tall and wore a simple linen robe with a leather belt and a small pouch. One of his hands rested on a walking stick. His face was suntanned and from the distance, his hair appeared light brown in color. The features were decidedly Mediterranean, with a straight nose, a high forehead and a strong chin. The beard and the mustache appeared neatly trimmed and the long hair, parted in the middle, fell to his shoulders. He gave the impression of a fit and healthy man. They could not see the color of his eyes but could not help admiring his delicate hands, which moved in natural gestures every time he spoke.

They were puzzled and anxious to be able to identify those who had followed Jesus Christ and who also had contributed to the enrichment of the Divine Message. The men around Jesus were all in their early thirties. They were of medium height except one or two who were over six feet tall. Two or three were of fair complexion and blond hair, while others were typically Middle eastern types, dark with well trimmed beards. The flowing robes of the paintings were nowhere to be seen, same as the elaborate turbans and hassayahs. They all wore similar clothes. They had a long shirt, tied at the waist with multicolored ropes or leather belts. Some had short trousers that reached to mid calf and wore leather sandals and stripped shirts. The fabrics were varied and colorful. The footwear was very much alike. Leather sandals with knotted tongs or cloth bands.

They turned to Eldon and asked him to help with the identification. Quickly, Eldon pointed to several of the men and pronounced their names, while Kathryn and Helen continued to stare at the group around Jesus. "I shall give you a better identification at the table," added Eldon.

They were terribly anxious to hear his voice. Somehow, they both felt that the voice would not only complement the handsome appearance of Jesus but would add another touch of charm and interest to the man. Ely and Eldon were also mesmerized and after a moment one of them said, "Talk about charisma! He conveys everything that is pleasant, just and true. I only regret that you cannot understand what he says. We'll do the best we can with the translation once he comes in."

After a while, Jesus and his companions turned and moved toward the house where half a dozen servants had set up benches and small earthenware washbasins at the entrance. Jesus grabbed one of the disciples by the elbow and motioned for him to sit down on a bench. As he kneeled, the disciple guessed Jesus intention and protested vigorously. Jesus turned to the others and spoke in quiet and moderate tones. Kathryn and Helen were dying to know what the conversation was all about. Ely came to their aid. "Jesus has just told them that he is going to wash their feet. It is an old custom to have slaves help the guests remove their robes, sandals and walking sticks and wash their hands and feet. They also apply perfume to their hair. You'll see all this in a minute."

Jesus proceeded to wash the feet of all twelve disciples, while others watched in profound reverence and silence. The symbolism of the act became clear to all.

When they finished, Jesus led them all into the house and ascended the stairs on their way to the Cenaculum or dining room on the second floor, while saying things that caused the others to smile and laugh.

The group entered the room and went directly toward the long table with the reclining sofas. As Jesus passed in front of the table where Kathryn and the others were sitting trying to control their nervousness and excitement, Jesus stopped. He smiled and nodded at Ely and Eldon, then turned to Kathryn and Helen. He stood in front of them relaxed and at the same time interested. He looked at them in such a way that both felt faint. The penetrating look from those gray green eyes and the faint smile playing on Jesus lips transmitted with incredible certainty a knowing message, impossible not to understand. Without a word he continued to the long table.

Kathryn and Helen were flushed with excitement and on the verge of tears. They had looked into the eyes of Jesus Christ who had acknowledged their true identity and had also sent a message the two women were still trying to unravel.

As the guests sat down at the table, with Jesus of Nazareth at the center, servants quickly served hot vegetable soup. They poured wine and then water in their cups. The four uninvited guests, Kathryn, Helen, Ely and Emosh sat at their own table a short distance from the main table, paying little attention to the food that they had been served by the ever attentive servants. Their eyes were riveted on the central figure of this historical event.

They watched while Jesus and his 12 disciples ate and talked animatedly among themselves. Kathryn, at one point observed, "Have you noticed the metal cups they are all using? They seem quite ordinary and do not resemble in the least the gold cups with precious stones that we see in the paintings about the Last Supper."

"You are right," added Ely. "The Holy Grail has been depicted in thousand ways. Actually, the cups they are using are made of a simple tin alloy with an engraved design on them."

Helen looked at her own cup that resembled those in Jesus' table. It was nondescript and the simple arabesque etched on it was quite common. "What I don't understand is how his cup became such a symbol."

Emosh raised his own cup and, looking at it, explained, "You see, later this evening, when Jesus talks to his disciples, he will use his cup to make the analogy of the wine and his blood. Remember He made a similar one about the bread they are sharing, and his body. What is known as the Eucharist, or loosely translated Thanksgiving. A symbolic gesture that has survived through the centuries. Well, Joseph of Arimathea, kept Jesus' cup. Somehow, when Jesus was crucified, Joseph of Arimathea who carried the cup in his bag used it to stem the flow of Jesus' blood from the lance thrust of one of the Roman soldiers."

He drank from the cup the mixture of wine and water and then continued. "Keep in mind that many Celtic pagan legends originated around the cup, or Holy Grail. At one time it was sought by King Arthur and described in medieval romances, especially Perceval by Chretien de Troyes in the 12th century. The legend also says that the Holy Grail will only be found by someone who is free of sins."

They remained silent for a while. The idea of the tragic and irreversible events that would take place in a few hours dampened their excitement. But, looking back in the direction of the table, their attention revived. As the dinner progressed, the visitors absorbed every detail and, expectantly, did not keep their eyes away from Jesus. He spoke with a strong voice, well modulated and extremely pleasant to the ear. His humor was evident by the smiles and the laughter that his words elicited.

Jesus now stood up and began to speak in a way that left no doubt about his sincerity and conviction. Eldon and Ely's translations were rapid and accurate and allowed Kathryn and Helen to absorb the meaning of every word as if they heard them in their native languages.

His was not a sermon. It was a very informal talk, punctuated by questions that Jesus asked of those at the table. He avoided the complex conventions of the language of that date and opted for simple sentences and clear concepts.

His soft but firm voice enabled him to capture not only the attention of his listeners but also to remove their doubts, instill optimism and renew their self confidence. His message was simple and adorned with parables, anecdotes and ancient quotations. Kathryn and Helen, in spite of listening through Eldon's interpreting efforts, were quick to fall under his spell. Nothing in their experience could compare to the way this man could in a few words create such strong beliefs and convictions. Nothing that could create such state of adoration and respect.

He talked about children first and from there he described social conditions in several places. Always relating to children, he touched upon many topics such as schooling, work ethics, family love and respect, helping others, tolerance toward the unfortunates and the observance of the Ten Commandments. He was able to combine vivid descriptions with subtle messages and teachings. Not once he referred to political matters or to the presence of the invading Romans, nor did he suggest any form of protest or rebellion. His references to God Almighty were measured and devoid of theatrics. His delivery, paused but passionate, projected a degree of sincerity and love that none of those present could ignore.

"Which one is Judas Iscariot?" asked Kathryn. Ely pointed to a short man with a striped blouse and a heavy black beard. He seemed nervous and did not seem to have any appetite. Then Ely proceeded to identify each one of the twelve apostles, explaining in each case their origin and recounting personal anecdotes.

Kathryn and Helen were seriously affected by the events at the main table. After everyone had left, they sat staring at the long table as if trying to relive some special moment. Most important in their recollection, was the extraordinary performance of Jesus of Nazareth. Even the more indifferent of those around the table could not resist the power of Jesus words and his ability to make every sentence a fountain of wisdom.

The four visitors remained at their table for a long while. Each one felt that words were unnecessary. What they had witnessed had left not only a profound impression but it had caused them to reflect, however swiftly, upon some of the truths and hopes postulated by Jesus.

They left the dining room and stood for a moment outside admiring a typical Spring night in Jerusalem where a starry sky and the fragrance of the garden helped them recover from an experience no one has ever had. There was also a sadness occasioned by the fact that they all knew what would happen to Jesus in the days following. Both Kathryn and Helen had tears in their eyes as they walked away from Joseph of Arimathea's house.

Eldon and Ely, sensing the emotion of the moment, delicately put their hands on Kathryn's and Helen's elbows and without looking at them said, "Time to get back."

They stopped briefly to return the robes and, in the next second, they were walking into the lounge in the pill above New York City. Helen stopped for a moment and looked at her loafers that were covered with dust from Joseph of Arimathea's garden. Tears flowed down her face as she entered the lounge.

Both Eldon and Ely made sure that the girls were comfortably settled in the lounge and, discreetly excused themselves. Kathryn and Helen got up and went to the luxurious Ladies Lounge to freshen up.

When they returned, Adam with Patrick and Richard were sitting around the coffee table drinking from soda cans. They all got up when the ladies returned and made room for them at the sofas. Adam spoke. "Eldon and Ely have just told us that you had an interesting, and also an emotional trip."

"Yes," replied Kathryn. "It has been a unique experience. To be present at the Last Supper and to listen to Jesus Christ in person is a dream come true!"

Richard said, "I only beg you to commit to paper this great experience. The moment we are all back on Earth, you must sit down and make as complete a description of this trip as you can. I envy you the great opportunity you have had. Let us make sure that we share it with the rest of the world."

A few moments later Adam suggested that they return to New York. The men had noticed the tiredness of the ladies and the somewhat let down feeling they were experiencing. The emotional impact of their visit had drained them of energy.

PART THREE
Back to New York

The first months of the year had been very busy for Richard. He had completed the first draft of another book and contributed a dozen articles to a half dozen monthlies; all this in addition to his weekly syndicated column. He did not remember the number of appearances in the more popular talk shows including those whose hosts delighted in discussing controversial subjects that allow them to expose on their own views.

To make matters more hectic he had been asked to chair a committee of the prestigious MMI Foundation in Paris and one of his immediate chores involved the supervision of a complex project about Morals and Ethics in Government. It had to be completed within a few months and required close work with a selected group of elder statesmen, educators and a few business executives. This initiative had received strong support from President Simonson who had enlisted other world leaders in what was becoming an unofficial crusade for honesty in public offices.

In the US, the moral quality of many leaders in Government and also in the private sector, aided by an irresponsible media, had compounded unbelievable scandals into webs of deceit and, worse yet, it had compromised the prestige of major institutions. It had began to erode deep into the puritan reserves of the country and, in the process, it forced subtle changes in the way justice, decency and respect for human rights was being considered and administered.

He was finding that his training as an Anthropologist and also as a Physicist provided him with some unique insights into the current socio-technical environment in the country. Without wanting it, he found that he was being solicited by politicians, public officials and that peculiar Washington breed, the Lobbyists. It seemed that the analysis reflected in his frequent columns were striking a chord and—he was pleased to note—were also creating a concern. For his columns were written in such a way that they would invariably review a subject, dissect it and without arrogance suggest available avenues of action, alternatives, but never solutions. He did not attempt to compile simplified lists of courses of action, or to assume the know-it-all attitude of many pundits. He encouraged his readers to think. In return they expressed their enjoyment of his honest and enlightening views.

His recent election as Coordinator for the UN in the current relations with the extra terrestrial visitors added to his many interests. He felt proud that he had been elected in a world election. He loved Patrick's comment when he learned about Richard's win: "The election of Richard Ferguson reflects the universal conviction that to deal with the unknown, it is always best to do it through someone who had spent his life dealing with it."

The press made a great deal of his reply to Patrick's congratulatory message: "This whole thing sounds crazy. Here I am going to work for the UN with a Mad Virginian as a boss, dealing with a space ship that looks like a cross between an egg and an Alka-Seltzer tablet, is crewed by a bunch of extraterrestrial yuppies and doesn't move at all!"

"Right! But you get to eat in the UN cafeterias, flirt with thousands of good looking secs and can park anywhere in Manhattan!" was Patrick's immediate reply.

He mentally reviewed the key events in the first half of the year and smiled when the project with Samuel & Schultz came up for review. He still could not figure out how he had been roped into becoming a Consulting Editor for a combination Television and Book project about History and Cooking. Blended together!

The Chief Editor, an old friend from their days at Princeton, had extracted from him his acceptance before letting him know the nature of the deal. The clincher came when he introduced Richard to Helen Lawrence the Coordinating Producer for the project. He still remembered the enthusiasm and conviction with which she described the project. He had not paid much attention to the contents but a great deal to Helen. After that he agreed to everything his friend proposed.

In a way, it flattered him that his culinary expertise had been taken seriously. For some time now he had unwittingly added the Gourmet and Cooking Expert labels to his reputation as an articulate author and a major conscience in the weekly column world. And it all happened because he had agreed to write a three column series about TV Cooking Shows. The first column almost created a civil war among networks, publishers, producers and Cooking experts. His mail reached an all time high. It all happened because he could not take the rash of cooking shows in Television seriously. His criticism was scathing and sharp. His usual moderate pen somehow turned into a sardonic, sarcastic and biting instrument. He remembered some of the lines and wondered what spices he had mixed in his salad the day he wrote those columns!

We should look forward to a few more hundred hours a year of Cooking Shows. At the rate we are going, we will have cooking shows that start with Breakfast Recipes from Tokyo, followed by Turkish Tidbits, Greek Grouse, Persian Sheep's Eyes, Moroccan Cous Cous a la Mode, Brazilian Bananas, Minnesota Barbecue Bear, etc. The network executives have enough unemployed relatives that they can structure thousands of cooking shows with them. All they have to do is to train said relatives to talk with a funny accent, expose an idiotic smile, learn the difference between cilantro and parsley and practice chopping onions and carrots with a sharp and menacing instrument without making a gory spectacle of themselves.

As far as the cooking itself, you can forget it in ninety nine percent of the cases. Who can follow and remember the numberless ingredients and the complicated sequences required to make poached eggs? There can be no great new trends in cooking just as there cannot be innovation in breathing. Food preparation has been and is, a common denominator to all cultures. It has been adapted to the rhythm and choice of evolving civilizations but it has retained flavors, aromas and texture. Roast lamb surrounded by pink wild parsnips in anchovy sauce, oregano-laden New Zealand tomatoes, fried banana peels with berries and M&Ms, is still roast lamb.

What we are being forced to accept is nothing but a simple convention turned into a ridiculous display of personal mannerisms, atrocious recipes and often disgusting attitudes. The answer: change the darn channel!

Funny enough, the added popularity brought with it a larger measure of respect from the public and the media in general. He found himself solicited in a scale previously unknown to him.

"Maybe you should stop trying to keep the national conscience fully awake and use your talents to help us improve the eating habits of this country of ours," Helen chided him at one of their working lunches.

"My dear, you should know that if this country ever learns to eat properly, its conscience will be overcome by the effects of healthy, tasty food and will begin a decline much more accelerated than we are experiencing now. Remember the ancient civilizations. Once they had conquered their neighbors and other surrounding tribes, and established a social and political order, the next thing they did was to devote their imagination to the pleasures of the flesh, one of which is of course eating…"

"What is wrong with that?"

"They made eating a ritual of exaggerated proportions. What happened next? Gluttony, which means lack of control. Next step, obesity, which brings laxity and laxity is the key ingredient of neglect. No more organized government! But the temptation is not limited to food as we have seen in recent years…"

"It sounds like you are talking about the chain of events that follow the adoption of a new political system in some countries," added Helen. "Once the new team is elected and firmly in control of their Government's purse strings, their devotion to the high and lofty principles of their revolutions fade quickly. The fading continued with the help of the bright and shiny Gold Visa cards that substitute the worn, dog eared party cards. All thoughts of social justice, honesty in public service, loyalty to the substance of the revolution and the support of their political philosophy, are quickly replaced by preoccupations with Hermés neckties, 5-hour, six-course, three-wine lunches, expensive mistresses, armored BMWs and a predilection for vacations in the playgrounds of the rich."

"Why limit such excesses to the those countries?" Richard enjoyed his discussions with Helen. He loved to provoke her into making those sharp and witty observations, invariably supported by sound evaluations. He continued. "There is a truth that is also a postulate, a thesis and an axiom that applies to all political systems, as well as to public or private groups, creeds or philosophies on the planet. That incontrovertible truth suggests that whenever someone is left alone in charge of a room full of goodies that someone will invariably end up getting his mittens on some, or all of them. It happens in this country in a million complex and sophisticated ways, and it also happens in the Vatican, the village council, the local PTA and all non-profit organizations, from here to Burkina Faso and back! Privilege in its many forms is probably more intoxicating than straight methyl alcohol. So do not be scandalized by the acts of a few. The question all along has been how to get people to accept the rules of proper behavior; then, to have people in positions of authority to behave responsibly, and finally how to convince those people in positions of influence and power, to behave decently. Maybe our visiting friends have an answer, don't you think?"

They both laughed and he said, "In all this, food plays a key role."

"Does it mean that better food brings worse government? You clever anthropologists should be able to come up with a cerebral dictum on the food-government inverse proportionality, or something."

Richard enjoyed the vehemence that Helen seemed to pour into any subject and also her unfailing good sense and sharp observations and judgments.

"You'd be surprised. Especially you who can talk for hours about the feasts of Medieval Europe, the banquets in Napoleon's court and the refined level of present day European cooking!"

"Speaking of European cooking, aren't you supposed to be heading back to Paris?"

"I just got here and you are already asking when I go back! No kidding, I returned to help get Patrick's committee organized and going. I also expect that there will be some action in the next few weeks and he has asked me to stick around. But, to answer your question, I'll be back in Paris the moment I see the coast clear."

He smiled affectionately at Helen and continued. "Of course I'll stay longer in New York if you promise to wine me and dine me and conduct a shameless campaign of conquest and seduction. Or, better yet, why don't you come to Paris with me when this is all over? The old place sort of seems faceless when you are not there."

"Not a bad idea, Professor. But I have stopped seducing academicians and keeping passionate encounters in Paris. Seriously, with this space ship situation I can't seem to get anything done. You know, in some quarters there is a feeling of 'what's the use?' The things above are probably preparing the sauce for a banquet featuring the human race, so don't worry about scripts, treatments, budgets and all that crap! My feeling is that this too shall pass. The question at the moment is when will this thing be over? If Paris is still there, I shall be the first to reach the departure gate. D'accord?"

"It's a deal! But when that happens, you and I are gonna walk down some aisle somewhere and be happy ever after, like the Beauty and the Beast!"

"Is that a marriage proposal?"

"What do you think?"

"For an anthropologist, physicist and pundit, your marriage proposals are as flat as the proverbial tortilla. Shoot, Richard, I get better proposals from the office boys. Gee, I expected some baskets of fruit, a couple of Tiffany samples, maybe a poem written on a silk handkerchief, a Gucci Agenda with dates penciled off and some cool champagne! The answer is yes!"

Richard laughed and holding Helen's delicate hand, kissed the back of her hand. Oddly enough, Helen observed through her own misty eyes that he had tears in his own.

Call from the Vatican

A few hours after Patrick had delivered his report to the General Assembly on his visit to the "pill" above New York, he received an urgent call from Cardinal Giorgio Beccaria at the Vatican. Patrick was expecting it. Already, Cardinal Ludlam in New York had diplomatically suggested that the Vatican would like to establish more direct lines of communications with Patrick, not content with the sporadic links provided by the UN's overworked and understaffed Press Group.

Cardinal Beccaria was recognized as the member of the Pope's inner council that had been able to reshape and bring into line the independent-minded Curia and to soften the voices of dissension and opposition within the Sacred College of Cardinals.

Since his days as Cardinal of Milan, Giorgio Beccaria had propitiated some of the more skillful resolutions that the Catholic Church had advanced in years. He was able to turn the more controversial issues like celibacy, women in the priesthood and abortion into objective issues that more than establishing a position or even allowing a glimpse at the complexities of modern day church policies, created a favorable attitude toward the church. Even the skeptical and hard boiled Milanese press had to admit that Cardinal Beccaria's deft touch could defuse any vociferous issue presented by any of the multitude of extremist groups and coalitions in the entire Lombardy. Besides, Cardinal Beccaria was known for his powers of persuasion. It was known that his conversations with Indro Montanelli had been a decisive factor in the latter's sudden support of Vatican views.

"Patrick, caro. So good to hear your voice!"

"Giorgio, what a surprise! It's been a long time. I been meaning to call you, but you must know that by now, our madhouse on the East River has been transformed into a frenetic madhouse on the East River."

Patrick and Giorgio Beccaria went back a long time. They had met when Patrick, still at l'Ecole, had spent a year In Milan working on an analysis of the "miracolo italiano," of the fifties and sixties. Giorgio Beccaria was at the time a student at the Monastery of Venegono Superiore, north of Milan. The apartment that Patrick had rented in Via Durini, steps away from piazza San Babila belonged to the Beccaria family and it was through this arrangement that the two met and, at once, became fond of each other. They also shared the same preference for Jazz music and became almost regulars at Santa Tecla, the underground jazz cave near piazza del Duomo and right next to the Palazzo della Nunziatura, or residence of the Cardinal of Milan.

At the time, Santa Tecla's ranking in the world of European jazz emporiums was very high. Most of the best musicians appeared frequently there and it was not unusual to listen in a single season to Chet Baker, Stan Getz, Charlie Byrd, Vandambrini, Paul Desmond, Sonny Rollins, Mussolini, Art Tatum, Thelonius Monk and many others. Its reputation was well earned and it attracted both musicians and cognoscenti from all over Europe. Santa Tecla's unique standing was also aided by the excellent service provided by Aldo and Lucca, the twin four and a half foot tall waiters and all around assistants.

Theirs was a deep and easy friendship that provided both young men with innumerable opportunities to review their own convictions and to seek those perspectives in life that in one form or another mold our later thinking and attitudes. They were fond of talking long walks in the Parco Centrale and of admiring the austere lines of the Castello Sforzesco, which reminded both of them of the past glories of Lombardy and also of the stormy episodes those walls had witnessed in the past.

More than once, Patrick had teased Giorgio about his addiction to Santa Tecla. "It must be the nearness of the Nunziatura, Giorgio. You will probably end up as Monsignor of Milano so that you can be near the Santa Tecla."

"Listen, in order to acquire sanctity I must be near Saints. Santa Tecla happens to be one of my favorites..."

Their paths eventually took their own directions and contact became less frequent. But they always remembered fondly the pizzas at Santa Lucia off Corso Vittorio Emmanuele and the peculiar charms of Milan's foggy nights.

"I know, I know. I've been keeping track of this entire episode. It is precisely about this that I am calling. You see, the Holy Father is concerned that this media offensive created by the arrival of the ships is keeping you and the UN as sort of their captives. He feels that the Church has a right to participate more closely in the evaluation of these events and, most important, in the orientation and guidance of the public. He feels, and I concur, that the Church has a role to play."

"Giorgio, I am a hundred percent with you. These events affect all mankind and I think that the presence of all religious groups is a necessity. I don't know what is going to come out of all this, but I suspect that comfort and strengthening of beliefs and large doses of faith are going to be needed. My problem now is that our Security Council and the Special Committee are going around in circles in addition to having to fend off the multitude of groups that clamor for the right to be included in the Committee and those who expect preferential treatment. You have no idea what we are running into. I have had to change telephones at home 3 times already."

There was a pause and Cardinal Beccaria came back on the line. "Patrick, I realize you are under great pressure. We do not wish to add to your burdens. But we wish to make a suggestion. Either as part of the Special Committee or as a sub-committee, we would like to see a grouping of world churches. Keep in mind that billions of people depend on us for guidance. We feel that we must get a little closer to you and the UN."

As usual, Patrick scribbled furiously on his note pad. He acknowledged that the suggestion was a valid one and that he would have no trouble putting it into effect. As long as the various religious groups in the US and abroad managed to agree among themselves. He mentally shuddered at the idea of having to group more than 500 religious sects into no more than a dozen delegates. He would have to leave that to the churches themselves, but he knew that while this would take a few months, the Vatican wanted immediate action.

"Giorgio, I think it is a great idea and I am prepared to put it into effect. However, keep in mind that the Catholic Church is a solid block and is not made of a myriad sub-sects like most of the other organized religious groups. Also, the Catholic Church has one of the best field Marshals in the business and can put a delegation together in minutes. I would not be surprised if you don't already have the names of the monsignors you want to join the circus here. The problem is that the other churches will debate and argue the matter for months. I also think that I would want a sub-committee made up of no more than half a dozen people, otherwise it will be unmanageable."

"I am very pleased that we both agree as to the substance of the matter.

I shall leave the form of it in your good hands. I know, like you do, that getting the other religions to accept the idea, debate it, set up selection committees, elections and what not will take forever. Unfortunately there is not much you or I can do about it, so I have thought of a way to, let's say, keep our finger in the pie while the others bicker and argue. I can ask Cardinal Warren Ludlam to attach himself to your staff in an unobtrusive way as possible. You know him and I also know that you think highly of him. We just want some eyes and ears near you and you know that you can depend on Warren's discretion and ability. He will not bug you about wanting to have tea with our space visitors nor will he be giving out interviews or appearing on Television."

Patrick thought about it for a minute and then replied, "I think it can be done. The only thing is that the others will raise holy hell, oops! excuse me, your Excellency. They will raise the roof!"

Cardinal Beccaria laughed out loud. He said, "Haven't heard that 'holy hell' in ages; sort of a contradiction. Around here I hear the latest profanities but good ole standbys like holy hell seem to have fallen in disuse. Well, back to Warren. The moment the others notice that Warren is near you they will hasten to put together their group. I think."

"Fine then; just tell Warren."

"Before you go, tell me one thing. Do you think that—in time—it might be possible to talk to these beings, you know, in person or through TV or radio? There are infinite subjects that we would like to discuss with them. You see, a portion of the Church's Dogma is liable to be found superfluous if these boys show us that there are other influences out there."

"Giorgio, everyone is asking the same question and it is one of the major topics that I will bring to them at my next meeting. And don't worry about Dogma. Remember our old arguments about how faith, belief and hope in one form or another are intrinsic part of man's make up?"

They spent a few minutes talking about the visitors and Kathryn and then said goodbye in their usual affectionate manner.

The White House

The President of the United States was beginning to feel the pressure of the last months. Since the arrival of the objects, his schedule had become unmanageable. In addition to his work load as President of the most powerful country on earth, he had had to shoulder a good part of the worries and planning work of the Emergency Committee created by the UN to deal with the extraterrestrial beings. He had managed to postpone any serious discussions with the leaders of the European Group and Japan, in spite of their insistence. Their aims to become a part of the Earth Team had, if anything, become more focused. They had also, probably under Elmo Sak's direction, put in motion an extensive promotion campaign designed to recognize the European countries as representatives of the rest of the world. They proposed joining with the US and the UN in the contacts with the visitors.

The confidential report on his desk detailed a number of Elmo Sak's initiatives and proposals before the European Union, the European countries and practically all the major corporations on the continent. It was easy to detect Elmo's subtle approach that in one form or another led the recipients to believe that by following Elmo's "guidelines," they would be doing the world a favor and could expect substantial returns themselves.

"Listen to this," he said to Ursula Walters, Alan Clayton and Mike Pashley who were sitting in the Oval Office.

The report had been carefully analyzed by the President's team and had concluded that underneath all the rhetoric about the best interests of mankind, the preservation of traditions and culture, the protection of our only living environment, there was a clear message about Elmo's wishes to be actively involved with the visitors. His eagerness to assess and take advantage of the newer technologies exhibited by the visitors did not escape anyone.

"Mister President, I am beginning to think that Elmo has ceased being a nuisance and is rapidly ascending to the threat level. I find him both brilliant and terribly egotistical. I wonder what makes people like him use other people and his own power to pursue additional power."

The President looked at Pashley and observed, "What makes a zebra a zebra?"

Elmo Saks

St. Michael's is a village on the Chesapeake Bay that claims a long and illustrious past. From colonial days, St. Michael's has enjoyed a discreet isolation that has made it one of the preferred areas for people who want to avoid the stresses of large cities or the inconveniences of summer resorts. It is a peaceful hamlet with a historical main Street and one or two major Hotels. Unknown to most of the residents, the large property on the north western side of the peninsula belonged to one of the more powerful and influential men on earth.

Highway 50 connects Washington, D.C. with the Chesapeake Peninsula. It is a widely used road, especially during week-ends when city residents make the short journey to their second homes in the peninsula. Some 12 miles past the Bay Bridge, just before coming to St. Michael's, a right turn and about six miles away there is a plateau that from the distance resembles a medieval fortress. The tall cypress trees and the vague shapes of several buildings partly concealed by birch, oak and pine trees at the top of the plateau give the impression of a medieval compound. As you reach the top, the road widens into a large park at the end of which a stone wall and a somber iron gate between two imposing structures let you know that a private estate begins at that point.

The 3 thousand acre property belongs to Elmo Saks, the retired Senator and at one time, a highly touted Presidential candidate. Elmo Saks is also President of Star Fidelity Bank and Chairman of the Wall Street firm of Michelsen, Murphy, Brown and Gillingham. He also controls or presides over a multitude of companies whose net worth has been estimated at several hundreds of billions of dollars.

During his years as a US Senator, Elmo had cleverly engineered multiple initiatives that had been forcefully steered through committees and more often than not, successfully turned into laws. His output was incessant and always reinforced with some aspect that meant material benefits to Senator Saks and the many groups that existed in his shadow. He used to say that "the US Senate was invented to function as a bakery. If there isn't fresh bread every day, the people will get their cookies elsewhere!"

Senator Saks became a household name in the country and abroad. While gingerly arranging for discreet management of his incredible fortune to avoid conflicts of interest, he continued to direct policy in his multinational companies through regular meetings at his St. Michael's estate. Elmo Saks had become a household word when he agreed to run for the Presidency of the United States thanks to one the most expensive and overwhelming personal promotion campaigns in the history of the country.

Elmo Saks had a background that he liked to compare to that of the famous families that had maintained a presence in American politics for generations. Families with names like Kennedy, Tallmadge, Taft, Adams, Rockefeller, Ripley and many others. This was an exaggeration resulting from his desire to obtain the acceptance of the snobbish East Coast society. His parents had been immigrants from England at the beginning of the 20th century and through hard work, perseverance and the unique ability of Myron, Elmo's father, had been able to carve not only a solid position for the family but also create a powerful financial empire.

It was a typical story of an immigrant family that through hard work succeeded in the new country. This fact plus the extraordinary opportunities available in a dynamic, growing world had enabled Myron to develop unique skills in the world of business and finance.

The immigration wave of 1900 brought a new vitality into the city of New York. While the amount of capital that flowed into the city as a result of this wave was limited to the modest savings of the immigrant families, other important ingredients of wealth had entered the economy. The diversity of personal habits and national customs stimulated the production of new products that rapidly evolved from homemade or artisan levels to full industrial scales.

The choice of products suddenly expanded to the point where they satisfied almost all tastes and preferences. Prices were set to make the products available to the average consumer, and rudimentary distribution systems were adopted so that the same brand would be available in New Haven as well as in Rutherford, New Jersey.

Where New York residents had been satisfied for some time with a limited choice of bread and bakery products, for instance, in a short time, they were confronted with an enticing variety of breads, pies, cookies, pastries and a number of related products. All of a sudden, fifty varieties of homemade pasta were available. Men's shirts, that up to that time had stuck to very laborious and expensive manufacturing methods, appeared in new styles and colors and at half the prices of the traditional Williams and Suntown poplins or the more popular Stern cotton softies, as they were called. Small food stores began to appear all the way from the Bronx to Long Island and with them came new brands of canned foods, cheeses and prepared foods.

Myron and Sarah Saks arrived in Ellis Island, New York in 1907 from the London suburb of Islington. Theirs was not a decision to emigrate born out of extreme economic circumstances but a result of a violent feud between their families. In that poisoned atmosphere, Myron found that a proper occupation and a tranquil family life were unattainable. He managed to save enough to apply for the exit visa, buy the steerage accommodations for himself and his young bride and go through the endless formalities required by the sponsoring agency in his district, and the US Immigration authorities.

Myron was determined to succeed in this important new venture in his life. He was prepared to bring into any job in the new world, an unwavering dedication and his desire for perfection. In this he was aided by the disciplines of a rigorous upbringing and a natural inclination toward mechanical problems.

Myron's first job was in a cardboard factory, cutting and assembling boxes. It paid enough to enable him to rent a comfortable furnished room in the Prospect Park area of Brooklyn. In less than a year he had introduced some improvements in the systems in use that would allow for quick and efficient moving, measuring, marking and cutting of large pieces of cardboard. This was promptly noticed by the plant superintendent who named him his assistant and moved him from the assembly floor to the glass enclosed offices overlooking one end of the factory floor. Wisely, the plant superintendent encouraged Myron to devote more of his time to devise improvements around the plant, such as the installation of conveyor belts, ventilation equipment and a new printing facility. While he was careful to give recognition to Myron, he slyly assumed before the management of the factory the major part of the credit for the improvements.

This promotion brought a substantial increase in Myron's salary and by consequence, an improvement in his living conditions. He found an unfurnished apartment in the same Prospect Park area and with Sarah proceeded to canvas the antique furniture shops in Brooklyn and the Lower East Side of Manhattan.

During this period, Sarah took advantage of the vicinity of a Bookkeeping Academy in Flatbush Avenue to study Bookkeeping, as Accounting was called then. She felt that this training would be helpful the moment Myron decided to strike on his own.

Their only son, Elmo was born three years after they first stepped on Ellis Island. This event stimulated Myron even more. His strong desire to succeed had not diminished an iota. On the contrary, it increased in intensity with every little triumph in his work or every moment of happiness and bliss with his small family.

After five years with the cardboard company, he and Ed Tyler, a colleague, decided to strike on their own. Aware of the low prices of fair quality wood planking available at the time from Pennsylvania, Massachusetts and Canada, they designed a simple wooden pallet that could be used for heavy-duty work at the docks and also for transporting fruits and vegetables. As in most successful ventures, the normally elusive ingredients of luck, coincidence or opportunity accompanied them. Their new product coincided with a large immigration wave that included a majority of Mediterranean peoples accustomed to a diet that included—and continues to do so—fresh fruits and vegetables. Street markets proliferated in a short time, along with itinerant sellers, street corner stands and all sorts of convenience shops. Produce had to move in wooden boxes and pallets.

That was the beginning of the M&T Company of Brooklyn, New York.

In time, Myron bought his partner's share and opened up his own sawmill in Eastern Pennsylvania. By that time, new means of transportation were helping create new markets and reach areas that up to that point were beyond their possibilities. Myron was quick to notice the impact of the growing automotive industry and, assuming a considerable risk, made a major investment in the new automobile industry. The payoff was quick and sizeable; high volume transactions at that time were often referred to as "pin the tail on the bull." Myron had placed the tail on the best part of the bull.

He was quick to see that stock swaps, trading and margin ventures allowed him to keep his capital in motion and, more important, in a steep growing curve. Through a process of acquiring small equity positions in middle size operating companies and then linking those investments he became active in trading and soon he was managing sizeable portfolios. His fortune had been made.

The fortune he accumulated was wisely protected through a complex system of updating investments, providing venture capital to new companies and the devising of a floating scale of assessment and evaluation that allowed him and his subordinates to modify positions in record time.

In addition to the great satisfaction that the money game gave him, the power over people was perhaps the greater source of contentment he and Millie had.

The only regret Myron had was that he did not have enough time to spend with Elmo, his only son, who was forced to grow up in the comfortable but lonely splendor of exclusive private schools, indifferent tutors, and a sense of aloofness. Perhaps as a result of his parents' devotion to their work and the time they devoted to the protection of their accumulated wealth, early in his life, Elmo developed a peculiar attitude toward his parents. This attitude translated into a subtle rejection of their company. Somehow he felt that being by himself insulated him from commitment.

Myron and Sarah had succeeded in business beyond their expectations but had failed miserably with their only son. They had given him everything he needed and wanted, except love. They had never established that current of comfort, trust and affection that a few well-timed caresses, embraces and attention are normally created between well-adjusted parents and their children.

His father's warmest greetings were limited to a handshake that did not convey any conviction and his mother's limpid pecks on the cheek were nothing but a careful gesture bound by concern about make up, hairdo and time.

While not conscious of it, Elmo developed a hard edge to his personality. He did not abuse his wealth but used it to obtain personal recognition and advantage. A ruthless strain became part of his character.

While he could not claim distinguished ascendancy like many of his classmates, he made it up by an attractive presence, a facility to convince and a peculiar charm that could quickly turn into uncontrolled rage and vengefulness. He had been actively involved in sports at the prep level and had been the captain of Amherst's football team and its star quarterback. Later he had rowed for Yale and made the Mortar Board Club. His wealth provided the passport to the ruling elite and to that special class that share the conviction that while the United States is a country of immigrants, with opportunity, liberty and freedom for all, it takes a breed of people, an aristocracy, to provide the exalted guidance and the leadership to institute the controls of a democracy. In the process, the elite protects its privileges and tries to keep the masses productive and happy. Which from a broad perspective makes the American democracy the best system ever devised in the history of the human community.

By the time Elmo Saks was thirty years old, he had enjoyed practically all that life had to offer. On a silver platter. The fortune that his father had amassed had continued to grow and Elmo himself had contributed a few innovations to the various industries that made up the vast holding. He was already well known in Wall Street where he had served an apprenticeship at Saks, Borman and Stafford, the investment-banking firm that guided his father's holdings.

Elmo's entry into politics was almost an obligation. His work in behalf of the Investment firm had brought him into contact with a number of non-profit organizations and financial institutions that, curiously, operated at very high profit levels. It intrigued him at first that a non-profit organization would become in most cases the last link in a chain of profitable investments. It sort of provided a touch of selfless compassion to the collection of companies whose sole aim appeared to be guided by uncontrollable greed.

His intimate knowledge and expertise in the control of investment accounts, transfers, market strategies, and the use and abuse of offshore transactions, coupled with his encyclopedic knowledge of the tax laws involved, enabled him to earn the respect of a number of Foundations and discreet financial groups operating throughout the country. His use of hedge funds in a consortium made up of some of the wealthiest investment firms, overseas banks and wealthy family trusts, had been an unparalleled success. The brilliant feature had been the self-imposed control mechanisms that he had devised to avoid excessive dependence on random investments and placements. It was through them that his involvement in public matters became the starting point of what would be a brilliant political career that at one point would reach for the highest office in the land.

Shortly after executing one of the more daring takeovers in Wall Street, he had the opportunity to spend a long week end at the home of senator Forsyth in Connecticut. The Senator had been a close friend of his father and had always shown special interest in Elmo's career.

The Senator was perceptive enough to detect in the young man, a peculiar strength of character and singleness of purpose. He guessed also that behind the refined manners and the sardonic edge to Elmo's behavior, there was a controlled touch of ruthlessness and even sadism. He also wondered about the evident lack of interest Elmo exhibited for the opposite sex. But, shunning these traits aside, the Senator felt that Elmo could develop as a first class politician. Besides, Elmo himself had already mentioned to the Senator that his involvement in political issues could no longer be ignored. He was anxious to have a heart to heart talk with the Senator, who in 35 years had managed to remain one of the austere and honest voices that were not only heard but also listened to in the Senate.

Elmo spent a memorable two-day weekend at the Senator's home in Connecticut. He arrived early on a Saturday and was mildly surprise to find that he was the only guest. The Senator had arranged for lunch in the enclosed terrace in the back of the house where they could enjoy the view of the pond and the deliberate maneuvers of the half a dozen or so ducks.

The Senator did not waste any time at the lunch table. After they had savored the avocado salad with shrimp and pineapple and the very delicate filet of sole, and toasted freely the Chateau D'Yquem, the Senator said to Elmo, "Any plans you might have about entering politics, which seems to be the direction where your activities are taking you, must be subjected to the most exhaustive scrutiny. Not only the plans but a necessary and very severe evaluation of your aims, your character, your personal history and a very realistic assessment of your capacity to react to true or imaginary charges. It goes without saying that you must also sharpen up your dialectic ability to enable you to say many things without actually saying anything and, just as important, to color or disguise public statements so that the truth is known only to you."

As an opening of what he expected to be a long and enlightening visit, the Senator's words produced the desired effect. Elmo was taken aback by the directness of the introduction and the path of responsibility that it implied.

"Senator, I have been more or less forced to make public statements and, as you know, to prop up financially some of the initiatives coming from some of the Foundations. To tell you the truth, I have enjoyed the public exposure, the TV talk shows and more important the possibility to deal directly with a number of Senate Committees, Senators and Cabinet members and be able to appreciate at close range the attractiveness that political power possesses…"

"You have discovered another facet of power. You already yield enough clout with your extensive investments and now, I am sure, you want to taste the sense of raw power that only Government can provide. It extends over the entire country and directly affects a quarter of a billion people on the planet. The question is whether you can become extremely powerful without appearing to be devoting your life to obtain and maintain that power."

"You seem to have a very cynical view of Government, which I frankly did not expect from one who has spent his entire life in the political arena of this country."

"Well, Elmo, it is inevitable that after a while you begin to realize that public service has little to do with public service. It is more like that fraternity devoted to the 4 Ps."

"What is that?"

"Protection, Preservation, Privilege and Power. You see, a great deal of important legislation that is genuinely aimed at improving matters in the community, are all too often left on the Senate floor, victims of the neglect or indifference of its members."

Elmo observed, "Well, OK. I realize that not all good deeds or intentions can come to an enthusiastic end in Congress. Those of us who have been or are peripherally involved in Government matters sense that most of the dynamics of the legislative bodies is stimulated by power and special interest blocks. Worse yet, we get the impression that without that influence, not much could happen. Am I right?"

"You are absolutely on target. Listen, you are a financial man and maybe my poor analogy can help you understand the system. If the banking community anywhere, becomes too involved in private industry, it runs the risk of becoming a slave to it, unwillingly. Example, the bank owns or controls equity capital in airlines, printing shops, shoe shine parlors, whatever. It will tend to favor the companies where its money is invested in detriment of other companies in the same sector. It means in many cases, cheap money to those companies owned or controlled by the bank, or other forms of investment strategies involving those companies. If taken to extremes, two things can happen: one, the competition is choked. Two, the loans get so large, or the obligations assumed exceed a prudent level that the bank, in the face of a commercial or financial crisis, is unable to collect or remain solvent and by consequence is forced to default on its own obligations."

"Or borrow like mad, which makes the hole deeper," injected Elmo.

The Senator continued. "Or get the Fed to bail him out. Yes, your free market economy and all the bull associated with its beneficial effects can and allows this to happen. Of course not everywhere. Keep in mind that the driving force is profits, profits, profits! And behind profits, there is personal greed, old boy."

Elmo thought for an instant and then said, "But isn't government supposed to provide the control mechanisms to prevent the type of climate you describe?"

"Yes and it does. But, keep in mind that the Government cannot bat a 100 percent. While many of us believe in principles derived from justice and fairness others get lost in the dizzying race of their own careers and loose sight of the real purpose of the exercise. Capitalism is supposed to create its own controls, but unfortunately it does not always happen, mainly because conditions change all the time and adjustments are always painful. I think the day will come when governments will have to regulate the extent of the power exercised by corporations, boards and managers. I also think that limits will have to be established to regulate compensation at all levels. I know that I am moving away from some of the free market concepts and approaching a more socialized environment, but the more complex the game, the more rules you need!"

He paused and then continued. "A nation's private sector assets like corporations, investment firms, labor groups, banking, transport, health care, telecommunication services, etc. provide the necessary resources to protect the living standards of the people. The Government on its part is there to make all this possible. Just like Religion serves to protect moral and ethical principles, Government is there to protect the creative resources of the country. The separation of church and state has worked since its inception. Something similar will have to happen with government and the corporate and other productive sectors. In other words, we should not have a Government that is run or influenced by industrial or commercial executives whose vision differs from true government service."

"But, how about their expertise, experience and knowledge? Are these not useful to the Government?"

"Definitely! But keep in mind that if you have a competent civil service, you have access to the expertise in many fields plus the usual formulas for counseling, consulting, etc. It just does not make sense to have, for example, an ex CEO of a pharmaceutical company run the Department of Health, or an ex CEO of a munitions company head Government departments dealing with military appropriations. Inevitably they tend to favor their industrial sector and influence the Senate committees and sub committees. There is a human angle that cannot be denied. Just like protecting your relatives."

"How about the other way around? All those retired admirals and generals that end up working for private companies?"

"Wrong practice again; they have the proverbial ax to grind. Again, go back to the separation of powers, not that there is anything wrong with that!"

They finished a desert of peaches marinated in Marsala, fruit juices, brandy and a touch of cinnamon, and took a short walk around the imposing grounds before settling in the large library. The manservant was waiting for them with demitasse coffee and a bottle of Courvoisier. They drank the aromatic brew with great relish and then savored the vintage Cognac. After a moment of silence, which implied lingering enjoyment of both coffee and cognac, the Senator pulled a gold trimmed leather cigar case from his coat pocket and opening it offered Elmo a cigar. They lit up the fragrant Havana specials and for a moment remained quiet, both savoring the intoxicating fumes and reflecting about what the Senator had said at lunch. At last, Elmo asked, "Senator, you are making the equation very simple. Centuries of so called development and civilization and all we have managed to achieve seems to be a permanent assignment to seek and refine ways and means of satisfying that undeniable quality some of us possess."

"Right and wrong, my boy! It is the same old scam since day one. But you are wrong about greed. It does not occur to a few, as you said. It is there in every human born of woman. It just surfaces when the opportunity extends its invitation. Greed is nothing more than the simultaneous application of two principles: that having more is better than having less and that to that end you can justify any means to have more!"

"That is an interesting definition. But you forgot obsession, Senator."

"Do not worry about obsession because it is also part of the package. To get more and to use whatever means to do so, implies a distorted form of concentration and single mindedness."

The Senator smiled and continued. "Listen, I have had opportunity to verify and classified greed in some of its forms. Let me tell you a little story that illustrates my point. I often take a walk around the park in front of my apartment in Georgetown. There is a small playground where children between 4 and 7 play. Well, the three swings are always in demand and that causes a bit of jostling and discussion. I followed one child that appeared more confident and aggressive than the others. He went straight to one of the swings and not so gently sent the occupant to the sidelines. After swinging a while, he noticed that a little girl occupied the swing next to him. He quickly sent her away. He now had two swings. He sat in one and would not let the other kids use the other. I noticed that he derived no satisfaction from enjoying the swing he was on or the empty one next to him. Nevertheless, he would not let anyone use the empty one, and to assert his rights, he would switch from one to the other. After a while the children moved to another part of the playground and our boy remained by himself with all three swings. He rejected any one trying to get at a swing. For more than an hour he kept all three swings to himself until one of the mothers intervened and forcefully placed her daughter in one swing amid the protests of our boy. Well, the story does not end there. The next day he did not show at the park, but one of the little girls that had been sent away the day before did exactly what our boy had done. In no time at all she had all three swings under her control. Now, what does all this proves?"

"The need for more swings?" asked Elmo as he let out a sonorous guffaw.

The senator laughed and finished. "Greed, my boy, is contagious; which also confirms my theory that the bug is built-in within the species."

"How about Congress?"

"Congress suffers from a similar ailment. Without corporate money, who more or less own the political system, I doubt that the system could survive. You see, representative democracy was born out of the necessity of preventing without bloodshed that one of your neighbors attempt against you and your property. Soon, you enlisted the help of the neighbors and since the system worked, others adapted it. Peace and some security were achieved. Later, great numbers of people could be counted on to pursue or prevent a certain course of action affecting the group. At that point the group had assumed a power that its member, individually, could not muster."

Elmo interrupted to observe, "Yes, collective thought began to assert itself as it developed into collective action."

"Right!" said the Senator. "A mechanism was needed to convert collective thinking into action. That mechanism was the vote which appeared naturally, and it worked for most purposes. If we can all vote, we can keep any abuse out of the system. The key to democracy is right there. The vote. If everyone is present at the election booth, the voice is strong and most societies have enough of a conscience to make sure that proper lines of behavior are followed and protected."

He took a small sip from his cognac sifter and continued. "Big deal, but it does not work as long as that vote is for sale. Which is something the Greeks, who were the first to fool around with representative government did not contemplate? Look at our history. Compromise and accommodation have been the silent allies of democracy, freedom, liberty and the old fraternité et equalité. Real estate companies and lobbies maneuver deftly to secure and protect zoning laws, subsidies and exceptions. Corporations use a legion of influential contacts to make sure that there is leniency if they are caught when they stretch the limits of the law, or that the face of government turns the other way and simply ignores the infringement..."

"The oil companies have always drilled on public quadrants without fees, royalties or lease costs, as they would have to do if they were setting up their rigs and gas gathering fields on extensions privately owned. I can go on forever on this tack. The lumber companies, the transportation companies, the pharmaceutical companies, the communications conglomerates, the food industry, all who can afford it, can buy his license to steal. The cost? Campaign contributions and, if clever enough, disguised payments and direct payola."

"I did not realize that the system was so thoroughly dominated by outside interests..."

"C'mon, Elmo. Don't tell me that from your Wall Street cockpits you never had to finance a little public relations with the SEC or any of the many Government agencies dealing with your money bags."

"Oh, yes. We have contributed to a number of campaigns, often disguising the transfers with other labels. There must be a whole encyclopedia on ways and means to do it. For instance, in addition to outright cash funneled to the Committee or person, you take care of car rentals, hotels, printing, insurance and a million other items that are not visible. We have even instituted scholarship programs to get chosen sons and daughters of friendly bureaucrats in top colleges and Universities. I don't remember how many sports outfits for girls' soccer, lacrosse and baseball teams we have donated. Creativity in contributions allows you to remain within lawful limits."

The Senator nodded and continued to engulf himself in a cloud of that aromatic cigar. He said, "You see, getting into politics in the United States is no easy matter. The process is no different however from that in use in Greco-Roman days, or in modern democracies and in not so modern or democratic states. Boiled down to its basic tenets it is simply a matter that involves three principles: the first, and most important, has to do with survival. A position that has been earned, inherited or otherwise arranged for, must be protected at all times without regard to personal convictions or beliefs. The rationale is that 'if I am not there to protect the masses, who is going to?'"

Elmo could not be more attentive. The Senator was providing a realistic summary of his views on Politics and Government. Elmo's agile mind was recording every word. After a pause, the Senator continued. "The second principle is just as important. It deals with political protection. It entails a complex and vast arsenal of actions and even attitudes. Knowledge of the colleagues and adversaries' strengths and weaknesses is essential, as well as the capacity to resort swiftly to accommodation, barter, reward and threats should anyone attempt to diverge from an established path, try to occupy a space that doesn't belong to him, or just exhibit a particular preference for stealing the show from its rightful owner.

"The third principle entails personal development. A politician is never born. It is a condition that gradually takes over the life and character of a perfectly well intentioned and innocent citizen. It allows for the unfortunate sacrifice of taking liberties with the truth, creating a convenient soul-saving storehouse of fabricated rationalizations and, above all, making sure that number one is taken care of at all times."

Elmo listened with a great deal of interest and fascination. He asked, "How about the voters?"

The Senator smiled and in a milder tone added, "In all this we must not lose sight of the fact the gist of political life in the United States is represented not by the voters but by those who enter politics, make the efforts and sacrifices to run for office, establish a power base, manage to obtain results in elections and ultimately become that small group of legislators that control the elements of power in the country."

As an afterthought he said, "Actually, I feel that it is easier to find out what voters think rather than try to pin down politicians in an effort to determine the basis of their beliefs. It is that kind of situation.

"Unfortunately, voters are not always present in sufficient numbers to really make a difference. That is why elections at municipal and state legislature levels are influenced by local political establishments that in many cases are light years away from the true aims of a democratic system. All that jazz about the fact that elections in this country are the true mirror of the people's aspirations, is just a convenient self-protecting slogan."

Not quite convinced about what he had just heard, Elmo observed, "You said a while ago that elections have been the avenue for democratic action..."

"Yes, they are, however, how certain can you be about the quality of the vote when, for instance, the national turnover in an election for President, seldom exceeds 50%. And those voting for Congress are roughly one third of those qualified to do so. Primaries command even lower percentages and those elections at local levels, are even smaller."

He looked at Elmo with a smile on his lips when he continued. "In my experience, I have come to the conclusion that most people cast their votes without having a clear idea about the candidates and, what is worse, about what those candidates stand for. Thomas E. Mann said something worth keeping in mind: The burden of proof is clearly on those who would argue that a significant part of the public is aware of their candidates."

By then it was mid afternoon. Time had passed quickly. The white-coated servant entered the ornate library bringing a large tray with coffee, tea and sundry pastries. He served tea to the senator and coffee to Elmo. As soon as the servant left, the Senator continued. "Don't forget that presidential elections take place only every four years. And for about an entire year preceding the event, the campaigns eclipse all other political events. However, in between the major events, there is a continuous succession of minor elections involving every community in the country that must elect governors, state legislators, members of Congress, City Mayors and a plethora of officials."

After a while, they both agreed that it was time to take a break, even if Elmo was fascinated by their discussion and would like to continue.

"Let us go up to our rooms, rest, shower and be back here in 90 minutes," suggested the Senator. "We can have a good dry martini and continued our session. I feel it is very important that you be aware of some of the good as well as the bad things in Government."

An hour and a half later, refreshed and rested, they met again on the ground floor and sat in the terrace amidst the gentle fragrance of the garden and the soft breezes coming from the bay.

Elmo spoke. "Senator, I still cannot understand how our system of government has evolved and how different and opposing tendencies have been kept alive."

The Senator sipped at the dry martini and, looking at the frosted surface of the glass, said in a thoughtful manner, "The currents of American political thought must be kept in mind. I would not venture to say such currents must, or can be, understood. It would a pointless task. You see, the substance of our political marrow, as in any other great civilization, is contradiction. A group of strong willed immigrants finds itself in a large continent sparsely populated, where they have the opportunity to practice their religion and live by their own principles. The environment however requires improvisation and new initiatives. To this you add the omnipresence of an unknown beyond, and you begin to experience freedom. On one hand you have strict religious principles and somewhat narrow minded attitudes and on the other you deal with large realities that demand flexible thinking."

He paused and, looking at Elmo, continued. "Successive generations were born in what would be a most liberal society, and everyone so announced to the four winds. You see, the essence of liberalism after all, results from patterns that could be termed conservative. Maybe it was the good intentions of a few that supported this view. It didn't last long. You see, liberalism had to have an opposite force, especially in a new society that had to deal with numerous elements of a conflicting nature. That is how radicalism and conservatism became part and parcel of the American political thinking."

Elmo nodded and commented, "What you are saying is that a balance was established. In my opinion such state of affairs has not been a bad thing. It has maintained a balance between political tendencies and has stimulated the introduction of responsibility in the formulation of competing trends and ideologies." Elmo paused and then continued. "In general, the exercise has been a positive one. We have a country that is blessed in numberless ways and is not reluctant to share its wealth and progress with others. To me, the present economic power and prosperity enjoyed not only by our people but also by peoples of other nations is another proof that the system has worked."

"Yes, it has." The Senator smiled and went on. "Take for instance our highly touted free market economics. It has stumbled from the beginning. In a way it answers to its own designs and it has not been until this century that some understanding of what makes the economy function has been glimpsed. These days, if it does not have the austere, and sometime sinister, supervision of the Federal Reserve, the SEC and others, it wouldn't last long."

"Why is that?"

"Without strict regulations that free market of ours would become first, a slaughter house where mergers, acquisitions, junk bonds, perverse credit and financing deals and other refinements, would do away with a large number of companies, depositors, banks and other financial fauna. Two, it would inevitably lead to the creation of cartels, monopolies and privileged business groups with the result that other initiatives and competition would be stymied. Remember, the driving force remains that old perennial: greed!"

"Are you saying that there is an implied morality in the type of conservative performance by an institution like the Fed and the other agencies?"

"Yes, sir! Most control actions have an underlying moral call, and keeping a rein on a potentially damaging situation, does answer to some form of morality. But we are getting too deep into these concepts and we may end up adding to our own confusion..."

"Right, but out of all this, it sort of stands out that greed, in spite of its censurable nature, does contribute to progress. Without those terribly ambitious and ruthless operators in Business, Banking, Commerce and just about everything else, there would not be much action, would there?"

"Absolutely. But keep in mind that we have been blessed in this country with scores of ambitious, ruthless and greedy citizens from the beginning, and that in one way or another these individuals have channeled some of their wealth and drive into the general welfare. Think for a moment that instead of just plain greed for material possessions, we had raised generations of people intent on conquests, glory, world domination and imposition of their own creeds. Political thinking would have been any convenient ideology espoused by the glory seekers. Shoot, we could have had a few centuries of chaos like in Latin America, absurd systems like Nazism, Communism, Bolshevikism, Anarchism, Fascism, Communism, Peronism, take your pick. Instead, our simple people, immigrants all, were guided by some sharp merchants and a strict Church, and soon found that by tilling the land and feeding the cows they could get a lot more than raising hell somewhere."

Elmo poured himself another dry martini and sat back with a thoughtful look on his face. After a moment he said, "Your analysis is quite sharp, Senator, but what happens if your greedy merchants exceed their own ambitions? Would they not corrupt the system?"

"Yes, it has happened since day one. You see, for a company owner, director, manager or caretaker, if suddenly faced with the prospect of increasing his wealth through unorthodox, or to say it plainly, dishonest means, his moral and ethical defenses are immediately challenged. If he is not able to dominate the impulses created by that latent greed we all possess, he systematically abuses those measures and also the guidelines that have been in place. In the process, he enlists those in a position to conceal, disguise or rationalize his actions. They become corrupted. Soon, the system is no longer a collective activity created to provide benefits and security for many and becomes a convenient source of wealth and power for a few."

Elmo could not help feeling the fixed gaze of the Senator on his face. It made him wonder if the Senator was perhaps thinking about some of Elmo's better known "coups" in the business and finance worlds. He mentally reviewed some of the sophisticated but doubtful mechanisms that he had used in his career and the careful web of rationalizations that removed from his mind any form of guilt or self criticism.

The Senator got up and said, "Elmo, I have placed a number of documents, photocopies and a number of highly classified reports and letters on my desk there. I think you will find them absorbing, if not shocking. There is also specific information about some districts that will likely figure in your initiation into the rat race."

Later that evening, Elmo returned to New York feeling both encouraged and puzzled. While the Senator had unquestionably strengthened his resolve, he realized that the demands of a political career would be all consuming.

Elmo's Political Career

Elmo felt that he had reached an important period in his life, even if he was vaguely bothered by a personal contradiction. In the midst of this new direction in his life, Elmo reflected, with some regret, on the ambivalent nature of his sexuality. At times, he wished that he had acknowledged the strange sexual urges he had experienced during his puberty. He felt that maybe he could have obtained some professional help if his parents had shown the slightest inclination to concern themselves with his emotional life and not worry to excess about his material comfort. While his relationship with his father had always been open and frank, he knew that he could not discuss sex with him under any circumstance. Perhaps as a result of his father's Victorian education, any talk about sex had a connotation that instantly evoked perversion, insanity and eternal perdition.

He was convinced that early treatment or at least open discussion of his doubts and fears about sexual relations, would have helped him understand the nature of the problem and also provide him with a personal insight and a better understanding of this most important of human relations. The funny thing was, as he remembered, that his interest in girls developed at a very early age. At 12 years of age, he began to feel tremendous curiosity about the opposite sex. With typical thoroughness, he enriched his knowledge of the subject by studying textbooks on Anatomy, reading from his father's library books about physical love and also those novels that contained spicy descriptions of love affairs and even some illustrations. He managed to obtain some girlie magazines, which he studiously admired. The excitement that he felt was new to him. Seeing the naked female body caused an initial sensation of confusion, awe and admiration. His excitement was not sexual as such but more a sense of satisfaction at having disclosed to himself some missing element of his intellect.

In later years, his love life—as he termed his very limited experiences in college—were not very satisfactory. He did not extract from the occasional partner, motel room, fifth of Bourbon and pack of Trojans, the sense of release and contentment he knew must be there. Nor did he find particular pleasure in the hurried groping with awkward coeds, in the uncomfortable contortions conducted in the back of his convertible. His young partners were as inexperienced as he was, and following the dictates of current American conduct, most of the girls rarely allowed him to admire their naked bodies, preferring to accept the sexual embrace only under the sheets and with the lights out!

The defining moment, as he knew would arrive one day, happened while he was in college. As member of Yale's Rowing Eight, in the sculling events, he kept in shape by following a rigorous training program and observing the essential precautions about diet, muscle building, and mental attitude. He loved to practice on the New Haven harbor late in the afternoon, generally by himself. Then, one day he ran into Gerald, a team member known for his quiet and refined manner. They decided to do a sweep round and proceeded to spend two hours in the tiring process of synchronizing strokes and maintaining perfect control of the sliding shell. They finished well past seven o'clock and after taking the shell and the oars back to the racks, they went into the shower room.

Elmo could never decide whether he had tried to dry himself too vigorously or if the nearness of Gerald's naked body contributed to the erection he sustained. Gerald noticed it and without saying a word, reached for it. They looked themselves in the eye and without saying a word began to caress each other with a rhythm and intensity similar to their performance on the shell. The excitement Elmo felt was beyond anything he had experienced before and at that moment he realized what his problem had been all along.

They spent the night together and in few words decided that theirs was a unique affair and that discretion was the key to it. American society had not yet in those days come to terms with the realities of its complex society, preferring in most instances to close its eyes to anything that strayed away from implicit norms of behavior, to ignore situations that required the complex involvement of personal values and the realistic appraisal of available solutions.

It was easier to ignore matters or to proceed to frame self-justifying condemnations.

Their love affair lasted well beyond their college years. They both moved to New York after graduation. Elmo joined his father's holding company and Gerald accepted a teaching assistantship at Columbia. They both felt that their homosexual love had many features that they wished could be made known to the general public. Homosexuality in America, like in many parts of the world, had often implied a deviation from nature, a thesis that found ample echo in the psychiatric community and the medical profession, not to mention the religious establishment. To them, their relationship had a number of rewards that they had not found in their heterosexual relations. Their similar intellectual makeup had enabled them to develop a base of mutual respect, affection and physical love.

In less than a year after deciding to enter politics, Elmo Saks had become a major political power in the country. In what appeared an effortless campaign for a Senate seat, he had secured the nomination of the Republican Party only weeks before election day and had gone on to win the election by an ample margin of victory. Pundits, political gurus and politicians of all colors took some time to recover from the overwhelming burst of energy that had characterized Elmo's campaign. Opinions were varied.

"Anyone with deep pockets can buy a Senate seat!" "If I had Reverend Toe herding crowds of religious people in this country, I could also become elected in no time at all," "Someone who can combine a religious crusade with a political campaign, deserves any prize he gets," "It's about time our state gets a Senator that knows how to pull the strings!" and so on.

In a short time, Elmo had become a national icon. In spite of strong opposition from the more conservative sectors of the Senate, he had managed to become the Chairman of the powerful Appropriations Committee and had proceeded to wield the power of that office to pursue a new style of what he termed "inspired control of the cookie jar." His energetic approach to complex bureaucratic procedures was admired and also feared. He was ruthless when it came to destroying those that opposed him or even attempted to put off or delay those pieces of legislation favored by Elmo. In the first couple of years he was indirectly responsible for the quiet resignation of half a dozen Senators, innumerable staff members and at least two suicides.

Elmo's extraordinary intelligence and cunning enabled him to use his newly found power to expand his business empire and to increase in exponential fashion his already immense personal fortune. A web of off-shore companies,

Foundations, Funds, Merchant Banks, industrial conglomerates and even investments in restricted accounts of foreign governments in Europe, Asia and South America, were cleverly disguised and enabled him to leverage not only financial but also political strategies. His influence had grown beyond anything he had expected.

During all this time, Gerald had played an important part in his life. Their love affair had matured into a solid and pleasant relationship; Gerald's gentleness and quiet and unassuming manner contrasted, or perhaps complemented, Elmo's blustery and forceful personality. Gerald had gently refused to participate in Elmo's political life and had also turned down attractive academic offers, secretly arranged by Elmo to move to Washington. But they continue to see each other as Elmo had leased an apartment in the same building on West 70th Street where Gerald had lived since moving to New York. They continued to exercise extreme care in their relationship. No one could even remotely imagine that their casual friendship disguised an intense homosexual affair.

In his second year in the Senate, with general elections approaching, Elmo was contacted by the party's leaders who bluntly offered him the chance to submit his candidacy for the Presidency. They would maneuver and arrange for a swift nomination at the Party's Convention and provide the necessary support in the general election. Typically, Elmo questioned them point blank about what they expected in return. They produced a long list that in Elmo's estimation, accustomed to grand schemes and megadeals, was merely trifles. He had no trouble agreeing, thinking all the time that he could always back out of any promise made or arrange for cancellation of any program they proposed that he objected to. As the seasoned politician he had become, he was aware of the convenient flexibility he could muster in the fulfilling of promises and covenants.

At the right moment, the political machinery was set in motion. Elmo's name became again a recognizable item in the entire country. He had an enthusiastic ally in Reverend Toe. Through the church's network of sanctuaries all over the world he was in a position to influence not only American public opinion but also world opinion. As a result, candidate Saks became a household name in most countries.

"Why should the United States elect a leader who, we know, will directly affect conditions in our countries, without lettings us have our say?"

The Reverend's clever reasoning, aided by the power and influence of his Sanctuaries, created both interest and expectation in other countries. Some sectors in Canada revived talk about Canada becoming part of the United

States. As in the past when a famous Sicilian bandit, Giuliano, proposed that Sicily be annexed to the US, some of the smaller countries or protectorates realized that becoming attached to the US was not an impossible dream. Encouraged by Toe and Elmo's circle of associates, places like Gibraltar, Montecarlo, Cuba, Singapore, Panama, Bermuda, Ireland, Iceland, Uruguay, Malta, Holland and even Norway, harbored movements of integration.

These movements, whose impact on world opinion did not go unnoticed, provided Elmo and the Rev Toe with substantial political support at home.

Elmo's position in the US political spectrum was by now firmly established. Elmo had reason to be satisfied and proud of his achievement. But at the same time he had began to acknowledge that his triumphs would acquire a sweeter taste if he could openly share them with someone. He was also aware that as candidate for the Presidency, a wife was essential but he could not bring himself to accept the complications of a marriage of convenience, other than the fact that he felt no physical attraction or desire for any member of the opposite sex.

It was enough of a burden to have to keep up appearances by appearing regularly with some striking female. He felt it was one of the sacrifices he had to make to maintain an acceptable popular image. To him, those dates were boring and stressful. He did not enjoy the vacuity of most of the women he was forced to date and could not stand their occasional displays of affection toward him and, in more than one occasion, the outright proposals to end the dates in physical intimacy.

Elmo had seldom sought any homosexual contact with a person other than Gerald. Over the years however he had been involved in a few discreet affairs in several cities but never in the Washington area and certainly not in New York. Of late however, after bouts of frenetic dealing and wheeling in the Senate, he began to experience periods of loneliness and, often enough, some restlessness that heightened his sexual desire. It was during one of these periods, when he was attending a party meeting in West Palm Beach that he ran into Ray. From the beginning Ray had been perhaps a bit too attentive with the Senator. As a volunteer in the local party headquarters, Ray had been asked to stick with Senator Saks and serve him as liaison, bodyguard, secretary and overall assistant.

At the end of a particularly lengthy session, and having missed supper, Ray suggested that the Senator come to his place where he would prepare a late snack. Elmo agreed and thought nothing of it. Midnight suppers, snacks and impromptu meals are part and parcel of a Senator's curriculum. He told his

Chief of Staff that he was going out to dinner with Ray and that he would see him in the morning. The crowd was quickly dispersing in twos and threes, as limousines and taxis created a minor chaos in front of the hotel.

Ray turned out to be a creditable gourmet cook. In no time at all he had prepared some salmon au papillotte, a green salad enhanced with three kinds of cheese and a smooth dressing of lemon, olive oil, mustard and chives. He produced a chilled bottle of an excellent Marques de Cáceres that was quickly consumed.

Ray explained that he was in the States for only a few months in order to acquire first hand knowledge of American Political Science. His parents, both Americans had lived in London for some years and Ray had the benefit of a mixed education. As a young lawyer, or solicitor as called in England, he was enjoying immensely his experience in Florida.

After the meal, they sat in the terrace overlooking the canal and drank from a fancy Brandy decanter that Ray had brought along with two goblets. Ray made the first move. "Senator, it is warm out here, why don't you remove your jacket. You'll be more comfortable."

"Ray, not only the jacket but also the necktie and the shoes," replied Elmo while wondering fleetingly about Ray's sexual preferences.

Ray then removed his jacket and necktie and also his shirt. His undershirt seemed glued to his torso. At that point Ray noticed, with that special intuition that homosexuality almost guarantees, that Elmo was looking at him with more than casual interest. Upon noticing a tattoo on Ray's arm, Elmo moved his chair closer to Ray's, ostensibly to examine the tattoo at short range. He reached for the arm and touched the tattoo. A look was exchanged between them and they both knew what was coming.

Elmo erased from his mind the episode with Ray. He had felt that Ray was not the type to expose or divulge their adventure. He stood to lose a great deal if their indiscretion was uncovered. His remorse was short lived; in all these years, he had been more concerned about Gerald finding out about his occasional promiscuity. He feared Gerald's reactions and was afraid to lose the mutual love and respect that anchored their relationship.

Several weeks later, he received a registered letter addressed to him that noted prominently that it was to be opened only by Elmo. It was postmarked in Chicago and had been left on his desk late that evening. He had returned from dinner and had decided to do some work in the peace and quiet of the off-hours office He opened the letter thinking that it would be another private request for economic assistance or one of the many he received protesting any one of his recent decisions. Inside, there was a small card and a black and white photocopy of a photograph. The photograph showed Ray and Elmo standing naked in front of a mirror. The card said:

We know about Gerald and Ray. We will telephone you at your home in two days.

For a full two minutes, Elmo Saks remained motionless. Gradually he recovered while noting that he had just undergone a tremendous emotional shock. He did not feel rational enough to make the effort to translate the substance of the message that the card and the photocopy conveyed. He reached for the water carafe and poured himself a large glass of water. He drank the water, all the while looking at the card and the photocopy, as if hypnotized by them.

After a while, his brilliant mind took over and began to separate and catalog the elements of the communication. First, the mechanical elements. It was a plain, ordinary envelope postmarked in Chicago. Second, it was addressed to him personally and his address was spelled and noted correctly. Third, it contained two parts; a card, handwritten in what obviously was false penmanship. The card was ordinary paper of about, he guessed 24 pound weight. The photocopy was also quite ordinary; the paper and the quality of it pointed to one of those public copying machines in perhaps a supermarket. He carefully placed the card and the photocopy back in the envelope using his letter opener. Just in case, he wanted to preserve whatever fingerprints could still be recovered from the envelope and its contents. He placed the envelope inside a folder and put the folder inside his safety box in back of his desk. He noticed that his hands were shaking and that his vision was a little blurry. He sat down at his desk again and began to analyze the meaning, purpose and ramifications of the communication.

In the next three hours, Elmo reviewed in meticulous order, first, those people near him who could have had occasion to link him and Gerald. Then those who might have discovered his brief affair with Ray. This last meant that the person had been in Florida attending the Party meeting. He quickly discounted the investigators and like fauna that were attached to the staff of other Senators and party members and whose role was to document any irregularities in the public and private life of prominent politicians. If the person knew about Gerald and about Ray, it must be someone close to him. Probably a member of his staff. He ruled out his Chief of Staff, whose loyalty had been put to the test in previous occasions. Slowly, he went through the list of people in his office and could not find anyone that could possibly know about Gerald.

He was about to give up when it occurred to him to access his computer and its infinite capacity to produce facts and establish links. Besides, he had access to a number of Government reserved sites that contained privileged information and data on members of Congress and their staffs. Other than his declared enemies, he concentrated on persons who might have urgent reasons to resort to blackmail. Political blackmail is generally conducted through the press and it invariably follows it own protocol. So it wasn't a political vendetta, nor a nosey reporter or a dejected suitor. His enemies were all powerful men whose methods were subtle and in general, involved strategies that included others. They were ruled out. This was in all certainty a personal initiative. Motive: money.

He began go reduce the number of suspects. The first list included those who had traveled from Washington to Florida to attend the meeting. He also listed the key staff members that had been to Florida. Patiently he studied each name and tried to imagine both a connection to his situation and a possible motive. He removed a good number from the list. He eliminated those who could not possibly know about Gerald. He desperately tried to remember any event or situation where any of those in the diminishing lists might have learned about Gerald.

The computer began to list current net worth of the names in the list. Most appeared normal, in the sense that there were no glaring differences or unusual conditions. He continued to explore the net worth angle in an effort to find anyone who might be in serious economic difficulty. The computer dutifully listed in reducing order those whose financial position was weak.

Another list was prepared. This time, it had no more than a dozen names. He quickly discounted those who he knew had not attended the Florida meeting. Next, he checked any possible connections with Chicago. The list was now reduced to 3. He stopped and concentrated on the three names. All of a sudden he hit his forehead with the palm of his hand. He checked the computer list. Sure enough, there was a name corresponding to someone whose financial situation was not only weak but desperate. He accessed more files and was able to learn the extent of current obligations, both long term and worrisome short term liabilities that suggested large expenditures of a speculative or gambling nature. He recalled a chance meeting in the lobby of the apartment in New York some months back with a Junior Senator. Later, Gerald had told him that several questions had been asked of the building superintendent about him and about Gerald. He had found him!

"How did you find out it was me?" Junior Senator Allen Post asked in a voice that clearly betrayed not only nervousness but also fear.

"It is not important. I feel that we have to talk, that's why I asked you to have lunch with me away from the old school. We can talk and not be disturbed. Besides, you'll save the 35 cents of the phone call you had scheduled for tomorrow evening."

"Elmo, I hope you are not about to do something rash. There is a detailed letter in the hands of the Editor of the Washington Post that is to be opened if anything should happen to me."

"That is good thinking, Allen. But nothing is going to happen to you. There must be a solution to this problem of yours. Money is no object."

Elmo's chauffeur, Remy, was aware that another unpleasant episode was about to take place. Every time he was asked to pick up the Senator and his guest or guests in the basement parking garage, something strange would happen. For one thing, the parking garage had several entrances, it was poorly illuminated and the car had tinted windows. Discretion and secrecy were almost assured.

As in previous occasions, Remy was prepared. He knew that once past the bridge on highway 50 he would have to turn into a country road that led to a farm house and a large barn. He drove directly into the barn.

A few miles north of the farmhouse there is a fishmeal processing plant owned by one of the companies within one of Elmo's holdings. The company imports fishmeal from Peru and Japan and formulates feed for the crab beds in Chesapeake Bay and some of the lobster farms down by Wenona and Crisfield. In addition to the blending and formulating equipment in the main plant, the facility also has a small-capacity unit in a separate building where residuals from meat and poultry processing are used to make enriched meal. Thus Junior Senator Allen Post joined the ranks of those who contributed to the rich protein diet of Bay crabs and lobsters.

The disappearance of Senator Post made the headlines of all papers in the country. While not a popular or an outstanding figure, the senator had a substantial following in his native state of North Dakota. All kinds of rumors were circulated. His brief fling with a British actress induced some to believe that he might be in England. Some of his relatives, aware of his financial difficulties feared that he had purposely disappeared and had assumed another identity. Both the FBI and the Metropolitan Police could not find any clues about his whereabouts. The case remained open.

Elmo counted on receiving another call. This time from the editor of the

Washington Post. He could not imagine that old Ben Branson would take action on such delicate matter without first confronting him. Elmo was prepared to deal with old Ben. The newspaper was partially owned by one of the companies in Elmo's holding and quite dependent on the generous facilities extended by one of its banks, also in the holding.

Elmo miscalculated. Old Ben gathered his editors, the Publishers and an independent and prestigious Washington law firm and presented them with the evidence contained in the manila envelope that he had kept in his safe for several weeks. After much soul searching and lively argumentation, it was decided that the matter had to be made public.

The scandal became an episode of epic proportions. The day the headlines aired the affair, Gerald committed suicide by ingesting a bottle full of Nucrazion tablets, the potent and effective blood pressure regulator. Wall Street reacted to the news with a substantial drop in the share value of some of the companies that were associated with Senator Elmo Saks, while at the same time arousing the interest of the usual trading sharks.

Elmo's chairmanship in the Appropriations Committee and all the other responsibilities within the Senate were quickly revoked, as the Senate negotiated with Elmo's lawyers to terminate as soon as possible the various aspects of the case. This time, the President applied the full weight of the executive office to recommend swift but quiet action and avoid the trauma of a national trial. There was no need to open any proceedings against Elmo even if some of his more vindictive enemies wanted as much public humiliation as possible. No one had thought to connect the disappearance of Senator Post and Senator Sak's disturbing exposure. In a few days, Elmo had been effectively erased from the rolls of public service.

Elmo retreated to his state in the peninsula and remained isolated for several weeks. Efforts to contact him were useless. A barrier of lawyers, assistants and friends managed to keep the media and others away from Elmo.

Elmo himself took matters in a philosophical vein. He overcame the depression caused by Gerald's suicide by throwing himself into a frenetic round of meetings overseas. He knew that exhausting work would keep him from digging into the clouds of guilt, self pity and contempt that invaded his soul; it would also keep him from bringing back the pain that Gerald's suicide had brought.

More than ever, he decided to strengthen the holding and streamline all operations. He paid special attention to the recruiting of powerful and influential people from all over the world so that he could, in any given situation, count with their active participation. A few months after his departure from political life, he began again to hold meetings at his estate in St. Michael's, where no more than a dozen of his associates would be invited at a time.

It was in this period when the world was shocked by the appearance of the objects over its major cities. Elmo's initial reaction was predictable. He applied the reasoning sequences that he had used so successfully in business and then in Government. First was credibility. Do not believe anything you hear, read, see or imagine. Next was suspicion. What do they want from me? What can I get from them? Then it was information and details followed by cross checking, evaluation, analysis and a vague plan of action.

Elmo's Aims

"I cannot believe that aliens from other worlds have installed all those ships on earth. We have not seen a single photograph of these beings, and I refuse to believe that Deschamps was not wired when he visited the ship! We only have his description of their physical appearance and we don't know what they sound like. It is not clear what they want but whatever it is, we must do it. We are totally at his mercy because he is the only one in contact with them and he can easily report and interpret anything at will. Shoot, it sounds like a giant scam. He can tell us whatever he wants!"

Elmo Saks looked at his small audience and smiled as he continued in the same agitated tone. "If you ask me, this is just another ploy by some of the industrialized nations to intimidate the people of earth. As we all know, the promotion of fear is and has been one of the more efficient tools of mind control. I am sure that behind this there is a well designed plot to go after something that the other nations have. It might also affect our globalization plans and the freedoms we have enjoyed so far."

The meeting had been secretly called by Elmo and all those that had been contacted were present. It was more of a summons than an invitation. Elmo Saks was known for his temperamental outbursts and the ruthless dedication to his beliefs. Those present owed their prominent positions in the Western World to Elmo Saks and were never allowed to forget it.

For years now, Elmo Saks had held secret meetings with 24 prominent members of the more important nations on earth. The group included elder and respected statesmen, retired ambassadors, bankers, economists, scientists and high ranking ex-officers. The tremendous wealth of Elmo's holdings had enabled him to assemble such influential group for the purpose of expanding his various enterprises and to help him manage wealth beyond anybody's dreams.

"Mister Gonzalez Bueno, you as one of the Deputy Directors of UNESCO must have detected some of this. After all, Deschamps relies on your organization for his political maneuvering and, I am sure, he keeps your boss, Ulderico Menor Tarragona, informed of everything."

Jose Antonio Gonzales Bueno was nervous and uncomfortable. He feared that in this case, he would be the one to shoulder the major part of whatever strategy Elmo Saks was developing. His prestige at UNESCO and the UN was a convenient tool for the Holding, who had used him a number of times to push through resolutions at both UNESCO and the UN itself. He was also convinced that the ships were really from another dimension and that Patrick's detailed reports were true.

He spoke in the usual measured tone with that trace of an educated English accent that journalists—and American women—found so attractive. "So far, Mister Saks, Deschamps seems to be so emotionally involved with this experience that I would be most surprised if this whole thing were a plot and he was a part of it. Besides, I do not think that the technology exists in our planet to place these huge ships at high altitude without moving. They certainly do not look like anything made by man."

"Exactly!"—Elmo interrupted. "His own honesty makes him convincing. Don't forget that deceit, to be successful, must be practiced by people of strong morality. And about technology, you forget that discoveries and inventions have always created speculation and that speculation is fertile ground for developing creeds and interpretations. Just imagine for a moment that someone had developed a helicopter in the 18th century. He would create such speculation in the minds of everyone that he could easily ascribe miraculous qualities to the object. Imagine for a moment the reaction of Louis XVI and his court upon seeing a helicopter fluttering about in the gardens at Versailles. The defiance of the laws of gravity of such contraption, coupled with its speed and maneuverability in the air, with no explanation that existing knowledge could provide, Louis would be ready to accept any convenient story."

Gomzalez Bueno, like the others present, did not feel like engaging in a discussion with Elmo Saks. He had too many memories of similar situations in the past where Elmo had prevailed in exposing his views but also had vanished in disgrace those who did not spouse them.

"All I can do, Mister Saks, is to keep attending the meetings of the Emergency Committee and inform you of everything that happens, as I have been doing."

"Well, I want more than reports. I think it is about time that we become involved directly in this matter. I want to see these so called aliens face to face. If they are really from other worlds, we must find out the extent to which they can be useful to us. The UN will never in a million years be able to take advantage of an opportunity like this one."

Dr. Erasmus "Corky" Gilbreath, the noted Harvard Economist and adviser to several US Presidents, cleared his throat and said, "Mister Saks, I agree with you. This entire episode could well be an artificially created alarm. For some time now I have been very suspicious about the Big 8. I have observed that at every summit some closed door sessions—totally unscheduled—take place. These are never reported or reflected in the joint communiqués. I have also noticed that members of some of the special agencies from each country are called at these meetings and after, they are quickly and discreetly sent away. I also recall that last year a number of top executives from Boeing, Sud Aviation, General Dynamics, Lockheed, Rolls Royce and Focke-Wulff happened to be having a summit of their own in the same city where the Big 8 Summit was held. At one point, the aircraft manufacturers hosted a dinner for the Big 8. It was attended only by the bosses. No interpreters, assistants or secretaries. We may be witnessing the appearance of revolutionary technology that the big boys wish to exploit by themselves."

Their discussion continued for some time. To many of them it was clear that Elmo's impotence at not being able to play a part in the contacts with the visitors, had turned to extreme frustration and rage.

At one point, Elmo Saks banged his fist on the table with great force. He leaned forward and, red in the face, yelled, "The only thing that is going to work is the use of extreme measures!"

Those around the table, used to his bursts of rage, remained quiet and waited for Elmo to regain his composure. But it was not to be.

"I have asked several of you to apply pressure to Deschamps, to the President and to that know-it-all Ferguson. But I got nothing! Nothing! All I get is excuses. George, tell us again about Deschamps."

George Sferza, CEO of one of the largest banks in the country, turned pale and, showing evident signs of nervousness, spoke in a low voice. "I finally got to Deschamps last week in New York. I was able to drag him for a cup of coffee after he had attended mass in St. Patrick's."

He was interrupted by Elmo, who said in a harsh tone, "If you talk louder instead of whispering like a decrepit priest, maybe we can hear what you have to say!"

George Sferza flushed and, with an effort, raised his voice to continue. "I explained to Deschamps that it was necessary that a special rapport be established with the visitors and that it was in the benefit of the Free World that an independent group such as our, assume a key role. I reminded him of our wish to remain independent, which would imply our preserving a position outside the reach of the major industrialized nations."

"What did he have to say?"

"He felt that it is too early to suggest any arrangements to the visitors. He mentioned that they possess powers well beyond anything we can imagine and doubts that they would be willing to discuss special alliances of a commercial nature."

"How about the carrot and the stick approach we discussed before you met with him?"

"Deschamps did not bat an eyelash. I even appealed to his patriotism and went to great lengths to describe the benefits that the deal we wish to work out would bring to the country, the world economy and, of course, the people. When he kept saying that the visitors would not be interested in pursuing any scheme of the type we have in mind, I reminded him that sooner or later they would have to modify their presence here and take active part in this planet's life. He also insisted that they are energy in themselves and proposals to develop new communication systems or improve energy sources in the world do not seem to interest them at all. I continued to insist that maybe if we could have the opportunity to discuss the matter directly with them, we could come to a better understanding. But he would not budge."

"All right. All right!" interrupted Elmo. "How about the stick?"

"I tried first to point to him that any arrangement he helped us make, would bring to him personally, untold benefits. Working on his transcendental inclinations, I stressed the fact that history would view his contribution as a major world event. But no dice. So I hinted at the possibility of working with the countries that attended the London meeting and had proposed by-passing the UN and making a deal directly with the visitors. Still no reaction. So I had no recourse but to say that if he was not prepared to work with us, we could arrange for some events that could force his resignation from the UN."

"What did he say to that?"

"Nothing really. He looked at me and shook his head. He got up, thanked me for the coffee and said, 'No Deal.'"

The meeting continued for some time, while Elmo insisted in pursuing new ways to have direct access to the visitors. They reviewed in detail, Patrick's recent life in an effort to find something that could be used as leverage to make him change his mind. A similar process involving Richard Ferguson and Helen Lawrence was pursued. Even Mercedes came under the scrutiny of those present.

That evening, Elmo dined alone and devoted the after dinner hours to serious thinking about the visitors and the strategy to adopt. The direct approach to Deschamps had failed. His maneuvering to get the European nations to propose his industrial group as a viable representative before the visitors had also earned no support. Gradually, an idea came to his mind. Why not substitute Deschamps? Peacefully? If he could manage to have Deschamps replaced by someone close to Elmo, he would eventually enjoy access to the visitors and would be able to carry on his ambitious plans. But he would have to stress the fact that the US deserved to take active part in the relations with the visitors in order to lead to a tactful replacement of Deschamps.

The next day, Elmo called the Reverend John Toe and asked him to come to St. Michael's.

"John, I am going to need a special campaign from you about these damned pills. I need the support of your churches and organizations to create a strong public feeling about them. You see, we have left the negotiating and contact with these visitors in the hands of the United Nations. Even if Deschamps has proven to be a most competent diplomat and administrator, I don't feel the United States should allow others to decide its future. I feel very strongly that we should be at the bargaining table rubbing shoulders with the visitors. After all, we are the major world power and our influence extends to all nations on earth."

"Yes, Elmo, but we are very much involved in the discussions with the visitors. One of our most popular humanitarians, that Ferguson character, is right in the middle of it. And he is working within a committee that includes a majority of Americans. Also, don't forget the UN's close ties with President Simonson."

"Right you are. But don't forget that a more direct channel with the US would result in better relations with these people, or whatever they are. Here is where you come in. This phenomenon has become a religious experience on this planet and it is along those lines that I wish to introduce criteria of what our country's role should be. If people are reminded of our importance in the well being of human society, and the right we have to be up in the pills instead of

Deschamps, we might be able to justify a change and have someone like you replace Deschamps."

John Toe looked at Elmo's necktie, afraid to look into his eyes and read what he was afraid had been there all the time. His mind raced back to the numerous times that Elmo had come to his aid and to those instances when Elmo had deposited all his trust in him with delicate matters involving the Foundations, the University and the highly successful Sanctuaries that had been built all over the world. *It is payback time*. His mind quickly unreeled that scene in *The Godfather* when Vito Corleone summons the mortician, who was in his debt, to request the favor of fixing up Sonny's shattered body. He made an effort to disguise the complacent feeling he experienced when it was suggested that he replace Deschamps.

It was a major compliment and implied recognition of his own worth. Both his ego, that mass of contradictions that subsisted thanks to his self assurance, his mental capacity, and his vanity, that nagging perception that seemed to inhabit his very soul, were deeply touched by Elmo's words. He slowly said, "I can start an immediate revival. It is not difficult to get people's attention nowadays. Our congregations are growing by the hour. Our services have been doubled since the appearance of those things and, funny enough, we are getting more offers for the coffers than ever before. People are streaming in desirous of becoming patrons, you know, make sizable contributions. I can devise the theme and develop the promotion in such way that very soon people will be clamoring for change. We can reach almost any country on earth, even China now where we have recently inaugurated 6 new sanctuaries. My questions at this time are many however. Elmo, what the hell do I do with these visitors in the event that I can replace Deschamps. Two, your involvement in this thing only means that there is a goal you are pursuing. What is it?"

Elmo Saks smiled and gently removed his Lott and Parrish eye glasses. He continued to smile without saying a word. He then put the eyeglasses inside a beautifully crafted Italian leather case and placing it on the small table with some decision, said to the Reverend John Toe, "John, the many years we have worked together are finally bringing a fabulous payoff. To both of us. As to what you do with the visitors, I wouldn't worry too much. They are intent on reforming a few things down here and you can surely help them do that. They will be happy to attach whatever spiritual values and religious fervor you can bring into their plans. It means that you will become the number one spiritual leader on the planet."

With excitement showing in his voice, John interrupted to ask, "And what about you?"

"Was about to tell you. Once we start working with them, it will be easy to convince them to let us use their communications technology to help them carry out their plans."

"What for? They can manage admirably, to judge by the way they turn on and off all screens on earth at will."

"Exactly! That is what I wish to get hold of. Imagine having instant TV, telephone, radio, computers, and all possible communications under control. What happens to all the mega empires in world Telecommunications? What would happen to television broadcasts, networks, radio, cable systems, satellite services, the internet, the private and secured message channels, all bank transactions, government secret lines, airline scheduling, traffic fines, credit card purchases, ATM operations, fiber optics, hertzian waves, microwaves, landing lights, traffic lights?"

He paused for a second and, with great vehemence on his voice, he continued, "I don't know how many other activities are conducted through the use of telephone lines, fiber optics, satellites, smoke signals, you name it. The idea is to control all these means of communication on earth. Between you and me old boy, instead of scores of multinationals with fat executive payrolls, one central entity staffed by loyal platoons of starched yuppies can run the entire omelet. For starters, communications would be the ideal opener.

"But, for what purpose?"

"I just told you!" He smiled and continued. "I suspect that these aliens, or whatever, will have to do some adjustments in our society if they wish to restore those balances and equilibrium that Deschamp reported. It sounds like they are talking about energy variations that they must correct. OK, I can put together an energy consortium in no time at all. You know about our holdings in power companies all over the world, oil companies, oil producing countries, etc. I can add our control of telecommunications companies all over the world, the satellites we operate and the network of television and radio stations. I can offer them a truly multinational network of companies, which is something the UN or any government is in no position to offer. They wish to rearrange energy distribution on the planet, they are welcome to it, as long as they use the means I control. In exchange, I want the communications parcel."

The Reverend listened with attention and then observed, "Elmo, we don't know what this talk about energy is all about. You are assuming that it has to do with electrical energy or energy fuels. From what Deschamps reports, the visitors are thinking in term of some abstract form of equilibrium, where energy is one of the elements."

"No matter. I can help them rearrange any energy profiles they wish. Keep in mind that we are in a position to exploit their technology better than anyone. One is Communications. We have that pretty well covered. Two is transportation. We have airlines, shipping lines, mail and delivery services, train and bus systems; it will be relatively easy for us to adapt their fabulous pills into commercial vehicles, whose comfort and safety will be unparalleled. And if they let us, we would like to get our hands on the kind of technology that enables them to place an electromagnetic shield around their vessels. In one stroke, we make conflicts obsolete and armies unnecessary. Instead we can organize police services the world over. You know, we keep every country in line and if anyone gets out of line, zap! we blast them!"

"You are talking about getting in bed with them so that you can run the show on earth. I know what you get in return but, what do they get?"

Elmo looked at the Reverend with interest and replied, "They accomplish whatever mission has been entrusted to them and in the process contribute to improving matters in this planet. Isn't that enough?"

John Toe had always considered Elmo Saks a brilliant manipulator that had amassed one of the largest fortunes in the planet. He knew what power meant to Elmo. It meant to be in control. To analyze matters in his own perspective and above all to plan, organize and direct entire worldwide strategies. His objectives had always been clear: to control key sectors of the world economy as a means of protecting and increasing his own wealth. But this time, the objects overhead and their unique characteristics had given Elmo other ideas. It appeared to the Reverend that good old Elmo was developing a Goldfinger complex. His ambition had started to acquire different bounds. He now wanted to reshape the world and for that he needed the help of the Reverend. With these thoughts in mind, he asked, "Elmo, your words confirm to me what I always felt was your ultimate objective: to find the way to influence, if not control, events on the planet. If your strategy works, you will be able to control world communications for a starter and from there who knows."

"Of course, if we start with communications, we are touching every nerve, commercial and otherwise, in the entire planet. I grant you that my own ambition and ego enter into the picture. Same as the knowledge I possess about communications in its infinite forms and its impact on society. Remember also that appealing to the senses in human beings is the quickest route to their intellects."

All the Reverend could say was, "I see."

"John, think of the way the boys in the ship managed to hold the entire world spellbound with their simple messages. They keep the screens empty for a period while everyone wonders about it. They create the suspense and the expectation. Then they deliver the message and then empty screens. Talk about shock value. And they had the audience in their hands!"

The Reverend smiled remembering his uneasiness and anxiety when the screens all over the world suddenly turned on. He said, "Well, yes. The power of the image is undeniable. Visual contact is the most powerful and useful tool we humans have. So is television! Thinking of it as only one sector in the world of communications I wonder what criteria and objectives must be developed to be able to make it an even more effective tool. More important, to keep the people watching."

It was Elmo's turn to smile and with genuine excitement continued. "Reverend, OK, let us look at television. To me, the analysis is simple. I base it on televisions original purpose, which was to entertain, inform and educate. So we look at world television today and what do we find? We find a very disappointing and inconsistent performance. We witness a great deal of trash, sex, violence, stupid contests, humiliating personal displays and the conception and coverage of outlandish events. A mammoth industry has been created that merchandises the dark side of our natures. By gosh! Even the techniques have changed."

As usual when dealing with a favorite subject, Elmo would pause and close his eyes and then would continue. "The few channels that started with good intentions and made the effort to provide a decent fare, have slowly deteriorated into the monotonous and boring showcases of fixed photography plus narration episodes they pompously call specials. Just get a couple of old photographs, pick up an unemployed scriptwriter at any bar on Second Avenue and you are in business. The janitor can do the close ups on the photographs with the studio camera and even pan and zoom in and out for minutes or hours if needed."

He pointed a finger at the Reverend and continued. "John, they have killed the plastic arts. Now, television with the aid of the computer and its infinite versatility, have done away with down-to-earth creativity. I am not saying that it should be abolished. I am saying that TV programs must be conceived and produced within criteria of good taste, quality and personal creativity!"

He stopped with a dreamy smile on his face then continued. "You see, here is the chance to shape and mold the minds of the human race. As in practically all other instances in the history of mankind, to really take a giant step, there can be no democratic play. The whole thing has to be run in answer to single criteria. In this case it will be mine."

"But you think people are going to sit still while you feed them whatever you think is best?"

"John, dear John," replied Elmo with a sigh. "I want to bring some sanity to the entertainment industry. It is the best way to enter, mold and condition the minds of the people. Above all I want to do away with the slob mentality in this country. I want to do away with those commercials that portray actors acting and looking like slobs. I am sure that people in other countries think that ours is a slob culture!"

"Well," protested the Reverend, "they all have their own slobs!"

Elmo looked out the window with that familiar expression that combined wistfulness and determination. Something like Evel Knivel's look just before opening the throttle. He took a deep breath and continued. "Think a bit. We have been going the way of old Rome. People are exposed to spectacles of all sorts as often as possible. And I am sure that there must be dark and smelly rooms in the posh network offices where horny, bald-headed executives devote their time to devising new game shows, talk shows, giveaway shows, scandal shows, mystery shows, funny video shows, behind the scene shows, cooking shows, travel shows and who knows what else."

Now that he got started, Elmo acquired a frantic tone. A look of disgust painted his flushed features. "Then, another gang is working the sports scene. Now we have senior this and senior that tournaments. Retired glories, and aging veterans all making fools of themselves. And the funny thing is that there are sponsors for every event imaginable. Soon, we'll be watching 6th graders competing in parachute jumps and nude grandmothers playing volley ball tournaments."

"But, Elmo," observed John, "if they keep doing it is because people like it. It is because there is an audience willing to support the products advertised and to provide the support the networks need."

"That is what you think! You yourself have employed some of the more refined techniques in the art of capturing and holding on to people's minds and preferences. Your campaign on the sanctuaries is a textbook case. I seem to remember that at the time, you concluded that people on this planet were ready and willing to be convinced about almost anything and that all it took was the right stimuli. Well, if I can control telecommunications of all kinds, I will be in a position to reach every intellect on the planet. I will be in a position to influence and control human emotions and human reactions, just like the promoters who guide the public into spectacles, action shows and what not!"

Their conversation continued well into the late hours of the night. And it was a fruitful interval. They agreed on a number of measures to influence public opinion in favor of the sanctuaries. It included effective steps to enhance the Reverend's image. Along the way, a strong but subtle campaign was to be waged in favor of having the US assume a leading role in the contact with the visitors. And in another lateral initiative, Elmo Sak's record of charities and legitimate good deeds was to receive special attention for the purpose of bringing a fresh image of his before the public.

The Visitors to the Ship Return to New York

While Elmo Saks continued to explore avenues of contact with the alien visitors, Kathryn, Helen, Richard and Patrick had concluded their most incredible visit to the ship and with some sadness prepared for their return to New York. Their short shuttle flight to the UN helipad was barely notice as it lasted about as long as the blinking of an eye. Before they knew it, they were in front of a large crowd that spilled over the gardens and the walkways. There were cameras everywhere, paparazzi and reporters three deep. The UN Press Officer managed to steer the four towards one of the entrances and, after checking with Patrick, stopped and, turning toward the anxious crowd of news people, asked for silence. "I know you are very anxious to learn about our group's trip to the pill above. We all are. There will be a detailed press release available this evening at the Press Office at 8 p.m. Right now, they have to rest a while and then report to the Council. Let me advance that they have had a most successful and fascinating visit. None of us will be disappointed. Thank your for your cooperation!"

He gently led the four into the open door and swiftly disappeared inside the building amid the protests of the reporters and others outside.

That same evening, the UN Press Office released a long statement describing how Kathryn and Helen had been invited to be present at The Last Supper in Jerusalem, two thousand years ago! It briefly noted the highlights of that unique voyage and noted with wonderment about how they had lived an amazing experience in a short New York summer afternoon. It also attempted to explain that while they went up to the ship at noon and returned at 6 p.m., they had actually spent more than 16 hours in the ship. The report went on to explain in not very clear terms, the ability of the visitors to arrange time at will.

As world interest grew, Patrick and the Council realized that the best thing to do was to have Kathryn and Helen report to the world through the UN's General Assembly. This was quickly arranged and a date set three days hence.

Both Patrick and Richard had had to spend precious time to establish some guidelines for the event. It wasn't often that private individuals reached world audiences through the General Assembly. With the help of Baron Carini and his staff they reviewed legal and logistical matters. They also enlisted Cardinal Ludlam's help in establishing some form of policy in relation to the religious forces in the world. Kathryn and Helen's report was certain to become a cornerstone of modern human history. Cardinal Ludlam quickly invited the visible heads of the Protestant, Jewish and Islamic faiths in the country to participate in the review of the Special UN report by Kathryn and Helen.

The President of the United States, accompanied by his wife, Earla Ann, flew to New York the day before the Special UN Session. Several Heads of State had also made the trip, most of them on short notice.

The day of the Extraordinary Session, the UN building was overflowing with delegates, guests, Ambassadors, Heads of State and their relatives and staff, and an army of reporters, anchors, commentators and even Sports figures. In this hectic atmosphere, the President of the United States took refuge in Baron Carini's office suite while Earla Ann was discreetly spirited away by Mrs. Nelson to Patrick's apartment where Kathryn and Helen were making notes for their report that evening.

It was inevitable that a number of informal meetings take place among Heads of State and their advisers. Most offices on the upper floors were "borrowed" by top officials from many countries for impromptu meetings.

Moments before the beginning of the Special Session, the President met with Simon Ross, the British Prime Minister in Patrick's office.

"Well, Simon," the President said, "our visitors seem to have gotten hold of the agendas, or should I say the reins of this affair. I can see that their scientific and technological level is well beyond anything we have on Earth. What I have learned from Patrick and Richard about this visit convinces me that whatever happens is going to be under their control."

The Prime Minister nodded in agreement and observed, "Our scientists and technical people, as you know, analyzed the circumstances of Patrick's first trip up to the ship. Their conclusions, in short, are that these beings are something out of outer space, and never better said. Their ability to manipulate matter, like the shuttle, and the darn pills is beyond anyone's comprehension."

The President had listened to the Prime Minister with obvious interest. He said, "I still find hard to believe that the ladies were taken back a couple of thousand years to witness an event that is a treasure of mankind. It was not done with mirrors or through hypnosis or some hallucinogen. Patrick showed me a roman coin, a linen handkerchief and one of the small spoons in use at that time. He told the visitors about it and they did not mind at all. You know what one of them said?"

The Prime Minister was all surprise. All he could mutter was, "What?"

The President smiled and tried to imitate a synthetic voice, as described by Patrick. He offered, "'Not to worry, you should see all the towels, soap bars, ashtrays, vases and even some spittoons that we all have collected, you know what I mean'!"

They both laughed. The President continued. "They assured Patrick that soon they would be able not only to answer questions about our past but show us how it was. Whatever they mean by that! My own conclusion is that they are capable of making almost any kind of change on this planet and don't seem to need some global conglomerate to tell them how! Even if they are only six energy equations!"

He smiled and finished his sentence. "I just hope the others in the Big 8 have abandoned their plans to make a deal with the extra terrestrials."

"Not quite. You know that I sort of withdrew from the whole thing when I learned that a campaign organized by special interests had been behind their decision to strike on their own. There was too much pressure from too many powerful groups. But more than pressure it looked more like a command."

"I thought so all along, Simon. And I bet I know who is behind."

The Primer Minister sighed. "Yes, good old Elmo. Pity such a brilliant mind cannot be used for more positive things."

"Speaking of the Session tonight, Patrick has given me a brief rundown on what Kathryn and Helen are going to describe. You know about their presence at the Last Supper. It is one of the most incredible things I have ever heard. So I am curious to hear their account."

"Well, same here. Our Archbishops have been calling non-stop since the ladies landed and it was learned that they had visited Jerusalem. However, this time their interest was purely historical. All I can say is that this incident is about to change many perceptions here on earth. God help us!"

With that, they both left the office and followed Baron Carini to the Assembly Hall.

Later that evening, at the UN Special Session before the world, Kathryn and Helen described the day they spent in Jerusalem. They did not spare details of their amazing voyage in time and kept the entire planet spellbound by their words. The recollection of their presence in the same place where the Last

Supper took place, was rich and full of color. As they mentioned Jesus of Nazareth and repeated some of the lessons and observations that he had made, tears rolled down their cheeks. Their delivery was charged with emotion and sincerity. It was a dramatic moment that would forever remain etched in the memory of all audiences.

Their report convulsed not only Christianity and all organized Religions and sects, but also that large portion of the population of the planet that lived with none or uncertain beliefs.

Among those who did not miss a single word of Kathryn and Helen's report were Elmo Saks and the Reverend Toe. They had agreed to meet in New York, hoping to be able to meet with Patrick, but had been unable to get hold of him. It appeared to them that Patrick was deliberately avoiding them and did not return any of the calls they made. They were also aware that Baron Carini had organized a dinner that evening after the session and that a small number of prominent figures had been invited. In spite of their efforts to obtain an invitation, they had not been able to contact the Baron who also seemed to be unreachable.

Never one to allow situations that would deny or ignore his wishes, Elmo quickly organized a series of urgent calls to some of the people that he knew would be invited to the dinner. He felt that even at a distance he could present his case to the President through third parties, hoping that the President would review the matter with the UN Secretary General.

In the last few days, the Reverend Toe had been busy elaborating the global plan he had discussed with Elmo Saks and that was to be put into effect right after the report to the General Assembly had been delivered by Kathryn and Helen. The Reverend assumed, quite rightly, that a wave of emotion would surge all over the world. He wanted to make sure that his ministers arrange for special popular demonstrations in most world capitals, set up open houses and throw the doors open of sanctuaries, retreats, schools and other installations to a public that he was certain would be affected by the report on the Last Supper and would seek reassurance and experience a confirmation of their religious beliefs. It would be the right moment to impress upon the public their ideas and hopefully start a world movement in their support.

Unable to obtain an audience with President Simonson or the Secretary General, Elmo and the Reverend Toe, decided to watch the television broadcast of the General Assembly session from Elmo's lavish penthouse right next to the Pierre Hotel on Central Park and Fifth Avenue.

Like everyone else they were genuinely affected by the report. The

Reverend Toe could not help shedding a few tears, while Elmo watched impassible but obviously mesmerized. At the end, Elmo turned to the Reverend and said, “You see, John, these visitors have not only the power to control communications at will but also the incredible capacity to go back in time. It means that they have solved the riddle of time and can manipulate it at will!”

The Reverend nodded, still under the spell of the scenes so vividly depicted by Kathryn and Helen.

“I find it so hard to believe, I am almost under shock. But you are right. These people, to call them something, possess technology that defies our understanding.”

“Just think of the commercial possibilities, John. More than ever we must try to establish direct contact with the visitors. I am convinced that some working agreement can be negotiated with them. We can deliver a large part of the population of the globe so that they can do their energy adjustment or whatever it is they wish to do. Mind you, it sounds like some involved scam. In any event, getting hold of some of that technology will allow us to change once and for all the way to do things in this planet.”

The Reverend had listened in silence. As usual, he made an effort to try to decipher Elmo’s words. He always looked for the real purpose. In this case he knew that Elmo was terribly anxious to acquire the power the new technology from the visitors could provide. It was also clear to the Reverend that behind the superficial desire to exploit the advantages of the new technologies, there was Elmo’s deep resentment against the society that had thwarted his political career and had condemned him to become nothing more than a footnote in the history of the country. The Reverend had perceived some time ago that Elmo’s motivation was largely a desire for revenge, and it scared the Reverend.

An Amazing Story

At Samuel & Schultz, where Helen worked, she became an overnight star. The Managing Editor did not waste time in proposing a succulent book deal. Television offers for documentaries, specials and even a Soap Opera came her way, in such quantity that she was forced to devote her secretary’s full time to handle such requests. Kathryn was also assailed in the same manner but in her case, media representatives from most European countries sought to obtain exclusive interviews, personal appearances, and involved publishing deals. The Madrid-based “Hola” and its London counterpart “Hello” offered

Kathryn and Helen 5 million dollars for a photo reportage. They were both glad to have Mercedes act as a buffer with the media, an untold number of universities, institutions and foundations of all sorts that wished to contact Kathryn and Helen.

World reaction to Kathryn and Helen's report to the UN General Assembly was instantaneous. Demonstrations were held everywhere, as people were anxious to express their admiration for Kathryn and Helen and to reaffirm their faith in Jesus. The churches, temples and synagogues could not accommodate one more person. Everyone felt that the report to the General Assembly embodied in itself a message of faith.

The dinner, held at the Plaza Hotel after the report to the General Assembly was a success. As in many other occasions, Baron Carini organized a truly magnificent evening. The event took place at the Ballroom of the hotel which had been decorated in a tasteful and sober mood. Since only 50 guests were present, the atmosphere was relaxed and conducive to more intimate exchanges.

Baron Carini greeted the guests with a short speech. He thanked Kathryn and Helen for their contribution to what he termed "bringing to life a meaningful episode in the history of mankind whose purpose and lessons have not always been remembered." He referred briefly to the responsibility assumed by Patrick and the UN, and praised the encouragement and assistance extended by the Vatican, the Council of World Religions, the governments of many countries and the special contributions of the President of the United States.

The President turned to Earla Ann and said, "There must be a term to describe our baron's ability to organize, manage or conjure up these fabulous soirées. Everything is just perfect, beginning from the guest list and ending with the way he is keeping many of the guests from making speeches. It shows that he understands the digestive process!"

"Well, the baron is an old hand at these things. Besides, he himself enjoys going through the frantic pace demanded by these events."

Soon, however, people began to approach the President. First, it was the Chairman of the Federal Reserve Board, then an Admiral, followed by the President of a prestigious university and finally a charming and popular movie star. In a moment when they were by themselves Earla Ann asked, "Say, Mister Prez, what is all this? They all seem to have the same message for you. Mind telling me, or is it classified?"

"One word, my love: Elmo!"

Good and Evil

The weeks following the visit to the ship, were busy for Patrick and Richard. Patrick had to arrange for a number of procedures established by the visitor. This involved detailed work with the Committee and with representatives of many countries.

Richard, on his part, had gone up to the ship a few times by himself. Adam had gently turned down suggestions to invite others to the ship.

Richard had had little time to himself. He had been mercilessly pursued by TV commentators, reporters, science fiction addicts, crackpots of all hues and officers from a number of Government Agencies.

Besides, the special committee that had been formed by the Secretary General, took up a great deal of his time. It was the committee's purpose to review and analyze every meeting with the visitors. The Committee was also responsible for daily communiqués to the media in general and special reports to the Security Council.

His meetings with the visitors—while not daily—usually left him as excited as he felt every time he went up in the shuttle. It was a strange sensation that stayed with him for hours. The physical weariness seemed to be overridden by the peculiar feeling of bursting mental anxiety. He tried hard to rationalize such condition and ascribed it to the powerful influence Adam and his colleagues had on him. It seemed that every word and every phrase spoken by them had unknown depths. Their mental processes enabled them to bring to any question an amazing capacity to discern and evaluate. Then, there were those touches of wisdom that he found so enriching.

After every meeting, he felt as if he had spent time with a fountain of knowledge that seemed to overflow his mental capacity. That explained the anxiety he felt. It was the desire to classify and order the thoughts and facts that had been received. The last session had been particularly tiring. But it had been a session full of passion and interest. This time, he had been accompanied by Patrick, whose sharp and objective mind had clearly earned him the trust and confidence of the visitors. Every situation confirmed the merit of his appointment as the brains and heart of the people of Earth.

About two weeks after their last trip together, they had boarded the shuttle early in the morning amidst the hectic complaints from the Media. They arrived in the usual milliseconds and walked into the familiar lounge. They quickly noticed that the original enclosure had been removed and that the entire area had been decorated in a very elegant and tasteful manner. A large marble topped table surrounded by comfortable-looking Italian leather chairs, had been added at one end of the area, for it could not be called a room as there was no immediate perception of walls, ceilings or the familiar sources of light. Lighting was a unique effect that varied according to unknown purposes, but it was always pleasant and it had improved a great deal since the initial visits when it was difficult to distinguish the features of the visitors.

A communications center on one side, contained telephones, a radio transmitter, large stereo systems and a bank of computers. There was also a large table set up as a buffet with a variety of hot containers, stacks of dishes, fruits, bread, cheeses and an assortment of soft beverages. A well stocked bar with a shiny counter and 6 stools stood to one side of the buffet table. It appeared as if the visitors had decided to make the place more comfortable for the earthlings and had set up this as a suitable work and meeting space. They had even included some fine Bohkaras and Tabriz rugs on the floors and, not having walls had installed a number of easels with pictures, photographs and cartoons. There was even a photo of Ross Simonson, the President of the United States, holding six small dolls that represented the six visitors, given to Patrick by the Mattel people to present to the visitors.

Upon arriving, Richard asked Adam about the bombing of a department store in a Middle East capital. Adam seemed to know all the details and his only comments were terse. "Again, we can see the confusing borderlines of good and evil that seems to be a characteristic of your species. For the terrorist, his act is one of accomplishment. He views the effects of the bomb—as repugnant as it might be—as a step in obtaining some forms of political credibility. He is convinced that by calling attention to his aspirations, he is performing a good deed in behalf of his faction. The victims however and the world in general see the evil of the act and condemn it."

Richard thought about it for a minute and then said, "But, Adam, what you just said is the simplest analysis of the matter. The real question we all ask is why such actions seem to be present throughout our history."

Adam had suddenly come to life. It was a topic he wanted to discuss with Richard, whose intelligence and boundless energy had impressed him greatly. He fixed his gray eyes on Richard and said, "You are talking about evil. Which on this planet is the opposite of good? I guess a smart young anthrophysicist like you has already found the key to the dilemma. You see, if evil exists, good must also exist. And vice versa. Good could not exist without Evil, as there would be no way to determine how good is good. Keep in mind that the abstract definitions of evil have been subject to so many currents of thought in your planet that I doubt if anyone can make any sense of it. Evil, per se is a complex matter."

Richard thought for a while before speaking. "True, from the dark ages—and before—the human race has always made the distinction between good and evil. I view this as a very important condition. I also think that such distinction—adopted by most religions and philosophies—has been a controlling influence in human affairs."

"Yes, it has been that way. I should tell you that the balance and equilibriums that we talked about before have a lot to do with the coexistence of these two expressions, or consequences of behavior. It has to do with the minimum acceptable ratios that must be observed in this neck of the woods. You see, it is partly the reason we are here. Your planet has been disrupting an energy projection beyond your universe. Remember, the game is about energy and believe me, a so called evil thought by a teenager is enough to shake the meters in other barrios, hombre!"

"You mean to tell me that evil thoughts if they outnumber good thoughts, or better yet if evil actions exceed good actions some energy level somewhere is disturbed?" asked a puzzled Patrick.

Adam laughed. "You bet your boots! Your species on this planet has believed for too long that their actions only had local repercussions. Oh, yes, you have looked at the stars and imagined all kind of things. Your imagination is really a good sample of a fine type of energy projection coming out of that shampooed head of yours and your co-humans. What I am trying to tell you, gentlemen, is that good and evil are like Romeo and Juliet, Romulus and Remus, Jiminy and Cricket, Pepsi and Cola, Union and Carbide and so on. There is an inherent affinity as much as there is an inherent repulsion between good an evil."

He paused for a moment and then, with some vehemence, he continued. "My friends, one way to look at all this is from the standpoint of balance. The founding fathers of the US set up a marvelous system based on checks and balances; one of the first applications of legal active and reactive actions on a social scale. Their intuition led them to deduce that life in itself is a matter of balance, and equilibrium. It is not a simple matter of opposites like full and empty, tall and short or, ugly and pretty. The very essence of these two opposites weakens the strength of any consideration that leads to absolutism. Well, we are dealing with a good and evil equation here. Translated into energy, of course."

In spite of the light tone of the conversation, Richard and Patrick were quick to detect the vague declaration of his visitors' intentions. They thought back to the original conversation with Patrick and the references to the balances and equilibriums that required adjustment. *Maybe*, Richard thought, *we have been screwing things so bad down here on earth that our evil doings are keeping the needles jumping in their meters.*

"Adam, evil has taken many forms. Theologians have long explored man's unique inclination to believe in symbols that would excuse him from assuming a direct responsibility when dealing with circumstances or situations that they judged negative."

"You must be talking about those negative influences that have assailed man from the beginning. Dealing with them has been both a relief and a pain. In the first case, it has been possible to freely ascribe any interpretation to a given negative influence and perhaps apply some guidelines of his own. The painful part would have been the need to develop the antidote or the cure."

"Please explain. It seems like an interesting evaluation."

"All right. A mother feeding her baby is a good thing for both the baby and for herself. If she does not do it is a bad thing. However, not doing it could be intentional or simply a result of neglect or forgetfulness. But still a bad thing to happen wouldn't it? Early civilizations catalogued these opposite forces and the myriad variations or reasons, or tendencies, and had a great time devising names and images."

"You are right. Evil was acknowledged and its manifestations assigned to a convenient variety of sources, including man, of course. The next step was to give it a personality. Thus, Satan!"

Adam smiled, if somewhat sadly, and said, "Satan. You see, in Hebrew, Satan means adversary, which again shows that the idea of opposition implies the existence of good. But the Satan that has been created here has been a great excuse for mankind. I grant you that you did not have another alternative. So for the last eight thousand years or so, the religions have taken advantage of such great shield to cover the deficiencies of those who failed to preserve good. As an excuse, evil, Satan, the dark One, the Antichrist, the Devil, the Demon and a lot of other colorful and fictitious characters and situations, have been useful in promoting the creation of religious bureaucracies on the planet. But instead of reinforcing the moral and ethical fiber of the species and providing guidance and compassion, they opted for developing the myths and false faith that enabled them to exercise some form of control over the people, and in the process—in most cases—provide themelves with a comfortable way of life."

"Fine, but how do you think it would have been possible to develop at least some form of moral discipline?"

"By denouncing evil. Religious groups have always had a strong ascendancy over people. Instead of converting evil into superstitions and legends they could have use the strongest weapon in their hands."

"What was that?"

"Simply the truth. Keep in mind that the roots of evil are firmly planted in denial. Twirl that hard disk you keep so active behind your frontal lobes and you'll come to the conclusion that evil in its many forms suffers from some form of denial. If it is a man hurting a child, the act in itself denies the truth of acceptable forms of behavior. The man himself ignores the harm he is causing and his act becomes an evil act. You see, from the first day, almost, human society, since its satellite days, established codes that responded to their instinct and of course to their environment. These codes, after a few million years, are as much a part of every human being as his lungs. By insisting on the truth, you lessen the impact of denial. In simple words, the religious groups could have enforced education and instilled an open desire for the truth instead of hiding behind myths and making poor old Satan the boogie man. But we are getting into deep subjects that are normally discussed at sunrise in some smoky parlor of a college campus."

After finishing some of the tasks that Adam had for them, Patrick and Richard returned to New York.

Elmo's Offensive

After delivering their report to the Security Council, Patrick and Richard found that Elmo Saks had been on the offensive. His campaign right after Kathryn and Helen's report to the General Assembly, brilliantly conducted by the Reverend Toe, had obtained very positive results. A global movement had been started and it bode no good for the UN and Patrick in particular. The world press had gotten hold of the key objectives pursued by Elmo and the Reverend, and had begun to question the wisdom of allowing only the UN and, worse, only Patrick and Richard to be the representatives of the human race. What started as a simple quest was turning into an indictment against the UN, Patrick and Richard.

In the United States, Elmo had obtained the support of a large number of Senators, Congressmen and some members of the Supreme Court. His approach this time was that the United States Government was being used by the UN to prepare statistics, arrange for reports and act as a clerical adjunct to the UN.

"I refuse to accept that our Government is devoting resources and time to comply with UN requests of a dubious nature. Who knows if the visitors really need all that material. I think it is time that we exercise some initiative. I am tired of seeing an elected President of this country acting like an office boy to the Secretary General of the UN!"

His offensive was well orchestrated. He had collected all the chits that he had in Washington. He had also used his considerable influence to secure the support of some of the most respected political personalities in the country. His ruthless approach betrayed his anxiety and desperation. In most cases it was a matter of going along with Elmo or placing ones head on the chopping block.

As a result, there was pressure on the President, reinforced by talk of impeachment procedures based on dereliction of duty. As expected, the opposition was quick to capitalize on Elms campaign against the President by adding its own innuendo, suspicion and doubt to the figure of the President. This climate was worsened by the increasing protest received from countries all over the world, coordinated under the capable hand of the Reverend Toe. There was no question that Elmo, the Reverend Toe and their close circle of collaborators had managed to change world opinion.

The President was concerned that Elmo had succeeded in swaying such important number of influential people. The media had quickly caved in before Elmo's attack. Practically all major world newspapers along with radio and TV systems were now clamoring for what some termed the "liberalization or deregulation of the UN-Visitors relations."

In this climate of unrest, the President invited Patrick, Richard and Cardinal Ludlam to meet in Washington. Also invited were the Vice President Ursula Walters, the National Security Adviser Mike Pashley an Alan Clayton, the Secretary of State. "This situation is getting out of hand." The President was obviously annoyed. "At a time when things are proceeding smoothly with the visitors, we have to face something short of a revolt. Saks has not given up on the idea of dealing directly with the visitors. He keeps on dreaming about the Goldfinger agreement he wants to negotiate with them."

Alan Clayton, whose training as a Psychologist enabled him to size up people and situations in record time, spoke. "Elmo has been a torn on the side of many people and also of entire countries since he was forced to give up his presidential hopes. He has some sort of vendetta in his soul. His resentment is deep and dangerous. He is not about to let up."

"Yes, but meanwhile, he is causing unnecessary conflict and confusion. His hordes of polished executives and the inexhaustible supply of pious souls produced by the Reverend Toe, can manipulate public opinion anywhere. It is a powerful combination of religious zeal and the jingling of many coins," observed Ursula Walters.

"Yes, this campaign is beginning to get out of hand. It bothers me when Elmo uses people's religious faith to mount what is obviously a personal crusade. I have received reports of proposals and plans that have been presented to some of the Vatican Authorities. It is typical Elmo. Gnawing bit by bit and all the while having Toe follow up with the sweet talk and the charities, or should I call them bribes? So, what is the latest?" asked the President of no one.

Cardinal Ludlam answered, "Yes, Mister President, Saks has contacted the Vatican, after making a thorough campaign with members of the Curia. He wants Cardinal Beccaria to head an Interdenominational Council in New York that could be in a position to assist the group that is to replace the UN. He has offered to place Rev. Toe's Church organization at the Cardinal's service, same as more than 5000 churches throughout the world, that include jus about every religious discipline. Further he counts with the vote of more than 100 countries at the UN."

"How could he accomplish that?" asked Patrick

"A world congress would be organized and a resolution adopted. They assured the Cardinal that they would have enough popular support to force a vote in the UN and replace it as the world's representative."

"And who would run the show? I don't think the Vatican would go along with such a scheme," observed the President.

"Absolutely not. The Vatican considers this affair as something that goes beyond human understanding and realizes that no one is in a position to dictate terms to the visitors."

"Glad to hear that," observed Clayton.

Cardinal Ludlam continued. "I think the Vatican's position has been made clear in the past few weeks. It recognizes the extraordinary nature of the visit by extraterrestrial beings and in this respect all it can offer is comfort to all. It also has made clear that it agrees with the role being played by the UN, the US and the few other countries making up the Emergency Committee. Beyond that, from the Holy Father down, there is the feeling that this event will change forever the nature of life in this planet and that in time there will be a better understanding of the matter."

"What does Cardinal Beccaria have to say? I think he is one of the sharpest cardinals to appear in a long while," asked Ms Tahaney. She had anticipated Elmo's plans and had conducted some discreet inquiries about members of the Curia and some of the more prominent Bishops throughout the world. She was quite certain about Cardinal Beccaria but wanted Ludlam to confirm it.

"You know, Cardinal Beccaria and I go back a long way. I have asked him point blank what he himself thought about this situation. As usual he went straight to the heart of the matter. He said that the Vatican would not under any circumstances support the overthrow of the UN. He also emphasized that his organization has specific instructions to refrain from making any commitment and to refuse any contribution, gift or charity from Toe. He feels, like I do, that this thing is too big for all of us and that only time will tell."

The President smiled and said, "I am glad to hear that Cardinal. While I do not think that our visitors need any help from us, we need to be sure of our own attitudes and reactions. Elmo is liable to create a problem that could involve a great many people."

As an afterthought he added, "And we don't exactly know about our visitors plans."

In the following days, the President began to feel Elms persistent attack. It put him for the first time on the defensive. Not only had the media become more aggressive in their judgments and opinions but they were beginning to espouse Elmo's ideas. Cleverly, Elmo had wrapped his arguments on patriotic notions, difficult to negate. It was a case of political opportunism when not waving the flag or questioning the Government policies, implied some form of disloyalty and even treason. The Reverend Toe on his part, had managed to create a strong world movement based on the need to show the visitors that they could count on a God-fearing and righteous human community. Subtly, it advanced the idea that the right world representative should be a man of proven religious convictions in stead of the pragmatic head of a herd of world politicians.

The President and Patrick decided to avoid any confrontation with Elmo or the Reverend Toe, and above all not to participate in the public debates that the Reverend Toe kept proposing.

"Patrick," the President confided, "I hope we receive some signal soon. Elmo and his troops are beginning to disrupt the functioning of the Government. Every day, we have to face requests from Committees, Citizens groups, Humane Societies, Religious sects and, what is worse I am getting delegations from schools throughout the country, the Armed Forces and even our own civil servants!"

"Yes, I have noticed the relentless campaign you are under because it is almost an exact copy of what I am going through at the UN. The Reverend Toe has succeeded beyond any expectations in creating not a wave but a tsunami!"

"I am going to suggest to you and Richard that you find the way to publicize Richard's reports on a grander scale. We have to fight fire with fire. I have noticed that every bit of information received by the press is the subject of untold speculation and creates much interest. The reports have been very concise and lucid, but they lean heavily on the scientific and philosophical, whereas the public wants to know more about the kind of sox the visitors wear, the kind of fuel the shuttles use and all those seemingly unimportant details that, in the end are important. This is no criticism of Richard or your Press Officers. It is just that we need a little hype. Maybe Helen Lawrence can help, She is one of the sharpest producers in these parts and she can dress up all those reports to make them more digestible. What do you think?"

Patrick was silent for a minute and then said, "Mister President, I think you hit it right on the head. I must admit, and so has Richard, that the reports have not had much impact. Except for the Last Supper episode, all other reports have been somewhat technical and have not had a great deal of appeal. I am sure Helen can make a discussion about tri dimensional epigrams in an ammonium atmosphere both exciting and informative. We shall give Richard's work a new look!"

"Excellent," said the President, "you know, just call me if I or our people here can be of help. Au revoir!"

In the next few weeks, Richard's visits acquired new importance. In no time at all, Helen had enlisted a number of specialists that were able to create tremendous curiosity and expectation about Patrick's and Richard's visits to the object above New York. DVDs, videos, booklets and inspiring TV shorts were produced and distributed. The TV shorts became an overnight success. Every night, Helen had some of the better liked and respected TV personalities review recent reports. Spectacular films of the objects in many parts of the world and especially composed musical scores, served to present statistics, scientific facts and thoughtful conclusions. Animated programs were also broadcast to make sure that children were made aware of the nature of the objects.

The message remained the same: The visitors wish to deal with the UN. They must know why. They have accepted both Patrick Deschamps and Richard Ferguson as the bona fide representatives of planet Earth. They are working on a program that is supposed to improve conditions on the planet. We just have to wait.

The strategy paid off. Most people began to realize that the visitors were in command of the entire situation. Changing the UN and Richard would not probably set well with them who had confirmed their enthusiastic support of both Patrick and Richard. In a sense, the threat posed by Elmo and the Reverend had been defused.

Meanwhile, the visits to the ship continued. Work proceeded on the collection and evaluation of data and, at the same time, interesting topics anchored the interest of Richard and Patrick as well as the visitors. Richard in particular did not miss any opportunity to touch upon topics whose nature remained as vague speculations on Earth.

Do You Believe in God?

For sometime Richard and Patrick had been carefully preparing a prologue that would permit them to approach the matter of the existence of God with Adam and his colleagues. They had not detected any reluctance on the part of the visitors to deal with any subject. On the contrary, they were so well informed about human thinking patterns and its ancestral history that they delighted in exploring subjects that they knew would interest Richard.

In this respect they were inclined to bring to the discussion very specific points of a technical nature, much in the way that a professor approaches a new and complicated subject This was especially so when talking about past events. They seemed to know intimately the past history of the human species.

They would talk in detail about the cave paintings in Altamira in northern Spain, for instance. Adam could describe the circumstances that led some of the tribes to record events of their daily life by painting the walls inside their caves. He explained that this had happened because bellicose tribes from the Pyrinees and the Iberian plateau had suddenly irrupted in the valley and taken away women and children, after killing some of the tribesmen. They had also stolen the skins and parchments that up to that time had been used to depict key events in their lives, like hunting for bison and deer, the taming of wild horses and chasing away mammoths.

When questioned about specific details, they seemed to have first hand knowledge. At one point Richard made an observation about the quality of the paints those early cavemen had employed. He wondered aloud about it. This prompted a quick reaction from Emosh.

"Didn't you know?" he joked. "They used plain ball point pens!"

Adam explained that it was common among the nomadic tribes in that area to live in caves where they could enjoy some protection from other tribes that had already tamed horses and could roam the plains at will. The cave dwellers were still a pedestrian lot. He explained that as the fires inside the caves covered the walls and ceiling with black soot—carbon black—it was scrapped off and collected. It was mixed with tree resin as agglomerate and also with fermented grape juices, or vinegar, which would act as a solvent. Colored pigments would be obtained from clay mixed in a similar manner or from the juice of various fruits. Other pigments were obtained from rock formations and some from sediment of the rivers and streams. This primitive form of art was widespread and reinforced the identity of tribes and family groups. He recounted that some caves were decorated like the fronts of some of the buildings in South Los Angeles. They were colorful and full of meanings. Most of the pictures recorded hunting scenes which were the major activity of people in those days. In time, the designs had faded away or the caves were destroyed by earthquakes or floods.

"See," observed Emosh, "graffiti is nothing new."

They however did not shy away from abstract considerations and seemed in possession of ample dialectic techniques. They would develop an orderly and well reasoned thesis and explained it in terms easily understood. Richard realized that it wasn't really necessary for them to go through reasoning exercises since they were in possession of the facts, or the truth. He felt it was done in deference to him and also in order to keep the discussion within the reach of Richard's intellect.

Richard felt that the questions he wanted to ask had to be programmed carefully. While he recognized that he was speaking to a greatly superior mind dressed in the flesh and blood uniform of the human species, he knew that its superior knowledge contained elements that were beyond the reach of human understanding. He also wondered about Adam's observation that linked the human race conception of the universe to its limited mental capacity.

As if divining what Richard was thinking, Emosh said, "Your conception of the Universe conforms logically to the reach of your mental capabilities. When I say you, I naturally refer to the human species. We are of course fascinated by the development of your theories about the Universe and your views on space and time."

Richard listened attentively. He was delighted that they had some time to engage in purely speculative chit chat. Especially after having spent hours identifying and reviewing historical records, statistics and a number of problems facing the planet and its inhabitants.

"Well, by now you should understand that our species has been a very curious one. I'd venture to say that the moment that spark of reason appeared, questions were asked. I don't know, maybe our good old amoebas were also subjected to the same inquisitiveness."

Adam joined them and smiling said, "You can be sure that some current exists, even in the amoebas. We find your early conceptions of your planet very interesting, but I shall not delve into their substance or tell you all I know about them. It would be too boring."

Richard smiled again, pleased that his hosts acknowledged some measure of intellectual value in him.

"Just tell me—in general terms—your view of our early perceptions."

"Well, it was interesting to note how thought developed on this planet. Once the neurological circuits were in place and reason began to influence instincts, it was fascinating to witness the progressive development of rational and associative thinking."

Richard interrupted him again. His Anthropological curiosity had to be satisfied. "I am most interested in the origin of civilization on earth. How it evolved and where. We can trace it as far back as 8,500 BC. Is this accurate?"

"No, it is not. You see, before your planet entered into its present phase, that is, its gravitational position and its placement around a star, the sun, Earth was a satellite of another planet. It was like the moon is to planet earth today. Earth was then a simple satellite to a much larger planet. Well, organic life developed in that satellite or today's earth, as a result of complex photosynthesis processes and the implantation of what you call life."

"I guess you are talking about the so called primeval ooze, or whatever its nature was, where life is supposed to have began."

"Yes. I can probably answer in two episodes." Emosh paused to smile and pop a Life saver into his mouth.

"Your scientists have made a great deal of progress in the last few years in tracing the electrochemical nature of some of the very basic organic elements of life. They have reproduced some of the more interesting synthesis that took place that first moment when multicellular organisms appeared. That ooze was a mixture of methane, ammonium, water vapor, hydrogen and a pinch of this and a pinch of that. I don't want to get too technical."

Richard listened with all his senses, as he used to say when his attention was attracted by especially interesting subjects. Emosh continued. "You know, under the right electrical discharge, these elements can produce synthetic radicals of the molecules of amino acids, which is probably the starting point of the process. Except that, somehow, those amino acids did have the key to the next tango which was the production of proteins. Keep in mind that the atmosphere in those days contained all kinds of chemical compounds, which in some ways acted upon the simpler cells. For instance, there were all kinds of derivatives and byproducts such as Formaldehyde, Peptides, Cianhidric Acid, Prebiotic acids and all kinds of mixtures. The matter is complicated as it is and even more so if I have to explain it. I sort of get lost when we look into the nature of DNA and the incredible extension of genetic code commands usually crammed into genomes. They all led to the creation of life on earth. This is the technical part of my answer."

Richard leaned forward and asked, "You just mentioned life. Maybe you could be more explicit and tell me about its nature and purpose?"

At this point, Adam, who had been also an attentive listener, replied, "Ah! This is going to confuse you even more. You and a few billion in your planet. Life is not easy to explain in your terms. But let me try." He reached into his pocket and produced a tube of Life savers.

"The force that makes things what they are in this neck of the woods is an energy formulation that can be instantaneously applied to any piece of matter. Think of a seed that has been sitting in a silo for years. At a given moment, and because you provide it with the appropriate conditions, that seed germinates. It just follows an energy equation. If the seed could think, it would worship you for allowing it to develop into a plant with limbs, branches and leaves and giving it the chance to enjoy the pollution of your atmosphere. Capish?"

"Yeah," retorted Richard. "But your seed was already an organism. I am talking about life for the human species; the initial command, Adam. You also said that a formulation can be or was 'applied' or 'assigned.' I ask, by whom? How? You mention that it could apply to matter, how about a piece of rock?"

"Same process, old boy. Which came first, the simple cell or the life that allowed it to multiply itself? Think a bit, if it was life, what form did it have? If it was a simple cell, how could it exist as a cell without some previous commands to make use of electrochemical energies and become a cell? If you think about the nature of both, the command and the cell, they are both energy. Deduction: they follow energy laws. Which laws? Ah! that is the part beyond existing references here. You see, the energy formulation follows certain principles existing beyond your so called universe. There is no single WHO. Or rather, a number of circumstances must coincide for the spark to happen.

And all this is not regulated by any one person, committee or entity but by energy configurations acting on dimensions not known to you, and, in your present state of development, impossible for you to conceive or understand."

"Okay, so, beyond our understanding, there exists a configuration or formulation or whatever that observes laws and assigns energy, let us say, energy combinations. Well, that is God to us. Something no one can really understand but it has been and continues to be the doorway to belief and faith."

"Well, in a simplified manner that is more or less the ticket. It ties in with your beliefs in a divine being or presence that is supposed to design, type and control everything that happens on your planet. Well, I am talking about your God. Believe me, as long as the human race retains its ability to think and to reason, there is a God on this planet, as real as Mount Everest! It is and has been the greatest influence in the development of your species. It has been a guiding and controlling feature. Unfortunately, the mental capacity of your species is such that it has adapted the idea of God to its own purposes, not always healthy."

This is getting interesting, thought Richard. *We are moving into very basic concepts*. He nodded and said, "Yes, you are probably right."

Adam looked at Richard with interest. And Richard could not help admiring the perfection of the synthetic composite in front of him. Then Adam said, "But, back to what I was saying before we got into God's territory. Incidentally, it is a subject I would like to discuss in more detail."

Richard immediately thought about the innumerable requests that had been received at the UN from religious leaders, theologians and scientists who wanted a chance to talk to the visitors about the nature of man and the forces that led to his creation. He remembered those lengthy sessions with Giorgio Beccaria, his favorite Monsignor, and with Patrick years before, when they would explore concepts such as the origin of religions in the world and, more often than not, their deep reasoning about the knowability of God and the views held by humanistic liberals, traditionalists and theologians of various hues.

He listened to Adam, "You see, one of the problems you humans have when trying to philosophize about God is that you run into that famous old limitation I mentioned sometime back."

Richard laughed and said, "Adam, we seem to have so many limitations that I lost track of the nature of some of them. Which is the responsible one this time?"

"Sorry, pal, but I think we did mention it to Patrick in some detail during our first meetings. It was a limitation that has to do with the fact that your mental development, on one side, and the existence on this planet of only some of the dimensions that are used beyond your universe, cannot allow you to understand the origin and nature of many phenomena that affect your planet. God is one of them. The idea of God on this planet, with the limited mental bounds of humans, is impossible to define."

Richard thought for a long moment. He was aware of the limitations mentioned by Adam and the other visitors, but still his intellect persisted in trying to reach some level of understanding. He observed, "OK, but to us believers, God transcends all material limits. It would seem that because of that, we should be able to have a better understanding of his essence."

"I see your point. Let me give you a hint. We talked about beginning and end once. Well, the essence of God is in many ways, related to those parameters whose nature is well beyond your understanding. Maybe some day, the human race will be in a position to appreciate, better than it does now, the boundless and infinitesimal influence that God has."

Richard did not want to become involved in a lengthy bout of speculative philosophy with Adam. He felt that he had his answer. And felt a heck of a lot better! He gestured to Adam to continue. "Keep in mind that the concept of God, as a supreme and eternal being that blends goodness and everlasting justice, took shape from Judeo-Christian beliefs of the last two thousand years. Not that God made his appearance at that time. Old YHWH, as he was referred to in the Old Testament, had been around for zillions of years!"

"How was the conception of a Supreme Being developed in early civilizations and cultures?" asked Richard.

"Without getting into deep theological speculations, the idea of God developed from unexplainable natural phenomena observed by the early societies. It complemented their natural desire to justify some form of harmony between the unexplainable and themselves. That in itself proves the presence of God. Remember the Greeks? They invented Gods for almost everything, same as the Sumerians and all other early cultures. Not satisfied, they created Goddesses and, like some of the more successful movies, they went after the sons of so and so. Gods all. But beyond the more immediate needs to identify Gods and Goddesses with natural phenomena—you will recall Ares, God of Thunder; Apollo, God of Light and Order, Mars, Venus, Aphrodite, etc. and many others, it helped associate the concept of GOD with harmony and order. Further, their perception recognized God as impersonal and omnipresent."

"I guess you are talking about later cultures like Mahayana Budhism and its Nothingness, or Indra in Hinduism, or Taoism, etc."

"Yes. They came to terms with the enigmas of their lives through God. The Greeks and the Romans from 200 to 1400 AD laid the initial notions of God, aided first by Plato and later Aristotle. But the bottom line, you will agree, is that all of them recurred to this unexplainable presence. The vehicle was reason, old bean. God was there!"

"Is he still here?" asked Richard with some anxiety in his voice.

"Yes, very much so. You see, every form of energy, in your case life, an interesting by-product, answers to God. Plain and simple. But it is not the kindly old man dressed in a white tunic that sits on a throne on some distant cloud. It is a presence that has been there always. Without that presence, dear Professor, there would be very little to explain."

"Yes, I know our limitations," added Richard with a smile on his face. "Somehow, the human race appears to be a bit behind in its dimensional development."

For the next hour or so, Adam and Richard discussed Earth religions. At one point, Adam asked, "Richard, we have come across an interesting religious leader on this planet. You probably know a lot about him. It is the Reverend John Toe. I have noticed that he's been very active promoting Elmo Saks before the UN, the President of the US and several governments. What's his motivation?"

Richard smiled and said, "Adam, the Reverend John Toe is a very peculiar phenomenon. Let me try to synthesize him and his impact on society. He is a combination snake oil salesman, glib provider of comfort and solace, extremely sharp businessman, convincing pitchman, a little too pious for my blood and a great seducer of good looking women."

"Does that make him the Spiritual leader of the US flock?"

"Well, it does. He's earned it. He has set up all those Sanctuaries that appeal to a large percentage of the population. He has managed to mix faith, religion, sports and a profit motive in the development of his Sanctuaries. To me it is just another scam or, if you wish, a pseudo religious entity with Wall Street aims and objectives."

Adam shook his head and nodded. "Is it money he's after, or power?"

"I think it is both. I also think that Elmo Saks, as his mentor from his college days, is his guiding hand. I am not surprised that the Reverend is agitating in favor of Elmo. He does have tremendous popular appeal and influence."

Adam got up and said, "Interesting."

With no further comment he led Richard, to the bar and poured a couple of hefty slugs of Jack Daniels. "Have a good trip back and say hello to our lovely ladies. If you have a chance, tell the President that we thank him for his help."

Richard drank the Jack Daniels and immediately felt the effect of the drink. His tiredness faded and the tension of the last hours subsided. He entered the shuttle and thought, *I think I earned that shot today. Maybe a couple more!*

PART FOUR
A Matter of Energy

In the next couple of days, Richard reported to the Committee and held a number of press conferences and meetings with key UN executives and, of course, with Patrick. Having provided the visitors with the first batch of detailed data and statistics requested, they both felt that some form of analysis of what was requested, could give them a better inkling as to the visitor's intentions. Richard suggested that they take advantage of Patrick's next day trip to Washington to meet in Richard's apartment in Fairfax Station. Patrick agreed readily and proposed that after their meeting, they meet with the President and bring him up to date on their most recent conclusions and observations.

Their analysis disclosed several surprising facts. The visitors were interested in all sorts of crime figures. They were also interested in detailed breakdown of crime statistics, records from Penal Institutions, data and statistics about court cases, terrorism, law enforcement, structure of police forces, rehab programs, etc.

"This looks to me as if they wish to evaluate the extent of crime in our planet," said Patrick.

"I also notice that they are reviewing the various judicial systems in the world, the Health Care programs, Welfare, Charity Institutions and the entire educational system. They also have shown great interest in corruption in all its forms, you know, from simple lies to deceitful claims, to major industrial contracts, government deals, health care scams and the unethical behavior of public and private institutions. Gee, they have even gone into sports records, churches and the so called non-profit foundations. I just don't know how they can absorb the masses of data we have provided."

"I guess," commented Patrick. "They are digging at the roots of all these systems to find the root of all those neg energy reactions."

"Well, yes and I suppose they'll draw their own conclusions and relate those to the Good-Evil considerations they stated."

"I suppose you are right, but I still wonder about what they plan to do. How do you rectify energy disequilibrium? Created by human beings?"

After many hours of discussion, they found no real answer to their queries. It was clear that some form of solution would be applied to the energy unbalance by the visitors but neither Patrick nor Richard was able to imagine the nature of the solution.

Late in the afternoon they met with the President, this time at the study on the third floor. President Ross was sitting by the window and greeted them with a big smile and a hearty handshake. A small buffet had been arranged, along with the usual cart containing fruit juices, soda drinks and liquor bottles.

"Glad you could come. We have matters to review, but before, let us fortify the spirit with properly mixed spirits!" He nodded to the uniformed waiter, who started mixing drinks.

"Well, my friends, I have to report some good news. It seems that in spite of Elmo's and the Reverend's offensives, the public is beginning to smell a rat. Also, and I must congratulate you both, your own campaign has brought quick results. Helen Lawrence has done an outstanding job. To me, it is still amazing how she has managed to produce a series of programs, specials and cartoons dealing with abstracts thoughts, historical references, and complex matters that in no time at all have become the favorite TV choices for people all over the world. You know, even that slow motion coverage of the shuttle makes you want to see the sequence over and over again."

Patrick smile and said, "Thank you, Ross. I guess it shows that in spite of all the noise and sanctimonious blah-blah fed to them by Elmo and the Reverend, people have the capacity to decide for themselves. And of course I agree that Helen has accomplished the impossible. She has been fortunate to have Mercedes and Muir lend a hand here and across the pond. To make television programs that do not rely on vulgarity and profanity and that do not show daring décolletages and insidious musical lyrics, is not easy; thank goodness our Professor here has been helpful in transforming a third degree equation into a lively but tasteful piece of gossip!"

They proceeded to discuss some of the conclusions that Patrick and Richard had discussed and outlined additional measures. The President however suggested that Richard take advantage of every working trip up to the pill, to discuss subjects that could enlighten the people of Earth.

"Patrick," he said, "I know that there are a zillion topics that can be reviewed with the visitors and it is a good thing that you try to touch upon as many subjects as you can. By having that information available, we are disarming Elmo's arguments. I have always believed that the truth is the best protection against the deliberate perversion of facts; sort of a cleansing fluid and a shield, if not a laxative!"

They stopped to sample the buffet, which, as usual was prepared to satisfy the more demanding tastes. It was night when they left the White House in one of the limousines that would take Patrick to National Airport and Richard to his townhouse in Fairfax Station.

Original Species

On his next visit to the ship, Richard carried the usual package of data that included printouts, CD-ROMs, videos and even photographs. The visitors seemed to want to see as much about our history of sins and peccadilloes as they could.

After a long session with Adam and Earle, they had a frugal lunch at a restaurant that resembled a British Pub, complete with darts and barrels of ale. Afterward they moved to the lounge and once seated comfortably and savoring a perfect cappuccino, they began one of their "heart to heart exchanges" as Adam named their long conversations about history, mankind and many other topics.

This time, Richard brought up a subject that had made him quite curious and puzzled. It had been the astonishing discovery that planet Earth had been a satellite to a larger planet and that the human race had its origins in that satellite.

Adam said, "In answer to some of the questions you asked yesterday, I thought I would expand a little on what happened to Satellite Earth before it became Planet Earth. It all happened as a result of a major cosmic calamity. Things seemed to be going great until one day BANG! and I don't mean the so called Big Bang your physicists have invented. The big planet overheated, so to speak, and after a while swallowed its own gravity. BANG! There she goes! All of a sudden, its satellite, now planet Earth, was cast adrift until the gravitational attraction of the solar system fished it out of space. But by then major climatic and environmental changes had done away with most of its inhabitants, except a few. You see, this happened about 100 million years ago."

Again, Richard marveled at Adam's unique grasp of current vocabulary and expressions. But he wanted to know more about conditions in the planet. "I remember that you mention this to me before. You also said that the dinosaurs disappeared as a result of the new orbit acquired by planet earth. But, were there still dinosaurs on the satellite at the time?"

"Yes, as a matter of fact they roamed some parts of the satellite, or Earth if you wish, but for the most part were left unmolested. You see, the human inhabitants of that period were not as plentiful as they were years later. Remember that each of them lived close to a thousand years and their aging process was very slow. Their reproductive process was a cyclical affair and not the instinct-driven performance of the newer race."

"But how did it happen?"

"Upon the destruction of the large planet, Earth received a number of shocks that created clouds of sulfuric acid in some areas, dust storms in others and shocks and tremors that affected even the inner core of the planet. Seismic waves ensued along with a basic change in the composition of the atmosphere. You see, Earth received all kinds of cosmic junk. Meteorites, particle clusters, gases and also varying gravitational inputs as it adjusted to a permanent orbit, etc. Its atmosphere suffered great changes as volcanic activity was rampant. Oxygen content dropped considerably."

"How about the major changes?"

"There were important ones. One, it affected the hormonal and neurological make up of the existing human species. It caused some mutations in the process of cell division and gave way to new combinations that have resulted in your present flora and fauna. These changes were aided by an entirely new gravitational profile. It did away with large mammals like dinosaurs, whose dependence on an enriched atmosphere was vital. Keep in mind that earth in those days was nothing but jungle. The forests had to be large enough to feed the plant-eating dinosaurs, who were in turn eaten by the carnivorous ones. Sort of a Wall Street chain, if I may offer you a gratuitous and cynical remark!"

Richard laughed. But there were many questions he wanted to ask. As he had felt since his first visit to the ship, he was aware that he had a unique opportunity to unlock some of the secrets of mankind. He was also conscious that his desire to learn was not motivated by a selfish edge but by a genuine desire to impart and share this unique knowledge with his fellow men.

"How did the existing humans manage to survive? Were they still on a thousand year visa?"

"Well," Adam said, "the original inhabitants were a crafty lot. Some remained in Africa, where the first humans had appeared while others remained in the areas where their civilizations had flourished. These areas were around the southern shores of the Caspian Sea, extending south to what is now Iran, then west toward Iraq and the Mediterranean, and north through Turkey. Remember, the dinosaurs lived in Africa, the American continent and parts of Asia. Keep in mid that the sea level was much higher than now and almost 90 percent of the earth's surface was covered by oceans. The Mediterranean as we see it now was a very large body of water. I would guess it extended inland about a 100 miles all around. That explains why sea fossils are often found in foothills and in places some distance away from present shores."

"How did they manage?"

"There was really little contact between humans and dinosaurs. The humans protected themselves against the clouds of volcanic ash and other elements and somehow a lot of them survived. When things settled down and earth was firmly parked on its solar orbit, they realized that they had suffered important transformations. At that point most of the large animals had become extinct as the oxygen content of the atmosphere and the barometric pressure itself had changed drastically. As for the surviving humans, they remained physically the same, about 5 to 6 feet tall, various skin colors and hair, but they noticed that they did not live very long. It was the price of adaptation to the new environment. Their longevity was around 30 to 40 years, as opposed to a thousand years."

Richard could not believe his ears. He was still having trouble in his mind accepting the fact that Earth had been a satellite to a large planet. It was hard to believe that the original man lived to one thousand years of age and that the physical characteristics of planet Earth were vastly different. The changes in oxygen content, barometric pressure and gravity were factors capable of altering practically every living cell on the planet. Adam continued. "Their mental powers had almost disappeared and in their place large a vacuum seemed to have invaded their consciousness. The survivors from the satellite age began to die a few hundred years after the change, while their children started dying relatively young. Another major change they noticed was the emergence of some instincts not known to them. Their instinctual configuration up to that time had been limited and totally subordinated to mental schemes that relied on reasoned parameters. They also noticed that the new earth had all of a sudden developed a great number of animal species and, worst of all, harmful strains of virus and bacteria."

"Hadn't they developed some form of health care or disease prevention before the Earth joined the solar system?"

"They had no great need of it. The whole thing began to look hopeless when earth became part of the solar system. There was a tremendous energy redistribution that affected every energy configuration in the planet. This accounted for the appearance of new species, the adaptation, or not, of old ones, and a lot of harmful ones. Besides man, of course."

Richard thought back to his knowledge of the very ancient civilizations. What Adam had just described made sense. It also explained a lot of things. Man did originate on earth. What he hadn't known, nor anyone else, was that man had populated the planet when earth existed under a different set of conditions. The species that inhabited that satellite was strong and resilient. It also had different mental processes. And it lived an average of one thousand years.

Adam interrupted his train of thought. "Some of the survivors from the satellite days had settled in what is now the Middle East. After a few million years they had been transformed—physically and mentally—into what you know as your species. They gradually developed social skills and began to organize their life in a quite orderly fashion. Remember, they were direct descendants of the satellite people, whose superior qualities were still in evidence. Some of those qualities remained with the new breed for some generations. That should explain to you the sudden emergence of organized societies in Mesopotamia and elsewhere in the Arabian Peninsula. Those people and I am talking about the Sumerians, still had a lot of the qualities of their satellite ancestors..."

"But what happened to those who were not living in the area when the changes took place?"

"They went through the same process and quickly adapted to the new conditions. Some existed here and there and developed along the same lines as the ones in the Middle East. They were small nomadic groups that eked out a precarious living from the chase and hunt of small game, fishing in the many streams and the gathering of wild fruits and roots. As hunters, they followed the herds. They were dispersed throughout the globe; from the savannas of Africa to the plains in America and the forests in Australia and Europe. They were all descendants of the long living humans but their basic mental capacity had changed. The new conditions in the planet, resulting from its new coordinates in the solar system probably caused the gradual deterioration of those marvelous mental processes that existed when the planet was a satellite.

As usual, Adam stopped after having delivered either his views or the facts that he had acquired. He continued. "In their place, your species became the only one on the planet with a capacity to reason. And, let me tell you, it developed some unique characteristics. Real lulus. A whole array of personal traits somehow grew within the new species. And the odd part of the entire process was that these traits became ingrained in each individual. You know, things like anxiety, greed, envy, hate, violence, jealousy, uncontrolled fear and the rest of that arsenal of mental and emotional twists you people keep within you. Talk about convoluted souls and dirty diapers!"

Richard laughed until tears came to his eyes. Not only at what Adam said but the way he said it, in that mellifluous voice half Placido Domingo and half Yamaha synthesizer.

"So, where was the first organized society and who were these first inhabitants?"

"Those were the Sumerians in the Mesopotamian valley, in what is now Iraq. They had been there for about 20,000 years. You see, the change from satellite status had already taken place and, by the time they began building organized societies as Sumerians, a lot of time had elapsed. They were already fully matured as a species, so to speak. All that biological development and cruising through the primordial ooze, as your eggheads call the original soups, happened ages before when this crate was a simple satellite."

"Earth as a satellite was probably better off than it is now. It took a few million years for the satellite, which is now Earth, to develop, create or formulate—take your pick—living organisms from which animal species developed. Humans, with the capacity to reason were next on the program. But these humans, actually one step before your evolutionary process, were substantially different from modern man, or from the humans now polluting this planet!"

Adam paused as he noticed Richard's intention to interrupt him to ask a question. "Those human species, I take it, were based on the same molecular combinations."

"Yes, starting with the presence of the old reliable carbon, hydrogen, oxygen and nitrogen molecules which allowed for a succession of complex bio-chemical processes so that living things could develop tissues, organs and also provide a necessary release or re-channeling of the energy generated."

"All right," injected Richard, somewhat excited as he saw an avenue of reasoning and actual facts that had great appeal to him. The idea that a human species had existed more than sixty million years ago, was still being processed in his mind.

"We know that all cells on this planet are made up of proteins, which are combinations of carbon, hydrogen, oxygen and nitrogen. We also know that the way these elements are positioned follow a genetic code. Now then, if these humans—our ancestors—had gone through the same processes as we have, why the differences?"

Adam answered, "They were as organic as you are, heavy on carbon, hydrogen, nitrogen and oxygen, but molecular interaction was radically different, the environment was also different and as a result their metabolism, cell growth rates and overall organic development caused them to live around a thousand years. The process, as you say was basically the same, except that they had to live under a different gravity pull to start with, an enriched oxygen atmosphere, climatologically diversities, diet, and a host of other circumstances. I don't want to get technical but let me emphasize a few items, that I am sure you people are familiar with."

He smiled and out of nowhere, produced one of those models of molecules that consist of colored balls connected to each other singly or in clusters. "You see, let us take plants, for instance. They produce these compounds aided by photosynthesis, which had different characteristics in those days."

He deftly maneuvered the pieces and built a complex model combining three of the elements.

"Chlorophyll, one of the important compounds serves as a catalyst and just like your solar calculators, uses the sun's energy. The chain of reactions takes place and you have six molecules of carbon dioxide mixing it up with six molecules of water to form one glucose molecule. This molecule, which is a sugar, is in itself an energy generating element. It releases oxygen or it keeps combining with the glucose to produce carbon dioxide and water."

He moved some of the colored balls, adding others and had a new and more complex cluster. He pointed at it and continued. "From there we go into the production of amino acids, that is, sugar molecules, which result from the reaction with nitrogen compounds. More mixing around and you have your proteins, and from there tissues and so on. But the major difference was that some of the physical parameters of the environment were slightly different, so that at the end of the chain, the results were slightly different. Plants were different then and humans were also different."

As he spoke, he manipulated the cluster of colored balls so that they represented the new compounds he was describing. It was a fascinating sequence that gave more meaning to Adam's words.

"Yes, I guess I can see where different conditions would yield different results."

"They managed quite well and after a few hundred thousand years they had created safe and comfortable conditions on the planet, even though they had to compete with and protect themselves from some animal species, such as giant mammals like the good old dinosaurs, reptiles and other Spielberg favorites."

"How different were those humans?" asked Richard.

"They were programmed differently than the present variety. They were not slaves to their senses and had what I would call interesting complementary thought processes; through which they were able to achieve many things."

Richard was a bit confused. So, contrary to knowledge acquired during the last five thousand years, earth had existed as a satellite some million years ago. And its people had "complementary thought processes," whatever that meant. It brought to mind the many theories about evolution some of which suggested that maybe a third human species had peopled earth some time back. Other than Homo Sapiens a relatively recent strain, there was the Neanderthals who lasted a little more than Sapiens. Erectus appeared to be another group that existed a couple of million years before the other two and probably were the first to walk on two feet.

"Would you explain a bit more, Adam. I am smart but sometimes I lose you."

Adam laughed and, pointing a finger at Richard, said, "Yes, I thought that complementary thought process went by you, high and wide! Seriously, it just means that those people worked as teams, and it started in their brains. Example: winter is coming, we must store some firewood. Everyone proceeded to get firewood. Somehow they all followed the same technique and achieved similar results. No one tried to get more, or play the wisenheimer and goof off. A little like the ants or the bees, you know. Neither singing crickets nor snazzy rabbits loafing during the race."

Richard, "How boring. Humans with sheep mentalities are really hard to visualize."

"Not if you knew what their brains considered achievement, satisfaction and contentment. Even if they looked like today's human beings, they were totally different. Their brain configuration was almost the opposite of yours.

Somewhere along their biological development the neurological circuits provided for a perfect equilibrium between what you call the conscious and the subconscious mind. This in itself enabled them to exist within the energy configurations that I mentioned earlier."

Richard observed, "But isn't it true that collective mentalities are as good and as easily influenced by the more developed and stronger ones. Don't they suffer from the backwardness of its slowest members?"

"Not in this case. While mental development varied among them, there existed an overriding instinctual sense that spelled order and discipline in favor of the collective good. This, unfortunately, is a trait that you rarely find in your species these days, right?"

"But don't we have any of those admirable traits?"

"Well yes, the human race has inherited some reflexive or instinctual things like your sense of self preservation, maternal affection, compassion, some control of biological drives and fear of the unknown."

Richard observed, "That is right. What you tell me reinforces the theory that such crash precipitated all kinds of changes on earth and gave way to the disappearance of dinosaurs and such. What happened then?"

"The few surviving humans, continued to live in Africa but gradually they began to loose the traits of the original race. In any case, after a while the old geezers disappeared completely and the human race as you know it now became the sole inhabitant of the planet. By then, strange tendencies gradually appeared in the emotional make-up of the race. These were characteristic that helped mold what you call the character or soul of your race. On the physical side, they developed the widespread use of brute force. Mentally, they began to adopt attitudes based on subterfuges and deceit They began stealing from others and to nurture an array of those virtues and defects—depending on who you are and how you view your own reality—that cling to your race like Tangas on the Leblon girls... They became increasingly carnivorous and in the process developed some revolting forms of cannibalism, involving children and other humans."

Richard could feel his own excitement mounting. It was like reading a text that offered nothing but answers to transcendental questions. He also felt that the knowledge he was acquiring in such informal manner had to be transmitted to people on earth. He quickly envisioned the wave of roundtables, the interpretations and even the idle reviews from semi literate pundits, commentators and word mechanics. Not to mention what Helen would do with such rich material. He looked at Adam, and asked, "Why were such traits instilled in man's character, or soul?"

"It was one of those distortions that happen all over time and space. I guess it sort of proves that perfection is nothing but an illusion. The bottom line is that your species was branded with some major flaws that, over the years have accounted for practically all the ills of mankind. Greed was one of them. Larceny, a close relative of greed was another, and selfishness, the essence of the two, was another. This whole cocktail was liberally laced with anxiety, an ingredient that stays with man from the first sucking experience to the final moment. The history of mankind gives irrefutable evidence that this is the case."

"Yes, but, how about the people in our history that have never shown such traits?"

"Simple, Professor. It is another proof of the existence of opposite or complementary reactions on this rocky planet. Those people are the exception to the rule!"

"You are talking about a genetic distortion of some sort, presumably caused by the new conditions."

Adam looked at Richard and nodded his head gently. Then he said, "Yup. How else could you explain a species that since its very inception in the new environment, as a unicell organism, started to figure out how to screw the cell next door? A species that has spent untold amounts of time and energy figuring out how to hurt, kill, maim and destroy other members of its own species. Think of the first wooden club, the first stone cast in anger, the first arrow aimed. As you move through your history, one of the unique constants is the preoccupation with producing, testing and using lethal weapons. You must admit that such thing reflects some form of evil, not to say defective thinking. Even today, when there is a surface feeling that major conflicts have disappeared, more than a dozen countries spend billions in developing the weapons of the new centuries. And now, they are playing with something more serious than fire! They are into biological doozies! These are more effective than your nuclear toys, your H-bombs, your Napalm and even your embargoes!"

"You sound bitter and down on our species."

"Well...Put yourself in my shoes. Look at the human race from afar. What do you see? A bunch of self righteous, carnivorous lunatics trying to do away with each other. Beings that lurk forever in the shadow of real, imaginary or conceived threats. You see all this and you feel like catching the next Greyhound out of town!"

Adam let go of a throaty laugh and winked at Richard.

"Well," ventured Richard, "I suppose that both the environment and the diet had a lot to do with all these changes, as negative and revolting as some of them are. Also, they probably got away from an exclusively vegetarian diet, when fire was discovered and game and fish could be prepared in a more appetizing fashion. From there to now it has been a simple process of developing and protecting sources of meat and fish."

Adam smiled and nodded. "Right. You people here eat a lot of dead animals and think nothing of it. You even eat each other; not so much now but it has been a common practice. I can understand that nowadays a human being on a menu would be hard to take. Think of those cholesterol clots, the petrified arteries, all the preservatives that accompany your food. Plus the oxidizers, nicotine, glutamates, esters, additives, preservatives, pesticides, etc. that go into your system."

Adam laughed and then added, "A professional cannibal of a few thousand years ago would not touch you with a ten foot fork!"

Races

Their exchange had been, like all their conversations, full of witticisms laced with revealing thoughts and comments. For Richard it meant having the proverbial fountain of wisdom at his disposal. Any question or concept that he wanted to make or expose would have an enlightened comment on the part of Adam.

Richard had thought long and hard about the origin of our species. While the theories were many, no clear link existed in the later stages of development of homo sapiens. Richard thought for a moment and observed, "Here on earth, or rather down below this ship, we have wrestled with the origin of our species since day one. As you probably know, much research and field work has been done to find where the first human appeared, what he looked like and what are the scientific facts behind the different racial characteristics of the human race."

Adam got up and went to the bar. He produced a Yellow Mellow can, raised it in offering to Richard and, when denied, took a healthy swig from it. He smacked his lips and replied, "Remember that your species appeared on this planet when this planet was a satellite to a much bigger body. That body was a huge planet but had no organic life or the type of energy configurations you term life. It was a few million years before the disappearance of the larger planet that life appeared on Earth, the satellite. The so called birthplace of the human species took place in what is now Africa. In time, fully developed and rational beings began the process of developing into social groups and performing collective acts that would protect them in one case, help support them in others. It was the beginning of civilization in other words. Their biological characteristics changed when Earth ceased to be a satellite as a result of the disappearance of its large planet."

He paused and then added, "To satisfy your curiosity I will show you a 3D holo of one of your very first ancestors, one of the very first living when earth was a satellite, I would say. We could take a little ride to the place where he lived and meet the boy personally, but we have little time just now, so the slide will do, okay? It will be like us stepping into his office."

The Caveman

Almost as Adam finished the sentence, a bright rectangle appeared to his left. It was like an illuminated room about 15 feet by 25 feet and some 20 foot high. All of a sudden, the room filled up with leaves and branches of trees and the walls turned into the rough interior of a cave. It was daylight but a small fire had been built near the entrance within a circular pit lined with rocks. Logs and kindling pieces were uniformly stacked nearby. In the center of the cave, sat a man scrapping a large bone with a sharp piece of obsidian looking rock.

The man appeared to be in his late twenties, was deeply tanned and had dark brown hair. Body hair was profuse and his face was covered with a beard that seemed to have been trimmed. He was dressed in a skin loincloth and had a leather belt wrapped around his body, bandoleer style. The cave was full of sharp instruments made of bone, rock and wood. It looked like a shop of some kind.

"Is this a shop of some kind?" asked Richard, still entranced by the scene in front of him.

"Not exactly. Just about every caveman had to prepare and make his own tools. At about this time, manual dexterity was acquiring an important role. Other than gathering things, these boys were beginning to make objects. Take a look at that water jug and the spoon-like pieces of wood. And check the small thing by the entrance; it looks like a doll. It means that this boy has children and knows enough to make things that keep the children entertained."

Richard could hear the slow breathing of the man in the cave and perceive a multitude of odors, some of which he could easily distinguish and others that were not very pleasant. The man had an elongated cranium and a thick lower jaw. His arms and legs appeared muscular and well tanned and his feet were covered by calluses and scratches, typical of the outdoorsman. On the far side of the cave he made out a sizeable area covered by straw, large dry leaves and some animal furs. He assumed this to be the bed for the occupants of the cave and was surprised to notice in one corner, neat piles of fur pieces and what looked like belts. Some form of basket made from leather pieces hung from the wall.

Richard stood by mesmerized at the "slide," which was more like a living holograph. He felt that he was actually within that cave, unobserved. He was aware that he was seeing something no one in the later history of the human species had seen. He turned toward Adam and asked, "How old is our friend here? How long has it been since the first cell appeared? How can you say he is one of the very first? Where is the location of the cave?"

The excitement in Richard's voice was palpable. Adam raised a hand and, pointing at the cave man, said, "He is 278 years old as we see him. His evolution has taken exactly 756 million years. That is, the period of time since that nothing in the mud all of a sudden absorbed energy from its surroundings and started the comedy we all know. What you are seeing happened at the time when there were only few beings in what is now Africa. I did not want to show you the very first because it lasted only a few hours. You know, it took many years for evolution to take place and end up with a specimen like the one you are looking at. You see, I am showing you one of the first humans that had developed associative thinking and was not hanging around trees eating mangoes and not having a thought in his head."

He pointed at the caveman and continued. "The group, to which he belongs, already thinks and act like human beings, that is, they communicate with each other, they recognize and help one another and show better coordination in their actions. Our boy here, we can say, has been down from the trees for sometime. Well, a few hundred thousand years really. He is 278 years old, remember. The cave you are looking at is located between Lake Victoria and the north of what is now Nairobi. Mind you, there were still huge animals around. Dinosaurs, some flying predators and some reptiles that Spielberg would love to include in one of his productions. And the earth is still a satellite with a different atmosphere and gravitational pull; its energy channels were also substantially different."

Richard listened to the explanation offered by Adam, and then asked, "When was this taking place?"

"We are looking at 73 million BC!"

"But what happened to the large mammals, the dinosaurs and all those large vertebrates? I mentioned that we have developed some theories about their disappearance."

Richard was interrupted by Adam who said, "In a way, the exit of the dinosaurs was the result of drastic environmental changes on earth. As the larger planet blew up, earth suffered tremendous changes. Chunks of it rained upon the satellite and added to the deterioration of conditions in it. Remember the piece that fell on the Yucatan peninsula and the damage it caused. In a short time, the dinosaurs had disappeared and other mammals took over, man being one of them.

"Yes. Field research and investigations have shown that the first lemur-like primates, apes and monkeys appeared around sixty million years ago, in what we call the Miocene period."

"Yes, I have read your research papers, a few thousand books on the subject, and have pored over a few years of National Geographic Magazines. I was curious about the lack of reference to the large planet and the fact that in all these years there has been no recognition of its existence or the important role it played in the development of your species."

"You see, no traces have been found of the old planet, except maybe a few rocks in Siberia, Mexico and a couple of places in Europe. Even the studies of strata and fossils do not show much."

Adam smiled and said, "It was a hell of a blow. It pulverized the old planet and sent earth spinning like mad for a while. When things settled down and earth was firmly parked on its solar orbit, conditions on earth had changed drastically. For millions of years there was a very slow process of, let us say recovery, but in other terms. Dust became rock, vegetation mutated; the previous oxygen content of the air was considerably reduced. Infrared and ultraviolet action was different. Gravity exerted a different force, global temperatures dropped... It was a rough episode. During all this time, only a few humans survived, along with some other species."

Richard could not keep his eyes from the cave man. He sort of enjoyed the concentration of the man as he methodically scrapped the bone in swift and well coordinated strokes. At times, he would breathe heavily and sort of whistled. Something between a sigh and a deep throat rumble. But it wasn't a frightening sound, more like the exhalations we sometime make when we wake up. Looking at the man, Richard wondered about its genetic make up and also about the mystery of the races on the planet. If this one was one of the first, what did the others look like? Were there Asians, Blacks, Redheads, Bolivians, then?

He asked Adam with some anxiety, causing Adam to look at him and reply, "You see, the entire monkey species, and man, descended from a mutant that lived some million years ago. As you can see, our hunter here—and he pointed the Yellow Mellow can at the holographic image—has many monkey features. Look at the shape of the head; his teeth have the thick enamel that is characteristic of your species and he is bipedal. Also, the bones in his legs, specially the fibula and the tibia are structurally developed to support the weight and exercises of a walking customer."

Pointing at the caveman, he continued. "It was a gradual thing for this species to learn to walk on two feet. It was also the separation of the human strain from the African apes. Things kept changing; the brain became larger, the limbs and the pelvis assumed new shape and positions."

"Where on earth were these changes taking place?" asked Richard.

"In Central Africa, Ethiopia, Kenya, in that area."

"Yes, findings confirm that biped hominid species existed in those areas. You know, we have a whole string of them, like the Australopithecus Ramidus, Anamensis, Afarensis, Ethiopicus, Africanus, etc. etc. But the question is if being bipeds is or not a fundamental human characteristic and why the early hominids stood up?"

"Environmental changes led to genetic changes. One was heat. Standing up you are exposed to less solar radiation than if you move around on all fours. Two, the jungle gave way to more savanna, which forced the hominids to move around more and look over the grass more. Do this for a few hundred thousand years and you develop a nice neck and learn to stand on tiptoe. There is movement and upward reach. Picking up fruits can be easier if you stand up; think of all those plums, apples, pears, figs, and a few nest eggs."

"How about their body hair?"

"When they began to walk upright, they did not need the protection against the heat in the form of profuse hair all over their bodies. Remember it was one hot, long season that lasted a few thousand years. To protect the brain, hair grew only on the head: it helps keep the cranial cavity cool. Even reproduction changed dramatically. Ovulation cycles changed in the female and along with that a new direction in the instinctual drive took place. The pairings became widespread and reproduction began to adopt another sense. In short, when the satellite became planet earth it already had the original human species. It was already walking on two feet and losing some of the good manners of the original human breed. As I said before, they did not live as long as the previous cats, but it did not seem to bother them. Your species can cause enough mayhem in few years! That is the actual race, dear Professor."

"You mean that there were two different periods and that during the first, the human species developed; then we had the blow up and we became planet earth?"

"You got it," replied Adam.

"What kind of people were they? If he was one of the first, how would you classify him? I know, a biped, but what racial make up, or was there such thing?"

Adam nodded and said, "This one belongs to the old planet really, where all of them were of the same genetic characteristics, development, color, etc." He paused for a moment and then continued. "Dear Richard, I understand your curiosity about the genetic or racial makeup of our fiddler here. I can't help perceiving that your curiosity is irremediably influenced by the thinking—and I guess also the feeling—of modern day culture and attitudes on planet earth. You are anxious to know—unwittingly perhaps—about racial classifications. A key cultural element on present earth is that represented by the various races and skin colors. I have noticed that in this planet, races and skin color seem to be the predominant identifying element among human beings. It is also a reference that brings with it all kinds of positive and negative reactions."

"Yes," observed Richard, "it is not only professional interest as an anthropologist but also as a member of a society that has maintained ethnic origin and race characteristics as weapons, excuses, blessings and curses!"

Adam smiled and said, "Damn right, old boy! From early on, man has used skin color as a key ingredient of social interaction. Skin color has had a lot to do with the early civilizations. They enslaved other peoples whose skin was of a different shade and made them instrumental in the building of their great civilizations. Later, as they acquired collective beliefs and creeds, their differences grew; they were no longer limited to differences based on race or skin color. They had more sophisticated excuses to accentuate the differences among them. But the funny thing is that they all come from the same Charlie. And the same Jane."

"Interesting. I suppose you know more about this than any one and yes, it is a matter of curiosity. Why are there men with dark skins, brown skins, slanted eyes, thick lips, tall, short, stocky, red hair, blond hair, curly hair, wiry hair if they all came from the same Charlie, as you say, and the Charlie I am looking at in his cave looks like a tanned Caucasian, as we call the honkies on the planet."

"My dear Professor," said Adam with a big smile, "I adore your sense of humor and your descriptions. It makes Anthropology sound like an earthy discipline, and forgive the pun!"

They both laughed. Richard was enjoying himself immensely. He felt that he was on the verge of learning things that had been the obsession of men for all times. The elusive power of the truth somehow kept entire human disciplines called religions, faith or plain superstition, under a sense of expectation and also hope.

He cleared his throat and asked Adam if he could have a beer. By now, Richard was used to Adam's incredible talent for producing things out of thin air. In a gentle sarcastic tone, but pleasant nonetheless, Adam asked the kind of beer Richard favored.

"Let us see how good a bartender you are, Adam. I would love to have a cool, crisp Cristal!"

"Hey, you know your beer. A fine Peruvian light ale coming up!"

Adam reached under the bar and came up with a tray with 3 bottles of the light and tasty Peruvian brew and some small bags of peanuts that had TWA logos printed on one side. Richard looked at the peanut bags and exclaimed, "Hey! Where did you get these? The airlines don't give peanuts anymore! And TWA ceased to exist some time ago!"

"Ah! We were friendly with some hostesses." He smiled and then said, "Now, about your questions. Yes, you all come from this Charlie or that symbolic Adam in your Bible. Genetically he is a unit. Due to the changes in the earth's condition as a satellite and later as a planet, some changes affected the superficial characteristics of part of the species. Keep in mind also that diet is a major factor in the physical make up of humans, meaning that food variety is different at different latitudes. You see, if our Charlie here was stuck in Alaska for generations, his grandchildren would not look like him at all. Try staying in a cold chamber for an hour. Come out and look at yourself in the mirror. The professor would look pale, wrinkled and tired. Both the hair and the muscular tone would show definite changes, due to the reduced molecular activity resulting from low temperatures. In time, assuming you continue to live in a cold chamber, the children you conceive in such environment would look much different than if they lived in a normal climate of earth. Their skin color might change and they might not have the breezy look you sport now, or the healthy, glossy head of hair you wear so well."

Richard smiled and asked, "How about the other groups?"

"Well, the same is true of the dark skinned groups, beginning from the blacks' skin pigmentation. How do you think the pigmentation—and its corresponding chromosomatic variation—came about. The sun, its ultraviolet, infrared and spilled stray light distortions played hell with our Charlies and, in time changed them. The slanted eyes? Well, they are not really slanted, but they are the result of inclement weather in what is now Central China. Some Charlies and their families settled there after the dinosaurs had disappeared. Do you remember the steppes, the Mongolian plains, the winds on the foothills of the Himalayas? All you do is squint your eyes. Do it for generations and the kids will no longer have the rounded innocence of your blue orbs. Well, seriously it is attributed to a genetic sideline, so to speak Hair and other characteristics went through similar processes. A simple pigmentation change due largely to diet and the ability of the body to develop certain enzymes and cell groups under certain conditions; and of course, thousands if not millions of years."

"You mean to tell me that the human races, as we know them, are the result of living conditions?"

"Basically, yes. Listen, the first humans that could be identified as such," Adam paused and pointed at the caveman, still busy scraping away at the bone, "were like this one. His descendants will move around and settle all areas of the planet. In the process, they would all adopt different living habits and, most important different diets. They would be affected by different climatic conditions and would develop immunities to other emerging forms of life in bacterial form."

"How about their diet?"

"It plays a very important role in their development. Think of the Eskimos who for ages have had a rich protein diet. This influenced their metabolism and by consequence many other characteristics. They started as dark skinned tribes and, in spite of the cold weather conditions, retained the pigments and their skin color. Not like some of the tribes in Northern Europe, whose diet was quite different and, somehow, allowed them to remain light skinned, blond and blue eyed."

"I guess you are talking about hormonal and biological changes."

"Yes, you see, diet, for one, can modify the body's content of carotene, hemoglobin and melanin. You know, skin color for one, can be modified through changes in melanocytes in the skin. But let us not forget that these wonderful human bodies react to the environment thanks to that great endocrine system you all have. Its various hormone factories, the pituitary, hypothalamus, thyroid, adrenal and gonad glands provide the ingredients needed to allow organs to do a particular task. But they are all affected by the environment, the diet and many other factors. As you change environment, you affect the way these factories operate and therefore change the end product, or if you wish to get technical, pave the way for genetic transformations and derivations."

"I guess that the process has taken several million years to arrive at what we are now," observed Richard, who was making an effort to absorb the comments made by Adam.

"You see, the differences among races or groups, from a base genetic standpoint, are nil. The difference among races in this planet is simply a genetic distortion. Unfortunately, it has always been a ready reference for establishing standards. For instance, for several thousand years, when you think of slaves you immediately think of blacks. The reason is simply that Africa was a very populous continent, as opposed to Europe where a few tribes of white skinned, blue eyed barbarians subsisted on berries, roots and small animals. Empires like the Assyrian, the Egyptians, the Romans and the Greek just tapped that pool of black people and turned them into slaves. Somehow the black color became identified with the social condition of slavery. It was easy to extend the inferior social level of that race to the race itself. So you see, it was just a matter of development, or as someone would say depreciation of appreciation."

Adam laughed along with Richard and then continued. "The Babylonians learned to raise crops, build carts and temples and work iron and copper. They also had better weapons than the tribes in the Upper Nile. Dominating and conquering those less developed tribes and forcing them to do slave work was easy enough."

He stopped and with a faraway look in his eyes said, "It could have been the other way around. Just imagine the white skinned people of this planet being identified as an inferior race simply because they spent millions of years preparing the fried chicken for their black or brown masters! The differences and the problems that exist among the races of this planet—in our view—are largely cosmetic, aided by the different degrees of mental and social development."

He paused for a moment and then continued. "There is of course the environment effect. Some races have remained isolated for centuries in places where living conditions were unique. Somehow, their physical and mental development has been largely conditioned by that environment. Now, however we have a different story. In the last few decades, this planet has become more knowledgeable about other cultures and people, thanks to your excellent communications. And people are no longer isolated; they know about others. Familiarity breeds acceptance and certainly, tolerance. The Japanese, for instance no longer consider the white races as uncouth barbarians and, like them, other ethnic groups have learned to accept other races and cultures. The age of globalization, as your economists are so fond of reminding everyone, is here: a new world environment!"

Richard had listened with great interest, but still he could not grasp in its entirety the effect that environment had played in early social groups. He observed, "Well, the changes in earth's atmosphere must have been considerable to produce such variations from the original man."

"Yes they were. But remember that these changes took millions of years. For instance, a surrealistic joke I heard concerns the kids of a family that live on the side of a hill. It seems that, after a while, they have one leg longer than the other as they always have one leg higher to the other when they go up and down the hill!"

They both laughed. Adam continued. "Keep in mind also that the changes that took place on the planet, especially in the last few hundred thousand years, caught some groups in isolated areas. Take the Khoisan of Southern Africa, which include the Bushmen and the Hottentots; they became a mystery. Consider those plain Charlies from Africa and the Asian plains. Or the Basques. They are a bunch that became isolated in what is now the French and Spanish Basque country. You know the fellows who have been raising so much hell in Spain lately, or rather some of the hotheads among them."

"Yes, we know about the Basques and their eternal claims to independence. Where did they come from?"

"They are a tribe that migrated from Central Europe and got stuck in that part of the world known as Euskadi, or that corner between France and Spain. You see, there was a great flood in what is now the Loire valley and changed the whole course of the Seine and the Rhone all the way to Provence and the Pyrenees, leaving our Basques isolated in that corner of the world for quite some time. As a result, the Basques inbred and developed some peculiar traits, including a minor genetic change that affects their blood type. Their race has the lowest frequency of Type B blood and highest in type Rh-negative and O in all of Europe."

Adam paused and this time produced a packet of spearmint gum from his pocket and offered it to Richard who took one. Adam winked and said in a strong and terribly funny western accent, "If you all hanker for some chewing tobakker, I'll be glad to oblige!"

"Adam, you have sketched in few words, the story of the races on this planet. What can you offer about the claimed superiority of one race over another? It seems that this has been one of the constant sources of conflict among humans."

"In trying to analyze this peculiar cocktail of races you got on this planet, you have to look at two fundamental references. One is strictly a function of chromo somatic development. In broad terms, there are strains that undergo genetic transformations and, by consequence, traits, as a result of the influence exerted by the environment. The children who are raised by the seaside have little in common with those that spend their lives on a mountain. Their diets are different, their living conditions are different and the challenges they face daily are certainly different. All this leads to the creation and observance of habits, customs and attitudes peculiar to the conditions of their environment."

Richard nodded. Adam had just touched on some of the more basic findings concerning the effect of the environment on the species. He said so and it was Adam's turn to nod. He paused and then continued. "Now, watch how conflict develops. The beach boy can catch and provide fish, while the mountain boy can make goat cheese. They start by exchanging things. But sooner or later, one or the other wants more, or disagrees with the terms of an exchange and as a result a fight ensues. The one who wins dominates the other, takes over his domain and his property and, after a while, he realizes the importance of his accomplishment and naturally feels superior to the loser. Small currents here and there and that feeling of superiority blooms into a belief. This in itself stimulates the need for more accomplishments. If successful, he now has acquired a degree of confidence and insight in his ability that enables him to seek new conquests. It is like feeding programs into the hard disc of your computer. After a while that expanded memory, or experience in our beach boy, gives him the confidence to embark on new ventures. The guy has become superior! Multiply this by millions of years and the imprint becomes genetic. I know that some of your eggheads are going to disagree with me on these theories, but let me continue. I mentioned another factor. It has to do with the family structure of the original band, tribe or group. As our beach boys extend their territory, a record of their exploits is more or less etched in the minds of the members of the group. The closer the family ties, the stronger is the message that is transmitted from generation to generation, giving way to a collective conscience, atavistic memory or group history. As a result in a few million years races develop their own traits and characteristics. Now, if they are faced with challenges, some collective instinct provides the necessary defenses or stimulus. Similarly, the moment there are no incentives, contentment sets in and things begin to sour."

"What happened to the losers?"

"Same enchilada, but in a negative way. The sense of defeat stays with them for a long time; multiply that by a few million years and the attitude and mental makeup of those people are much different from the victor's. And the same can happen when you are a victim of your environment. It obstructs development in many ways. That is why tribes in remote places retain the same level of development."

"That is an interesting theory, or should I say, assertion? Since you have had opportunity to look into the intimate details of our entire human race, you are probably just exposing a series of true facts. What you are saying also makes a lot of sense. Greek, Egyptian, Romans, Syrians, etc., at the beginning of civilization followed a familiar pattern. Origin, growth, cultural and social development, era of privilege and then decline. I guess it could also happen to us, Americans, huh?"

"Well you live in a different social climate. Like all previous empires, yours will face some challenges that in one way or another will affect your very nature. It can continue to improve and remain a dominant force or it can begin its decline. But do not think for a minute that those levels that you have achieved are guaranteed to last for eternity. If you wish I can let you listen first hand to the Asyrians, Egyptians, Babylonians, Greeks, Romans, French, Otomans, Mayas, Aztecs, Incas, English, Spanish, Austro Hungarians, Germans and all those who had created great empires and who believed that their empires would be eternal. Without going back many years, remember old Hitler and his 1,000 years. Napoleon and his innumerable generations, Communism and their 1,000 years again."

He smiled and concluded, "Time, in addition to being a great dimension, is also the most effective laxative of human history!"

Richard laughed enjoying the unique references and especially the punch line.

"Listen, Adam, I would love to stay here and continue our chat for days on end, but I am expected down at the shop. Besides, I must have spent what seems like 6 or 8 hours going over the data. But when I look at my watch, I see that only two hours have elapsed. Besides, I have not seen any clocks up here and none of you wear wristwatches. Could you enlighten me?"

"Well," replied Adam, "a simple trick to make sure that your physical integrity remains protected. See, when you come up here, you become subject to our time frames. That is, you can spend 10 hours up here but when you look at your wrist watch, only two hours of earth time have elapsed."

"Why is that?"

"We just wish to keep the wear and tear on your body to correspond to a suitable time period like the two hours your watch shows. Otherwise, if allowed to age according to our time frame up here, you would be many more hours older. We decided to keep the time difference at about two hours. That is also why the shuttle always arrives at the UN between two and three hours after it comes up. Follow me? As for wearing watches, we really do not need them; time to us is like breathing to you. It acquires a physical dimension, almost. Every time we go exploring however, we get ourselves some fancy Rolexes or Patek Philippes or some trusty old Timexes."

"Amazing," muttered Richard as he picked up his computer case and a rolled parchment printed in one of Guttenberg's early efforts, a gift from Earle. He moved to the end of the room where the shuttle seemed to be waiting for him.

At the White House

The day after his return to New York, Richard accompanied by Patrick boarded the executive jet that the State Department had placed at their service in La Guardia Airport, and flew to Washington to meet with the President.

While both Patrick and Richard were satisfied that Elmo's attack had been somewhat checked by Helen's excellent campaign, now titled "A Look Beyond," they knew that Elmo would not give up on his designs and that the Reverend Toe would continue his frenetic promotions all over the world.

Elmo had continued to create a wave of support from a number of multinational corporations, church sectors in places as disparate as Australia, Norway and the Philippines. He had also managed to counter any of the White House diplomatic initiatives. His control of some of the major publishers in the country enabled him to continue to influence public opinion in favor of his and Reverend Toe's proposals.

The President, annoyed at first, was now worried. Through the pressure received from prominent members of both houses, he had been forced to meet with Elmo twice. At the first meeting, he felt that having such meeting was a small concession to some of the conservative lobbies and that he stood to gain in the exchange. Elmo had been forceful and straightforward. His exposition however was not devoid of a subtle threat, which the President chose to ignore.

First it was a "strong recommendation" to consider having himself and Reverend Toe appointed independent observers for the United States. Next, it was another "helpful suggestion" that he be included in the UN Emergency Committee. And another proposal that Elmo head a so-called "Tech and

Commerce Team" to deal with the visitors, presumably without interfering with the UN group. The idea was based on technology exchanges for which the UN team had made no substantial allowances, as they dealt more with social and moral issues. The President promised to review these matters with his advisers and also made it clear that the visitors above had the last word. He took advantage of the occasion to remind Elmo that additional campaigns could only result in confusion at the time when discussions with the visitors had reached a critical stage.

A day later, the President met with Patrick and Richard to discuss Elmo's visit.

"Elmo has been very convincing. He has met with almost every President and Primer minister in Europe and right now he is working Southeast Asia," informed the President.

"It is clear to me that his purpose is strictly commercial, and worse, quite personal. He is disguising his appetite for the visitor's technology with all sorts of benign pronouncements about sharing the benefits among all nations."

Richard added, "Let's not forget that his campaign is very well organized. I don't know how many Ambassadors pay homage to him and how many heads of State are in his debt. But, you know, all this hasn't happened as a result of the appearance of the pills. He's been doing this for years. Ever since he had to withdraw from the Presidential race, he's devoted his time and his considerable means to enlist a large number of influential men from many countries. He is a boy with a fixed idea in mind!"

"Well, not only that but he also has a great ally. That Reverend Toe seems to be everywhere. His powers of persuasion are limitless, it seems. Just last week he obtained the support of several Protestant groups to back Elmo's aspirations. But that ain't all, friends. He's also working on the Armed Forces of most major nations and, hold on to your seats, he is campaigning in the Vatican and also in Israel, Syria and Iran!" added the President.

Patrick, who had remained silent, spoke up. "While we cannot lose sight of Elmo's maneuvers, we should not worry too much about him. For one thing, it is the visitors who establish the pecking order. Let us not forget that they are in a position to make any changes they want. Their power is really beyond our comprehension. I feel sometimes that at if at any moment they decide to drop the entire project they can just freeze our energy bonds and the whole planet is toast, as the saying goes!"

"You are right," agreed the President. "But what bothers me is the confusion Elmo and the Reverend are creating and the strong foothold they have acquired in the world's power structure. Once things get back to normal, if they ever do, they will be damn near unmovable. I for one do not believe that their charitable and humanitarian inclinations are 100 percent sincere. From what I hear, our Reverend is more concerned with the receipts from his holdings than with the assistance, both material and spiritual his organization is supposed to provide to the millions of his followers. And Elmo is no different. I am convinced that his aim is to attain total control of some key sectors of the world resources, like communications and transportation, and assume a level of power never seen before."

They spent the next few hours examining reports from the NSC that dealt with the Reverend Toe's and Elmo's various activities in several continents. With a great sense of discretion and also good taste, all three chose to skip a discussion on the way the information had been obtained and the implicit responsibility they shared in its existence. Whatever undercover service had been involved in keeping tabs on the Reverend and Elmo had done an excellent job.

Their interest, as the President underlined, was to be sure that no attempt was made against the national security, the existing international agreements and the protection of the existing order. Elmo's sudden interest in the members of the Supreme Court was puzzling, same as the Reverend's quiet relations with prominent people alleged to be connected with the drug cartels.

They agreed that surveillance should continue and that periodic reports should be made to the President. No one felt that the matter should be brought to the attention of other members of the Government.

The President summed up their meeting. "Now we not only have to worry about restoring that famous energy balance but also spending some energy by keeping and eye on these two!"

The Future

The following days in New York were spent by Patrick and Richard in a succession of meetings and appointments. The UN's global network had performed admirably and had supplied the visitors with the data requested in record time.

The work load of the Committee increased as additional data was received in the form of computer printouts, diskettes, CDs and plain typewritten reports. Not only was it necessary to organize the data but also to provide the summaries requested by the visitors. At one of the meetings of the Special UN

Committee, Baron Carini asked, "Why can't the visitors do their own compiling and summarizing? You might think that with their control of most physical elements on this planet they could set up their own Statistical Department. Haven't they heard of IBM, Microsoft, the Library of Congress, and Office Depot?"

Richard laughed and explained that the visitors insisted on receiving data directly from human beings. It seemed that there was a strange component whereby human inputs aided in classifying and identifying the data.

As the work proceeded, Richard found time to meet with the visitors as often as he could as he wanted to discuss as many topics as possible. He felt that here was the chance of a lifetime to uncover many of the secrets of civilization. Other than reporting to the Committee, he had gathered a small academic group that made use of videoconferencing regularly. He had invited Professors, Academicians, and experts from all over to share with him every one of his discussions with the visitors. And there was Helen, forever anxious to receive additional information for her program.

On one of the real hot days in Manhattan, he was glad to have scheduled a trip up to the ship. The combination of high temperatures, high humidity and the canyon feeling the skyscrapers produced were good reasons to "go upstairs," as he had become fond of calling every one of his trips to the ship. He only regretted that not enough time was devoted to Helen, who also seemed extremely busy with the TV project and her other duties at S&S.

Upon his arrival, he found Adam in the lounge. "I see you are having another hot day down there," observed Adam. "You know, I thought our pill would provide some shade and lower the thermometer but it does not seem to work."

Adam remembered their last conversation about Time and seemed willing to continue on the subject. Sitting in front of an elaborate marble fireplace, Adam took the piece of chewing gum from his mouth and holding it between the thumb and index finger of both hands, slowly stretched it until it broke. With a look devoid of expression he said, "Chewing gum can give us a clue. It holds for a while but then..." He pointed at the broken pieces of gum. "In a way, time is like gum; but not on this neck of the woods. As a dimension whose limits are not quantified on any existing scale on this planet, it acquires another character where we come from. It stretches at times, it can be molded and, at times it can break, or be interrupted or started anew. Confusing, isn't it?"

"Absolutely! You could have explained all that in ancient Mongolian and I would have been just as enlightened!"

They laughed and Richard took advantage of the pause to ask something he had had on his mind for some time

"Adam, since you have the ability to understand and control time, I guess you can also see into the future. You know there are whole industries on Earth devoted to the future, you know, psychics, seers, magicians, the lot. Maybe you can tell me about the future of our country, or at least let me have a glimpse of what is in store for us."

Adam carefully put together the two pieces of gum into the fingers of his left hand, made a ball of it and deftly propelled it to the waste paper basket in the other end of the room. He smiled pleased with himself, and exclaimed, "Three points!"

"Professor, one of the items we agreed on among the six of us when we landed here, was not to allow humans to glimpse into their future. You see, it sort of throws in a special energy syntax into our procedures which may not be advisable. We could show you all you want, but we are concerned about the unpredictable reactions of your people. Imagine the cosmic picnic we would have if everyone wants to see what will happen to his investment portfolio, or be able to see his great grand children or maybe find out who will win the series, or the number of the Powerball? But as a special attention to you, dear Professor, I'll show you a few things. But only a few, mind you!"

Richard was almost under shock. It was too unreal to be able to see into the future. He felt strange. He could not define the sensation that took over him. It was a combination of anxiety, curiosity and fear! He found he could not say anything and just nodded. Adam turned and took a few steps in the direction of the corridor. In a second, a huge screen, of the same holographic quality of previous occasions appeared on his right. All kinds of sounds and smells could be perceived. Richard looked at the scene and felt faint and dizzy. He vaguely recognized the place, but such was his anxiety to register every minute detail that his dizziness persisted. He remained motionless and took in the incredible scene in front of his senses.

A succession of images appeared within the frame. He could hear voices and comments spoken with lightly accented English and, in the background, traffic sounds, occasional barking of a dog and even felt the slight breeze that came from the box. The images continued for a few minutes, while Richard remained motionless in the sofa. His mind was having a difficult time adjusting to the unreal scenes that were projected.

"Have you seen enough?" Adam asked after a few minutes. Without waiting for an answer, somehow, he caused the scene to change several times.

Each time, Richard's amazement grew in geometrical proportion. He began to feel the tension and exhilaration that such spectacle was having on him. As if sensing the effect that the "shows" were having on Richard, Adam suddenly turned and grabbing Richard by the elbow, led him gently back to the parlor. "I guess you have seen enough," he said as he helped Richard to a sofa. "It is certainly an amazing thing, isn't it?"

Richard remained silent with a faraway look that denoted surprise, perplexity and awe.

"Time for a Scotch," said Adam as he moved toward the bar.

It was more than one Scotch that allowed Richard to regain his composure. He had felt excited but at the same time some measure of shock had entered his system. To see your life and yourself as time passes was perhaps too much for the human mind. Adam, however, had been careful in showing scenes that would not inflict too much of a shock.

At that moment, Patrick arrived accompanied by Emosh. He greeted Adam and Richard and made a beeline for the bar. He poured himself a Scotch and asked Emosh if he wanted one. Emosh declined and excused himself.

After a while, as they reviewed US Statistics, Richard asked, "And how about us Americans? I mean Native Americans. What is the real story?"

Adam drank the last drops of Scotch and also allowed a couple of ice cubes to remain in his mouth. As he chewed on them, he pointed at his mouth and motioned to Richard to wait. Once finished eating the ice he said, "Three major groups or tribes from Asia walked over to the American continent when the Bering Strait did not exist but was a frozen mass, some million years ago. From there, Alaska today, they kept walking south and populated the entire continent. In time they developed some superficial differences. An Eskimo from Hudson Bay is different from an Aztec, or from a Shoshone or an Aymara from the Andes. But they are blood differences and slight chromo somatic variations. Remember that they all come from the same Charlie. In this respect the symbolism of most of your religions is correct when they assure you that you all come from a single couple or the same source."

"We know that," observed Richard. "We have always theorized that nomad tribes from Northeast Asia moved across the frozen bridge into North America. It is a good theory but it lacks some tangible support; you know, fossils, artifacts, etc. These are hard to get because the whole area is now under many feet of sea water."

"Well, that area evolved into large marshy plains that supported vegetation and forests. This attracted other forms of life like goats, bears, reindeer, rabbits, wolves, birds, fish and some of the Ice Age species. There were still mammoths, mastodons and woolly rhinos roaming around so the tribes had enough life support to keep moving east and south. The initial troop of 21 men and 34 women, was followed by thousands who managed to follow and get to the other side. A few thousand years later, the two continents were again separated by the sea as the ice from glaciers melted and caused the sea level to rise again."

"I see. From there, I guess, the migration to the south was natural."

"Exactly. The further south they traveled, the larger the variety of fauna and flora. Also, the milder climates in the lower latitudes enabled them to do some farming and to establish permanents settlements that, in time, developed into admirable civilizations. But the majority remained a nomadic society. As you know, they kept moving south until they ran out of steam in Tierra del Fuego; they also ran out of land."

Patrick nodded and said to Adam, "What you say confirms many theories and hypothesis about the original inhabitants of the American Continent. You seem to have seen these things happen, or you have memorized a couple of encyclopedias, Adam?"

Adam laughed with his slightly metallic resonance and said, "It is a simple mental process that I can use. It involves some of the time-space equations of my level—or species as you would say—and it borrows the human brain I have acquired to do the translation. A little like using a computer where you can recall many items from installed software, such as the encyclopedias or on-line info from the many services you have now. Complete with video clips and enhanced with aromas and flavors."

"You must admit that the brains of our species can be very useful," joked Richard.

"Well, you'd be surprised. Your rudimentary brain can beat any computer that you have developed so far. Your problem at this time is that you have not learned to use it. It has ample storage capacity, instant recall and can interpret all kinds of inputs. Using the brain that I have borrowed, for instance, I was able to see just a moment ago, that first bunch of nomads walking across unknown marshes simply because they wished to follow the tracks they had found. They kept following the tracks and, in the process found birds and animals that were strange to them. Also, they found various kinds of forage for their own beasts. I could feel the cold winds and smell the cooked rabbits and fish. And I could also listen to their conversations. I could have taken a reading of their thoughts and gauge their instinctual feelings, but there is no need to really know these people that well."

"I have one question," said Patrick who had been busy making notes. "You mention 24 men and 34 women as the first to cross into the American continent. Is there any meaning to those figures?"

"Glad you asked," replied Adam. "You see, they figure that on a long journey some women would become pregnant, bear children and be otherwise occupied with their offspring and would not be 100 percent available for the many tasks a nomad group had. The additional women were reserve labor, if you wish."

"I have been fascinated by the way you have conjured up images from the past and would like to know if I can ask you to let me see some of my choosing."

"Certainly," replied Adam. "The reason we haven't used more images is that we are aware of the effect they would have on earth once Helen Lawrence has subjected them to her magic treatment. The DVDs we prepare for you are of course to be shown to everyone. The only reservation we have is that these images do not create conflicts among you humans."

"What sort of conflicts do you see?"

"First, and let me use my Harvard legal training, there is a small matter of rights. In truth, the DVDs are given to the UN and therefore become the UN's property. Technically, it is the transfer of an asset from us and I don't know how your tax lawyers would treat the transaction. There is also the matter of assessing the value of the asset so that subsequent depreciation and amortization quotas would make sense. However, it could also be treated as inventory in any case."

"You sound like old Arthur Andersen himself!" interrupted Patrick and then, "The UN is out. I have dismantled a Film, Radio and TV Division that cost a few hundred million dollars a year and was neither 'ni chicha ni limonada,' as they say in Seville. It produced some documentaries more for internal consumption and for the expensive massaging of the ego of a number of aficionados, than as serious public services. Besides, I always felt that the media is a highly specialized field and should remain in the hands of professionals in the industry. I saw no role for the UN in the indiscriminate sponsoring of strange movie and video shorts about even stranger topics. So I did away with it."

"How about Helen's program? Who is underwriting the costs?"

"We created a special fund, administered by and independent auditing firm. Practically all nations contribute so that their actual disbursements are small. There is no rights deal of any sort and anyone can copy the programs, edit them, fill them with commercials or turn them into a travel show. PBS agreed to use their network to air the programs and link up with worldwide television. I have made every effort to avoid the temptation to apply those incredible bureaucratic practices to a simple video deal."

It was Adam's turn to nod and he said, "It is really something to behold the way you people create procedures, methods, checklists, manuals, instruction books, summaries, abstracts and a million other ways to complicate matters that can amply justify the application of bureaucratic practices."

"Such as?" asked Richard.

"Well, look at your Health Care organizations. The simple task of providing medical aid to one or all has become an industry with layers upon layers of procedures that answer to special interest groups. While Medicine in your country is without doubt the most advanced, it is corrupted by its own effectiveness. Richard, if Christopher Columbus had tried to make his voyage in these times, the lawyers, the corporate elites, the bean counters and the technonerds would have kept him busy ashore all these centuries arguing about business and strategic plans, marketing plans, uncharted waters maps, investment recovery, transponder links, venture profitability, human resource evaluation, P&Ls, ROIs, NPVs and depreciation schedules!"

They stopped to enjoy a mid afternoon snack. As usual it was a tempting array of dishes that would make the Chef of the Pierre Hotel proud. Earle pointed out that the mid afternoon snack had its origins with the Sumerian priests. It seems that they were expected to spend long prayer hours after sunset and in order to prevent serious hunger pangs decided to have the snack just before entering the temples. The conversation then turned to the various cycles of evolution prompting Richard to comment on the genetic make up of the Sumerians compared to modern day man.

Adam thought for a minute and then said, "No major changes. Perhaps some research could clarify some of the modifications to cellular structures and ultimately to DNA chain reactions, which after all rule the whole process. Some of these changes do have great repercussions in the ultimate nature of any cellular compound."

Richard stopped Adam in mid sentence. "I guess you refer to major changes in the biological makeup of the human race and the genetic changes that go deep into the substance of man. In terms of biological science the base sequence of the DNA chain was altered at some point. In other words, it could also be that nucleotides increased or decreased in the DNA chain and changed the number of nucleotides in a gene. If this happened, was it limited to the human species, and what triggered the change in the genetic code?"

"Gee, Richard, you are getting technical on me," replied Adam in his usual pleasant and well modulated tone.

"In genetic terms, as an organism becomes more complex its genes become more segmented than in the case of, let us say, a bacteria whose entire gene is contained in an unbroken DNA molecule. A simple mechanism to prevent extensive mutation is that of having the genetic code in segments. It is like tearing a dollar bill in two or more parts."

"What happens to the pieces?" asked Richard.

"By themselves, the pieces have no value but when they get their act together you have your greenback. Same with the old molecules. As you know, genetic code sequences can be altered if bases are added or deleted. Let us not loose sight of the fact that each gene is responsible for making a particular protein which in turn causes a certain trait to develop. And, once coded, it stays there for all succeeding generations."

"How about other forms of life?"

"As to whether genetic changes in the past few million years also affected other forms of life, yes. The why is another matter. Here I have to go back to energy, gravitational forces and intermolecular attraction in the planet. These are all physical characteristics that have suffered numberless changes in the last eighty million years or so. If one changes, it modifies the others, and don't forget my dear Richard, that before all the bullshit about chromosomes, genes, codons and polynucleotide chains of RNA, which are the elements you have to go by, it is those forces I mentioned that keep the human race from falling off this decrepit planet of yours!"

Richard laughed, still amazed at Adam's unique way of explaining complex subjects in an easy and even cheerful manner. But he was intrigued by the changes that had occurred to the human race and, in particular to the drastic transformation from the original man who developed on Earth when earth was a mere satellite of a much larger planet.

"You are right of course. Our interest has been to define the mechanisms that triggered the changes and, to some extent you have clarified that for me. I can see that there is lots of work ahead of us, especially if that work involves the blend of Biological and Physical Sciences."

He stopped to give himself time to formulate his next question in as clear a manner as his excited thinking could make it.

"Adam, I follow you when you explain that original man was transformed by the physical changes that took place in his environment when the large planet exploded. I can accept that present day man, having lost many of the traits of the original version represents a model that has adapted well to his new environment. But, coming down to more recent times, how have a few humans, parked in the middle of the African continent have managed to create a lineage that lasts to this day? How indelible was the change?"

Adam listened to the question with obvious interest and answered, "Well, we already talked about the genetics of the race and the fact that changes, or mutations if you like, do occur. Tracing a specific strain is another thing. Some thousands of years ago, humans began to travel. As time passed, some stayed put in some areas while other kept traveling. I think that eventually your scientists will be able to trace the various groups in the many places where humans have settled."

"I suppose you are right. A great deal of study is being done on fossils, human remains and artifacts. They all are clues about the way humans disseminated throughout the planet."

Adam nodded and said, "Well, you have a wonderful tool at your disposal. If you follow the Y chromosome trail, you will find many answers. For instance, take the European continent. Today, a Y chromosome analysis would reveal that most Europeans come from the Paleolithic people. These were the first humans to settle in the European continent."

"But, how solid is that kind of f research?" asked Richard.

"Quite, old boy, quite," replied Adam in a passable imitation of a British accent. He continued. "Using the Y chromosome is playing it safe. This chromo is one of those who almost never changes. It has about 60 million DNA base pairs that seem to remain unchanged. Thus you can rely on it when you do comparison charts. It stays the same for generations and sort of establishes a clear origin. You know that the Y chromosome produces a male when it is carried in the sperm that fertilizes an egg. By the same token an X chromo from that sperm produces a female."

"It makes sense," observed Richard. "We know that Stone Age humans migrated into Europe around 40,000 years ago, even though their exact origins have never been firmly established."

"You can stop wondering. They came from the Middle East and Central Asia. But after a while, the last ice age brought the huge glaciers into the continent and forced our boys to take off for the soft belly of Europe, like the Balkans, Spain, Turkey and the Ukraine. That is where some of your fossils come from, and with them that reliable Y chromo that indicates pedigree, I should add."

"What happened next?" asked Richard.

"A long time went by. Well, long by your standards. Something like 16,000 years before the ice melted and our tribes were the able to move back to other areas of Europe. Time passed and about 8,000 years later, a new wave of people arrived form the Middle East. These were more advanced and introduced many improvements in the continent. Things like pottery making, irrigation, bridges, agriculture, metal working, etc. They helped make life better. They also brought their own Y chromosome, which you will find will pinpoint the descendants of that group of immigrants."

Richard nodded, pleased that more pieces of the great puzzle were being revealed in every conversation with Adam. He commented, "It is amazing how history can unravel from just a modest chromosome. Not only that but how the human species has developed on a number of fronts, while maintaining a basic genetic structure. Like other human races in the Universe."

Adam had listened attentively and, raising a hand, made a point that, to Richard, was conclusive. "Now you are talking, but I must confess that your species, as developed as it is, has consistently assumed that all forms of life in what you call the Universe are somewhat similar to you."

Adam laughed, and continued. "In that respect, the human race is a little conceited. You can only see the inhabitants of other worlds physically resembling you. I noticed that some of your science fiction TV shows delight in designing humanoids with pointed ears, bumpy complexions, horns, halitosis and other idiotic traits. Even worse, one of those shows reaches the height of the absurd by having the crews of their space ships wear some ridiculous tee shirts!"

To Richard, it seemed that Adam did not miss an opportunity to emphasize the flaws of the human and other species on the planet. But always in an amusing way. It was not in any way demeaning, or patronizing and it usually lead the discussion into areas where Adam offered definite enlightenment. Richard thought that he was before a master of inductive thinking. Adam's technique stimulated both scientific and personal curiosity. He asked, "Alright, but tell me are there other planets in the universe as we conceive it inhabited by people like ourselves?"

"No way, José. I am talking about the collection of rocks around that hydrogen-helium furnace you call the Sun and those burning cinders beyond. Some of them are raw energy pockets without much value in the general scheme of things. But I don't want you to think that you are unique in what you call the Universe, which to our eyes is a small, accidental system that lacks some major dimensions and elements, and produces a confusing level of consciousness. It is possible that through a time-energy mirror effect, there may be a planet somewhere with people like you. You see, you are a bio-electrochemical product, which, frankly, ain't very popular beyond your neighborhood."

"Why? Are there other forms or products as you say?"

Adam smiled and explained, "The most obvious is energy, of course. Energy takes many forms even if in this planet you recognize it more as an effect than as a cause, or simply the capacity to do work. It is hard to explain, but energy in some levels of existence, can be as flexible as chewing gum and therefore can be adapted to outside inputs. This means that things outside your neck of the woods can take forms that are hard for you to imagine, like for example mental energy entities, time-energy quantums and a variety of mixtures that involve other dimensions."

It was an incredible explanation. Richard and Patrick were thankful that Adam did not explain things in highly technical terms. It was just as amazing to listen to that melodious synthetic voice use all kinds of colloquial expressions and a most agreeable inflexion when describing complex topics. Richard also wished that some of his friends at Princeton and at King's College in London, renowned physicists, could have been present and could have participated in this discussion. He felt that even though he could draw from his deep knowledge of theoretical physics to ask the proper questions and to follow Adam's explanations, his colleagues were far more qualified than he was and could benefit a great deal more. He thought for a moment and answered to Adam, "I guess you are right. We have always considered energy as a scalar quantity, depending always on measurements within the limitations of the dimensions we know in this planet. You see, most of the theoretical work on energy has centered on the three components of linear momentum and single four dimensional vector quantities. But we begin to get dizzy when we interpolate the time element which we have considered as one aspect of the four-dimensional space-time-continuum."

"Well, you are on the right track. However, you would have to go beyond your present reasoning and interpolate new elements to be able to glimpse at the essence of energy. Because you are in a system that cannot, or does not have, such elements, you will always be stuck. Something like 'what you don't know won't hurt you' kind of thing. Also, it is clear that you are not equipped to fool around with the substance of another important element, or dimension, such as time. We could get really philosophical about all this. Which is the natural consequence once you have exhausted all possible rational explanations for a given phenomena. And from there, dear Professor, we go into Religion."

A Matter of Energy

Mentally, Richard was carefully filing away each and every one of Adam's comments and explanations. He knew he would have to rely on his extraordinary memory to transcribe all that had been said. While this burdened his level of attention and assimilation, he was conscious that what he heard from Adam stimulated his own imagination. He was not only recording but also thinking. Here, Adam is talking about energy that can be manipulated because it coexists with other dimensions and, presumably, is used to create other forms of energy susceptible to be converted into matter at will. And the suggestion that time was not a one way street! And the proof was that Adam and his colleagues had witnessed earth's evolution taking place during millions of years in a period of 90 days while parked above New York!

Observing Richard's concentration, Adam smiled and said, "Richard, please do not let me confuse you. Most unfortunately, I don't have the answers to the million questions I am sure you have. I can only make a painful comparison to illustrate my own frustration in not being able to accommodate you and all those nerdy physicists on earth. If you try to explain to a slice of pizza Einstein's Theory of Relativity, you'll find that all the pizza does is get cold. But you cannot blame either yourself or the pizza if the dialogue does not go anywhere. In short, there are, out there"—and Adam raised his arm and pointed at the ceiling—"things that are impossible to understand like levels where time can be made to start, twist, turn and go back to the beginning. It magnifies the meaning of your zero. Then we have those funny dimensions that convert other sources of time and energy into levels where consciousness and other conditions are the predominant forces. And the common applications that bend back and forth what you call the beginning and the end of things. I am of course simplifying the whole enchilada. I would not be capable of translating the cases I have just mentioned into meaningful equations or theorems. They are really way out, man!"

The explanation given by Adam had left Richard and Patrick in a deep pocket of wonder and amazement. Even if they realized that their own mental capacity could not possibly cope with the physical features of that world, or universe, or whatever, described by Adam, they felt that at least they could ask questions. Even stupid ones. "Adam, you have referred to time, one of our dimensions as just one of those that exist in your so called level of existence. What is your understanding of time? Is it a vectorial concept or what?"

This time Adam reached under the table and came up with a bottle of a 1983 Chateau Montrachet, three fine goblets and a plate full of Spanish "tapas" on a large silver tray.

"Before we waste too much time on time, let us taste this wonderful juice. Confidentially, I am becoming something of a lush, totally addicted to earth's wines. I still wonder at the amazing manner in which the sun's energy becomes this liquid marvel."

As Richard and Patrick admired the appetizing collection of Manchego Cheese, Spanish tortilla, salmon slices on toast, chicken croquettes, anchovies in olive oil, chicken livers, blood sausage or morcilla, fried minnows, stuffed olives, fried calamari, mussels, fried pieces of swordfish and chunks of freshly baked bread, they realized that they were hungry. Adam poured a full glass of wine, offering the comment, "I know it is not good style to fill the glass, but I am sure you will be glad I did. This wine must be drunk in proper doses. Timid sipping won't do!"

They quickly finished the "tapas," and most of the wine, before Adam continued. "Well, about the dimensions. Your universe, in your case, is a four dimensional animal. The more immediate ones like height, length and width are considered somehow related to time, at least mathematically. However, while you can go up and down—and backwards and sideways—in the three, you can only go in one direction when it comes to time."

"Yes but Einstein's equations of motion, when the direction of time is reversed, work just fine, even though no one has ever been able to take a little trip back in time."

"I am aware of such theoretical calculations, whose only possibility of reaching some reasonable foundation is to take Einstein's reasoning further and assume that time and space will suffer some distortion if their motion approaches the speed of light. Also, the same reasoning implies similar distortions if the dimensions are influenced by almost infinite mass values. From there you can develop some correlations that conceivably could lead to manipulation of time. That is, traveling in time."

"And what is wrong with that?" asked Richard.

"Really nothing. It proves the brilliancy of Einstein and his herd of physicists. However, such thing is impossible if that line of reasoning is pursued. To fiddle with the speed of light and with mass, would lead you to the concepts of infinite density, which in itself is some homerun, or fooling around with related forces like infinite gravity. There is no need for that. The whole cake is greatly simplified if you introduce what I would call fresh energy catalysts that would enable to control the direction of time."

"And what are they?" Richard was not only curious but also terribly excited. He was getting a glimpse of other dimensional energies beyond those that rule the physical makeup of our universe. He realized that he was on the verge of learning about key concepts that existed beyond our universe. It also meant that he could obtain a better idea of the energy configuration claimed by the visitors.

Adam thought for a moment, obviously trying to find an easy way to answer. After a moment he said, "Let's go back to time. Think of a river flowing downhill. Think of the water in the river as time. First of all, it has a certain shape as long as it stays within the bed of the river. Also, it moves along if the bed of the river has a certain inclination. The steeper the inclination, the faster the water will flow. Follow me?"

"Yes, I follow you swiftly," said Richard. "Paddle on."

"Well, Richard, the water in that river is TIME in this environment of yours. You flow because it goes downhill. Time then goes on. You cannot go back on it. Remember it is going downhill. You cannot affect it otherwise because it flows within an established bed or shape. To that flow, you here on earth attach all the other dimensions that you have and you find yourself with a finite-infinite equation. You cannot change time here. Now, if you can change the inclination, you can change both the speed and maybe the course, if the bed is fixed. But if the bed is flexible you can spread time over many acres, couldn't you? If you change the inclination high enough, you are liable to get your water back where you were a while before, right?"

Richard was making a tremendous effort to make the necessary translation of the analogies and to try to visualize what Adam was saying in terms of some basic correlations.

"Well, Adam, your analogy is clear up to the point where we have our water flowing comfortably within a river bed. You lose me when you start changing that river bed inclination and throw the water outside the river bed and conceivably make it flow backwards. How is that possible?"

"Elementary, my dear Watson. Down here you only have one direction of flow, one river bed, one inclination. We don't. We have other energy-related elements that enable us to move that water any way we want. We can control the rate of flow. We can keep it in a narrow course or a wide one. We can make it turn back. We can store it. We can make it do things for us. And all that, using energy-related references that unfortunately are beyond the frontiers of human understanding."

Richard thought for a moment and continued with another question. He could sense that Adam was making an extraordinary effort to explain matters in simple terms and he could also detect some generous acquiescence on Adam's part to please Richard. He said, "I understand. I mean that if you go beyond the analogy I will not understand a radish. It is fine with me. I just have one more question that keeps bothering me. What is the beginning of your river, and where does it go?"

"Hey!" exclaimed Adam as he produced a box full of Callard and Bowser Mint Toffees, and offered them to Richard. "Good question, old boy! Here we part company in the matter of both criteria and speculation. To you, there are two essential elements in your existence. These elements have been detected since the beginning and have sort of ruled your entire essence and that of your environment. I am talking about those two concepts of Beginning and End."

"You mean to tell me," interrupted Patrick, "that where you come from such elements do not exist?"

"No, I haven't got there yet. I am talking about your planet and your universe. You attach a great deal of importance—understandably—to let us say the beginning of things. Unable, for the reasons I have mentioned, to rationalize such concept you have created a number of versions that at least remove some of the uncertainty of your existence and possibly reduce the inherent anxiety of the species. Like I said before, at this point we face religious beliefs and also some well constructed physics parameters such as the Big Bang and a host of related theories about the beginning of Creation, as you pompously call it."

Again, Patrick interrupted. His curiosity was overriding his innate politeness. "I follow you, but I get lost when you get to the Big Bang. If it did not happen, what happened? If it did, what made it happen?"

Adam laughed good-naturedly and said, "Boy, you are sharp this morning! First, there is no such thing as a Big Bang. For it to be the beginning means that your so called nothing existed before, which is a gold-plated contradiction! But nothing in our farm is a combination of elements in a continuum. That planets, galaxies and stars blow up, you can be sure. This universe of yours has been suffering from a long list of energy deficiencies and it is not unusual that some equilibriums are often reached through energy releases and exchanges. I must tell you that beginning and end, like time, obey some conditions not easy to explain. Let me just say that the concepts of beginning and end only exist here.

It ignores the fact that your entire neck of the woods, or universe, expands continuously and applying static parameters to it, or even thoughts, don't jibe, old boy!"

Richard thought for a moment, wondering at the same time if he would be able to remember this session with Adam. The wine was going to erase some of the points that he wanted desperately to etch on his mind. Again, as if guessing his thoughts, Adam said, "Listen, Prof, when you are ready to return this evening I shall give you today's DVD that contains everything we have discussed today. Complete with photos, video and lovely little maps and graphs. The only thing that is not shown is the hour or so we spent with the wine bottle and the 'tapas.' I don't want to be accused of leading earthy UN bigwigs and anthropologists to perdition."

At that moment Emosh returned with Patrick and both went straight to the buffet table where they prepared some sandwiches. They sat down and listened for a minute to Adam's and Richard's discussion. Emosh nudged Patrick and said, "The professors here are back at it. I would love to hear what they are talking about but we better get back to our numbers." Then, they both got up and left.

Still laughing, Richard asked Adam, "Now, about the Big Bang or the beginning of our comedy. How about the expanding galaxies beyond the Milky Way? What do you think is the age of our universe? What is the universe made of?"

"Well, Richard, your people have been guessing at all this for many years. Every time they detect a weird neutrino, out come the great theories, hoping that a Nobel Prize will be the reward. Of course the universe is expanding, There is no static object in this universe. They all shag ass at a good clip and do so in rates expressed in the ever popular kilometers per second of recessional speed per megaparsec of distance. The energy confines—not the beginning, my friend—I can estimate at 90 billion years in all directions, but keep in mind that the expansion it operates under can cause distortions in time. No big bang, only energy rearrangements, which are as common as combing your hair. Besides, your people have developed all kinds of theories based on limited observations. They check the life and death of a little star somewhere and with help of a little old spectrometer, a scanner and a K-Mart Electronic filter, pinpoint its chemical components and from there develop some computer models. From there you come up with some numbers which are plugged here and there and come up with more sets and sets of numbers. Unfailingly useless. It is like memorizing the first 30 of Shakespeare's Sonnets. That and two bucks will get you a cup of coffee."

Richard could not help letting out a sonorous laugh. "What about the composition of our universe?"

"I guess I sound like a stuck record, dear Richard. It is energy in many and varied forms, but essentially, a cute little situation that combines subatomic particles and gravity in the moving train that is the expanding universe. It affects the simple clusters of galaxies and the superclusters and everything in the neighborhood. It plays hell with dark matter. You see, even the smallest particles have a say in this song. Those in dark matter gradually accumulate mass until they are big enough to exert a gravitational pull. At that point the equation changes. Your next question, I bet, will be about when we are having another energy rearrangement, right?"

"Yes, sir!"

"Having one right now. Problem is that your universe and its solar system are tangential forms of energy, and other than projecting some vibes—so to speak—are far removed from the scene of the action."

"And how does all this relate to your mission here? You have mentioned that some form of equilibrium has been disturbed in our planet and that you wish to take the necessary measures to re-establish that equilibrium."

Adam changed imperceptibly. From his nonchalant, cheerful demeanor he subtly became somber and thoughtful. He answered, "Richard, remember when we talked about Good and Evil?"

Suddenly aware of the thin edge of sadness in Adam's voice, Richard nodded slowly.

Here comes, he thought.

"Well, planet earth has been experiencing a serious distortion in its energy projection. It affects energy levels in other, let us say, areas."

Richard interrupted to ask, "How long has this been going on and what is it exactly that we are doing wrong?"

"Well, these distortions were noticeable as soon as earth became a planet and the mutant species—the human race—became the dominating species after Earth was no longer a satellite. We are talking a few million of your years. And as far as what you are doing wrong, dear Richard, just let me say that damn near everything!"

"Please give me some examples. I can see that this is going to be a difficult report to deliver. Perhaps, it would be best if I can get Patrick here."

"Right! We should sit down and go over the list of things we would like to ask of you at this time."

Adam got up and left the lounge where they had been sitting. Richard was grateful for being momentarily alone. He tried hard to dominate the wave of apprehension, if not outright fear, that had come over him. He could also compose his thoughts and prepare for whatever remedies Adam was about to propose. A momentous climax like this was without doubt the greatest event in recorded history. He got up and stood in front of the buffet table looking at the tasteful arrangement of the tempting dishes displayed there. He moved to the bar and poured himself a healthy shot of old Jack Daniels in one of the cut crystal glasses. He splashed a bit of water from the fancy carafe and dropped two ice cubes. He looked at the color—his method of determining the strength of the offering—and then took a long drink. He was savoring the familiar taste when Adam and Emosh, preceded by Patrick came into the area.

"Prosit!" said Emosh in his cheerful voice. All Richard could do was to lift his glass and smile.

They sat down at the long marble table and for a few uncomfortable seconds no one said anything. Adam, cleared his throat and said, "You know, in the short time we have spent on earth, that is, above earth and in the time we have come to know you two, we have developed a special feeling for the human race. You people are so special that we never imagined that we could find some common levels of interest."

He paused and smiled. "You do have a cozy arrangement in this remote corner of the energy quantum. You see, by adopting human shapes and, more important, by immersing ourselves in the essence of man, we have been able to understand and evaluate the way the human race thinks, feels and lives."

"You mean that you have experienced the variety of human virtues and defects?"

"Well, not exactly. We have become aware of them, just like you and other humans do. We recognize virtues and defects, but not necessarily experience them; hatred for example. We know what it is and have even realized how useful it can be when we have seen something evil taking place on your planet. It is curious to watch how hatred develops in the average human being. To see how surprise changes into amazement, on to indignation, then revulsion and then hatred. Those are unique chain reactions in that electrochemical reactor you have in your brain. However, hatred is a negative thing and it can be contagious. You see, you have a catalog of negative feelings and attitudes that are not balanced by an equally evident collection of their positive counterparts. And this is where we come in. We are going to need the help of your Committee and of the people of earth. We must ask you to gather some more information. Just a few odds and ends that we need to come up with the appropriate solution."

Patrick raised his hand and said, "You know that you can count on our unconditional help. And I might add that having known you, Emosh and your other colleagues is really a privilege and an honor. For energy configurations, as you call yourselves, you score high with us. But it is not clear to us, the extent and nature of the measures you plan to apply to our planet. In short," and he turned to Adam, "dear Adam, what the hell are you going to do?"

"First, we have to do more data gathering. As you know we have already spent some time making a historical assessment of man's impact on its universe. While we are equipped to conjure up all kinds of situations in all measures of time, we need fresh inputs when it comes to some of the characteristics of the human race. You know we have already received a great deal of information from your Committee. We have gone through population density figures, ethnic details, distribution, age comparisons, social development, etc. But there are some more elements we need. We need some profiles on crime and punishment through the ages. This also involves the penal system and what you call justice. There are also many other pieces of information that we would like to have."

Patrick and Richard were a little surprised at the nature of the request. They recalled Baron Carini's comment about the capacity of the visitors to obtain information on almost anything by themselves. The visitors had proven their incredible capacity to learn human history and to register all kinds of information from the very beginning of life on the planet. They had already received large amounts of material in the form of records, books, computer inputs, videos and all sort of historical and educational aid. They could use their peculiar powers to conjure up that information, or even go down to the nearest Barnes & Noble, Borders, Brentanos or any public library and transfer that information to one of their CD-ROMS or DVDs.

As if divining their thoughts, Adam smiled and said, "I can guess what you are thinking. But you see data from existing records, libraries, bookstores and textbooks is useful to us up to a point. It lacks an element that is related to the type of energy that makes up your race. When we have humans put this data together, there is a starting energy input that we find extremely useful. It shouldn't take your people too long to get this data for us. You see there will be an energy fingerprint from every country on earth. That helps our purpose."

Richard nodded and observed, "I see, it is more than just cold data that you are after. I guess you wish to feel the human psyche, is that it?"

"Yes. You see people on this planet seemed to contain an element of fear and a tremendous disposition to create barriers among themselves. The fear is ever present and can be triggered into emotional states by the right stimulus. But just like fear, there is hope, which in most people takes the form of faith. But the puzzling part is the importance given to those barriers that are continuously created. Religion, race, social status, paycheck, golf scores, beer capacity, etc. Each of these differences has a tremendous effect on the character of the people, and in most cases leads to rather negative results, my friend."

Emosh produced a couple of spiral bound booklets and handed one each to Patrick and Richard.

"Here is some work for your Committee. It shouldn't take very long."

Adam said, "You must be patient. You must realize that fixing this old crate must be done in a way that guarantees the type of performance that is expected. We will discuss the details when the time comes meanwhile we really appreciate your help."

Noticing the tired looks in Patrick's and Richard's faces, he concluded, "Boys, we have kept you too long. And what is probably worse is that we have talked your ears off. Time to get back to the Big Apple and watch a good wrestling match. That is what we are going to do!"

A few moments later, they were escorted out of the lounge and entered the shuttle when it materialized in one of the walls. There was a Lord and Taylor's shopping bag full of DVDs, photographs, two or three video cassettes and a leather-bound album sitting on the floor. A note from Adam said, "Helen will love this!"

Patrick and Richard were back in Patrick's office in a few short minutes. They noted the time as 18 hrs, which led Richard to comment, "I don't know but I get the feeling that once we are in the ship, time loses its zip. I am still amazed at how these fellows stretch time!"

"Exactly my feelings. They keep a special time slot for us. No matter what we do while we are up there, meetings, holographs, visits, meals, etc. they all happen within a precise time limit!" Richard looked at his wristwatch and shook his head.

"Well," began Patrick, "let us take a look at the homework and have someone check on the contents of the bag and advise Helen. She can give us a good report on its contents. We also have to go over the requests included in the notebooks Emosh gave us. But before, let us put together the report for the Security Council tomorrow morning."

They spent some time summarizing what they had discussed with the visitors. Carefully, they divided the report into the topics that had been discussed and added their own observations. The report would then go to one of the Committee members for editing and polishing. Eventually it would find its way into the press through the appropriate releases and Press notes. It would incorporate Helen's comments on the material sent by Adam and Helen's evaluation of the DVDs and other material sent by Adam.

Once finished with the Report, both of them studied the booklets and made notes. Once finished, Richard said, "I guess now we can pass all this to the Committee. Our visitors seem to want more detailed statistical analysis of a number of activities and situations related to the people of the plane with particular emphasis on morality, ethics, the criminal mind, etc. It looks like a major Sociological survey. Nothing that our group cannot put together in a reasonable period of time," Patrick agreed and said, "Fine. I'll have copies of my own notes sent to you. Meanwhile you can get your people cracking on this. By the way, are you going up tomorrow?"

"Yes," replied Richard, "I have to bring some of the latest figures, maps and illustrations that were not ready for today's trip. Are you coming?"

"No, I have too many things to prepare. I also have another show at the General Assembly. Have a good voyage!"

They headed for the elevators.

Reliving History

As planned, Richard was back in the pill by noon the following day. He delivered the data to Adam and Emosh and was glad to note that they had already set up the lunch environment for the day. This time it was in front of a rocky beach. In the background an old monastery and a dock could be seen. The sound of the waves and the salty breeze added a touch of realism to the place.

"Where are we?" asked Richard.

"It is called San Fruttuoso and used to be a Monastery. It can be reached by boat from Rapallo or Santa Margherita or, if you have goat capabilities by a mountain trail from either place."

At that moment Emosh offered Richard a drink, saying, "We thought you would like some rustic atmosphere. Spending too much time in New York turns your lung filters the color of chocolate chip cookies. This Negroni will help you absorb the local contaminants!"

They enjoyed a meal of Spaghetti alle Vongole, Mixed Fried Seafood, Sabaione and coffee, all of it under the auspices of a cool Verdicchio. They moved to the lounge and prepared to continue the dialogue of the previous day.

Richard took a long pull on the Cohiba cigar and said, "The Mediterranean cultures created more legends in their kitchens than in their battlefields, it seems. That meal was a real treat and it is simple fare after all!"

"Speaking of legends, I wish we had the time to visit Sumeria, one of the real cradles of civilization. Their vitality, inventiveness and imagination were admirable. Their cities were splendid and, above all, orderly and crime-free. But we can take a peek."

The usual brightly lit panel appeared and for the next hour or so showed scenes of a thriving city. The great Zigurat, the other temples, the irrigation canals, the use of the wheel in carts, milling and other activities illustrated a vital urban site. Richard was amazed to observe the neat farming grids that extended miles in the distance. He was also impressed by the appearance of the citizens, their homes and their schools. The temple services were impressive and transmitted a sense of peace and security. Once finished, Richard nodded and observed, "Sumeria had lasting influence in the beginnings of organized society. Also, some of the Sumerian legends were adapted by the pre-Islamic tribes in the Middle East and survived a long time. Things like the epic of Gilgamesh and Enkidu in Uruk, which gave way to an entire chapter in early mythology. Some of the concepts were even assimilated by the Jewish and Christian movements and remain a part of the dogma and ritual of these religions."

Richard paused for a moment and then said, "You know, our schools neglect the study of civilizations as essential as this one. Now that I have seen what they were, what they built and the incredible social interaction among their people, I regret that not enough attention has been given to its history. Their social discipline is both an action and a reaction to their religious fervor."

Adam listened and after a moment said, "Right you are. You see, in your world, the impact of religious disciplines has been very powerful. Just think, for all practical purposes your origins are generally perceived in terms of religious events, except the Jewish people who count the years from the creation of the universe. You will remember that the Musulmans count their beginnings from the march of Mohammed from Mecca to Medina. And then we have the Christians who set their beginning from events that occurred two thousand years ago."

"I agree. We could do better by starting to study our history at the time when the Sumerians established this marvelous civilization. But you know, many currents of thought throughout the years have attempted to impose their beliefs, albeit unsuccessfully. For instance in recent times, the French Revolution and the Russian Revolution were seriously proposed as the starting points of human history. And other events have also triggered similar propositions."

For the next few hours they reviewed the latest statistics and checked on a number of reports from penal institutions, churches and schools, apparently looking for common thread linking those accused of crimes. Time went by quickly. Finally Adam said, "Professor, you must be tired by now. We have been prowling around Sumeria, doings stats, checking reports and putting together more data. Let us take a break and continue our statistical work in a couple of days."

As he finished the sentence, the shuttle appeared. As Richard was boarding it, Adam presented Richard with a small gift bag with the Lord & Taylor's logo.

"Teach," he said in his happy monotone, "this is for Helen, with my apologies for keeping you away from her so much."

"What is it?"

"You'll see!"

The door closed and in a second Richard was back at the UN heliport.

A Welcome Return

The following evening, Richard presented the gift to Helen. They were having dinner at a newly opened "brasserie" in the Upper East Side.

"This is from Adam and his team. He apologizes for keeping me away so much of the time."

Helen looked at the bag and exclaimed, "Lord & Taylor's! I might have known! They are having a sale these days." They both laughed as Helen deftly opened the damask-wrapped package inside the bag. She found a small ivory box with exquisite carvings and gold inlays. Again, she exclaimed full of admiration and delight. Inside the box, on the fine cloth that lined the box was a silver and gold collar of incomparable beauty and design. Helen was ecstatic.

"Okay, Professor, give Adam and the boys my thanks. This is really the mother of all necklaces. I guess they have realized that they are responsible for keeping you gallivanting through the ages, while I go nuts with the TV program and don't have anyone to tell my problems to! Mercedes is on an assignment on the West Coast and will not be back for another week or so."

"Yes, they know they are keeping me away from you. They seem to sense love in the air. Emosh mentioned it to me recently. He joked about my spending too much time with the President and with Patrick, when you and I could be savoring our private paradise, as he put it."

"He probably read my mind. I just hope that soon we can return to some form of normalcy. I feel that I am aging fast."

Richard laughed, enjoying the moment. He leaned over and kissed Helen on the lips. The reaction was instantaneous. Helen returned the kiss with some unexpected passion, not that it surprised Richard but made him a little self conscious. Compromising displays of affection in public was not something that neither Richard nor Helen cared for. But the moment had gained such intensity that both were momentarily beyond any sense of propriety.

In a voice that betrayed her mounting excitement, Helen said, "Professor, pay the bill and let us get out of here. Too many eyes checking up on you!"

"Me? You are the one provoking this tired celestial messenger!"

In a few minutes they entered Richard's suite at the hotel and in a frenzy of kisses caresses and discarded clothes, they made love until morning.

In the next few days Richard and Patrick held a number of conferences with representatives from several countries, religious groups and their own committee. They were all working to complete the data that had been requested by the visitors. They puzzled over the emphasis the visitors placed on all sorts of irregular or out of the ordinary situations that made up the history of many countries. This emphasis centered on wars, internal strife, civil liberties or the lack thereof, border conflicts, the nature of education of children, the penal system, crime statistics, environmental protection guidelines and even odd items like liquor consumption, drug abuse and production of pornographic movies and books.

As they feared, Elmo Saks and the Reverend Toe had been unusually active in the last few days. Many countries, under Elmo's urging had collected the data and information requested but instead of sending it to the UN Regional Centers, had turned them over to Elmo's representatives. There were urgent calls from the Vatican, and most of the UN's Regional centers. This time an organized effort had been made by Elmo to enlist a hard head count of countries that would back his requests before the UN Security Council.

"How is he getting the support of all these countries?" asked Richard.

"As I understand it, it is simple blackmail. Campaign promises, the carrot and the stick, pie in the sky, subtle and not so subtle bribery, and all the other refined techniques that he and the Reverend have developed over the years.

Which small, poor country can afford to turn down special aid programs, foreign investment, free rides with the IMF and the World Bank, not to mention the corporate giants ready to set up shop in the country? All this artfully supported by a religious footnote, almost impossible to ignore. You see, the Reverend conducts a parallel campaign that darn near forces the government of the country to comply with the wishes of a large part of its citizens. The approach blends economic perspectives and the religious fervor of the people. It is a great formula, my friend."

"What do you think is next?" asked Richard, who all along had felt that there was a need to confront Elmo before he caused further damage and confusion to the work of the Committee. He was reluctant to discuss Elmo with the visitors even though he was convinced that they were aware of Elmo's and the Reverend machinations.

"Well, he will probably try to blackmail us, the committee that is, by negotiating some sort of deal in exchange for the missing data. He desperately wants to meet with the visitors and feels sure that he can make a deal with them. Fortunately some of our people have been aware of Elmo's aims and made sure that the same information retained by Elmo, has been relayed to us."

Patrick thought for a moment and then said, "The President is also quite incensed about Elmo, but he tells me that the backing he has is formidable. He is gradually gaining support by using his patriotic approach, that is, his insistence that the US take over the work the UN is doing. So, he's got influential Senators, members of the Supreme Court and many others that do no cease to bombard him with hints about Elmo's indubitable qualifications and capacity to assume an important role with the visitors. He feels however that we are almost at the end of the road and that in a matter of days, the visitors will present us with their solution to the energy unbalances."

Patrick closed his notebook and with a sigh concluded, "Time to go home, in my case, and your cozy suite at the Essex House in yours. Let us worry about all this in the morning. We can discuss our next visit to the pill at that time.

Back at the UN, Patrick and Richard closeted themselves with the other members of the Council and drafted a detailed report that was to be broadcast within the hour. The report explained that the visitors had more or less completed their preliminary assessment of the energy problem and that in the next few meetings would outline and explain the measures they would take to correct the energy problem.

As tired as they were, they decided to review the report in Patrick's apartment. In spite of their willingness to examine diverse theories and hypothesis about the famous energy unbalance, they were not able to pinpoint, except in vague terms, the exact nature of the problem the visitors wished to solve. The imbalances that existed on earth were so many and varied that they could not establish the type of measures that could be applied in order to arrive at a solution.

"I can only surmise that the imbalance they are talking about has to do with good and bad. I guess you would call it vibes. What puzzles me is the translation from an abstract condition to a pedestrian thing like simple old energy. Or does the abstraction possess some slice of energy somehow?"

Richard realized that Patrick was talking aloud. He observed, "You are getting close. I think that the consequences of good and bad vibes, or whatever, are measurable and tangible. Somehow, these two conditions co-exist within some sort of equilibrium or balance. If you have more of either one, you are distorting the equilibrium or balance, thus the problem."

"Could be, could be," mused Patrick, "but why the equilibrium or balance? If you have more good than bad, I should think it would be a desirable condition, don't you?"

"That is one of the parts that throws me. If you only have good, bad is non-existent or vise versa. An equilibrium, such as we imagine, is therefore lost. And that seems to go against some mysterious energy equation."

"Now, let us for a minute assume that it is we who must balance out this planet's energy status. We have collected good deeds from day one and also bad deeds. It seems that the bad deeds, or bad energy to use their reference, exceed the good deeds by a long margin. Now, that bad energy is all created by humans, so to reduce the effect of the bad deeds you have to reduce the bad humans?"

"It would appear to be so. The question is how can that be accomplished and what sort of energy profile will the world have if bad energy is eliminated? Will they transform the bad energy generators into good energy generators? How? Will they just eliminate them? How?"

"Good questions, Richard. But perhaps we are taking the energy equation too literally and they use the opposite concepts of energy as the framework of a more complex solution. As I understand it, our planet is throwing a bad echo to other levels of the universe. They found it is due to ill conceived actions and to the entire catalog of human defects. Would it no be easier just to do away with the whole enchilada?"

"I certainly hope not, Patrick. I would hate to just evaporate without having seen my future grandchildren and perhaps a new world where some of the misery we have created no longer exists."

"Listen, we can spend the next semester speculating about this. Cardinal Beccaria, same as Baron Carini feel that the ultimate solution might be a brain wash of universal proportions, leaving a world less wicked. But, who knows?"

For some time they continued their analysis, but were not able to reach any meaningful conclusion. It was late in the evening when Richard left the apartment.

In the morning, the press had analyzed the Council's report on the latest visit by Patrick and Richard and had prepared its inevitable rash of sensational headlines. The alarm had been set.

"They are going to fry us!" "Payoff time is here, humans!" "The pill dwellers about to collect," "What is going to be the price?" Helen produced a special that tried to be objective about the recent news from the pill, but could not escape a touch of concern. The Television networks rushed to program all sort of specials, interviews, panel discussions and the like. Uninterrupted coverage began early in the morning. Experts of all kinds appeared in most programs and tried hard to appear as if they knew what they were talking about. The hosts and panel moderators enjoyed one more of those days when they could talk and say nothing for hours on end.

Public reaction was quick. Prayer and discussion groups were organized. However, no preparations could be made since no one, including the UN Committee had any idea what the adjustments would be or how energy balances could be re-established.

Breakfast Above New York City

Two days later, Patrick's driver picked up Richard at his hotel a little after six in the morning. They expected to be at the ship by seven, which would be a decent breakfast hour. They both had wondered what sort of breakfast awaited them.

As they stepped off the shuttle in the already familiar lounge of the ship, they were immediately regaled with the unmistakable aroma of frying bacon and the more subtle emission of percolating coffee. There was even soft background music that seemed to come out of one of New York's FM stations.

Adam appeared, flanked by Emosh and in the back, Ely, Eldon, Evan and Earle. Patrick and Richard were warmly greeted by all and led into another room in the ship. To Richard, the visitors appeared like a good natured group of young to middle age executives meeting in a Hilton Head hotel for a management or sales meeting. Two of them appeared to be in their early forties, while the rest were definitely in their mid thirties. The older ones were dressed strictly Madison Avenue. Hickey's, Armani's and a couple of British cut masterpieces from Maliphant & Whickley. Adam and Emosh, from the younger gang, were dressed informally.

It was a spacious dining room with a beautifully set table in its center. The selection of silverware, crystal and china was perfect. The subdued reflections and shines blended together in a most pleasing manner. The color schemes and the flower arrangements denoted refined taste and great decoration talent. On another table on the side, an array of chafing dishes, trays, hot plates and pitchers with all sorts of fruit juices, was responsible for the aromas that permeated the entire area.

Richard could not help commenting, "Adam, you must have hijacked the chefs from the Pierre, the Majestic in Cannes and the Dorchester to arrange this marvelous setting and prepare all those dishes."

Adam smiled and said, "Since landing on earth we have found that breakfast is the most important meal of the day to most people. And Supertramp was right, 'Breakfast in America' is a great experience! We have become so accustomed to it that often we eat breakfast two or three times a day. You see, we are not overly concerned with the dangers of excessive food intake and, besides, our room service is the best in the West!

"Yes, I wondered who your caterer is."

"No caterer. We just will it. The only deficiency here is that we have no waiters, so we have to serve ourselves. I share the opinion that a good table requires good service, but unfortunately we do not wish to abuse earth's hospitality and use some of your wonderful waiters or waitresses. If we do, we are liable to be accused of illegal exploitation of aliens by aliens, and will have to appear in court, receive a fine, be damned in the press and will have to pay social security charges and exorbitant legal fees! On top, the lawyers will be asking for life and accident insurance, IRAs, vacations and bonuses for our waiters, health care coverage and, what is worse, we would be prevented from running for office...And don't forget that anyone we hire, will end up writing his or her memoirs about the experience with the 'visitors.' Shocking revelations would be included about Emosh's obsession with the NBA, Ely's addiction to Computer Games and my own inclination to read and memorize every newspaper printed everyday all over the world! A sale to the Enquirer or similar sensational paper would be made, the fellow would make a pile and we wouldn't get a single sous!"

Visit to Ancient Rome

They had a memorable breakfast. Both Patrick and Richard had been exposed over the years to the best cuisine on earth and were in a position to appreciate and judge good food and better service. Ely was acting as the head-waiter and did an admirable job of it. Emosh related a short visit he had just made to Imperial Rome. This prompted Patrick to ask him, "How did you manage? Did you use our airlines or flew on your own?"

"Well, I did not make myself clear. It was a trip using our energy relocation process, as your scientists would call it. Just flew back in time. The trip I took was to Imperial Rome at the time of Augustus. I have a special curiosity about the Roman Empire and last night things were quiet around here that I decided to take a peek."

Upon hearing this, Richard suddenly leaned on the table and, with a look in his eyes that betrayed both curiosity and awe, said, "Emosh, I must ask you to bear with me and answer some questions. I have always been intrigued—and fascinated—by the Roman Empire. I have read every book that has ever been written and have also traveled extensively in what at one time was the Roman Empire...I have been up and down the via Appia, Emilia, Aurelia and have checked places outside the Italian peninsula like Ampuria Brava, Tarragona, Les Baux, Segovia, Chestnut Hill, Browmley, Cusia and a many other places where the Romans settled. There are many things I'd like to know."

"You know, Richard, present conditions in the so called industrialized countries, with another style of course, resemble Rome in its heyday."

"How is that?"

"Well, in those days Rome was clearly divided into well defined social groups: The Patricians, the Politicians, the Clergy, the Merchants and Artisans, the Generals and their Armies, the Plebeians and the Slaves. All right, you asked for it! Now, today, the ruling classes or the influential families with the exclusive schools, large holdings, extended investments and, often, good manners, own or control more than 90 percent of the wealth in practically all of your so called developed countries. Like Russia at the beginning of this century, where the Czar and a handful of families, owned just about every square inch of land. Remember what happened to them?"

"It is a distant comparison, Emosh."

"It depends on the way you look at it. To me it is a very valid case. Think about the class system, which most will deny but nevertheless exists. The politicians are forever the same breed. I have checked. The Consul from the distant Provinces of the Roman Empire behaved in exactly the way your Senators and Representatives act today. Lots of lip service, promises and unabashed compromise. Your Yuppies, speculators, corporate demigods, sports idols, entertainment freaks and the like, correspond to the Merchant and Artisans class. You know that the Generals and the Armies have not changed a bit. They all want to instill, maintain and promote the so called military virtues: be prepared to defend the country. Be prepared to attack, offense is better than a defense; build a bigger catapult, aircraft carrier or missile and blast the hell out of the enemy! And if there is no enemy, find or invent one! Then the Plebeians. The guys working the 8 to 8 shift. The underpaid school teacher, delivery man, bus driver, the Government clerk, the overworked nurse, the tailor, the beer-saturated truck driver, the abused social worker and the lowly news reporter are all identical to their equivalent counterparts in Roman days."

He paused for a moment. Richard took advantage of the silence to ask a question.

"How about the slaves? the clergy?"

"Glad you asked! The slaves are still here, sir. Think of all those people that emigrate to more prosperous countries. In 9 cases out of ten, they are exploited, mistreated and discriminated against. It could be a few Poles in Portugal, West Indians in Manchester, Mexicans in Southern California, Senegalese in Morocco, Moroccans in Spain, Orientals in Melbourne, Bolivians in Buenos Aires, Turks in Dusseldorf or Texans in Boston. How long do you think it takes them to reach a satisfactory standard of living? How about their traditions, children, family ties, beliefs? You don't call them slaves anymore but treat them just as bad or worse."

He paused and added, "As for the clergy, they have always existed in one form of another. The Romans had a class dedicated to decipher the future and provide some guidelines on morals and ethics. Nowadays you have tons of fast talking ministers who claim to talk to God every day; ministers who also can dispense with unending and strident sermons about evil that people hear but don't listen to."

There was more silence. Then he said, "And here comes the clincher! At one time, Rome had just about one day of popular festivities for every day of work. Think about the present. The ever presence of sports in today's life can only be compared to the almost daily dose of competition that in one form or another kept the Roman masses focused and excited. In this country, you have developed a unique web of events, fueled by nothing but greed and admirably aided by the NBA, the Baseball Leagues, the PGA, FIFA, the Olympics

Committee, the Baseball Season, the Soccer Season, Wrestling, Tennis, Hockey, Skiing, Ice Skating, Cycling, Hunting, Rodeos, Swimming, Frog Jumping, Trailer Pulling, Ass Kicking, and so many other competitive sports that in many ways keep the masses away from using their brain circuits in more useful ways. Not to mention television, which is a separate chapter my friend. The gladiators were no different from the strong and superbly fit morons that make up the current sports universe in your planet. You will excuse me, Richard, but I see them all in the same light. The only differences are in the form. The content is the same. And you know what happened to the Roman Empire."

Emosh smiled and served himself some more coffee. Richard said, "I want to inquire about something."

"Inquire away!" shot back Emosh with a big smile.

"I have always been curious to learn the details in the lives of the patricians and the populace. How they lived, what they ate, where they lived. How the state was organized. You see, Rome has had such a strong and durable influence on western civilization that it should be studied in more depth. I am convinced that we would be able to enlighten modern society if we can verify that many of today's customs, habits and defects can be traced back to those times. The comparison you just made is an interesting one, and very accurate. History—as some sage said—repeats itself endlessly. Now, I would love to know about everyday life, the Senate sessions, the Circus, etc."

"Please tell us about it. What is the general atmosphere like? Did you have a chance to talk to anyone? Where in Rome did you go? Did you eat well?"

Emosh looked at Richard and smiled. "Once an Anthropie always an Anthropie. Well, it was fascinating even if I only spent about a week there."

He was interrupted by Patrick. "But you said you went there last night. How could you have spent a week in Rome?"

"Elementary, dear Watson," he retorted. "Time can be stretched, remember? The reason I stayed for a whole week was because a new show was opening at the Coliseum and I did not want to miss it. There was also a sort of fair featuring cooking from Iberia, new wines from Galia, and fresh slave gladiators from the provinces."

Adam interrupted Emosh to explain to his visitors, "You see, since coming here, our Emosh has taken a special liking to things like the NBA, wrestling, soccer, bullfighting and even aerobics with Jane Fonda. I would not be surprised if he even tried some of the net and trident encounters when he was in Rome. Or perhaps he met some cute Roman chick with her own place."

Emosh interrupted him to say, "I have a better idea. Why don't we drop in on our Roman friends? Let us follow a Patrician from the moment they get up until they return home and go to bed. It will be better than any description I could muster."

By now, Patrick and Richard were used to the unconventional if not unique behavior of the visitors, but to learn that they could travel back in time at will, never ceased to amaze and fill them with awe and admiration.

Emosh got up and asked his visitors and Adam to follow him. He stopped in front of a wall and a large closet materialized. Hanging inside were a number of fine cotton togas, and on the floor leather sandals and the small moccasin-type slippers that Romans used. He stepped aside and pointing to the togas and the sandals, said, "Please wear these. You know, when in Rome.

They all laughed. A bit nervously, Patrick and Richard took their pants and shirt off and in their underwear put on the togas. Each selected a pair of sandals and felt comfortable but awkward. The visitors did likewise. Then, all four looking like well dressed Romans, led by Emosh walked to one end of the lounge. He pointed at the empty wall. Instantaneously, the old familiar door to a shuttle appeared. They all entered the peculiar vehicle and in a fraction of a second had arrived in Rome as it was in the year 10 AD during the reign of Augustus. The door opened and they filed out into a small plaza from which several roads leading away from it gave the impression of a major center. They looked at each other with some surprise. Adam smiled and said, "We look like four prosperous Romans. Emosh has been wise enough to select togas and sandals of some quality. I feel better as a prosperous Roman than as a poor one! You know, in this town at this time, class distinction began with the togas!"

Patrick laughed and, turning to Richard, said, "Without my wallet I feel sort of naked, you know."

Richard squinted at the bright sunshine and replied, "What I am going to miss is my sunglasses!"

They looked up at the unmistakable blue Mediterranean sky and felt the moderate temperature of the day. They were in a corner of a city, which by all signs and appearances was Imperial Rome. Their sudden arrival at one discreet corner had passed unnoticed by those nearby. The shuttle vanished the moment the last of them had stepped out. The noise assaulted them at once. In addition to the loud conversations in the shops around the plaza, there were the unique cries of vendors, children playing and someone singing in Greek.

Somehow familiar were the symmetrically placed stones on the pavement, and the narrower paths for pedestrians. The clear sky and the gentle aroma of orange blossoms and freshly baked bread provided the proof that they were indeed enjoying a Roman morning. Patrick pointed to two deep impressions on the center of the pavement.

"There must be a lot of traffic on this road to have worn out the pavement!" exclaimed Richard, still amazed at the way they had so quickly gone back in time.

The handsome markers on both sides of the road were also a Roman signature that spoke more of their preoccupation with the assistance the markers could provide to visitors and strangers, than any esthetic purpose. The markers had Roman numerals and letters and presumably identified the district and the street. They looked at one that said Via Triumphalis which they identified as a major thoroughfare. The facades of the houses were of stucco of different colors and the roofs were neatly placed tiles on wooden beams. Iron and bronze were used profusely. Windows were barred with elaborate and intricate iron works.

The time was about 10 in the morning so there were a lot of people going about their business. Richard and Patrick observed the action with a sense of admiration and surprise, as if a mystery had been suddenly revealed.

"Well, here we are!"

"By the way," asked Patrick, "what is the date, Emosh. C'mon, give us some information."

"Sorry," replied Emosh, "I am not being a very good guide. So, I'll try again. I don't want to miss a good tip! We are in the year 7 AD. These are Empire days and the Emperor is Augustus Caesar, previously known as Octavian. You know, Augustus means 'imposing one' in Latin. It was during his reign, which began in 27 BC, that the Roman Republic became an Empire."

He paused to point at one of the streets and motioned for them to follow. He then continued. "You see, by now, Rome had conquered just about everything. Rome's power extended to the Eastern Mediterranean and even the Middle East. Not to mention Northern Africa, Iberia, Gallia, Anglia, etc. There was even a province, Asia, that was freely transferred to the Roman Empire by King Attalus III of Pergamum. It included the city of Ephesus, where the temple of Diana was built. It was a wealthy and prosperous province and a welcome addition to Rome. This province was near Galicia and Galatia and north of Bithynia in what is now Northern Turkey."

"Sounds like a nice gift," chimed in Patrick

"Yes, it was. It also reflected the admiration that the Romans elicited from the peoples and cultures surrounding the Roman holdings. Some of the integrations were voluntary as in the case of Asia. Some fall under the maxim that if you cannot beat them join them, as in the case of Cilicia, Bythinia, Cyprus, Syria, Numidia, Crete and others."

Emosh smiled and added, "Today is a holiday. Keep in mind that at this time of Roman history, there was almost one holiday for every working day!"

"Gee," interrupted Richard in his usual cheerful manner, "the Unions here must have been worth joining!"

"How did they get any work done?" asked Patrick, who could not take his eyes from a street vendor that offered fruits, some pastries and a creamy concoction in clay jars placed inside a larger container full of crushed ice.

"They worked in shifts. And don't forget that out of one million people in this city, about one third were slaves. And you know what happens to slaves; they slave away!"

Emosh shook his head in clear disapproval and continued. "All city services continued to operate during the holidays, and also some public markets. The funny thing, thank Goodness, was that the public baths never ceased to function, same as some specially licensed restaurants or refectoriums."

He stopped in front of an imposing structure which he identified as Pompeii's Theater. They admired the clean lines of the building, especially the ornate dome and the solid marble columns. "We are going in the direction of the Imperial Palace," advised Emosh.

"From there it is a short walk to the Circus Maximus."

They walked down one of the roads until they got to an area where there were houses and few or no shops. There were also fewer people around. They stopped in front of one of the more impressive houses to admire its marble facade and its carved wooden roof beams.

After a while, a portly, middle aged man appeared at the elaborate wood and iron door and stood by the curb, obviously impatient. He was dressed in a fine cotton toga with delicate embroidered designs in its edges. His sandals were shiny black with metal buttons and thick leather soles. His hands were adorned with rings and he had a large silver chain around his neck from which a golden medallion hung on his chest. It looked like the effigy of an important person.

From his shoulders a wine colored cape was carefully pinned to the toga giving the man a very impressive and handsome look. Moments later, a woman in her early thirties appeared and joined the man at the sidewalk. She was also wearing a toga, but the material was lighter and the cut was such that her generous figure showed in a most attractive way. She was also bejeweled; her hair was carefully braided and coifed into a large bun at the top, fastened by gold clips. Her eyes were clearly made up. Her lashes were black and there were soft blue tones around her eyes. Her face was well powdered with a very light peach color and her lips were deep red. She said something to the man, who frowned and continued to pace the sidewalk. She signaled to a vendor with an elaborate pushcart to approach and he did so. She said something to him and he quickly produced two cone shaped containers made of thin bread crust. He filled each with the cream from one of the jars sitting on a bed of ice chunks and gave one each to the lady and her husband.

"The old ice-cream vendor!" exclaimed Richard. Patrick also expressed his pleasure at recognizing the existence of a present day treat in the distant past.

Seeing the interest and obvious enjoyment that Patrick and Richard showed, Emosh approached the vendor and in fluent Latin ordered four cones. The vendor looked at him with some amazement and without saying a word prepared the four cones.

"Anyone got a credit card handy?" asked Emosh as he turned, smiling toward Adam and Patrick and Richard. As they laughed he reached into his leather purse and produced several roman coins, which he gave the vendor. They tasted the frozen creamy paste and were pleasantly surprised to find that its fruity flavor was delicious. It appeared to be a combination of fruit sherbet and cream, with the consistency of modern day ice-cream.

"Remember, vanilla, chocolate and pistachio had not entered the picture in those days," observed Emosh.

"Now, where are these two going?" asked Richard. Emosh pointed at the other end of the street where an open carriage pulled by two horses was approaching. The carriage was painted a bright blue color with gold trim. The seats were covered with a heavy fabric and there were pillows all over.

"That is their private transportation. Before going to the games at the Circus, they are probably going to eat somewhere. There are interesting contests today. There is a special race scheduled today between teams from Greece, Gallia, Alexandria and the famous Victorius Velocis, a local favorite team."

"What is going on at the Coliseum today?" asked Richard.

"Not working today since the Circus has a number of special events. The Coliseum will have some interesting contests tomorrow, with newly arrived gladiators from Sicily and Africa."

Emosh then described in detail the events of a gory afternoon at the

Coliseum. "Thank goodness there are no Christians these days to feed the beasts," he concluded.

"I told you already that the Roman calendar in this period included one holiday for every work day and that, in order not to run out of entertainment, and having more or less decimated the ranks of gladiators, Christians provided much needed fare."

They all watched as the matron and the man climbed in the carriage and were quickly driven away by the driver who was busily eating something resembling a briosce.

"Listen," said Emosh, "let us follow these two. They will probably lead us to a good restaurant."

The had no trouble following on foot. As they approached the more crowded areas, the carriage had to slow down and at times it had to stop while other carts maneuvered in the narrow streets.

Patrick and Richard did not fail to observe the poor state of the road and the amount of refuse all over. Other than the luxurious villas along the way, there were quarters where two and three story buildings seemed to contain half of Rome. After a while, the carriage turned into a wide road and stopped in front of a large building surrounded by carefully tended gardens.

Around the front and back of the building there were tables and benches, while on the terraces surrounding the place, there were several tent-like structures but covered with beautiful silk curtains. The floors were covered by fine Persian rugs and the more popular cotton weaves from Egypt. Inside there were reclining sofas, called triclinia, and small tables. There were some smaller enclosed areas within the tents, covered with black curtains that were clearly used as convenience corners. The place was almost full of gesticulating and laughing people, evidently enjoying themselves. Clay and crystal wine pitchers were everywhere.

"This is the pre-game crowd," observed Emosh. "Now, let me see if I can get us a table. Watch this!"

He walked into one of the terraces and approached a man, whose toga and tablet in hand, denoted some authority. He was evidently the Head Waiter. Emosh caught his attention and dipping his hand in his purse, produced some coins which he gave the Head Waiter with a smile and some comment the others could not hear. The Head Waiter laughed loudly and accepted the coins readily. At once, they were all taken to an area between two of the large tents that had reclining sofas and small tables. Then, two women servants approached them with small washbasins and pitchers full of perfumed water.

Their meal was a unique experience. The servants were busy bringing hor d'ouvres in the form of figs, olives, goat cheese rolled into thin slices of ham, small fried fish and biscuits with honey and nuts. Wine mixed with water was served. Richard observed with great curiosity what was happening at the tents nearby, where whole families and friends kept welcoming an incredibly parade of dishes and pitchers full of wine.

The only instruments they had were several spoons of different sizes and shapes, two knives and a bunch of large metal, wood and ivory toothpicks.

Two hours later, they all felt as if they had eaten the most elaborate meal in history. The usual menu that day consisted of seven courses featuring fish, veal, pork, vegetable cakes, lobster, chicken, small birds, large artichokes in oil, pickled mackerel, grape jellies, and so many other delicacies that they soon lost track of them.

"Listen, to give you an idea of Rome's cosmopolitan make up, I'll try to list some of the things we have eaten. First, the fish. It is of course from the Mediterranean, near Ostia, same as the shellfish and the small snails and sea urchins. The forests of Laurentia and Ciminia abound in game of all kinds, from boar to deer, rabbit, and a wild kind of edible dog. Around Rome, the fields provide domestic flocks and herds of various animals, plus milk and many varieties of vegetables. Then there are the cheeses of Trebula and Vestini, places famous for the quality of their dairy products."

Emosh looked at the others and smiled. He was obviously enjoying his role as host and guide. He went on. "On the southern edge of the city, there is Picenum and Sabine where fine vegetable oils are produced. You will notice that there are many kinds of spices; well, they come from Asia Minor. The pickles come from Spain and the pork from Gallia. The wines come from several places, I have tasted Greek, Spanish and Gallian wines. The apples and pears come from Chios and the citrus fruits and dates from Africa. Plums from Damascus, honey cakes from Egypt and cider from Sicily."

"Sounds like any international Parisian restaurant of our time!" chimed in Richard.

As they reclined comfortably after the meal, and the servants had removed the vestiges of the feast, they could not help observing the couple that had unwittingly led them to the restaurant. They had eaten in a reserved alcove off to one side, which privacy was barely protected by some embroidered curtains. They had also finished their meal in the company of other couples and were now under the influence of too much wine. Some of the men began to caress and kiss the women amid jokes and laughter. Their play became more intense and erotic as women appeared to encourage the attention they were getting. Soon, couples were indulging in foreplay without concern or regard to the others. The women removed their gowns and allowed men to caress them in the most uninhibited ways. For their part, the men had also disrobed and allowed long sessions of fellatio with some of the women; they embellished the act by pouring honey and wine on their intimate parts and celebrated with expressions of joy every time one of the participants achieved a climax.

Richard turned to Patrick and said, "This is really a disgusting spectacle. Let us get out of here!"

Emosh and Adam had watched the episode with detached interest, as if they were used to such debauchery. Adam said, "Yes, Richard, this is for the birds. Unfortunately we have seen so many scenes of this kind, and much worse, in the course of our research. We have material for one thousand porno films, but let us get out of here."

Emosh paid the bill and they all left. Back on the street, Patrick asked, "What next?"

"Normally, after the meal most people go to the public baths before going to the Circus. You know, the Emperor Augustus has decreed that you must wear a toga at the games, so people take time to spruce up."

"Wish we had something like that," observed Richard. "The last time I went to an NBA game, I felt in another planet. There were people without shirts, painted faces, ugly shorts, no shoes, ridiculous caps and they all drinking and eating. It was disgusting!"

Emosh looked at Richard and said, "Ah! forgot to tell you. Augustus also forbade eating or drinking at the games!"

The rest of the day was an unforgettable interlude for Patrick and Richard. They saw the baths, and visited the libraries there and were impressed by the family rituals in the baths. After, they walked to the Circus and, thanks to Emosh expedient ways with his bag full of sesterces, were able to secure a comfortable box on the second level. It had an excellent view of the arena.

"People come to the Circus, or the Amphitheater, as a religious custom. The games combined a liturgy with rules of etiquette," said Emosh as they all sat in marvel at the splendor of the occasion.

The spectacle was full of color and beauty. The arrival of the Emperor was a spectacle in itself. Guards, priests, royal guests and generals made their appearance amid the blaring of trumpets and drums. They saluted the crowd, who threw flower petals and waved white handkerchiefs. As they entered the royal enclosure or pulvinar, great multicolored smoke rings were released to the delight of the crowds.

The initial parade, included elephants decorated with multicolor adornments, zebras, white Arabian horses, the impressive parade of a detachment of the Imperial Guard in full parade uniforms, and its multitude of flags and battle banners, the squadrons of legionaries and the columns of gymnasts and acrobats. The large images of the Gods that were paraded atop large carts drawn by oxen did not fail to create a powerful impression on all those present. Of special impact was the enthusiasm that the sculpted images of dead Emperors evoked.

They witnessed a full afternoon of 2, 4 and 8 horse chariot races, sports events, competitions of various kinds until late in the evening, when the Circus acquired a unique aspect due to the torches and candles lit all over the place.

Emosh explained that the races would continue until the next day and asked Patrick and Richard if they were ready to leave. They all looked tired and quickly assented. They left the Circus and walked toward the Tiber. Once they reached a discreet corner, Adam stopped and said, "Let us go back to our pill!" The shuttle appeared from nowhere and they quickly entered it. In no time at all they were back in the ship. Patrick and Richard changed into their clothes and thanked Emosh and Adam for the most incredible afternoon they had experienced.

"Well," asked Adam, "what do you think of Rome now?"

Richard smiled and quipped, "Not much different from spending a day in Washington: great food, uninhibited sex, outstanding circus, a strong smell of political power and submissive masses being fed sports and entertainment!" They all laughed.

They all moved to the lounge to pick Patrick and Richard's cases. As they stood in front of the large coffee table, Adam said in a serious tone, "My friends, please come up day after tomorrow. This time—and more in keeping with proper New York habits—I would appreciate it if we can have breakfast together. I would like to devote the morning to a review of the data we have gathered and the conclusions it suggests. We can also define the key elements of the energy distortions on this planet so that you have an idea of the relative urgency of the problem. Also, I would like to sum up the research done so far and outline the options we have to solve the problem of energy imbalances on this planet."

Silently, Patrick and Richard moved to the corridor and the shuttle. Again, in seconds they were at the helipad of the UN gardens. Only a few people were around hoping to catch sight of the shuttle, which by now had become a popular piece of real science, no longer fiction.

At the UN

As in all previous occasions, Patrick and Richard went immediately to Patrick's office and sat down at the round meeting table. They summoned Mrs. Nelson and began to dictate detailed descriptions of the momentous experience they had just lived. Mrs. Nelson could not conceal her amazement but remained attentive and deft as she took down the story in her laptop. At one point, Baron Carini entered the office and, without a word, sat down in one chair, lit a cigar and listened full of wonder as Patrick and Richard described in rich detail their incredible visit to Rome.

Patrick raised his hand and observed, "This was a fantastic trip. To see Rome the way it was is a unique experience. It is a shame that we could not share it with others."

Baron Carini exhaled a cloud of aromatic smoke and said in an ironic tone, "Yes, it must have been a great experience. Even today, walking around the relics of the many palaces, temples and buildings in Rome you wonder about the glory of the Empire. However, gentlemen, we have not heard about the energy adjustment program. I hope it was discussed in between chariot races, orgies and the other activities that our two prominent representatives of Earth seem to have enjoyed."

Patrick laughed and answered, "Yes we did talk about it. But it was before the orgy. Adam said that he did not want us to miss the chance to see Rome and that he himself was intrigued when Emosh mentioned his brief escapade. He said that Evan and Ely were working on the final part of the program they would present to us. He suggested that we return day after tomorrow. The rest of the time was spent admiring the marvels of the Roman Empire. Hope you forgive us, Baron. Next time we'll ask Adam to get you a seat on his peculiar time machine."

It was the Baron's time to let a big guffaw.

Later that day the President called Patrick and both engaged in a long conversation. Patrick was anxious to let the President know that a solution seemed imminent, while the President informed Patrick of the measures that had been taken, at least in the United States to prevent Elmo Saks and the Reverend Toe from creating additional uneasiness and tension.

"I share your concern about the energy solution," said the President. "If we study the good-bad criteria of the problem, I am inclined to believe that some drastic measures are in store for this planet. Also, let me say that the entire concept of good and bad energy reflects some flexible parameters totally unknown to us and beyond our comprehension. In all reason, any adjustment involves both good and bad but how? And to what extent is the human race responsible for the unbalance?"

"Ross," said Patrick, reverting to their familiar terms, "Richard and I arrived at more or less the same conclusion. The question is how? Who? What?"

"That is what you have to find out, old mon Secretaire General!"

PART FIVE
The Verdict

This time, the trip up to the ship in the shuttle, did not create the excitement and anticipation of the previous journeys. Both Patrick and Richard were especially apprehensive. Beyond the cordiality shown by the visitors and the impeccable treatment they had received, there remained the declaration made during Patrick's first encounter that their purpose was to re-establish some form of balance and equilibrium that seemed to be off on earth. Adam had been emphatic when he bade them goodbye at the end of their last visit. "We would like to move into the final phase of our stay here. We can probably implement the measures we have outlined, at our next meeting."

This time, they were received in the main lounge and quickly served coffee and pastries. All six visitors were present but it was clear that their jovial attitudes had been replaced by a serious if not somber mood.

After one more cup of hot and aromatic coffee, they got up and, led by Adam went into another room that resembled the Board Room of a New York bank. A solid oak conference table about 15 feet long was surrounded by leather backed high chairs whose excellent design and finish matched the paneling on the walls and the elegant copper lamps on the walls.

The six visitors sat on one side of the table and invited Patrick and Richard to sit across from them. Leather covered portfolios had been placed on top of the table in front of every chair, along with a Papermate ball-point pen. In the center of the table there was a large silver tray with several plastic bottles full of water and half a dozen glasses.

As soon as they were seated, Adam cleared his throat in the best tradition of Board Chairmen everywhere on earth, and said, "Dear friends, I am going to dispense with long speeches about our being here and who we are. That has already been covered. I wish to come to the point and explain in detail the reason for our presence and the measures we wish to take. As you know, we have identified a number of problems in this planet that are interfering with the energy balances outside your known universe. You see, the whole thing, here in this universe and in the other levels, obeys to simple balances of energy inputs. When these balances are disturbed, adjustments have to be made. I realize that the matter is complex and that it is difficult for you to understand. I shall try my best to explain."

He looked around the table at the grave and serious faces, and continued. "Let us say that there are positive and negative kinds of energy. Let us say that equilibrium in this neighborhood is necessary for some other forms of energy outside your system, to exist. You can wonder about positive and negative energy. We have talked about it. You can compare it to good and bad, to high and low and, if you wish, to ball and strike or, for the golfers among you, bogey and par. If at one time you begin to get more negative energy, or have more balls than strikes, you either give the pitcher a new set of coordinates or ship him back to the bullpen. Or lose the game. What is happening here is simply that this planet has been producing an excessive amount of neg energy. It is beginning to screw up the works someplace else."

Patrick looked at Adam and not detecting any special look in his eyes, said, "I suppose you mean our wars, our constant struggles, crime, delinquency, etc. These are unfortunately the result of traits that have been with the species since the beginning. How can you evaluate and measure such negative actions and attitudes?"

"I believe we have talked about energy content before now. Maybe I can put it this way: everything on this planet is energy of one kind or another. The air you breathe, the thoughts you have, the sounds you hear, the dreams you have. I mean absolutely everything. Go back to the first thought your ancestors had in the cave, or the first grunt. They are both energy and have to be accounted for, classified, dry cleaned and inserted into other e-forms. But if you begin to produce more negative loads than positive ones, the desired balance is disrupted."

"I more or less follow you," stated Richard. "But what I cannot understand is how you first classify what is good and what is bad and, second, how you transform them into energy outputs and classify them as positive or negative.

You see, from what we know of our species, the entire game has been a constant struggle between two opposing forces. Like the principle of action and reaction. The catching of the first fish, or the killing of the first rabbit could be said to be negative acts because they deprived some living forms of their existence. But if you used that food to feed and nourish newborns, old men and people in general, you were performing a positive action because you were preserving life. Do they balance each other or do you have to weigh the fish, measure the rabbit and check that once they were broiled, eaten and digested, they contributed the exact measure of energy to induce someone else's cells do their act to keep the person going."

Patrick interrupted with a question of his own. "Okay, by following the same line of thought, it could be argued that by ingesting the fish or the rabbit, some harm might come to the person who ate them. Things like a spine stuck in a young throat, or an excessive load of cholesterol from a fat rabbit. In which case, we have two negatives: killing the animals and harming the hunters. You could add bad cooking too!"

All of them laughed at the comment. Adam turned to Ely and said, "You are the expert in quantum energy. See how you get out of this one!"

Ely smiled, poured himself a glass of water, drank some and, pointing at the half full glass, said, "Is this glass half full, or half empty?" Everyone looked at the glass. Ely continued. "You see, some sort of equilibrium exists between a half full glass and a half empty glass. Same with Richard's example. The negative and positive parts of actions and attitudes in general respond to their own balances. To stay with the fish and the rabbit, you have to take into account that other factors enter the equation. Think of a very general and essential axiom that supports the existence of your species. It is its survival. It has to be a positive element, otherwise you would not exist. All right, within this element—which incidentally applies to the fish and the rabbit as well—a whole natural cycle is developed. Also positive. And a balance is established ultimately. Is it not? The fish eat smaller fish, the rabbit eats leafs and grass, that are living things, and you eat all of them! What this means in this universe of yours is that there is always an overriding consideration that both regulates and explains the nut and bolt nature of your lives. In the case of the energy emanating from this planet, we are the control factor at the moment."

Richard seemed to have been waiting for this statement. He asked with a touch of anxiety in his voice, "Yes, I understand. But, tell me, you are saying you are acting as control. But who sent you? Certainly you must answer to some 'overriding consideration' as you call it."

At this point, Evan, an athletic-looking 40-year-old, dressed in Armani from head to toe, spoke for the first time. Both Patrick and Adam could not fail to notice the smooth demeanor and the familiar way he held the Cross 18k gold pen in his left hand. Down on earth, the Gold Cross Ballpoint pen in the corporate world was a shield, a pointer and a mental crutch. It enabled the holder to argue or defend a position by holding the pen in a vertical position and moving it in a motion similar to that of priests spraying holy water. It fixed an audience's attention by moving it as a magic wand. More often than not, the pen kept the hands busy by the process of shifting the pen among one's fingers. This would attract everyone's attention so that the holder could take advantage of that brief moment to order thoughts, prepare answers and formulate ideas.

As if expecting the question, Evan looked at the pen and answered, "Here is where the going gets a little sticky." His accent was pure Boston. He tapped the pen lightly on his leather folder and continued. "The rearrangement and processing of energy, so to speak, conform to some physical reactions that fall within a dimension whose characteristics are beyond the understanding of our earthly cousins. Please, it would be useless to even approximate a definition. Just let me illustrate by describing a situation that would be so meaningless to you as to seem absurd."

He breathed deeply and went on. "You are all travelers in one of time's vectors. But in this planet or energy pool, you just go one way. Now, in the outer reality time is a point in space. You could travel in any of its vectors and even do so laterally, up or down. What does it mean to you, let us say, to travel laterally in time? Probably nothing. Your conception of time and the way it works down here would not allow you to understand what lateral fiddling of time means."

"Just for kicks, what does lateral time travel mean?"

"Well, it means an infinite repetition of the time-space-object sequence. Now then, to make any change in that lateral frame, you have to use other dimensions, right? These dimensions exist in other energy levels."

Predictably, Evan raised his hand with the pen and pointed it at the ceiling. He paused and then went on. "We are not sent by anyone, we are an energy reaction. We fiddle with the dimensions so that we can come down and help you straighten yourselves out. I guess you could call us a team of troubleshooting ergs!"

"But how can our species create energy problems in a universe so vast and complex. We admit that our species has had problems from the moment it appeared, how come they come to your attention now?"

Adam replied, "Remember that your species comes from a strain that existed when earth was a satellite. Those people, while physically identical to your present shapes, were psychically and emotionally different. Their energy balances were normal. Then, you will recall a major change took place and the human race in its present version took over this planet. Since then, there has been a flashing red light in the control panel. I think I have already talked about them. Your species is just playing hell with the balances and equilibriums outside your bailiwick."

Patrick sat listening intently to what was being said. He understood most of what Adam was trying to explain. His scientific training on the one hand and his sense of belonging to the human species, now under indictment, on the other created some hesitancy in his manner. He looked up and asked, "I more or less follow your argument, Adam, but how can you differentiate good energy from bad energy. I can see the difference between a good pitch and a bad pitch; they both represent energy outputs. They may end up inside or outside the strike zone but they are still energy. How can one be good energy and the other bad energy? Are we talking about effects solely?"

"Not at all. The moment the pusher knowingly gives a 10-year-old a pill that he knows will start that child on the way to drug dependence, bad energy is used. The moment the switch blade cuts some flesh as a result of fear, intimidation or just plain meanness, bad energy is again used. Sometimes, even when a cop gives you a traffic ticket—and depending on the circumstances—the energy quality may be of one type or the other. You see, down here on this planet, you have a catalog of bad vibes that is almost as extensive as the New York City Yellow Pages!"

"Yes, but what about the good vibes? The clean energy?"

"Buddy, there is so little of it that you have to look very hard to find it."

Again, they all laughed heartily. In spite of the informal and cordial atmosphere and the light humored way in which the visitors treated such transcendental matters, both Patrick and Richard, were uneasy. If there was a major energy screw up, the measures would be of a corresponding magnitude.

There was a moment of silence. Patrick placed both hands on top of the fine leather portfolio and said in a voice laced with gravity and depth, "I, like a great majority of people on our planet, have been taught to believe that in the end goodness, fairness and justice prevail over those traits and qualities that are the opposite. In a sense, it is a hope that has been sort of built into human beings. Faith and religion have their 'raison d'etre,' in that hope. Now then, I agree that we are going through a especially painful period in the history of humanity. It is also magnified by the larger numbers of people we now deal with. Where three hundred years ago, a famine in an African country would take one thousand lives in a year, in our times it is one million. Same with wars, crimes, terrorism, etc. It is a larger scale. According to your assessments, there is more neg energy, as you call it. But, how do you plan to rectify this situation?"

Adam looked at both Patrick and Richard and in a light tone replied, "We are going to give the human race a new face. And probably a new soul. We could easily recover all the energy that makes up this planet in one modest bang and re-establish that equilibrium somewhere. You wouldn't feel a thing. The kind of disappearing act like 'now you see it now you don't.' Copperfield would love it! We have discussed among ourselves the options we should consider. We all agree that the ' bang you're gone' option is out. We all kind of like some things on this planet and would like to do something, huh, positive. We do not wish to destroy anything on this planet. We have identified the nature of the energy problem and have elaborated a proper solution."

There was absolute silence around the table. The expression on all six visitors was sober and even somber. Patrick and Richard sat motionless waiting for a verdict that they knew was coming since their very first visit to the ship. Adam continued. "I should point out that most measures will be directed at the human race, as the living community responsible for almost the entire equilibrium condition. We are starting with those people that have been directly responsible for the death and the suffering of other human beings. This is a large order as the percentage of people that have attempted against the welfare of others—in any form or manner—seems inordinately large. At least that is what we conclude from the data you have been furnished and our own analysis. We have been painfully surprised to find that almost the entire species exists under three of the flaws we pointed out before. Greed is just about a reflex action with most people. Larceny is almost unstoppable and selfishness is the order of the day. Violence is often the recourse of any of them."

Patrick, in a low voice, asked, "How serious do you consider these attributes to force you to take corrective measures?"

Adam stood up and went to the bar. He poured himself a good measure of Chivas, added a couple of ice cubes and returned to the table. With a sad smile, he invited his guests to join him in a drink. Patrick declined but Richard and Emosh got up and mixed their drinks and returned to their seats. Adam continued. "Very serious. Please let me illustrate the general idea. In your species, we find that it takes thousands if not millions of years to achieve changes in mental, physical and even emotional levels. While environment is important, social conditioning has been a major factor in the transformations that have occurred. Without going back centuries to the Asyrians, the Egyptians, the Nubians or the Romans, just look at your own neck of the woods, this great country called the United States of America. A neck of woods that we have learned to appreciate and to identify as one of the best examples of positive behavior in the history of the species."

He paused as if to make sure that every word he said was heard and understood. "Let me focus on just one set of circumstances permanently etched in the history of the country and the psyche of its people. It is a contradiction hard to understand. For almost two hundred years, this country practiced slavery. Or it forced slavery upon other human beings. Let us forget about skin color for a minute. What happened? The generations born in slavery had to accept a set of rules that was vastly different and greatly inhuman as compared to the rules under which other humans lived. In time, slavery and a black skin came to signify an inferior class of people. Remember we said this before. As they were denied opportunities to learn and to become free to choose their occupations or even follow modest personal ambitions and dreams, the black race retreated into a passive, subservient role. It was conditioning at its best. But it was also negative from all aspects. The tragic part was that an entire continent, Africa, was affected and the races that inhabited it had to carry with them the stigma of being a commodity rather than human beings. Talk about inhumanity to man! When later, social changes occurred, the black race was not prepared to cope with a society that had ignored, mistreated and abused them for generations. Call it a complex, resentment, pain, revulsion, hatred, etc. what the black races felt. Slavery was responsible for such feelings and attitudes. The black child who grew free in his native Dakar, never experienced these feelings until he had his first contact with the white man. For the white man was also conditioned to view the black race as a different race and one not deserving of equal treatment."

He paused for a moment and then continued. "We find ourselves with a dilemma and a contradiction concerning this subject. On one hand we have a heartless bunch of greedy merchants who institute a labor system based on slavery. The system aids in creating a great nation that provides opportunities and a home for millions, including non-slaves and peoples of all races. It just does not jive. Where the hell was the Christian spirit of the people? Nowhere, my friends. It was an exercise in greed and hypocrisy and the sooner this is understood and accepted, the sooner a more equitable society can be built. Another hundred thousand years?"

Richard listened with a mixture of surprise and regret. Regret that the entire slavery condition in the United States was an indelible wrong that would probably never be totally removed from the minds of the people of the country. And he was surprised at the tone of condemnation implied in Adam's words. He could only reply, "True. There is no question that a most shameful situation was created and, worse yet, it involved the more developed countries of the time. Those were countries that lived within a peculiar morality and impressive religious fervor. But you probably are aware that from the beginning of slavery in this country, and others, there was a strong voice against it. There was a widespread opposition to slavery, strictly on humanitarian terms. The Abolitionists sought by all means to put an end to slavery and so did a number of organized groups in France and Britain. So there was always a strong element of compassion and justice during the period in which slavery was practiced in this country."

Richard felt that looking at both sides of any question was always the guarantee of the soundness of any judgment or criteria. He also wanted Adam to understand the currents that for two centuries had torn the country apart.

"Yes, I am aware of all that. There was of course a large part of the country who opposed slavery on moral and Christian terms. No question that the work done by Benjamin Lundy, the Colonization Society and some of the Founding Fathers tended to maintain the question very much in the public eye. I also know that some of these movements crystallized in the Free Soil Party and that it eventually became a major political party."

He paused and, pointing a finger in the air, continued. "Still, dear Professor, it was a wrong action that took centuries to correct. And you know what the driving force was?"

Richard had of course many ideas on the subject and was well aware of the confrontations that had existed on all fronts at the time, but he wanted to hear Adam's usual sharp dictums or opinions.

"What was it?"

"It was greed, my friend, greed. Slave owners had found an easy way to convert human beings into highly productive and profitable assets. The profits that resulted from the use of inexpensive labor industrialized large portions of this country and the funny thing is that every slave owner knew in his heart that he was doing something wrong. But he was never reminded of it when he attended services on Sundays. He ignored that voice of his conscience when he worked to shape and defend a Puritan outlook based on principles he was betraying. To me, it was a strange case of organized hypocrisy."

He turned to Richard and, smiling, said, "Water under the bridge, my friend. Besides, the moral perspective of the age, like in any age, was distorted by the pressing needs of the nature of the life and circumstances of the time. But let us not get mired in what was really a thorny issue in your country, because even today you people live under a cloud. A Black cloud."

Patrick and Richard remained silent. It was a serious indictment that they accepted. Patrick, as a descendant of French immigrants was well aware of the harsh dictates of French colonial policies in Africa and in Southeast Asia and the centuries of injustices and abuse that were practiced by cold and indifferent governments. Richard mentally reviewed the many colonial efforts by most European countries and also China and Japan that resulted in the enslaving of natives and the denial of their basic human rights.

Crime and Punishment

Adam drank some more coffee and in a grave voice said, "As a first measure affecting the present reality we are removing from planet earth those human beings that have contributed to the negative energy values in your society. It is a dry cleaning job, really. We are accelerating that conditioning process that would normally take thousands of years to achieve. We will leave a planet with a changed race that has gotten rid of its more toxic components. I expect that future generations will gradually stick to the traits of the race we leave on this chunk of solar rock, and that somehow, negative energy is kept to a minimum. Otherwise..."

He paused for an instant and then, "As of this very moment, those persons on this planet that have been responsible for the resent energy conditions, no longer exist. Presto! They are now energy inputs being recovered and recycled! Take a look."

He turned to one of the paneled walls and pointed a finger. The wall sort of transformed itself, like a movie fade in. In a large portion of it, around twelve by sixteen feet, an image appeared. It depicted with holographic quality the death row cells in a Texas Penitentiary. The image showed several cells where inmates were sitting, reading, lying on the cots or standing around smoking. A digital clock ticked away in the lower right hand corner of the image. Then, the inmates disappeared. The image suddenly showed empty cells.

A few moments passed and then all hell broke loose. Alarms started to screech and armed guards appeared from all sides. Patrick, Richard and the visitors were witnessing one of the visitors' first energy adjustment measures!

Surprisingly, some of the guards themselves disappeared. The next shot showed the warden's office where he and three officers were meeting. As the camera closed in on the warden, he disappeared from view. The camera moved along the table and two of the three officers vanished leaving the other officer motionless, unable to believe his eyes and beginning to exhibit the effects of a major shock.

The image suddenly switched to a panoramic view of a section of a city in the Middle East. It was a good professional establishing shot, complete with leisure pan and moderate use of the camera optics. It began zooming in on an apartment building in the outskirts of the city. It kept zooming and finally focused on a lavish apartment on the top floor. The image just went through walls and furniture and showed a well furnished living room where a large man, elegantly dressed in a perfectly cut Savile Row gabardine suit, was at that moment pouring himself a drink from an expensive cut crystal decanter with a solid gold identification tag and chain. Standing next to him were two younger men in their late twenties, dressed in jeans and black leather jackets. Both sported the familiar half unshaven beards and the solid gold chains hanging from their necks. Again, all three disappeared from the image in a wink.

"Terrorists," murmured Patrick.

The next image was a long shot of Miami. It panned almost the entire coast line, beginning with Key Biscayne and going on up through Miami Beach and into Fort Lauderdale. It began to zoom in on a large ocean front mansion complete with a well appointed dock that included a gas pump, winches, hydraulic lifts, utility connections and other accessories. Properly anchored was a 60 foot Larson yacht where two men were busily scrubbing the decks.

The zoom continued into the house. Two more men dressed in loud colored shirts were sitting in a small hallway talking in low voices. Each carried a 45 caliber Thorn and Simms automatic pistol in black holsters in their waists. Then the image moved quickly through the impressive living room, the bar, the library and up an elaborate marble, bronze and glass paneled staircase that led to a large foyer on the second floor. The image continued to move along as if providing a guided tour of the house.

Finally, it stopped in front of an elaborately carved wooden door and then switched to the interior. It was a very large bedroom furnished in several styles of expensive chairs, sofas and small tables of dubious taste. The image then centered on the luxurious triple bed, complete with black satin sheets, that took up one corner of the room. The bed was occupied by a nude barrel-chested man with a tremendous erection, and a shapely naked blond that laid on the bed almost unconscious, while the man seemed to be about to devour her. He was running his hands over her large breasts and her flat stomach and making strange gurgling sounds. He then leaned over her breasts and avidly kissed them and then sucked at the nipples with great enthusiasm while running one hand between her legs.

Patrick and Richard gasped. The man was General Azpiroz, the butcher of Villa Solana, personally responsible for the murder of more than 300 persons, including women and children in one of the more dramatic episodes in the recent history of one of the Latin American countries. As recognition came to their minds, he too disappeared leaving the semi conscious partner vaguely aware that the caresses had stopped. Her drugged mind had trouble connecting thoughts. She looked at the mirror on the ceiling, saw herself alone on the bed and then turned around and went to sleep.

At that exact moment one of the men on the deck handed a large pail to his companion but was stopped in mid motion as his colleague disappeared. He could not believe his eyes; eyes that a millisecond before were looking into the dark eyes of Manolo. He gasped and walked rapidly toward the house.

In the hallway, one of the men had just lit another cigarette and was returning the lighter to his companion. As the lighter was grabbed, the man disappeared and the lighter fell to the floor. The other man could not believe his eyes. He remained motionless for an instant and then got up and hurriedly moved to the back of the house where Señor Pedro Gaviria, the General's personal secretary, and the man whose betrayal to his Commander in Chief had precipitated the violence unleashed by General Azpiroz, was lazily lobbing balls at two young ladies on the tennis court. The camera followed the man to the tennis court and caught his surprise and the hysterical screams from the two girls as Señor Gaviria vanished before their eyes.

The next image showed Elmo Saks, sitting on one of the covered terraces of his estate in St. Michael's. The Reverend Toe sat across from him in one of the comfortable rattan chairs. The coffee table in front of them contained a silver coffee service and a plate of doughnuts. As if listening to the best high fidelity system, Adam, Patrick, Richard and the others could hear every word of their conversation: "You see, Reverend, it will not be long before the President will have to tone down his support of the UN. Our campaign has gained many adherents who have reason to be suspicious of the Secretary General and that Know-it-all Ferguson. All these trips and the fancy Television documentaries are no match for your fear campaigns. People rather react to fear than to reason; otherwise there would not be any need for religion."

The Reverend smiled, used as he was to Elmo's discourses. He added, "I think that the time has come for the visitors to let us know what they plan to do. I imagine it will be some sort of universal revival where we all get a sermon and advice about the environment, child care, traffic lights and cholesterol. Also, it is clear that some form of deal will be made about their technology and that is where we come in!"

"Right! I can hardly wait to have one of those pills to myself. They say that their cooking is out of this world and never better said!"

They both laughed when all of a sudden they both disappeared. Just at the moment when Remy had entered the terrace. Remy's last image was of the two men laughing and then vanishing! Then, he himself disappeared.

For the next thirty minutes, Patrick and Richard saw murderers and people of all kinds in all parts of the world disappear as they turned into energy outputs. Some of the scenes were grotesque and unexpected. Famous physicians, politicians, priests and ministers, athletes, bus drivers and even a sickeningly large number of teenagers from the ghettos in Mexico City, Atlanta, Beirut, Marseilles, Liverpool, Bogota, Medellin, Bilbao, Los Angeles, New York and a hundred other cities on the planet.

Especially impressive were the scenes dealing with one of the most repugnant of criminals: rapists. A young, pretty nurse was shown leaving the hospital at night with another nurse. They each got into their cars and left the hospital parking lot. The young nurse drove to her home in an apartment complex in a quiet section of the city. She parked her car, closed and locked the door and, with the keys in her hand, walked quickly around the flower beds and went up the few steps to the door of the apartment. As soon as she had opened the door, a shadow materialized from the bushes next to the wall and pushed her brutally inside the entry hall. She was so surprised that she had no time to scream or yell. By the time she realized what was happening, it was too late. She was inside the house and a strong pair of arms were holding her own. She dropped her purse and the keys which the intruder quickly retrieved and pocketed, after locking the door. She was terrified and unable to utter a word. Her assailant spoke for the first time. "You will probably come out of this alive, sweetheart. Just keep quiet and do as I say. I have a knife and a gun. I know you live alone here so we are not going to be disturbed."

His tone was even and denoted excitement, whose nature she preferred not to identify. His accent was neutral and she could not detect any specific inflexion. She managed to say, "Please, what do you want? I don't have any money or jewels or anything of value. Please leave me alone!"

He did not reply and instead half pushed, half carried her to the bedroom. Once inside, he pushed her toward the bed and repeated with some finality, "If you want to stay alive, just do as I say! This is not going to hurt you any more than when you do it with all those doctors at the hospital or those frat boys at your gym. Maybe you'll learn a couple of new twists!"

"Please, don't do it. I don't go around with anyone. Don't you realize that?" She could not finish the sentence as he slapped her in the face, hard enough to emphasize the warning.

"Just keep quiet. Women who talk too much end up at the bottom of the river."

The only light in the room was that which came in through the voile curtains of the two windows in the bedroom, so she could not clearly see the features of the man. Her training helped her form a quick image of her attacker. He was a white man about thirty years old or late twenties, close to six foot tall and was dressed in jeans and a sweater. She fought with herself to maintain her self control and mentally tried to remember all those things she was supposed to remember in a situation like this one.

He sat on the bed, still holding her arms tight and buried his face in her hair. "Uh! Your hair smells fresh with maybe a little bit of anesthetic in it." He then pulled the light cardigan she had on and took it off in not too gentle fashion. Next he pushed her on the bed, while she began to offer some feeble resistance, as fear and terror began to take hold of her. All she could do was shake her head to keep from screaming.

He took his sweater off and at the same time produced a 4 inch switch blade which he held in his left hand. With his right hand he pulled at her blouse and ripped the front in one quick gesture. He seemed to be in a frenzy and his breathing was short and quick. He then pulled at her skirt and, when she resisted, he brought the knife's point to her face and whispered, "You want to keep your face the way it is, or do you want me to carve my initials on it? Don't be stupid; this shouldn't hurt you. Besides, women like it this way also, don't you?"

She could not reply. He had removed her skirt and also forced her to remove her shoes and her stockings. By now she was dressed in only her bra and her panties. She could not stop from trembling and shaking her head. She looked into his eyes but he turned his head away. He began to caress her breasts over the bra and after a few seconds used the knife to cut the piece between the two cups. His breathing took on a more accelerated rhythm. He stood up and removed his shoes and his jeans. He was not wearing underwear and his erect penis seemed to be fighting to take off on its own. He caressed it slowly and with his right hand forced his victim to turn her face and look straight into his erect member. Suddenly, the nurse was staring into the empty space in front of her. She remained static for a moment and then, realizing that the danger had disappeared, started to sob and shake uncontrollably.

At that moment, Adam stood up in front of the screen and said, "Our rapist will never threaten anyone anymore. But our nurse is liable to suffer from serious emotional and psychological anomalies. This is one of the more shocking and hurtful experiences that can be inflicted on anyone."

Patrick and Richard remained silent, in their own way sharing the revulsion and the terror that the scene they had just witnessed had provoked. The girl continued to shake and sob inspiring not only concern but also pity. Adam moved to one side and said, "I am going to rectify this horrible episode. It is happening right this minute."

As he spoke, the screen went back, as if a reel had been rewound, to the point where she entered her apartment. As the door closed, the shadow in the bushes suddenly disappeared. She was not aware of anything and, once inside the apartment went through her usual routine. Adam sighed and smiled. "She can now live a normal life, without knowing how close she was to living out the worst drama a woman can endure." As Adam sat down, the screening continued.

Scene after scene illustrated the extraordinary range of human wickedness. Some scenes were hard to take. In a flash, a session of the US Congress was shown as more than half its members disappeared amidst the puzzlement and alarm of their colleagues. The same scene was repeated in Rome, Tokyo, Buenos Aires, London, Bonn, etc. Then, quick shots of another scourge of mankind: the child molester. Their disappearance however left some small measure of satisfaction in both Patrick and Richard. No part of the world was spared, it seemed. From New Zealand to Oslo and from Alaska to Capetown, banishment acquired a subdued rhythm and all that could be heard in the room were the exclamations of surprise by those who remained, and in some cases, muttered thanks and sighs.

The silence in the room was ominous as the images began to fade out and the paneling reappeared.

Adam stood up and reached for the water pitcher. He poured himself a full glass and drank it thirstily. His expression was somber and dark. He pointed at the panel and said, "Done! Every murderer in your planet, along with those who have committed crimes against humanity in this planet, have just been turned into their very basic component."

Richard was almost speechless. The succession of images and the identity of some of the people in them had left him wondering about the quality of the human race. He finally asked, "How many of these people have been, uh, reprocessed?"

"About five billion."

"Five billion?" asked Richard in an incredulous tone. Patrick, next to him remained motionless and seemed speechless.

"I am sorry to say that, yes almost 90 percent of the population of this planet have with their acts contributed to a distortion of its energy levels. And as I said when we first met, that distortion has caused a few problems elsewhere in the system. It was imperative that the problem be solved…"

"What happens to the ones left?"

"Actually not much. In time, their notion of good and bad will begin to fade and be substituted by more ingrained characteristics of a positive nature."

"What do you mean by that?" asked Richard in a tone of voice that betrayed his unmistakable state of surprise and even shock.

"Well, maybe I can explain with an example. Lying for instance. Up to now, it has been a ready choice for many. It has been a valid alternative for others and it has also been the key ingredient in the behavior of large numbers of people."

"Such as?" inquired Patrick, also still shocked by the incredible scenes he had just witnessed. That "clean up" job had been as shocking as it had been final.

"Gee, so many. Let us start with lawyers, salesmen, advertising executives, TV pitchmen, CEOs, building contractors, hairdressers, mail order catalog editors, teachers, doctors, nurses, preachers, bus drivers, cops and the cream of them all, politicians!" He smiled and continued. "Well, as conditions have changed on the planet and the people left are presumably upright citizens, the need to deceive will slowly fade. Don't forget that successful lying is based on adequate reception. The moment a lie is delivered, that transmission is forever tainted. See what I mean? The receptor accepted a truth that turned out to be a lie. It upsets its essence. But from now on as there is less need to lie, the very composition of a lie begins to transform itself into less deceitful manifestations. If the politician realizes that people no longer require, nor accept, exaggerated or false information he begins to analyze, review and propose solutions that contain no hidden meanings and that reflect his true assessment of the problem or situation. Eventually, he has no need to lie."

He looked at Patrick and Richard with a mild look that revealed nothing of whatever he was thinking. This time, Adam's impersonation of a hermetic human was excellent.

"The technique begins to fade from his consciousness and he becomes as truthful as Mount Everest."

He stopped and for a long while looked at Patrick and Richard with obvious concern, as if he wasn't certain that his explanation had been completely understood. The silence continued, if such thing is possible. The other visitors barely moved and their expressions did not hint at anything. Both Patrick and Richard were still under shock and incapable of recovering their composure. Adam spoke. "We must not feel that we are witnessing mass executions. This is not the case. We are only beginning a process of removing from human society those elements that have contributed to, let us say, its downfall."

"What happens to them?" Richard could not help wondering. To see these people disappear with such finality seemed to him unreal and at the same time puzzling. To Patrick the act contained an uncertain air of violence even if the disappearance was instantaneous and surely painless. His legal mind questioned also other parameters; evidence, trial, due process, attenuating circumstances, etc.

Sensing the doubts that the images had sown in his guests, Adam said, "They are converted instantaneously into an energy pool and from there assigned to the appropriate level. This is of course a simplification. I am aware that the solution seems drastic and may even offend your sense of justice and, I notice that it has awakened in you some measure of compassion. Just let me say that these people are only the beginning of the process. There are many successive steps that we must follow before we can consider that planet earth does no longer pose a threat to the other circles of existence. It is important that you understand what we are doing so that you can properly explain it to your peers. We don't want this entire exercise to be counterproductive. By removing a negative portion of the equation, we don't want to create another negative pool in the form of animosity or rejection."

"I did not realize that we had so many criminals in our midst," observed Patrick. "I cannot comprehend the incredible extent of evil in our society."

Richard added, "I am still baffled about seeing Dr. John Fielser, a Nobel Medicine Prize winner in the killer category."

"Let me show you." Adam again pointed his finger at the paneling and an image suddenly appeared. It showed Dr. Fielser carefully withdrawing with a syringe about two cubic centimeters of an oily liquid from a small vial. He then injected them into a half full plastic container of an intravenous saline solution of the type normally administered to critical patients. He closed the small vial with the oily liquid and replaced it on the shelf of the cabinet in his office, where it became another undistinguishable bottle among others. He carefully locked the cabinet. He walked across his office and, after making sure that no nurse or other personnel were around, entered the room next door where special medications were stored and labeled. He placed the plastic bottle in one of the trays marked Jenkins and quickly returned to his office.

"My friends," said Adam, "Dr. Fielser has been speeding up the departure of a number of people for some time now. The reason? In some cases, he has been under contract from greedy relatives impatient to get their hands on inheritances, properties and deeds. In others, he just wanted to have immediate access to the grants and endowments that some of his wealthy patients had agreed to donate posthumously to his clinic. You will recall that a year or so ago, there were some questions raised by the relatives of one of the deceased about the premature demise of their loved one. However the inquiry did not go beyond the Clinic's boardroom. Nothing came out of that and Dr. Fielser has continued to arrange for the deadly drippings in about a hundred cases."

Richard looked at Patrick and commented, "I see. But the other sequences show that a number of people were murderers by accident. Take all those hit and run drivers, traffic controllers, nurses, train conductors even lifeguards who were out taking a pee while some child drowned."

Patrick nodded but did not say anything. Ely sat up and said, "Yes, it appears a bit unfair, but you have to accept the fact that the death of another human that occurs as a result of negligence, incapacity of some sort or, as you say, just plain bad luck causes a direct energy conflict. But ask yourself the question, did the guilty ones have or did not have the option to prevent the end result? A bus driver who exceeds a speed limit is in effect attempting against the safety of his passengers. The lifeguard who takes a moment to empty his bladder without having someone replace him is neglecting his duty and therefore the only one responsible for the drowning of the child. Here we can go into direct responsibility, non-intentional behavior, accidental causes, etc. I know that your defense lawyers would find a million attenuating circumstances, including I hear, the effect of genetic characteristics, to let those people go free. To us this is a clear situation. If you go into a room where you know there is a gas leak, you don't strike a match, do you? Well, same deal here. Whatever the chain of circumstances, the end result is the death of a human being. And the one who caused it directly or indirectly, is guilty. Period."

"I still think it is kind of drastic," observed Richard, who suddenly had become very uneasy. "How far do you reach in this, huh, energy rearrangement, as you call it?"

Ely, with a grave expression in his handsome face, replied, "Every enhanced living creature on the planet."

Richard interrupted to ask, "Enhanced living creature?"

"Well, a euphemism for humans. You see, humans have the capacity to reason and are clearly liable for their actions, or inclinations. Animals live on a balance of their own, more or less. Within our rearrangement program, a child who lies to his parents, or to his teachers, sends a signal that triggers an instantaneous projection of what his later years would be. If the projection is negative, that is, if later in life he graduates from lies to cheating other persons and causing them pain and suffering, he is a clear candidate for reprocessing. Those people remaining on the planet are better off, now and in the future. I think it is a simple equation and, while drastic, it provides nothing but safety for the human race. Think about it."

Patrick, who had been in deep thought, raised his head and asked, "Is what you are trying to do, or doing, the equivalent of something like 'ethnic cleansing'? Except that the cleaning in this case is done on moral and ethical grounds and it means the salvation of the planet."

Adam replied, "It works that way. The process is somewhat similar to the elimination of rotten apples in a barrel. Get the rotten ones out and there is a good chance that the other apples will retain their freshness a longer time. In your case, there are too many rotten ones. If stricter parameters had been applied, this planet would have been left with only a couple of million humans!"

Adam paused and, looking at Patrick, said, "We are adding another ingredient to the cure. Gradually, your genes will blend and eventually erase one of the major differences that have been the cause of conflict among humans. We are adding a common denominator that will soften the drastic physical differences that have separated humans all these years. You will see."

He smiled and embraced Patrick and Richard.

At the White House

At the same time that Patrick and Richard were witnessing the disappearance process in the ship above New York, the President was meeting in Washington with the Vice President, the National Security Adviser, and his Secretary of State. Also present was Baron Carini, representing

Patrick Deschamps and Cardinal Ludlam. They were still trying to interpret or at least make sense of the avalanche of information provided by both Patrick and Richard. The last few weeks had seen almost daily visits to the ship above New York by Patrick and Richard. What they reported to the Emergency Committee and to the Security Council was simply astounding.

The whole world had been shaken when the TV programs produced by Helen Lawrence with material from the ships above began to appear almost daily on the world TV screens. The programs showed the visitors in the ship and toured some of the rooms that had been created to meet with Patrick and Richard. Under a crisp documentary format, the programs included all the visits made by Patrick, Richard, Kathryn and Helen. It also provided a fascinating record of the conversations held during the many visits and numberless visual sequences that complemented the matters discussed.

Helen Lawrence's deft touch was evident in most takes. She had worked hard with Evan and Earle to blend her own material with the incredible footage provided by the visitors.

With an unusual sense of accommodation, the programs were aired in each country's native tongues. The programs enabled the world audience to visit the first cavemen in Central Africa, to admire the clean architectural lines of ancient cities like UR, to participate in the discovery of America, to walk with Jesus to the Mount of Olives, to be shocked and enraged at the sight of the Japanese fleet steaming toward Hawaii, to watch Michelangelo handle hammer and chisel, to listen to Lincoln at Gettysburg, and to witness infinite episodes of the past that up to that moment had been known only through textbooks and in few instances, photographs. It let people see Roman days in the heyday of the Empire and to weep at the events leading to Jesus of Nazareth's crucifixion.

The impact of these incredible sequences, enhanced by the latest visual technology, was beyond anything ever witnessed by the people of earth. They began to mold a new understanding of history as the episodes shown diverged from existing accounts. Especially those dealing with historical situations that had been conveniently modified by historians and politicians. But in general, they underlined the dramatic tone of most historical episodes and the beauty of other great events and cornerstones in the history of mankind.

"It seems that in few short weeks, the visitors have managed to review the entire history not only of civilization but of the human race. But after the latest conversations with Patrick and Richard, we seem to be coming to a conclusion."

The President sounded worried and somewhat uneasy. Ursula Walters, the Vice President, said, "It is also my impression. On one hand they have given us a good glimpse of what we are and many historical footnotes of great interest. They have also outlined the imbalance equation they mentioned at the beginning and, I suppose that right now they are going over the final details with Patrick and Richard."

Pashley observed, "I think that they are probably discussing the solution to the problem. My question is how the heck you transform, modify or eliminate negative energy?"

The President got up and, looking out the window, sighed. "I am afraid that our energy inspectors are about to turn this planet upside down. As much as I try to justify some of the horrible things that humans have inflicted on other humans, I cannot find enough good deeds that may offset some of that bad medicine. What the heck can we do?"

"Mister President," remarked Ursula Walters, "whatever they decide to do, it will probably result in an improvement. Please don't forget that all along they have shown great consideration for the peoples of the planet and a large degree of understanding. To me they always sounded compassionate and sincere."

At that moment, Mrs. LaVance burst into the office with an expression of horror in her face. She was almost speechless. Right behind her, appearing disheveled and terrorized, Pan Rossi clung to a cellular phone, a handheld palmtop and earphones connected to a satellite radio. Alan Clayton, the Secretary of State quickly reached Mrs. La Vance and led her gently to a chair. Meanwhile Ursula Walters was pouring glasses of water from the pitcher on the small bar in back of the room.

"What is going on?" asked the President.

"The people. They have disappeared. They have vanished! God help us!"

Mrs. La Vance could not control herself. She was in the throes of a nervous convulsion and could not say any more. The President turned to Pan Rossi, who had also sat down and was drinking from a glass. "Pan, what the heck?"

Pan swallowed and some of the color returned to his strained features.

"All of a sudden people started to disappear, Mister President. We have lost some people in our staff. We don't know what is happening. It must be something the damn visitors are doing!"

They all moved quickly to the conference room where the large screen television had been on for some time. They all looked at the images that were beamed to the entire world by the ships above. Not only were the images nerve-shattering but the audio portion was crowded with cries, yells and the hysterical screams of people shown on close ups.

What people were watching was beyond understanding and it caused anxiety and terror. People on the screen suddenly disappeared without any trace of motion. Even those who appeared comfortably seated and at ease, vanished in a microsecond, leaving those around them in the throes of surprise and fear. In a way the images resembled a well edited travelogue. A lovely shot of Laguna Beach quickly faded into a lavish office where one or more people would disappear. Then, on to a street in Singapore where the traffic policeman would suddenly vanish. Then, a shot of the Mediterranean and a close up of a lavish villa in Cap Ferrat. Again, an entire family would vanish, leaving only astounded servants.

At one point, the images showed the Rockefeller Center area from the 5th Avenue side. As people moved across the screen, some of them would simply vanish. Cars and taxis cruising the area suddenly stopped and the drivers would vanish. Even some of the elegant women seen entering or leaving some of the fancy stores on the street would suddenly disappear, while packages, bags and poodles were left by themselves.

Just as shocking were the scenes of ministers, priests, gurus and spiritual advisers of all types that, in a millisecond, ceased to exist.

For the next few hours the world was in the grip of uncontrollable terror. The disappearances were unexpected and happened with such finality that most people were not able to understand the phenomenon.

Finally, the television screens all over the world lit up in the peculiar color of the objects overhead. It indicated that a message was about to be shown. In less that an hour, the message appeared:

Peoples of Planet Earth. Please do not be alarmed. What you are witnessing is nothing more than a measure taken to insure that the people of this planet will hereafter be able to live without fear and anxiety. Think of the future. Forget the past and concentrate in raising a new race, a new understanding of your planet and a new hope for all. There is a God that looks after all of us. Let us make him proud.

Our task is almost complete. We leave your planet with sadness in our hearts. In the short time we have been here we have learned to appreciate and love many traits of the human race.

We are confident that Patrick and Richard will be able to explain matters in more detail. They can do that much better than us.

The atmosphere at the Oval Office was heavy with amazement and fear. Besides, the telephones had not stopped ringing, same as beepers, cell phones and all the other devises of the time. Wives, relatives and friends called trying to speak to those who were with the President. They were able to say a few words and in return hear a few words of reassurance. Including the President who asked Earla Ann, his wife, to come down to the Oval Office.

All those present were stunned. For the last few hours their attention had been absorbed by the strange fascination offered by the scenes they were witnessing. Mike Pashley whispered to no one in particular, "I feel like the small jungle rabbit that is hypnotized by the boa in the tree and remains motionless while the boa takes its time coming down to swallow him!"

"Exactly what I think," added the President. "There must be some unexplained compulsion that keeps us seeing a spectacle that is both horrendous and according to our visitors, necessary. I never realized that people on earth contained such charge of ill will, malice and evil."

Clayton got up and, still looking at the screen, said in his gravel voice, "I think that this solution might be a good one after all. Now, all we have is good apples and we must make sure that we can take care of them. I also wonder what happened to Elmo and the Reverend."

"Not to worry," said the Baron. "I saw them at the very beginning. You'll be able to see them in the tapes. They were together at Elmo's home and all of a sudden they were gone. I remember watching the expression on Elmo's chauffeur but it only lasted a second as he himself disappeared!"

The President got up and moved to the table with the beverages. He poured himself a tall glass of ice tea and thirstily drank it all in one quick motion. He turned to the others and said, "I think I now understand the philosophy behind the touted energy readjustment. It is a simple deputation of bad and evil people, as they are mainly responsible for the conflicts that beset the human race and everything that is sordid and wicked in our society. Kind of drastic though. The visitors are just purging our planet of bad eggs. All I can say is that we are still here, so it means that we have all been classified good, or something. But, my friends do not think for a moment that this episode is over. This rearrangement I am sure goes beyond what we have seen. In the next few hours or days we will be able to appreciate the extent of the changes that the adjustments have brought to us. Whatever they are, we must be thankful that we have just inherited a new world!"

They were silent for a while. They were obviously shocked by what they had seen and found it hard to come to grips with the grim reality and the finality of the "energy readjustment." The Vice President, Ursula Walters in a quivering voice said, "We must wait until Patrick and Ferguson return to get more details on this cleaning job. It will be interesting to know how many people have been 'de-energized,' or is there another term?"

"Yes," added Pashley. "Also, it will be interesting to learn about the criteria employed to classify the energy features of those vanished. I expect Deschamps and Ferguson will be able to tell us more about it."

The President smiled sadly and said, "Whatever the explanations, details and even the techniques used to clean up our planet, we must be prepared to face a tremendous change in our lives. The implications of this event will stay with us as long as the planet exists."

Cardinal Ludlam, whose face was flushed with the excitement of the moment, observed, "Think of all the new parameters of Philosophy, Religion, Ethics, Education, Government and even Sports, that will require an immediate reform. Does this also mean that those left on the planet are good? How in heck do you maintain a 'good' status? What are the degrees of goodness? When do you reach the opposite?"

The President put his hand on the Cardinal's shoulders and answered, "Warren, we still have God!"

EPILOGUE
A Different Look

Richard looked at Helen and said, “Helen! What a beautiful tan you have!”

She approached the mirror and looked at herself, pleased with what she saw. Her light blonde hair had turned a lovely light brown color that provided a most pleasing contrast with her softly slanted—light brown-green eyes? They used to be deep blue. Her complexion had changed. She no longer had the rosy hue that allowed her perfect features to make her face a work of art. Instead, her complexion was now slightly darker, more like a tanned color, and the effect was as attractive and alluring as the previous skin color.

She then turned to Richard and said, “Have you looked at your own tan? You know, you are even handsomer than the boys who advertise Calvin Klein underwear!”